LONELY
SPIRES

LONELY SPIRES

AN EPISTOLARY NOVEL

RAE SENGELE

Snakeshead Press

Copyright © 2024 Rae Sengele

Published by Snakeshead Press

Cover Design by Rae Sengele
Cover photo of a wave by Tim Marshall on Unsplash.
Cover photo of lighthouse by Joshua Hibbert on Unsplash.

ISBN: 979-8-9907878-0-3 (print)

Printed in United States of America

1st Edition, 2024

CONTENT GUIDE

Note: This is not an exhaustive list and may contain spoilers

Lonely Spires as a whole is an exploration of grief, depression, and self-sabotage, if you're not in the place to sit in those feelings, be good to yourself. I'll have other books. Other strong themes/topics are suicide/suicidal ideation, cheating, and a secret pregnancy/child. There are also depictions and descriptions of domestic abuse, a toxic relationship, drowning (both literal and metaphorical), sexual content, and alcoholism/binge drinking, as well as, brief depictions of homophobia and smoking.

LISTEN TO THE
LONELY SPIRES
PLAYLIST ON SPOTIFY

For Mama,
The lighthouse through so many of my storms

Marc—

I've always struggled with beginnings.

Then again, you already know that, don't you? You read all my papers, after all, in the writing center at TAMU-CC. Every one I would bring you, you would say I needed to fix the beginning.

"But beginnings are hard," I would complain.

"That's what makes them so important," you'd tell me with that smile that brought lightening to my stomach, the electricity crackling along my bones for days after.

Where exactly am I supposed to begin, though?

The day I left? The night I slept with Jonathan? The day I met him?

But there was so much more to it all and I'm still not sure when it all began.

Did it begin with my mother's suicide? The postpartum depression that caused it?

You were there for some of it, but not all of it.

I wish I could begin before those days; back when life was still normal. Back when all my mother wanted was a king sized bed for Christmas. Back when all we worried about was schoolwork and whose house to spend the night at. Or even back to those days in the writing lab, when I would "forget" my outlines and I would "forget" what was on them just to spend extra time alone with you talking about Shakespeare, Dickinson, Blake. You would quote Keats for me and I would try to impress you with my Nirvana and Gorillaz albums.

I could even begin back in a time before those blissful honeymoon years. Before my awkward lonely teen years without you, each underscored by my mother's depression and multiple breakdowns. Back to when Scott, Mack, Tate, and I were children; congregated in our parents' room, sprawled out on the queen sized bed. Back to when we had been small enough to all fit. Seeing who could jump the highest, dancing to our father's collection of classic rock and 60's psychedelic bands, our mother's anti-war folk music and 70's pop songs: Pink Floyd and Boston; Syd Barrett and Donovan; Bob Dylan and Simon & Garfunkel; ABBA and the Bee Gees. Back to when we had spent our days hiding under the sheets with our mother while our father was at work, midday sun filtering through the fabric making anything possible. Back to when she would tell us tales of magic and faraway places, treasure and adventures, monsters and ghouls, love and heartbreak.

I wish you could have heard those stories.

I wish Tegan could have heard those stories.

I wish Lucas could remember those stories.

Then again, I have to wonder whose story this really is: mine or my mother's. The two intertwine like tangled vines. My mother's jasmine knotted with my own bougainvillea. If this is my mother's story, then do we begin with her depression and anxiety—those monsters that had strapped themselves so tightly to her you could see its markings on her bones? If so, then we'd have to go back to the days when the panic attacks first began. Back before you and before me. Back to her days in Vermont. Back before she had met my father. If that really is where her story began.

And what about my father? This is just as much his story as it is ours. It's my brothers' stories, it's yours, Tegan's. It's as much y'all's as it is mine, for without you my story would be empty, echoing in upon itself. Like a symphony your stories complete my own. Individually, each of our private songs are beautiful, yes, but uninformed—a single note without a chord. But together, each of our melodies ebb and flow, playing off one another as the greater story crescendos into being, bringing with it that static that moves beneath your skin like ocean waves along the surf.

But this isn't a story, is it?

You know, there are days that are harder than others, days when I can't look you in the eye. All it takes is a passing comment, a reminder of those years without you, those years I kept her from you, and suddenly I'm back there, I lose my footing, I can't take hold of you, of Tegan, of Lucas, of Hope or Kurt. My hands become waterlogged, the fog becomes too thick, the stars

disappear.

Roxie says I need to move forward, Sara says I need to release the past. That's what I'm hoping this will be—an apology, an explanation, my penance for the things I did in that destructive haze. Maybe if I relive it all on paper my regret will be immortalized. It can continue to live on these pages so I can move forward, look you in the eyes without wanting to beg your forgiveness, hold our daughter without apologizing for keeping you from her for as long as I did, be in the same room as my family without the guilt echoing in my ears, wondering if somewhere deep down they still hate me for abandoning them, for abandoning you.

My mother's forgiveness I'll have to continue to carry with me. I'll never know why she left me—why she left us—but I do know that I could have helped her, could have tried harder, could have fought for her. I could have told her we needed her, could have said it more than I did. I'll always live with that regret. I've accepted it as my penance for letting her go. But that's the punishment I've placed upon myself. The reparations every mothering deity demanded from me I paid while in purgatory: that haze which drove me away from you.

I'd like to begin with New Year's Day, 2007, even if just because it was the last time we were all happy and, for once, together. That had been when Scott was still moving as though to stay in one place for more than a few weeks would cause him to become stagnant and deteriorate. That changed in LA. I still don't know if it was to keep me afloat or to finally be where Joss was, maybe it was a little of both. Either way, I was glad for it. During those years of his constant movement, I had felt as though I'd had a limb missing. Phantom itches and all. I missed him. I needed him. At least in those days I'd had you to steady my balance. That phantom limb feeling only got worse when I left. In LA it was multiple limbs, my entire lower half—a mermaid without her tail, a siren without her song. Scott carried me through those days. In Austin, I had nothing. I was an empty torso, a ghost ship drifting in and out of reality. Tegan was my only light in the fog, if only because she was yours.

But on that day, in 2007, we were together.

I was whole.

We were happy.

I had been out running that morning, had left you at the house to sleep.

I know you know that road, that house as well as I do, but allow me the space to remember it. None of the subsequent owners ever could bring it back to the way it was, the way it had been when it had been the Matthews' house.

Not even before the fire.

Everything changed after Her.

My morning runs always took the same route less out of convenience and more because I loved the feeling of coming home from that direction: the ocean at my back, the sand beneath my shoes, surrounded by dunes, the roofs of the neighborhood peeking over the tops. The path would change to pavement and the dunes would be exchanged for tall, coastal homes on their strong, salt air weathered stilts, each painted some form of pastel, each lined with palms and oleanders, flowerless and dry that day in the winter cold.

Then there was home. Painted sky blue and towering an extra story above the others in the neighborhood. Rocky, not yet his full Maine Coon size, stretched out from under one of the ferns flanking the mailbox to purr and circle my legs while I tried not to trip over him between walking along the driveway and up the sun bleached, wooden steps. Mack's REM leaked through the screens of the open kitchen windows, him caterwauling along, Meg laughing and begging him to stop.

I'm still not clear when my parents had bought the house after moving back to Texas from Vermont after Mack was born, before Scott and I were.

All I know is that this had always been home.

All I know is that I'm sorry Lucas never got to experience it the way the rest of us did.

All I know is that I'm sorry Tegan never had a place that was always home.

As usual, Rocky had beat me to the door that day, had rushed in the second I had opened it, had leapt easily onto a barstool by the counter where Mack and Meg had been cooking and had stared hard at the food waiting in an assembly line across it.

"Alex," Mack had groaned. "You let him in."

"He's just hungry like the rest of us," Meg had insisted with that cutesy voice she always talks to Rocky with and lifted him off the stool to cradle him against her shoulder that was only a light fawn color because of winter, it would darken to a deep shade of tawny brown by summer. She took him to Mack, her thick, black ponytail swinging behind her like Rocky's tail. "He won't hurt anything. Will you, Rocky?"

"But he will. Won't you, Rocky?" Mack had returned, lowering his Matthews dirty blond head close to Meg's, his Matthews deep set, light blue eyes even with Rocky's.

Rocky had reached out to paw at Mack's nose bringing Meg to giggles.

"Give the cat a break," Dad had said, stealing a piece of pineapple from a bowl of mixed fruit at the end of the island counter then letting Rocky lick the juice from his fingers.

"Should he be eating that," I had asked.

Dad still feeds Rocky things without thinking.

"A piece should be safe," Tate had said from the couch in the living room without looking away from his DS.

Dad's eyes had gone wide with mischief. "You hear that, Rocky? You can have a *whole* piece."

While he had been reaching for the bowl again, Mack ready to protest, the water down the hall had shut off and Dad had turned before Rocky could get his treat. As he left for the hall, he had tapped my shoulder with his fist.

"Your turn, stinky." He had given me that fatherly smirk I never thought I'd miss; I never thought I'd have to live without. "Drag Marc out of bed while you're at it," he had added already headed for the master bedroom down the hall with the new king sized bed.

"I'll get Scott," Tate had nearly shouted and tore from the couch to rush past me for the stairs.

"Don't get your head bit off," I had called after him as I followed.

Back before you, before Scott's wanderings, the bedroom next to mine had been his. I'm sure you never noticed then, but there was a vent connecting the two. When it had been decided we were too old to share a room, it had carried secret messages in the dead of night when we were supposed to be asleep, each perched on the edges of furniture to get as close to it as we could manage. During the day, we would shout through it to call into the other's room. Once, I had tried to cover it up when I was mad at him, not realizing that vent had had a purpose other than our childhood communications.

After Scott, after it had been a guest room for years, after Mom's belly had begun to swell again, it had become the nursery. The walls had been painted a sky blue with a large, goldenrod yellow sun in the top corner stretching its rays out across the room. It had been Mom's idea—so the new baby could wake every morning to the sunshine no matter the weather. The

whole family (minus Scott, plus Meg, plus you) had spent a day measuring out and taping off the rays while Mom had supervised from the rocking chair Dad wouldn't let her get up from.

That rocking chair had been nearly three decades old then, is closer to four now, had been stripped and repainted a new color with each child: a basic, baby blue for Mack; green and yellow for Scott and me; Mom had had fun for Tate, each spindle a different color, spirals and dots painted along each one. That day, as she and Dad had directed us around the room with painter's tape and rulers, she still hadn't painted the rocking chair, still hadn't known how she wanted it.

It hadn't been Scott's room anymore. He hadn't even slept in it when he had come home for Christmas, instead sleeping on the pull out in what used to be Mack's room, in what was then officially Mom's office, unofficially the library. Mom had never used it unless she was writing emails or talking with her agent. She never had done her best work at a desk. Her best poems had always been written in the big overstuffed chair out in the living room, on the bench swing out on the deck, in the sand out by the water, on the rocks out on the jetty, on the various piers around Port A, in the only coffee shop on the island watching the people drift in and out between lines, in bed by the light of the big window in what was once my parents' room, in what I had thought would always be my parents' room.

In my room, our room on the nights you stayed over, I had slipped into the bed next to you. You had been on your stomach, your olive face with the dark stubble buried deep in the pillow, one arm above your head and your thick, always wild, black curls sticking out in every direction, the other outstretched among the side of the sheets I had occupied that morning before sneaking out. I had lifted that arm and slithered in beneath it while it instinctively wrapped around me.

"You stink," you had muttered through half-sleep and pressed your long, pointed nose against the crest of my forehead. (Don't you grimace at that. I know you hate it, but I love it. It's yours.)

"I love you, too?" I had giggled and nestled against your thin chest with the wispy, black, curly hairs.

"It's a good stink," you had insisted, your eyes still closed, your lips against
my skin. "I like your stink."

Already, I'm regretting what I will have to write. Already, my heart is

refusing to allow my hands to continue. Already, I want to write I'm sorry over and over until the ink blurs with the blood draining from my raw fingers.

I regret that now every moment of us like this, from before, has been tainted by my fear to stand still, my fear that to do so would have allowed the barnacles to take root and weigh me down until each breath was a burden and I followed my mother to the dark depths of nothing.

I'm sorry.

I need you to hear that.

I regret the truth which is that Jonathan never said things like that to me. Jonathan never made me giggle like that. Jonathan never would have tried to convince me to stay in bed a little longer like you did that morning, would have never tried to coax my clothes off despite my sweat and smells, would have never insisted between deep, genuine kisses, "I don't care. I just want you." Jonathan never held a candle to you, which somehow made it easier to be with him through those nights when I didn't deserve to see the stars.

I know now I was stupid to leave you.

I need you to understand that.

I regret that after She left I believed I didn't need those things. I believed what I needed was indifference. I believed what I needed was anyone who wasn't you, anyone who didn't know my depths, anyone who didn't know what I could possibly inherit even if it meant never knowing that tender understanding that only someone so familiar with my currents could provide.

I love you.

I need you to know that before I get to the parts I'm already regretting.

Until then, let me linger here where everything was serene, when that storm was nowhere in sight, not even out on the horizon. Had we been sailors, we would have known only by the red morning glow.

But we weren't.

And we didn't.

Instead, we had filled ourselves with bacon and egg tacos, fruit, coffee, orange juice all between overlapping conversations filled with laughter and high energy.

Everyone was there in the spaces of our home:

Tate with all his teen awkwardness, not yet used to that length he, Scott, and I had each inherited from our mother, not yet in control of those gangly limbs she always managed to use to her advantage like a creature who wasn't

limited to muscles, tendons, or inflexible bones.

(I was probably the only one of us four to get away with missing that stage, though I never have come close to her grace. Hopefully we can still help Lucas to, as well. When Scott and I were little, four, maybe five—no, it would have been after that. Mom had hit a low point after Tate and we were five when he was born. It must have been the next year. Well, Mrs. Hernandez from down the street. The woman with five daughters all close in age. I can't remember if you had ever met them. I think most of them had gone inland for school by the time you had left Fort Worth. Alma may have been the only one to stay in Port Aransas, but I want to say she studied something to do with math, so I'm not sure she would have come through your classes after Freshman Comp. Either way, Mrs. Hernandez had found out that Mom had kept up with dance after moving to Vermont and had begged her to set up classes for the kids on the island. I think Mom had only agreed because she had wanted me to try it. The classes had stopped when I was around fourteen. Something had happened and Mom just couldn't take it anymore, couldn't take much of anything anymore. But the lessons still stuck. Unlike my brothers, I had learned that my limbs were my own, no matter how foreign and uncontrollable they felt. If only I had learned to take that inward: to recognize that my thoughts, my emotions were my own no matter how foreign and uncontrollable they sounded. Maybe things would have been different. Maybe I wouldn't be writing this to you.)

Along with the awkwardness, school and books had no longer been enough to sustain Tate, though he had continued to absorb everything like a sponge—still does and hopefully always will. Scott had been his idol in those years. He had never said those words to any of us, but he had never needed to. All we had needed was to see the way he would listen to Scott's every word with that wide eyed intent, the way he would rush to sit next to him, would master *Mario 64* and *Mortal Combat* to impress him, would pester out where Scott had been, where he was headed (though even Scott rarely knew) so Tate could spit out with an excited rush everything he knew about the place off the top of his head.

The moments that would make his eyes shine, though, would be when he'd make a joke (whether intentional or not) and Scott would let out his genuine, burst from the depths of his belly laugh. Tate has never been the quick wit sort of funny, he's always been better building off someone else's quips,someone like Scott who seems to move through every moment with a casual comedy coursing through him that makes cracking jokes look like

nothing more than the natural way of things. But Scott does that with most things. The only thing I've ever seen him struggle with is the act of staying still. Even in his sleep his body screams with that innate need to move. As kids, back when we shared a room, I would fall asleep to his shifting and turning and in the morning he'd always be in some knot of limbs and sheets, if he hadn't left the bed entirely.

And his body seems to need that movement the way the tides need the moon. It's always been in him, ever since he was young. You missed the majority of those fifteen years when family trips were planned around the wind's secret conversations with Scott's feet. The way Mom would get anxious and withdrawn if she went too long without writing, Scott would become snippy and disinterested in anything that would come near him if we went too long without piling into Dad's Station Wagon and drive anywhere that wasn't Port A or Corpus Christi. He never seemed to care what it was—a nature reserve, a city, a camp site, an amusement park, a jungle gym off a bike trail, a mall—he just needed to move, to be headed somewhere else, to touch his feet to ground that hadn't already been claimed in the name of Home.

That had been the beginning of his wanderings, the reason he had stopped calling anywhere home. I know December of '06 and January of '07 had been hard for him, but his Christmas present to Mom had been to stay still until the baby had been born. We had all wished he would stay longer, but that morning in the kitchen, his feet had already begun to itch and, though still in good spirits, our words and actions had already begun to snag along the hidden rocks below his surface as his tide crept lower and lower.

I wonder how much of it had been Mack's idea. If he had secretly hunted Scott down just to convince him to stay more than a week when he came in for Christmas, if he had kept talking and hinting until "stay until New Year's" had become "stay until the baby's born." It seems like something Mack would do—go out of his way to bring us together, convince one of us to sacrifice a little if it meant we'd be whole again.

Because, if Dad is our ship's captain, Mack is the first mate. He's always been the responsible one, the one keeping us in line, the one keeping us safe. Even in high school, when Mack had been a sophomore, Scott and I freshmen, Mack had kept an eye on us.

Mack had been the one to make sure we were on the bus in the morning.

Mack had been the one who had always known where we were between classes and after school.

Mack had been the one the office would call before our parents when

we were sick or in trouble, that is, if he wasn't the one getting into trouble for us.

October of our freshman year, Scott had been caught flirting with sophomore Jennifer Reid, the girlfriend of senior Elijah Torres. A fight had broken out, Scott only avoiding getting hit because in those years he had had the body of a scarecrow who had grown tired of his perch, flailing and dodging with little rhyme or reason which had truthfully just confused Elijah into missing every swing. But then Mack, with Dad's sturdy build that could cement him to the ocean floor while the rest of us would be swept away with the softest tug of the undertow, had taken over and punches had landed. Elijah had lost a tooth. Mack's nose had been broken. It had been understood from that day forward that a fight with the Matthews twins meant a fight with Mack.

It had been while waiting for Mom in the nurse's office that Mack had met the new girl who had forced herself to throw up to get out of cutting frogs in Biology. In my fourteen year old mind, Meg had been entirely too cool for Mack. Meg who had lived outside of Texas. Meg who wore threadbare Ramones and Led Zeppelin concert t-shirts she had bought off Ebay. Meg who listened to actual punk bands and knew Pink Floyd had recorded more than just *The Wall* and *Dark Side of the Moon*. Meg who could wear heavy, broken in Doc Martens one day and pristine ballet flats the next without ever looking like she was trying to be cool, because she just was. She could beat Scott at *Mortal Kombat* and discuss Joyce Carol Oates with Mom. She could listen to Dad talk about porpoise population sizes without her eyes glazing over and hold her own in our family Scrabble tournaments.

But I'm realizing you know all this, don't you? After all, you had met Mack and Meg at TAMU-CC before you had met me. For a year, I was just the kid sister always trailing behind y'all after school trying to hide all the cliché things I hadn't wanted you to know you made me feel because for you I wanted to be something more than the seventeen year old in the sharpie scribbled Converse and Tori Amos t-shirt. For you I had wanted to be the girl in HEB wearing the thrift store sweater and John Lennon glasses who you had stared at from over your shoulder between checking off items on Mack and Meg's Thanksgiving shopping list. For you I had wanted to quote poetry instead of song lyrics, read Virginia Wolf instead of Stephen King, drink fancy coffee instead of Big Red. You were the reason I had applied to TAMU-CC, you were the reason I had minored in English, you were the reason I had grown my hair long and stopped wearing smudged black eyeliner.

I had wanted you to see me the way my father had seen my mother back in Vermont: the twenty-something with grace filled limbs who didn't know how to dress for New England weather, always reading books with poetic titles, always scribbling in leather bound notebooks, always matching his Philip K Dick with Vonnegut, his Asimov with Anne Sexton.

I had hoped that one day you'd look at me the way my father always looked at my mother, the way he had looked at her that New Year's morning: as though she alone brought the waves to his shore.

And that morning she had looked back at him as though he alone had brought the rhythm to her rhymes. She had been happy that morning—she always was when she had all of us in the same room—and she had watched every one of us with her large, deep-set green eyes that ended on either side in perfect points creased with a smile that stretched out the precise heart which was the center of her lips. Her caramel waves had been clipped out of her warm, winter's ivory face and flowed down her back. Her belly had been round and heavy under the weight of the baby who was to arrive, as we would continue to say for a few more weeks, any day now.

I have to admit, I had to consult a photograph to remember that. Her skin is a pale white in the photo on the back of her last collection, but I remember it only ever as varying forms of sunkissed—a simple glow during the winter that would deepen to a soft amber by the end of summer.

She's fading from me.

That smile did come back the moment I looked at the photograph, but I had to look to remember. There was a time when she had been seared into my memory. Her voice had been etched along my bones, her movements had echoed in my muscles, her touch had been stitched into my skin. Beyond the Matthews dirty blonde hair and hooded blue eyes, I had been every inch her daughter, just as, beyond the Caro black curls and olive skin, Tegan is every inch mine.

I know one day she'll lose me and I'll fade from her bones, her muscles, her skin, her memory. I just hope she'll be older by the time that happens, that she'll have children of her own, that I'll leave her in a place of peace, that she won't ever have to ask why I left her.

After breakfast and card games, someone (either Tate or Scott, may have even been Dad) had remembered we still had fireworks leftover from the night before. We had walked to the beach in a staggered group talking and

laughing between our clumps while Tate carried the plastic milk crate where the last of the roman candles, Catherine wheels, and bottle rockets clattered around in the bottom. While you men folk started with the smaller fireworks, Meg, Mom, and I had abandoned our shoes to brave the winter waters. It hadn't been long before Mom had settled into the sand at an angle where she could see both the ocean and her boys, her tired, swollen feet outstretched in front of her.

No matter the weather or the season, she had always looked most at home on the beach—the wind begging her long hair to dance, her eyes quietly exploring the horizon or following the gulls, her long hands behind her in the soft sand. Sometimes I would almost forget she was my mother and not Calypso surveying her land.

Y'all had moved on to the larger of the fire-toys pulling Meg to watch at Mack's side. Mom had smiled up at me and watched as I lowered into the sand next to her. I can still feel her fingers combing my hair away from my face, her head on my shoulder while we watched the fun, y'all's whoops and laughter, the roman candles' pop and crackles echoing off the dunes.

She had lifted off my shoulder and sucked in through her teeth. I had turned my head to see her with one eye clenched and one hand on her belly.

"I can't tell if he likes it or is trying to hide," she had said with that laugh like wind chimes.

"How're you feeling? Baby wise?"

"Ready."

"Thought of a name yet?"

Before answering, she had taken me in with that small, lingering smile that only mothers have when looking at their children as through preserving us down to our smallest gesture, our deepest molecule.

"Lucas," she had finally answered.

"And if it's a girl?"

They hadn't wanted to know the sex, after four kids, hadn't cared.

"You know he won't be," she had told me with a smile.

She was right. I knew it in my bones. Had known it before she had. Had felt him humming around me before she'd begun to examine her own body for signs. You had thought, maybe hoped, that he would be ours, but I had known even then—our first would be a girl.

I had rolled my eyes and tried not to groan the way I had all three trimesters.

That wind chime laugh had burst from her. "Sorry I disappointed you."

"Not you. Dad. Tell him I'm ready for a sister."

She had laughed again followed by a sigh as she leaned back against her hands. "Pretty sure this'll be the last. Besides," she had looked me over again with that preserving smile then reached up to reorient a strand of my hair the wind had caught. "I don't think she'd be able to take the pressure."

"What pressure?"

"Of competing with you."

A laugh had sputtered out before I had been able to catch it. "Mom, stop."

She had leaned against me, her arm loose around my waist, her chin on my shoulder, her belly against my hip, her jasmine perfume cradling me. "It's true, though. You're the only girl I need."

"What about Meg? Or whoever Tate ends up with?"

"No girl for Scott?"

I had shaken my head, so sure at the time. "Scott won't ever stay still long enough for one to catch him."

"There's one out there somewhere. He'll be cruising by and she'll catch him off guard. Make him reverse all the way back to her."

"If you say so."

"You'll see. She'll be everything he needs. And he'll be everything she needs. And she'll be part of the family, just like Megan, just like whoever Tate brings home, just like Marc...but they'll never be mine." She had squeezed me tighter. "Not like you."

Why did I do this to myself?
Why did I start here?
Why didn't I just start with Jonathan?

I don't know anymore.
Maybe I'm just stalling.
But, at the same time,
You need to know.

You need to understand where my head had gone.
Where my heart had gone.
Why I couldn't yet give them back to you.

They were with Her.
For five years they were lost with Her.

Lucas was born in mid-January.

I wish I could say it would be months before the signs presented themselves, but, looking back, they had always been there. They just hadn't been obvious. They had been things we'd been able to easily dismiss. Things we attributed to the baby and that laborious act of giving birth.

When, in the hospital room, we were all celebrating and Mom had sat quiet, watching us with eyes that were sometimes there, sometimes not—she's just exhausted.

When she had slept most of the hospital stay—she needs her rest.

When she would give us short, often one word answers—it's the hospital with the nurses and doctors and sounds, she's always been easily overwhelmed.

When she had barely eaten—once she's home with real food, Mack or Meg's cooking, she'll eat again.

Then she had come home and while she had bounced back to some degree, there had still been something there that, looking back, I can now say had been different, but a kind of different we had seen before. You'd think that would have made it easier to spot. And in some ways, it had. We had been able to see it before the end after all, even if it had been too late. But sometimes you see something so often you stop seeing it altogether.

I still believe that first week had set a false precedent for us all, especially Dad who had already seen her through three pregnancies and four babies before Lucas. Between work and school schedules, we had gathered at the house as much as we could through that week. Scott had spent it mostly with Mom, his camera constantly around his neck. Those are still some of my

favorite pictures of us all, maybe my favorite pictures of her. But I think I say that about all of Scott's pictures. Scott does have a way of doing that, after all. He sees things through that lens, things I always manage to pass over. He got that from Mom (Tate, too, we've come to find): the ability to see the world as paint on canvas.

Even through the crying and diapers and near sleepless nights, Mom had managed to see the stars through the clouds. I think she had seen them because of Scott. With him there it had felt like a family event, all of us gathering around to get as much of him as we could before his inevitable exit. With him gone, it had been too easy to slip back into our separate lives.

Not that I blame him for leaving.

Not that any of us do.

Not that Mom would have.

I've told him that.

I'm still not entirely sure he believes it.

But, because of that first week, when the wind had blown and Scott had left in his unceremonious way, leaving behind only pictures and a slip of paper with a scribbled name and phone number, we had thought Mom's outlook would continue. Had we thought to keep paying attention, we'd have seen those heavy, grey clouds steadily beginning to black out the night sky.

But that blacking out of the stars had been gradual.

Then again, it almost always is.

Isn't it?

In the beginning, there are always more good days than bad. Enough that when the bad days hit, you're able to shrug them off, hold out for the sunrise that you know will be on the other side. But as time moves on without a way to clear away the clouds, those bad days stack up until a few become a few in a row, those rows become several, you start to wonder where the sun had gone, you start to consider the possibility it'll never return.

But here's the thing that, on the bad days, I still find carved into my guilt:

None of this had been new.

By that point in our lives we had thought ourselves experts in my mother's weather patterns.

And we were.

And we weren't.

And on those bad days I want to shake each and every one of us, even Tate who either hadn't been around for the previous episodes or had been too

young, the rest of us insistent on shielding him. How could we have so easily ignored the truth? We had known the signs. We had been her watchers. We had become masters of her signals. Why this one had been any different, I'm still not sure.

I'm starting to think I never will be.

Though, maybe it had been because she had always pulled through before.

Maybe it had been because we had all been so distracted with our own lives.

Dad had gone back to work at UTMSI, grumbling about lectures, and pouring over data that he brought home and frequently left out on the dining room table. Luckily, his campus was within walking distance from home. I think he came home to Her more than the rest of us.

Tate had started back at high school. He had been re-acclimating to his routine, balancing homework with friends, planning dates with that girl from his astronomy club.

Mack and Meg had just bought their first house together a few months before. They had gone back to unpacking and painting, driving inland to antique stores to replace their first apartment furniture with real "grown-up" pieces on the weekends and around Mack's return to high school history curriculum and assignments, Meg's restoration jobs, business school night classes, and playing phone tag with her father and his contractors.

You and I had been settling into the spring semester, bouncing from your apartment to my bedroom, sitting on your couch or my bed or your balcony reading from stacks of textbooks and writing out essays, trading them back and forth for feedback. You had started as a TA that semester, had still been holding on to part time shifts at that tiny bookstore in Corpus. I had started that work-study job in the English department where professors lamented teaching Shakespeare or Modern Lit before not so subtly asking how long Mom's maternity leave would last.

We had all been living our lives as though nothing had changed, each passing through that house like ships in the night. The only constants became Mom and Lucas, lighthouses begging us to come home, stay still.

And then I trip.

I know the script I should be telling myself. I know the words people want me to say.

This wasn't our fault.

We couldn't have predicted something none of us wanted to happen.

We did everything right.

We did what we were supposed to do.

But simply sensing that script on my tongue, I want to yank it from my mouth and set it on fire. That deep, hurt, still lost part of me that's been left to the elements until it's raw and bleeding and waterlogged knows that fucking script is a lie. It's what we tell ourselves to remove the burden, cleanse ourselves of the guilt, move forward for one more fucking day. There are still days when that part of me wins, when I don't want to move forward. I want to tether myself to the stilts of that house and refuse to keep moving because to keep moving would mean to leave Her behind, to lose Her forever, to once again leave Her alone on that island with nothing put pen and paper and a red felt tip flare gun.

Maybe I'm having one of those days.

It's in the fog of these days when I'm glad to have Tegan, to have you. Without either of you I'd have anchored myself to the ocean floor of that pain a long time ago.

Tegan may have been the only reason I ran.

Both times.

I was running towards her even when it was away from you.

I realize how that sounds, but you have to understand the things I could never successfully put into words back then when I still wanted you to hate me:

In those days you and everything around you screamed my mother, my guilt, my failure as a daughter. To remain in the echo chamber of that screaming would have meant falling behind Her.

I had felt it in my bones.

I had read it on the wind.

I had seen it in the stars.

Even if now I know it had been a lie.

I think it had finally begun to culminate somewhere between late January and early February.

"Has Mom come out at all," I had asked Dad in a hushed tone in the kitchen so Tate couldn't hear from the couch.

I had been with you over the weekend the way I always was, had been in a blissful ignorance. I had been home a day and Mom had spent it either in Lucas' room or in her own as deep in the covers as she could get.

Glancing at Tate, Dad had shook his head then sighed and turned to lean back against the counter, his hands gripping the edge behind him.

When he had taken too long to answer, I had asked, "You don't think...?"

"No." His eyes had shot up to meet mine with that fatherly reassurance that used to work even when I knew it wasn't the truth. "Not yet. It's too soon to tell."

The assured feeling had rushed away though the moment he had said the words *too soon*. "Dad."

"I know," he had rushed to say before I could continue. "I know. But..." He had glanced at Tate, at the stairs, at Rocky rubbing against his calves. "We need to hope for the best."

I knew he was right, but after that I had set to getting hold of Scott anyways. I'm sure you remember those days. The ones before Scott had a cell phone. It's hard to imagine now how he had managed as long as he had without getting one. Before Joss he was always moving, always hopping from one couch to the next, one world to the next. He would always give me the number of the first couch.

From there he'd leave a trail of numbers and names some of which didn't always work out.

My attempts to follow his trail like Poseidon stalking Odysseus had started as a secret, waiting until everyone else had gone to sleep or first thing when I had arrived at your place. The number in Atlanta had led me to a guy named Charlie who only knew that Scott had been heading up the Appalachian Trail with a pair of photographer friends. He hadn't known where they were going to be stopping, so I'd been left with digging up a map and my old notebook of numbers I'd called in the past, trying each one that fell along the mountain range. Finally, I'd hit Rosalie in Roanoke who had said he'd headed out to Charleston, West Virginia. I had then been sent to a noisy room in Nashville where someone had quickly given me a number to someone out in the Ozarks. That was as much as I had been told "somewhere in the Ozarks."

It had taken me a week to get that far. I hadn't been in a rush then.

Now I wish I had.

I had been at the house for Sunday dinner. It had been one you had skipped. I think that was the night when your father had called right as we were leaving the apartment, not that that narrows it down any. You hadn't had the heart to cut him off, had let him go on ranting at you in that way I wish you wouldn't. He shouldn't put that on you. But I guess I'm not really one to talk. While he ranted in your ear, you had written out on the back of some paper that I should go without you, tell everyone you said hi and sorry, that you'd see me the next day on campus.

Reluctantly, I had gotten my stuff from the corner of your apartment that was the bedroom, let you kiss me goodnight, and left without you.

(I'm stalling again, aren't I?)

That night at dinner without you, Mom had floated in and out, sometimes using Lucas as an excuse to disappear, sometimes just slipping away without a word the instant our eyes were diverted. When she had been with us, her eyes had kept slipping into the distance. When we had managed to hold her attention, her smile had been only half hers, half a trick of the moon against the fog.

It hadn't been a good night.

It hadn't been the first.

It hadn't been the last.

At some point between kitchen timers, Dad had gone off to look for Mom, Tate had gone upstairs to get his laptop charger, Meg had slipped into the bathroom, Mack and I had watched them leave.

"Alex?"

I had looked at him, but, in truth, he hadn't had to say my name or catch me alone. I had been waiting for the same moment to slip out onto the deck hopefully unseen. Though, once outside, words hadn't been necessary—I had known his question and he had known my answer—and we had avoided exchanging them while sitting on the bench swing staring out at the ferns nudging the empty oleanders.

But eventually, he had needed to ask it and I had needed to say it.

Finally, he had dared to begin, "Mom?"

"Yeah."

"How long?"

I had stumbled, realizing I hadn't had a solid timeline. "I first noticed Monday."

"Dad?"

"He's hoping we're wrong."

Mack had let out a long sigh and slid down against the bench shaking his head. I had pulled my feet up onto the edge and hugged my knees to my chest, my lips and chin pressed against my jeans.

"Scott?"

"Started calling around Monday night."

"And?"

I had shrugged, trying my best to remember where I had left off without the hidden notepad of slowly growing names and numbers in front of me. "Colorado, I think. Ronnie."

Mack had made a noise. He was always uncomfortable with Scott's wanderings. Before he could comment, the door had opened with a cautious speed and Meg, after glancing back over her shoulder, had stepped out. Once on the deck, the door closed behind her, she had only to look at the two of us to know the topic and what direction it had been headed.

With a long sigh that had matched Mack's she had gone to him and slid into his lap, his body accepting her without words, mine aching for yours.

"How bad is it," she had asked me what Mack had been avoiding.

"Hard to tell yet," I had admitted, though it had been only half the truth.

If I had been entirely honest the way I should have, I would have told them it had been worse than before, had moved with a silent speed like a shark once it had smelled blood in the open water. Though, I can't remember anymore if I had actually known that then—if I had still been mistaking the fin for a porpoise.

Meg had let out a long sigh, her demeanor collapsing to match ours. "Y'all think maybe…?" She'd glanced at the door again. "Maybe it's time?"

I'd looked to Mack who looked to me.

I don't know how much we've ever really told you about what had happened in late 2004.

Meg had been there, of course, had been there since 2001, had jumped into the dark waters to keep us afloat without hesitation or question. That's why Mack had proposed to her once it had all been over, because even seeing us at our lowest hadn't scared her away, had only made her dig her heels into the wet sand and fight for us.

But you…

You had been new back then and we'd all hesitated to show you just how bad it had really gotten. I had only admitted what I had to you at the time because Scott had been in Washington with Connie touring college campuses. I had been without a limb, had been at risk of losing another, and I had wanted you to be someone who could support me the way Meg supported Mack even if we were still a year out from you looking at me as anything other than Mack's kid sister. But I still remember masking the truth, still keeping you from seeing just how dark those waters were, still afraid they might scare you away.

"When's the last time she's seen Preston?" Mack said, pulling me back from the edge of those waters, already searching the choppy waves for my own reflection.

I just shrugged.

With the pregnancy, Mom had stopped seeing her therapist entirely. She'd had a distraction, something to occupy her thoughts and move her forward. Her sessions had become more check-ins than they had active work. She'd stopped seeing the point in them and none of us had wanted to question her. We had all been just as distracted. Then Scott had come home and she'd been so happy, light as air. The skies had been bright. Though, now I wonder if she really had been that happy; if it had all just been one more trick of the light.

Mack had sighed and Meg had looked to him then me then Mack again.

"Is that the next step then? Call him?"

Chewing the inside of my lower lip, I had nodded and Mack had done the same, his arm tightening around Meg's waist and, from my peripheral, I had seen him slip his nose under her hair and to the space just below her ear. It had made me miss you, had made me want to leave the deck right then and there and walk barefoot to your apartment. You always knew how to make everything so nearly right with only your touch, cradling me close in that way that felt like a ship's hull—I knew the water was right there on the other side of your arms, but I trusted that you would keep it all at bay.

I hate that we lost that.
I'm grateful we found it again.

We had waited until after dinner to tell Dad.

Had waited until Tate had gone upstairs to call that astronomy club girl.

Had waited until Mom had slipped away yet again.

Had waited until Dad had spotted the three of us sitting quiet at the table staring at various spots around the dishes.

He had sat with a weight like an anchor hitting the ocean floor then pressed his clasped fists against his lips and the bottom of his nose. We had each glanced at him, none of us wanting to be the one to start.

"Spill," he had finally said, also staring at the table.

Mack and I had looked at each other, hoping the other would break first.

"Don't make me drag it out of Meg," Dad had said looking between us with a shadow of his usual smirk.

We had both taken in simultaneous deep breaths then met the other's eyes hoping it had meant we wouldn't have to say the words. Then Mack had nodded to me.

"It's Mom," he had finally said.

"I know," Dad had said and the three of us had turned our heads to look at him.

Mack glanced at me when Dad hadn't continued then took in another breath. "We think it's time to call Preston."

Dad's eyes had closed before Mack could finish his sentence, but he hadn't protested.

"It's just..." Mack had tried to start. "You know it's better if—"

"We catch it head on," Dad, back to staring at the table, had said for him.

"Yeah," Mack had sighed.

Meg had reached over to take his hand before pressing the back of it against her lips. That ache for you had come back and I remember fidgeting with my phone fighting the urge to call you right then and there.

"Al," Dad had said and I had looked up away from my longing for you to meet his eyes. "You get hold of Scott yet?"

I had just shaken my head.

"How far out did you get?"

"Ronnie."

"In Colorado?"

I had nodded and so had he. Then he had taken in a long breath and leaned back in his chair, his eyes back to watching my thumbs running along the buttons on my phone. "Go ahead. Tell Mom goodnight first?"

"Dad," Mack had said. "What about—"

"I'll call in the morning," he had said, his voice a heavy sort of numb. "Doubt they're open this late."

Mack had nodded, but neither he nor Meg had moved from the table. I hadn't been able to take it any longer and had stood before going to Dad to hug him around the shoulders.

"You sure," I had asked him.

"Yeah," he had told me, his big, calloused hand on my forearm. "Tell your mom—"

"I will," I had assured him before letting him go.

Upstairs, my shoes on, my overnight and school bags repacked, I had found Mom in the library staring at the couch that had been a bed for the previous two months.

"Hey, Mama," I had whispered to her.

She had looked up at me in that way she did when she had been pulled out of a stream of thoughts: with her lips softly puckered, her eyes wide, her brows lifted. Those wide eyes had traveled to my shoulder, my hand, my keys sticking out of my pocket.

"You leaving me, too?"

All I had been able to do at first was blink. "Just for tonight, Mama. I'll be back after school tomorrow."

She had nodded and looked back at the couch. Watching her, I had felt

suddenly guilty for needing you more than I needed her. I know now, that wasn't true, that I needed her in a different way, just not the way that I had needed you in that moment. But it doesn't matter what I know now. That night, in that moment, seeing her already slipping away from me, I had been knocked off my feet with the guilt, with the ache for you to make everything very nearly right.

Leaving my bags at the door, I had gone to her side and started to kneel, but she had taken me around the waist instead and pulled me into her lap. It hadn't been easy. It had been years since I had been small enough for her to cradle.

With me finally settled, she had sighed and adjusted her arms around my waist. "When did you become an adult? I can still remember when you fit perfectly in my arms." She had tucked her chin against my shoulder, my head leaned against hers. "I could envelope you. You had been all mine."

I hadn't known how to answer and instead had stared at the couch with her. "Scott isn't gone forever, Mama."

"Might as well be."

"Do you want me to stay tonight?"

Her body had inflated against me along with her deep breath that she had swiftly let out again. "No. Go to him. Tell him I said hi." But she had hesitated in letting me go, her voice becoming soft next she had spoken. "And tell him to keep you safe for me."

Again, I hadn't known what to say. "I love you, Mama," had been all I had been able to come to. "You know that, right?"

She had pulled away from me and smiled, tucking my hair behind my ear. "Of course I do."

Looking her over, I had felt entirely unsure of what to do. Finally, I had nodded. "I'll be home tomorrow. I promise."

"You better." She had kissed my cheek then guided me to stand.

"Goodnight, Mama," I had said, giving her a proper hug before leaving.

"I love you, baby," she had told me.

By the time I had made it to you, I had been numb.

I had tried not to think about that conversation with my mother the entire way back to you, The Killers on full blast from my car stereo while I did my best to drive away the thoughts I hadn't wanted to be thinking, the cycles it had been too easy to fall back into.

It had been so easy for us then.
For me to fall into you.
For you to carry me.

I'm sorry we lost that for as long as we did.
I'm sorry I made it so easy to.

But on that night, on nearly every night over the next few months, you had taken me in without question. You had let me fall into you, had told me everything was going to work out, that everything was going to be fine.

And that night, we both believed it.

It's such an easy lie to believe until nothing's fine and nothing can be taken back. Only once it's too late can we understand those words to be a lie.

But on that night, it hadn't been too late yet, the lie had felt like truth on your tongue, your ship's hull arms around me.

Everything was going to be fine.
Everything was nearly right.

Dad had talked to Mom that night, had convinced her to go see Preston, had made the call for her, had gone with her to the appointment a week later and sat in the waiting room with his knee bouncing, I'm sure, staring at the coffee table and the fake plants, pretending to read those month old gossip magazines he hates mixed in with the Psychology Todays and the Yoga Journals he was indifferent to, trying to chat with the receptionist who would politely return the conversation before shyly returning to work.

Afterwards, he had told each of us, excluding Tate, what Preston and the office psychologist had decided:

Postpartum depression.

But that was nothing.

Right?

One in nine mothers develop postpartum depression. That's what we had found on the internet the next day when I had met you in the English department's TA office for lunch.

One in nine.

That's common.

That's treatable.

That's recoverable.

That's nothing.

So lost in the lie we had been telling ourselves, we had forgotten that one in nine is nothing when it's one in nine women who aren't already prone to these things; women whose brain chemistry wasn't off kilter from birth; women who hadn't already been committed; women who weren't familiar with breakdowns; women who hadn't watched their own mothers go through

the same thing; women whose families weren't trained in rotational watches.

Dad hadn't helped the lie, either. He had told us how Mom had gone through levels of postpartum depression with each of us, had dropped to lows that had worried him, but that had gotten better with time, with support, with love. Had we not been so focused on believing the lie, we would have reminded him that that same time, support, love only helped when she was open to it, when the night sky was clear enough for her to see even some of the stars, just enough to keep her going.

But how were we supposed to know?

But how could we not have?

And the family watch had begun.

Mom would never be left home alone. We'd structure our schedules around her. That had been the easy part. We had done it all before. What hadn't been easy, what had made this one different, had been that Dad hadn't wanted her to know it was happening, hadn't wanted her to think it was because we hadn't trusted her. So, we had perfected our lies. Mack had just been stopping in to visit. Meg had just wanted to help out around the house so Mom could focus on Lucas and writing and sleep. You had just wanted to talk through your thesis with her. Mine and Dad's lies had been the easiest, taking over the watch in the morning and at night, nothing out of the ordinary.

What we hadn't anticipated—though looking back, I'm not entirely sure how we hadn't—was her catching on, her being just as familiar with this rotation as we were.

She had figured it out with you.

She may have started to suspect something with someone else and I'm sure you had done everything right, had said all the right things, avoided all the wrong wordings and topics, but one of those afternoons in March she had for some reason picked me to get the truth out of.

I had come home to find you and my mother in the library talking. Everything had seemed fine, normal. I had joined you and we had talked a little longer before she had sent you downstairs for something. That's when her face had shifted as she had met my eyes.

"Spill," she had said without elaboration.

My eyes had gone wide. "Spill what?"

"What did Preston tell your father?"

I had stumbled. Like any mother worth her salt, she had always been good at making me lose my footing. "What—when—I don't know—"

"Alexandria." Her eyes and mouth had been stern, staring at me hard while I had scrambled to think how Scott would have answered.

But I'm not Scott. He had taken all the wit, all the quick-footed thinking, all the ability to say just the right thing at just the right time all the way back in the womb leaving me with a stumbling, short sighted tongue that loses all contact with the radar tower just when I need it most.

"Mom," had been all I could think to say.

She had looked away from me, closed her eyes, let out a long sigh.

"Mama, I—"

"I'm not that bad off," she had insisted. "I'm not stranded."

"Not yet."

Her eyes had snapped onto mine. "You don't know that."

"I—Dad said—"

"And you told Marc? And Megan?"

Of course we had. But I hadn't been about to tell her that.

"How long," she had asked.

"How long what?"

"How long have they known?"

I still hadn't understood what she was asking, had tugged at the cuffs of my sweater and avoided her eyes. "Known what exactly?"

"About—" Our ears had perked towards the baby monitor where Lucas had made a sound but then fallen back into silence. Before continuing, she had let out a long sigh. "About me, Alex. About...all this."

I had shrugged. "I think Meg's known since high school."

She had lowered her elbows to her knees and heavily ran her palms against her face.

"Marc since...since last time."

Taking in another deep inhale, she had dropped her hands to interlace her fingers then looked to the hall. "I should've figured as much."

"I'm sorry," I had muttered, not sure what else to say.

She had shaken her head. "I guess..." The words not ready to come out, she had instead continued to take in and let out long breaths through her nose, her lips pursed before finally parting just enough so those words she hadn't wanted to face would crash onto the carpet between us. "It's best...if

they're—" Her eyes had refocused when you had stepped into the doorway " where you had hesitated, looking between us with wide eyes. "If you're going to be part of all this."

"Part of what," you had asked.

"Part of us," She had told you and nodded you into the room. "If you're gonna stick around…"

I remember you taking my hand from between my knees and clasping it between both of yours. I remember my entire being becoming suddenly buoyant. I remember needing to be closer to you, pressing myself against your side to keep from floating away entirely. I remember wanting to slip into your chest, wanting to wrap myself around your heart, wanting to never be apart from you.

I'm not saying these things in retrospect. I realize how it could sound that way. But I'm not.

I was conscious of those things then.

I was conscious of them after.

I was conscious of them without you.

Never once were you less than everything to me.

"I guess, then it's best that you know," She had said then, watching you watch me as though I alone brought the waves to your shore, watching me depend on you.

Reading that back, I know that's not how she had actually felt. I may not have wanted to know it then, but some part of me had. Like Mack, she had always insisted on carrying her burdens herself. Accepting that you and Meg had been shown those burdens couldn't have been half as easy for her as she had insisted it was.

I wish I could say that I always knew better, that I had learned from her mistakes or even that those cycling currents had skipped over me, but we both know the truth. Maybe the thing I learned from her drowning, from her mother's before her, was to finally grab hold when someone thrust their hand beneath the surface.

I wish I had learned it sooner.

I wish I had learned it with you.

That night, everyone had learned that Mom now knew of the watch.

She had asked us each to promise her one thing, however: to keep it all from Tate.

We already had, but it had been an unacknowledged action. Once it had become a spoken rule, my stomach had begun to turn every time I was around him, the words scratching at the base of my throat. It hadn't helped that he had started to notice the way the house had been almost never fully empty, the way Meg had begun coming over early in the afternoon to start dinner with Mom, how Dad had stopped packing lunches to take to campus, how you had begun hanging out at the house without me or Mack or Meg. It had only been a few weeks before he had gotten the truth out of me, as well.

Somewhere during those weeks I had finally gotten hold of Scott. He

had been in Nevada documenting the behind the scenes of a friend's film. It was a friend we've never met, not unlike most of Scott's friends. I hadn't even recognized the name when Valor, his friend in Arizona (one of the few of Scott's friends we had met in person, who we'd stayed with for that awful week when Scott hadn't come home after a two night trip to Kofa, who still has my number logged into her phone after all these years the way I still have hers) had given it to me along with a number she had told me was actually for a state park's office, but that someone named Jose would know how to get hold of the film crew for me.

After talking to Jose, it had taken two hours for Scott to call me back. I know I had told you all that when it had happened, but I'm still in varying levels of disbelief that that had been the only way to get hold of him, that I had grown so used to it that, at the time, I hadn't thought twice about it, that none of us had.

I also know you were there for this next part, but I need to recount it, need that reminder that before everything I've yet to get to, before everything I still regret, you had carried me all the way to the end, had continued to make everything so very nearly right.

"When do you think you'll be able to head this way," I had asked Scott from the corner of your couch I had tucked myself deep into, your house phone cradled between my ear and my shoulder so I could pick at the blown out knee of my jeans.

I should have been making that call at the house, but I hadn't wanted to hide, hadn't wanted to do it alone huddled in a corner of my room hoping no one would over hear from the hall. Besides, I had wanted you there with me, had wanted to feel you against me the instant you got home.

I hadn't needed to be in the same state as him to see his shrug. "Depends. Why?"

Before I could answer, though, you had come in the front door. Catching sight of me, you had stopped and looked me over with that smirk beneath those furrowed brows. All at once my heart had tried to shove its way out of my chest to meet yours.

"Scott," you had asked.

I had nodded.

"Marc," Scott had asked.

"Yeah," I had told him.

"Tell him hey."

"He says hey," I had told you.

"Hey," you had returned loud enough for him to hear with a wave between hanging up your keys and unloading your school and work bags while my eyes never once left you.

"Alex?" Scott had said, but I hadn't wanted to be listening to the way his voice had shifted from casual amusement to sibling concern.

I had wanted to hang up, to fall into you when you collapsed on the couch next to me. To rip your clothes off, let you rip mine off, feel your skin against mine, your ship's hull around me.

"Why'd you give Jose Marc's number?"

I had wanted to say it and I hadn't, my mouth struggling between the two. You had watched me, your arm wrapped around my knees, your hand running back and forth along my thigh. When my chin had begun to quiver, you had let go of my knees and reached across to guide me to your chest where I had curled without question.

"It's Mom, isn't it," Scott had easily guessed.

"Yeah," I had muttered from your hull.

On the other end, I had heard him shift and breath deep. "How bad?"

"Still around five."

"But who knows how long that'll last," he had finished.

Silence had taken over while Scott had processed it all, I had burrowed myself against you, you had tightened your arms around me to compensate for the molecules of space my burrowing had cause between your limbs and my body.

"Preston?"

"Postpartum."

"She got through it with Tate."

"She'd had *all* of us."

He had taken in a long breath and let it out again, but had still taken a few more seconds to answer. "I gotta finish here." The phone had shifted. "Feel like shit if I took E's money and ran right before everything was done."

"Kay."

"Give me…" Papers had shuffled. "Two weeks? Yeah. There abouts. Hopefully no more than that."

"Kay."

A shop door bell had rung.

"Hey, uh. Sorry, Al, but I, uh, I gotta go."

"Alright."

"I'll call you when I leave? And when I hit El Paso."

"Okay."

"Hey," he had added, his voice serious and, knowing him by heart, I could just see him ducking his head down to meet my eyes, "don't you get stranded, too. Not until I get there. Kay?"

"Marc won't let me."

"He better not," he said with a chuckle then took in a deep breath. "Kay. Love you."

"Love you."

When I had hung up, you had taken the handset from me and tossed it to the end of the couch before wrapping both arms tight around me again.

"What won't I let you do?"

"Get stranded," I had answered into your shirt.

"Never."

And you hadn't—not there on the couch or in your bed not long after or in my bed that night when you hadn't wanted to leave me alone after the dinner Meg and Mom had made for all of us.

And even after that day you had continued to try, but it's near impossible to keep a ship at sea when the captain keeps steering it into the storm.

I refuse to blame you for that.

Scott has never blamed you for that.

No one's ever blamed you for that.

No matter how much you wanted us all to.

But I'm stalling.

It had been a week later that I had fucked up.

Or maybe I hadn't.

I still can't say if Tate knowing had been a good thing or not.

There had been an accident at one of the properties Meg's dad had been flipping. She had been on watch that day, but hadn't trusted her dad to work everything out by the books and not in a way that could have left them liable

again. So, Mack had managed to grab a temporary sub while I had started my way from Corpus to Port A. It had already been one of those days that had felt as though I had been tangled in sea weed that would wrap itself back around one ankle the instant I had freed the other.

By the time I had gotten home, Mack had been on the front deck with Mom and Lucas and I had still felt that slippery claustrophobia.

"Sorry," I had shouted up the stairs. "You gonna make it back in time?"

He had already been headed down. "Not for the last bell, but it should be fine."

"You two do know I can be alone for ten minutes, right?"

There had been annoyance under sarcasm which had made us both stop at the middle steps and look first at her, staring squarely at Lucas who was grabbing hold of her fingers between pulling them to his mouth, then each other. Scott would have known what to say. Would have known how to make it into a joke that would have reminded her we were buoys not prison wardens.

"Mom—"

But she had done her best to smile and wave my words away before I had had a chance to say them. She stood and adjusted Lucas against her shoulder. "It was a joke, baby."

Rocky had sped up to slip in around her feet, the front door had closed behind her, Mack had turned back to me, I had met his shrug with a nod.

I hadn't had to ask and didn't bother, Mack answering anyways.

"Meg said she was somewhere around a six all day," he had told me while starting down the rest of the stairs. "Kind of ruined that when I came when Meg had to leave. And when I wouldn't leave 'til you got here."

"Now?"

At the bottom, he had shrugged, fidgeted with his keys, and looked back up at the door. "Not a four yet." Then back at me. "Not exactly a five. Four and a half?"

I had nodded then followed him to his car. "I really am sorry. Getting off campus was hell."

"I remember," he had assured me with a smirk between sliding into the driver's seat.

While he had closed the door and rolled down the window, I had stared up at the house with my arms crossed tight over my stomach that was slithering itself into a knot.

"Think it's been ten minutes," I had asked him with an attempt at a smirk.

He had returned the attempt. "Give her five more. But don't be…somewhere else tonight? She's always in a better mood after hanging with you."

"Mack. I'm Alex. Remember?"

"Oh, right," he had laughed and hit his forehead with the heel of his palm. "Alex, girl. Scott, boy. Sorry, I don't know how I keep mixing you up." He had smiled up at me then reached out to pat my arm. "But seriously. She is."

"Sure."

He had just smirked at me then pulled out of the driveway.

In the street, he had waved to me and then Tate who had walked up from the street corner where the bus had dropped him off.

"Hey," I had called to him with my arms still crossed. "Nothing after school today?"

He had shaken his head. "Why was Mack here?"

I had glanced down the street after Mack's car turning the corner then to the house and shrugged. "Hanging out with Mom, I guess."

He had squinted at me. "In the middle of a school day?"

I had just shrugged then started for the front stairs, avoiding his eyes.

"He called in a sub for last period so he could just hang out with Mom?"

I should have said something, should have at least stopped, but I hadn't. I had felt too guilty about lying to him, about leaving him alone on the island while we went out to man the lighthouse.

"Alex."

There had been an impatient sternness in his voice that had made me stop, but not enough to turn to him.

"What's going on?"

Still trying not to look at him, I had just stood there only partially facing him, picking at a splintered spot in the wood of the railing. "Nothing," I had tried to tell him.

"That's bullshit."

I'm still not sure why those words had triggered me to finally meet his eyes, but it had. Only then had I realized how tense his shoulders had been, how tight his jaw, how pink the whites of his eyes. With a long breath, I had

gone back down to him then pulled him by the shoulder towards the street. He hadn't said a word, just followed me down to the beach while gripping the straps of his backpack.

When I had stopped on the other side of the dunes, safe from the view of the house, I had stopped and turned to face him, but hadn't said anything, my arms crossed tight while I stared at the sand between us.

"What," he had asked.

I had opened my mouth, but the words hadn't wanted to come out. He's my baby brother. It's my birthright to protect him, to keep him from having to face things like that.

"Stop it," he had nearly shouted at me forcing my eyes to meet his again. "Stop acting like I can't handle anything."

"Tate—"

I realize now the gentle tone of my voice had been a bad decision. I realize now it had come out as condescending even if that hadn't been how I had intended it. I hadn't realized it then.

"Don't talk to me like that, Alex! I can fucking take it."

"You don't want to take it," I had told him without thinking.

"That's not for you to decide!"

"Yes, it fucking is! You don't know!"

"Because y'all won't fucking let me!"

He had been right.

But I hadn't wanted him to be.

"You won't know what I can handle until you let me fucking—"

"Fine," I had shouted over him. "Fine! Mom's having a fucking breakdown, Tate!"

He had stared hard at me, his entire body tight.

"She's fucking suicidal! You think you can handle that?!"

From down the beach, sea gulls had cried out, people had continued about their lives. They may have been staring at us. They may have been ignoring us. I hadn't bothered to look, hadn't even considered it. I had been too focused watching Tate in front of me.

"How-how long?" He had stopped shouting, his voice instead distant, almost lost.

"This time?"

He had blinked. "This time?"

"Yeah, Tate. Is that what you wanted to hear?"

He had glared at me. "Of course not."

I had known that would be his answer, but I hadn't wanted to know it. Hearing it however, had forced me to face it and had forced the tide back down along with it.

"Sorry," I had sighed and closed my eyes. "I'm sorry."

"When…How many…?"

I had shrugged and turned to sit against the bottom edge of the closest dune, Tate dropping his backpack before following me.

"'04 was the last bad one."

At first, Tate had just nodded. We had both stared at the waves. The gulls and terns had called over the wind.

"And this time?"

"Mack and I noticed it late January."

It had been a moment before he had continued. "How do you know…?"

"Preston told us. Back in February."

He had nodded. "Is that why she went back?"

"Yes and no. We had to suggest it."

"Why?"

I had picked at a scab near my elbow before answering. "Makes it easier if you catch it before it gets too far."

He had stared at the hem of his jeans, twisting the fraying ends around his fingertips. "Has she, I guess, tried to…?"

I had watched his fingers while avoiding answering his question. "Once. That I know of. Kind of. Dad figured it out before she could actually try anything."

He had turned his head enough to squint at my sandals. "Was that when…?"

"Yeah. She, uh, she wasn't on a retreat."

He hadn't responded, just blinked at my shoes.

"It was her idea not to tell you."

"Would you have?"

I had looked him over for a moment. It hadn't hit me until that moment how little he had resembled the kid he had been back when Mom had last been committed.

"I don't know."

He had nodded, but not in agreement. It was more of a "of course you wouldn't" kind of nod.

"You were so little."

"I was 12."

"And you didn't need that on you. No one that age does. I don't even think you need it on you now."

"I'm part of this family, too."

"Tate. We know that."

"You don't act like it sometimes."

"I'm sorry. I am." I had taken in a long breath and let it back out into the wind. "You've been the baby for so long. It's not an easy switch to make."

He had nodded, though I don't know if he had really taken what I had said to heart yet. "Is there anything I can do? To help?"

"Maybe. You can't take off school—"

"I can miss a few days."

"Maybe. But, after school might be better? Maybe if you come straight home, you can…fill in the gaps? But, Scott'll be home soon, so he can—"

He had perked up a little. "Scott's coming home?"

"He's finishing up an assignment in Nevada. Said last Thursday to give him two weeks. When he gets here he's gonna try and stay home with Mom during the day."

What little pep the idea of Scott had filled him with had flickered out then and his face had grown serious, already aged by years I didn't want to count. "I want to help."

"I know. And we'll find you a place. For now just…be there for her. Let her know you love her."

That's so much easier said than done, though.

Everything about those days was.

I wish it wasn't.

I wish it wasn't so easy to forget that loving someone whose brain chemistry has taken away their ability to see that love is hard. Forgetting that only makes it that much harder and not just for those of us on the outside.

But I guess you know that.

I guess I was the reason you learned that firsthand.

I hope Tegan was too young to have learned it, too.

I'm worried she wasn't.

I'm worried she learned in those years how it feels to watch someone you love be ripped away by the undertow, be battered by the current driving them in cycles that take years of endurance to break, that can take lifetimes.

I shouldn't have put that on her.

I shouldn't have put that on any of you.

I should have just given her to you from the beginning.

I should have…

But that would have broken her more.

Wouldn't it?

Would have left gashes where, hopefully, there are only faded, barely memorable scars.

At least I did one thing right in those years:

I never left her.

I never let him take her from me.

And when the undertow had been too much,

I managed to come back to her.

I fought that cycle

For her.

It had only taken a few days for Mom to figure out that Tate now knew about the burdens she continued to insist on carrying by herself even with us all around her offering to take them from her.

I can't remember anymore what Tate had done or said, but it had been enough to make Mom grow quiet. Then, the moment he had left the room, she had rounded on the rest of us.

"Who told him?"

"Told him what, Anna?"

She had glared at Dad. "You know what."

"He doesn't know," Mack had insisted.

"He does," I had said somewhere between hesitant and defiant.

Mom had looked at me with wide eyes and tight jaw. "Why?"

Avoiding looking at her, I had shrugged. "He could tell something was going on."

"That wasn't for you to decide, Alexandria."

"It was his decision. I didn't *want* to tell him."

"And yet you did."

"I'm sorry. He could tell there was something going on. He was mad we weren't telling him."

She had clenched her eyes shut and shaken her head. "He doesn't need this."

"I told him that."

She had met my eyes.

"He said he still wanted to know. Mom, he just wants to help," I had

added when she had let out a long breath. "He just wants to be here for you. Like the rest of us."

She looked at her feet. "He doesn't need this."

Before anyone could stop her, not that anyone had really tried, she had turned and retreated to the bedroom.

I know I keep saying it, and I'll probably continue to say it, but I still don't know if anything we did in those days was right. That's what I'm supposed to tell myself, isn't it?

That we did everything we could.

That we said all the right things.

But did we?

I don't know.

Is there any way of truly knowing?

Roxie told me the other day that I shouldn't dwell on it. "Can't change the past, Al. It's done. No point in trying to come up with a different ending."

The look on Sara's face had told me that she hadn't entirely agreed, though she hadn't said anything to disagree either. Maybe it was just the way Roxie had said it that had made her right eye scrunch up along with the matching corner of her mouth the way she always does when something doesn't entirely sit right with her.

Because that's the thing, Roxie *is* right. Even if I do want to believe that it's easy for her to say, she does know better, I guess. She let go of the past a long time ago. Let go of all that anger and self-destruction. Opened up her sails for the wind to take her exactly where she's meant to be. And she seems infinitely better for it—light as air. You'd almost think she could walk on water.

But it still doesn't change this guilt I've been carrying for the last ten years and it still doesn't change the way that I want to believe it's all easy for her to say.

Roxie barely knew her mother.

Roxie didn't let hers slip from her fingers

Roxie didn't have to find hers cold.

It doesn't help that the guilt over Her is and will always be a direct line to the guilt over you and over Tegan. Even over Lucas. If we had done things differently, if we had said the right things would she still be here and would

what I'm currently trying not to get to not have happened? Would I have finished that semester the way I had started it: utterly indifferent to him?

And here we are.

It's stupid how I keep avoiding this part and it's not even the worst of it all. It is, however, the first link towards the part which still gnaws at my ring finger whenever I think of him. I try not to, but that's not how memory works, is it? We don't get to dictate who slips in through the cracks nor how, nor when.

It's been days and the only progress I can seem to make with this letter is to stare at that word: *him*. Every time I sit down to continue, my arms go numb and I stagger through disjointed thoughts that I eventually erase because none of it actually leads to him, not the way I need them to so you can fully understand. Every night I've given up with no progress made. I've returned to the hall, passed Tegan and Lucas' door, passed the twins', to our bed where I've slipped under the blankets to press myself against you and fought every crying whale inside of me that wants to wake you, apologize to you, beg you to hate me, beg you to love me.

And yet, that love is what makes this all so hard.

If you hated me, if you yelled at me, if you banished me to a prison atop some rocky island with no way back to you it would make all this so much easier. At least then I could beg for your forgiveness, throw myself at your feet, beat my chest, cry out *mea culpa's* the way I deserve. Here, in our home in a whole different city, with you in our bed, our children down the hall, I'm knocked off my feet every time the wind drags him along my memory whispering *fraud* until all I can do to relieve the guilt is to cry back:

Mea culpa

Mea culpa

Mea culpa

But then you wake and you look at me from over your shoulder, those warm eyes still fuzzy with sleep, that half-awake smile so quick to appear, your arm slipping around me as you roll over, your fingers, your lips searching out mine in the dark.

And then you love me.

So easily, so effortlessly.

And then I realize,

Roxie's right.

And so is Sara.

I need to let him go.

I can't change what I did, what he let me do to you. It's done. And if you're going to keep insisting that I don't need to be forgiven, then that leaves no one but myself to search out forgiveness from.

Doesn't it?

I'm not sure anymore where in all this it had happened, just that it had been after midterms and before Scott had come home. I had gotten back an assignment with a grade that had been barely passable with a red ink note at the top asking me to stay after the lecture.

The entire remainder of that lecture had passed with my mind, as usual, entirely focused on everything else: wondering how Mom had been doing that day; what she and Meg had decided to do; trying to remember if you'd had a lecture or office hours next; if I could get away with skipping my next class to go spend it with you or maybe even just go home, spend the rest of the day with Mom and Meg.

Maybe I should have.

Maybe things would have turned out different.

So mentally gone from campus, by the time everyone around me had begun packing up their things, I had already forgotten about the red ink note on my paper.

But he hadn't.

"Alex," Jonathan had called to me before I had reached the door and I had looked to him with raised brows and wide eyes. "You have time to talk?"

No.

I had nodded and moved to the side of his desk at the front of the classroom where he had been stacking up papers and filing them away into his expensive looking leather messenger bag.

"How're you doing," he had asked me between tucking books in alongside the papers.

I had shrugged. "Fine?"

My answer had made him stop and meet my eyes. "You sure?"

I had just shrugged again, avoiding his eyes.

"'Cause your grades took a real nosedive recently. The kind of nosedive that comes with not being fine."

I had shaken my head. "No. Yeah. I'm fine. Everything's fine."

His eyes had narrowed at me, but when I had refused to give him any more, he had nodded and gone back to packing up his bag. "I know it's probably weird to say, but, if you decide you need an impartial ear, you know my office hours." He had lifted his bag off the table and held it at his side while his free hand had slipped into his pocket and he had looked me over for a brief moment. "You know this class is only offered in the spring, right?"

I had crossed my arms and nodded.

"And that I'll give you shit if I have to teach you all this again just because you were too stubborn to take help when it was offered?"

I had lifted my eyes to see his smirk then, despite myself, had given him a small smile and nod.

I wish I could tell you there was more to it. That everything else to come hadn't begun with a simple check in from my professor over slipping grades. That I'd had more sense than to let someone like Jonathan take me away from you for as long as he did.

But what's done is done, right?

There's no use trying to come up with different ways it could have happened.

I'll just have to live with it.

Or you can just let it go, Roxie would tell me. *Move forward, Al.*

Or you could just forgive yourself, Sara would say. *Let the past stay in the past.*

And I want to.

I want to move forward for you. I want to move forward for the kids. This is probably the worst of ways to do that, but it's the only way I can think

of that allows you to fully move forward with me. I want us on even ground from here on out. And that won't happen with me holding all of this inside me, carrying it on my own.

I just hope you'll still love me when I'm done.

I just hope you'll still want to help me carry it.

It had taken three weeks instead of two for Scott to finish in Nevada and come home.

Tate had started to become anxious, asking me every chance he got if I had heard from him. Of course, I hadn't. I had debated calling the park again, but the idea of pulling Scott away from a job that could be done or could be far from it seemed like a daunting task.

But, finally, towards the end of April, Scott had finally called me.

"We're headed out now," he had said over a crowd of chatter behind him. "Just gotta find Ryan and make sure the email I got's still good then I'm driving away." He had said that last bit louder than the first and a female voice had moped from near enough to hear. "Sorry," he had said to, I assume, the voice with a chuckle.

The next morning, I had woken to a voicemail—him half-yelling over the sounds of whooshing traffic in the distance, occasional convenience store door dings, family chatterings drifting by. He'd hit El Paso. Had twelve more hours to go before he'd hit home.

"Don't tell Mom," I had told Tate when he had nearly lifted off the ground over the news. "I want it to be a surprise."

His eyes had been as wide as his smile and it had seemed like everything that had happened over the past month had already begun to melt away. "So, he'll be home by dinner?"

"Hopefully."

Though, when dinner had started without him, Tate's mood had begun to tarnish.

"He'll get here," I had whispered to him at the kitchen counter while he

grabbed another soda. "He's always later than he says he'll be."

And sure enough, just as everyone had been getting full and Tate had all but given up, Rocky had jumped up in Mom's lap to turn in excited circles, purring like a boat motor, his yellow eyes large and never leaving the front door where a key had eventually turned. Mom's brows had furrowed then her eyes had gone wide when she had seen Scott standing in the doorway, bag slung over his shoulder, that lopsided grin across his face. When she had stood to greet him, her eyes had lit up the way they used to and her shoulders hadn't been half as heavy as they had been before.

For the first time in months, the stars had come back out from behind the clouds.

I had wanted to hope they'd last, but, unfortunately, I had known it wouldn't, that it wouldn't be long before the clouds would sneak back in again.

But for that week, maybe a little more, everything had gone nearly back to the way it had been. Scott had spent time with Mom during the day and had gone out to visit old friends and haunts late at night after Dad had gone to bed and before Mom had snuck back out of the bedroom to sit on the couch with me (sometimes us) or up in the library reading, writing, sorting.

The rest of us had returned to our routines.

I wonder if maybe we shouldn't have;

If maybe we should have continued to show her we wanted her with us.

On one of my days off, Scott had been itching to get out of the house. Mom had been at around a seven that day, had made breakfast for us, had sat on the living room floor with me while playing with Lucas, had started talking about submitting some poems, had even sorted through a few while Scott and I had sat on the couch in the library giving our opinions, Rocky sprawled out on his back between us, stretching and pawing for our attention, purring loudly when we would pet him.

When Scott had suggested going down to the beach, she had initially been hesitant, but I had reminded her how many days it had been since she'd left the house, Scott had made a joke to make it sound less like a reminder of her shortcomings. Which it hadn't been, but her brain chemistry had been skilled at taking something harmless and making it into a blade.

Half an hour later we had walked down to the water.

It had been one of those blessed few weeks of Texas spring: the cold and rain had stopped, but the hundred degree, humid days had yet to hit.

Scott had wandered off to take pictures (and to follow after a woman he had been eyeing) while Mom and I had sat at the edge of the swash where the waves would just touch our legs before drifting back out into the surf. While I had entertained Lucas, who had been fascinated with the ebb and flow of the waves, laughing every time the water had licked at his toes, Mom had been building a castle in front of us, the wet sand gathered in her fist to drip lonely spires standing nearly as high as her shoulders kissed with constellations against those beginning stages of amber returning to her skin.

A clump of seaweed had washed up against Lucas' and my feet. When he had tried to reach for it, I had picked it up by the stem to show him. With curious eyes, he had run his splayed out fingers along the small berries and leaves of varying yellows and oranges while I had spun the small bundle. When he had grown bored with it, instead focusing again on the frayed edges of my shorts, I had begun to pick the seaweed apart and tuck the pieces into Mom's braid that had run down her back to end along the bottom edge of her bikini top just visible through her lacey cover.

"What are you doing back there?" She had laughed, making Lucas babble and reach out for her.

"Making you a siren," I had answered with a smirk.

She had turned to us with that sentimental, preserving smile before running her fingers along Lucas' temple, his blond curls from the salt and sun, while he had smiled up at her with stars in those hooded Warren green eyes.

"Do you want to hear the story of the sirens," she had asked him with that loving excitement she had always initiated her stories with.

He had laughed and reached up for her. But instead of lifting him from my lap, she had taken his hands, kissed the tips of his little fingers.

"Well," she had begun and plucked a clump of seaweed from the water. While she told my favorite of her stories, one I had heard so many times I nearly know it by heart, she worked seaweed into a ring:

Once upon a time, before the rise and fall of the Roman Empire, there were creatures called sirens.

The sirens were ugly, violent creatures with the heads of foul crones, the bodies of eagles, and talons so sharp they could rip through steel. Their favorite prey was the meat of sailors who had the unfortunate chance of crossing the sirens' paths.

But with time, the sailors had learned to avoid their territory. The sirens, craving the feeling of flesh beneath their talons, had to think of a new way to lure

their prey. So, they flew across the lands of men disguised as seagulls, watching, observing. It wasn't long before they discovered the weaknesses of these men.

Armed with this new knowledge, the sirens returned to their rocks and coves in the sea to wait.

Once the ships set sail again, the sirens dove beneath the waves. The salt shredded their feathers, the foam softened their skin; the water twisted and massaged their torsos until they were long and lean, supple breasts emerging from their now naked chests; the undertow pulled their wings and talons into graceful limbs; the fish knitted seaweed into their hair until it mimicked the waves above them, moving and swaying with the current.

One by one, the sailors spotted among the rocks merging with the cliffs and the sea, beautiful women rising from the surf. And when the boats drifted towards them, the sirens began to sing. Echoing through the cliffs and caverns, their haunting songs bled longing and heartache, beckoning to the men with curled, seductive fingers.

"Closer. Closer," the sirens sang.

The sailors were unable to resist.

"Come closer. Come," the sirens cried.

The sailors obeyed.

Closer and closer they came until their ships began to scrape against the rocks. But they took no notice and continued closer, closer. Loud cracks and creeks intertwined with the singing. Water began to flood their hulls. Slowly, the sailors realized their mistake. Just as they began to shout and call to their captains, begging to retreat, the sirens' bodies and faces twisted into the grotesque creatures they truly were. Unfortunately for the sailors, this would be the last image they would see before the sirens tore the men to pieces.

She had reached out to place the crown of seaweed atop my head. From nearby, Scott had stalled in coming back to us and crouched in the sand, watching us through his camera's viewfinder.

"You are so beautiful," Mom had told me while adjusting my sea salt twisted hair into just the right design. "Could tear a man's heart apart with just a glance of those eyes."

I had looked away from her to Lucas who had been watching Scott with that three month old's intent stare. "Mama?"

"Mmhmm?"

"I always wondered why the sirens didn't just stay beautiful women."

"Why's that? You think it would have made their killing easier?" She had given me a smirk.

"I don't know," I had laughed. "Maybe."

"Well," she had answered slowly yet matter-of-factly while continuing to style my hair to match hers. "You can't hide who you truly are forever. Eventually, the real you has to come out. It's better to just…let it happen, I guess. Better than forcing yourself to be something you're not."

I wish I could say there was more to that answer, that there had been hidden meaning beneath the words which I could have deciphered and used to save her. But I don't think there had been. I mean, I can try and dissect it all I want, pull the words apart and thread together meaning, but that runs the risk of connecting pieces that weren't meant to go together, runs the risk of putting words into her mouth that I had wanted to be there, but that, in truth, hadn't.

Unfortunately, I think her explanation applied to me more than it had her. Not that she had known it would. Just that it did. For so many years, I had tried to be something that I wasn't:

I had tried to be okay.

I had tried to be stable.

I had tried to be a housewife.

I had tried to be a Peterson.

I had tried to be no one's.

I had tried to be anyone's but yours.

I'm still not entirely sure I've figured out the real me. She's in there somewhere. She just needs to find the right song that will lower my defenses long enough for her talons to rip through my flesh. The closest I've ever come to finding her has been with you.

But, like I said, the stars hadn't lasted.

I thought this part would be somewhat easy. I mean, I knew writing it would hurt, but I figured it would come easily. It's the part of all this I think about the most. Yes, even more than Jonathan. But, I'm realizing now that we never talk about it.

Not just you and me, either. None of us do. We talk about Her and we talk about our lives with and without Her, but we never talk about that day. Scott and I talked once about the week leading up to it, but only once. And even then, we stopped short.

And now, I've allowed this letter to linger for more than a week. I had begun to think that I had said all I needed to say, but then realized I haven't gotten to any of the parts I need to tell you, the parts I took from you.

Today at lunch, Roxie said maybe it's a sign that this is what I need to truly move forward. That maybe I can't because I, and the rest of us, won't allow ourselves to really, truly let Her go.

And then Sara made that right-faced squint, and I understand why.

We wouldn't actually be letting Her go, would we?

I don't know what we'd be doing instead, but right now, by not talking about that day, neither acting like it didn't happen nor acknowledging that it did, we're making it…almost sacred. I realize that sounds strange, and maybe it's still the wrong wording, but what I'm trying to say, I guess, is that we're giving it a power that it shouldn't have.

Or maybe it should.

I don't know anymore.

Maybe I never really did.

I do know that it had started nearly all at once. It's like they say: when it rains it pours. The part they leave off is that sometimes that storm is in truth a test of our strength, and sometimes some of us have been pummeled for so long by the rain and the hail and the wind that we no longer see it as a passing storm. Suddenly, it's just life. Suddenly, we realize this isn't living. Some of us pack up our bags and move for drier climates. Some of us lost the keys a long time ago. Some of us drown before we ever find them.

Mom had figured out that Scott was just home to watch her. Truthfully, I think a part of her had known, but that same part hadn't wanted to acknowledge it. Scott's feet had already begun to itch and Mom had sensed it.

I've never bothered to ask Scott what had started the argument, but one day I had come home from work and an anxious tension had already flooded the first floor, had been working its way up the stairs. Tate had been outside on the bench swing with Scott, both staring at nothing.

"What's wrong," I had asked, but neither had explained.

Tate had just shrugged while Scott had avoided looking at me.

Inside, I had found Dad talking to Mack in a low voice on the couch. When I had stood in the entry way they had both looked up at me.

"Go talk to Mom," Mack had said and nodded to the bedroom.

"Why? What happened?"

Dad had taken in a long breath and leaned back against the couch. "She and Scott got in a fight."

"About what?"

"Alex," Mack had said before Dad could explain further. "Go make Mom feel better."

Looking back, I hadn't wanted that responsibility. I had wanted us all to share it. But I also hadn't wanted her alone in the bedroom while everyone else had sat outside the door waiting for her to save herself.

Though, I guess that isn't fair, is it?

They had tried to save her, had wanted to. No one had wanted to leave her to fend for herself. But sometimes you get hit by splintered shrapnel so many times you start to believe the best thing to do is to just get out of the way.

You know, I had all but forgotten about this, and it's probably nothing, probably faulty memory…then again, you always like to point out when those weird moments happen, when I get those feelings that I always try to dismiss, even when you laugh and nudge me when those feelings, those…visions, I

guess you could call them, turn out to be right. But, when I had touched the door knob that day, I had been hit with the smell of ink, had heard that scritch and scratch against paper, had seen the thick red loops and squiggles of Her handwriting.

When I had opened the door, there she had been, in that king sized bed mostly under the covers, her back pressed against the headboard, her notebook against her knees which were practically under her nose, the red felt tip pen she edited with scribbling across the page so fast I had had a hard time imagining the script would be legible. Her lips had been wriggling against each other, her bangs had been shoved back so many times they were nearly standing on end, the whites of her eyes had been as pink as her nose and they hadn't moved when I had entered the room, instead solely focused on the marks of her pen. Rocky sat at the end of the bed like a gargoyle watching the door, his tail flicking from one side to the other. Looking up at me, he blinked deep and slow before continuing his watch.

"Mama?" I had whispered and climbed onto the mattress to crawl to the headboard next to her.

But she had just shaken her head, otherwise ignoring me.

At first, thinking she was just in the middle of a thought, I had let her go on writing, curling against the headboard and stack of pillows next to her. But she had kept going. It had only been when I had leaned against her shoulder to try and sneak a peek that she had snapped her notebook shut with a rush.

But she still hadn't looked at me.

"Sorry," I had whispered, but hadn't moved from her shoulder.

She had let out a long sigh then placed the notebook on the side table. The felt tip she had held onto, flipping it in circles against her knee while I watched.

"No pen?"

"Ran out of ink." She had nodded to the wall on the far side of the room.

Not too far from the baseboard had been the pen she usually kept in the side table drawer.

I had nodded then settled close to her.

"What happened Mama?"

She had shaken her head, tapping the red felt tip against her knee. But after a few tense seconds, she had taken in then let out another long breath.

"Scott shouldn't be here."

"He's here because he wants to be."

"No, he's not," she had said over me. "He's here because of me."

She hadn't been wrong. "Is that such a bad thing?"

"I shouldn't be keeping him from what he's supposed to be doing."

I had tried to argue, but she hadn't let me.

"This isn't how it's supposed to be. I'm supposed to protect *you*. Not the other way around."

What had I been supposed to say?

She hadn't been wrong about that either.

Even if I had wanted her to be.

"Well," I had tried my best, "it is the way it is, Mama. And we're not gonna just leave you because of it."

"Maybe you should."

I had shaken my head and burrowed deeper against her. Her entire body had inflated then deflated against me while the breath audibly passed over her lips.

"I'm sorry," she had said. "I shouldn't be putting any of this on you."

And that's the part that confuses me the most.

In so many ways, she had been right. It's the same reason I roll my eyes when you let your father rant about your mother at you, the same reason I try not to let our kids and Lucas see us at our lowests, the same reasons Mack and Meg try to leave the room on the rare occasions they argue—some things you shouldn't put on your children.

But, at the same time, I had wanted her to put it on me. If that's what it would mean to get her through the storm, to hang on long enough to see those stars again, then I would have been more than willing to take that for her.

I had wanted her to depend on me the way I had always depended on her.

Even if it had meant losing sight of some of those stars, as well.

It's so easy to look back now and see how this was all going to end, but in the moment, it's the last place you want to go. Still, some part of me must have known because my drifting had amplified. I had started skipping classes and calling in to work more and more so I could stay at home with Mom and Scott or you on your days off. You had never questioned me through that, had never made a remark about the very real possibility I'd have to take each of the classes I was skipping over again, had just loved me on those days off, had just let me sit in the TA office on the days I had managed to, at the very least, make it to campus. You had let me drift through those days, even if we never talked about the thing neither of us had wanted to talk about.

And yet, that same part of me that had known where it all was going must have wanted to say something to someone. Why it couldn't have been you, I'll never know. Maybe because you were too close. You weren't a lighthouse, you were there in the boat with me.

On one of the rare days when you had been able to convince me to go to class, it must have been pretty obvious how far I had been mentally from campus, because while everyone was filing out, Jonathan had called me over again.

"Walk with me?" He had said with that half-smile when I had made it to his desk.

I had crossed my arms and shrugged.

In the hall, we had mostly walked in silence. I remember being surprised by how comfortable that silence had been. Like you, Jonathan hadn't pressured me to fill it, had just patiently waited for when I was ready to. It hadn't been until we had reached his office that either of us had said anything.

He had placed his leather messenger bag on a table in the back corner then fell into his desk chair and looked up at me. "What's going on?"

I had stared down at him. "What do you mean?"

Leaning forward to cross his arms on the top of his desk, he had raised his brows at me. "Things aren't getting better. I'd ask if you're okay, but I'm pretty sure the answer would just be 'fine' again."

I had started to tell him that I was, but for some reason the words wouldn't come. Instead, I had let out a long breath and slid into the chair across from his. And he hadn't said anything. Not *I knew it*, not *I told you so*, not even a smirk, he had just watched me and waited for me to speak.

"My, um, my mom's having—I guess, it started as postpartum, but...now I think it's another...another breakdown."

"Another?"

I had nodded, but hadn't continued, hadn't elaborated.

"And how's your family handling it?"

I had shrugged. "Best we can."

"Which is?"

I had shrugged again. "This."

"Sure that's healthy for you?"

"Does it matter?"

"Of course." When I had blinked at him, he had continued. "You can't expect to pull someone else from the water when you're drowning yourself."

"She's my mother."

"I'm not saying let her drown. I'm saying make sure you're in the lifeboat, too."

I wish I could say that I had taken what he had said to heart, but it would be a long while before I would. If there's anything good that came from Jonathan being in our lives, I'd say it would have to be that. Without him I don't think I'd have ever learned to stay in the lifeboat.

Then again,
It had been those early attempts to stay in the lifeboat
That had led me towards self-destruction.

I had told myself that Jonathan had been right—that I had been too

focused on my mother; that I needed a day, just one single day to not think about any of what had been going on at home. So, I had convinced you to spend the day at your place with me.

Shut away the outside world.

Nothing but a day of your flesh against mine.

I don't know why this is so hard.

I don't know why I can't even commit this to paper.

They're just words.

And maybe that's what keeps making this so hard. Because so much of me wants to hold onto this. Wants to carry it on my back, trek barefoot through the desert. *Mea Culpa.* But Roxie keeps telling me I'm not a martyr. Sara keeps saying She wants me to move forward, to forgive myself, to be everything I can for Tegan, for Lucas, for Hope and Kurt, for you.

But I'm scared, Marc.

What if by doing this I lose Her?
What if letting go of it means letting go of Her?
What if this is all I have left of Her?

I know it's not.
I know that's ridiculous to think.
But fears are almost never rational,
Are they?

And then there's a whole other part of me that's afraid that to relive this all will be to drive me away from you again. Who's to say that reliving this guilt won't also retrigger all the lies I told myself in those days, all the ways in which I believed I didn't deserve you? What if now I also believe Tegan doesn't deserve me either? Or Lucas? Or Hope or Kurt?

I left my mother.
I left you.
How long before I leave my children, as well?

Sara and Roxie keep promising me I won't. You keep promising you won't let me. You have gotten better at that, haven't you? At recognizing when it's safe to let us drift with the wind and when you need to attach an anchor to my heels.

I love you, Marc.
I love everything we've grown to be.
I love everything we've built together.
I love everything I am because of you, because of the kids.

I know She'd thank you. I know She'd be grateful to you for keeping me safe, for carrying me when I could no longer carry myself, for taking me back even after everything I did to you. Because you're everything I need and the kids are everything I wanted. Without y'all, I'd drift back into the storm to splinter against the cliff side. You and the kids are the light through the fog, the stars in the dark. I'm sorry I was blind to that for so long.

I guess I should stop stalling. Even Sara's stopped answering my messages. Roxie probably told her to. How she knows me so well after so little time I have no idea.

I'm sure you want to relive all of this as little as I do.
But Sara says I need to say it out loud. That I can't keep holding onto it like this. But I'm still not ready to take it quite that far.

So, here we are instead.

I don't really know where to start.

It was May.
Tegan might be the only reason I don't retreat entirely through that month.
It was just before finals. It was a wonder I had made it as far as I did without dropping my course load entirely, how I had passed at all. I was with

you at your apartment. It was well past noon and we had yet to leave your bed. Your hand was between my legs. Your mouth was locked with mine.

When the house phone rang, you reluctantly left me, though you never turned your back on me, watching me with that smirk while I continued where you had left off and watched you back.

It was Scott.

He asked if my phone was off.

It was.

He'd been trying to call me, had a question about the grocery list.

While I talked to him, I turned my phone on.

I wish I could say I did it because I had gotten some sort of sense that I should, that something greater than myself told me that She needed me. But, in all honesty, I have no idea why I did it. I have no idea why of all the times for those stupid moments, those stupid maybe visions to not happen, it had to be then.

I hate the world for that.

Three messages.

One from Mrs. Hernandez:

Alex, Mija. Your mom just dropped Lucas off at my house? I asked if she was okay and she said everything was fine, but…I don't know. I'm-I'm sure it's nothing. Anyways, I uh, I tried you dad? But the school said he's out on a boat with a class or something? I don't know. I shouldn't be worrying you with this, I'm sorry. But, just maybe…I think maybe you should check on her if you can. I think. I don't know. If you can. Okay. Sorry.

I shot up from the floor and started searching for my jeans.

One from Scott:

Hey, uh, sorry, I stole Mom's cell. Figured this would happen. Anyways, I tried the house, but Mom's not picking up, so, you're the lucky winner. What's…blue bottle soap? If you don't call me back in…ten, I'm calling Marc's. Don't care if you're fucking or not.

You were already asking me what was wrong.

One from Mom:

Alex. I…Baby, I'm sorry. I just…I'm sorry. Fuck. Maybe this is… (That silence. No single word can properly explain the way it made my head spin and my heart race and my lungs ache and my arms go numb and cold like heavy steel.) *I love you, Baby. I'm sorry. I love you.*

I still hear that voice sometimes at night when it's too quiet and you're already most of the way towards sleep and I feel too guilty about waking you to make it go away. The waterlogged sound of it. Everything underneath it that she had been trying not to say. Her arms all but reaching through the phone for me, trying to call me home.

And what was I doing?

Trying to stay in the lifeboat while she drowned just out of my reach.

The fifteen minutes it took us to leave the apartment and get to the house were somehow the most frantic and yet the longest fifteen minutes of my life. I remember scrambling for the rest of my clothes; throwing yours at you while you tried to get me to explain; yelling at you because I couldn't find my keys; nearly tripping down the stairs; dropping my keys because my hands were shaking too hard; fighting with you because you insisted on driving, but I was the one who was letting her down, I was the one who needed to be there, I was the one who needed to get there.

You told me not to go in, told me that you'd tell me if it was safe. But I didn't listen to you. I rushed out of the car before you had even parked, then up the stairs, through the front door. You yelled after me the entire

I can't, Marc.

I can't.

You were amazing.

I've never told you that.

I don't think I ever even thanked you for everything you did that day—for taking over while I was useless on the floor. There are times when I doubt my own memory of what happened over those next few hours. The EMS, the police, Scott, Mack, Meg, the debate of who would go get Tate, who would call the college, who would say the words so they could radio Dad—it was all a hyper-realistic, kaleidoscopian blur.

I remember it all, second for second.

And at the same time

I don't.

Unfortunately, the thing that imprinted itself onto my flesh, that took three years to wash off, was the way you held me against you, your shirt soaked with my grief, your hull shaking around me while cannon balls took all your safety away from me.

I should have never asked you to be stronger than me.

I see that now.

But in those days I had splinters in my eyes.

And it took me three years to dig them all out.

Did I ever tell you the history of the Chapel on the Dunes?

In the '30s, this poet from San Antonio would stay in Port A every summer with her husband and kids. She had the chapel built for herself, a place where she would "meditate and find inspiration", as the historical tours will tell you, but Mom would always whisper to me that they were basically the same thing and that it was pointless and wordy to try and separate the two. The poet always wore white dresses—was known as the White Angel. From what I've seen online there doesn't seem to be many pictures of her, but ever since I was a kid, ever since Mom first took me up there, sometimes without the tour, just rang up the owner who would walk us up there to sit for hours in the chapel staring out over Port A and Mustang Island, I've always imagined they were the same person—caramel waves in the wind, amber skin against white organdy, green eyes set on the horizon, words only she could hear whispered along the waves, across the dunes, through the bristlegrass and sea oats.

When Mack called, he didn't even have to ask, the owner insisting we hold the funeral in the chapel.

"It's where she'd wanna be," he said over the phone, Mack poorly holding back tears, nodding before clearing his throat and forcing out a thank you.

She was admittedly confused by our refusal when she offered to help find a preacher. Dad's religion was the sea; Mom never liked the dogma of organized religion. But she loved that Chapel with its white stucco and watercolor murals, its crooked staircase outside and the view of the island from the top even as it became more and more surrounded by houses. In

some ways it was good without the preacher, just Tate's ipod playing Her favorite songs over a junky little speaker, the sound of the wind in the palms and shrubs over the ocean outside, all of us together in that room, even if we were all silent, staring at nothing, only coming back when someone came up to pass around condolences or stand in front of the altar to read out one of Mom's poems, a quote they remembered her liking.

Then "Wish You Were Here" started. That was what broke Dad. He just got up and left. We watched him through the window, standing far enough from the stairs and the Chapel that the visitors coming and going would be less likely to spot him, would see by his demeanor—the constant rubbing at his face and shoving at his hair between crossing and uncrossing his arms, dropping his head to press his hand against his eyes—that he wasn't in a place to talk. The song played through, but before it ended Scott went to the ipod, cycled it back to play the chorus a second time. That was what broke Meg, Mack just holding on to her, trying not to break himself.

Connie was late, as usual, and dressed in that Dallas/Fort Worth way that was almost designer, almost chic, but toned down to not stick out among our salt and sand worn Walmart and Goodwill wardrobes. She spent the whole time trying to get us to talk about Mom, trying to get us to stand up and say something. None of us were in the mood to argue, but none of us were in the mood to listen to her either.

I don't know if I've ever explained this to you, if Mack ever told you, if you ever figured it out yourself from Mom's writings, but Connie wasn't her birthmother, didn't even really raise her. Mom and Connie had a weird relationship that way. I guess being only ten years younger than your step-mother doesn't make it easy to bond with her no matter how hard she tried to make it happen.

That part, I'm realizing, you do know, did know then. It's the rest of it that I don't think we ever told you. We weren't really allowed to talk about it. The only reason we knew was because of persistent child curiosity. When you become aware enough to be able to do the math, realize there's a reason your mother acts so strange around your grandmother, the why and the how hum around your brain until you find the person who'll answer. That person was Dad who, after Mack had worked up the nerve to just ask before Scott or Tate did it in a less tactful way at a less tactful time, walked us down to campus and sat us in his office, explained to us that Grandma Warren died when Mom was ten, that Grandpa Warren had married Connie when Mom was fourteen.

Over the years we learned the full extent of it from hidden conversations

with Dad, curiosity driven dissections of Mom's poems and essays, late night decipherings of things Mom, Dad, or Connie said in discussions that ended the instant they realized we were listening—Mom was part of a cycle, a cycle I'm still so terrified I could possibly continue.

And it didn't begin with Grandma Warren or her mother before her or her mother before her. Mom figured it out once. It was in a junk spiral notebook she thought she'd emptied before letting us use it for Pictionary. A multi-generational timeline that went back as far as the records would allow her at the time. A straight line of mothers and death and daughters left to pick up pieces they weren't taught to carry in the first place, pieces I was struggling to carry that day at the Chapel while we sat on those benches, Mack holding the box that held Mom's ashes, Dad unable to do it himself.

You tried your best to help me carry them. I could feel it. But you never learned to carry pieces that sharp either and each of us stumbled through it all that day. Looking back, the only thing that kept me from collapsing entirely was Lucas who slipped in and out of tears that I'm not entirely sure he understood the source of. But holding him, caring for him, it was a distraction I was partially grateful for.

After the funeral, we saw Dad less and less.

I don't know where he was in those days, just that he was never home, out there somewhere on a waveless ocean. He went to work in the morning and came home long after dark, more often than not sleeping on the couch. Sometimes we'd be downstairs when he came home, most times we were already upstairs isolated in our rooms, Scott always with me if I wasn't with you.

Scott stopped sleeping in the library, instead sharing my bed like when we were kids. Granted, it didn't feel the same. No late night whisperings, no what if games, no books and flashlights that we passed back and forth across the pillow; just silence and darkness, just guilt and trading tears, just Lucas' keening over the baby monitor.

I remember at the time being frustrated, even angry at Dad. Didn't he know his children needed him? Didn't he know that, despite being mostly adults, we still needed to know that we had something to hold us together? Didn't he know that we didn't want to do it by ourselves?

Now...

Now I understand.

I understand that he lost something you can never get back.

I understand that asking him to care for Lucas was the same as asking him to sleep in that king sized bed night after night, was to ask him to hold the pain that he was still trying so hard to not face.

I understand that, in one way or another, we each reminded him of Her, that that house reminded him of Her.

While the rest of us were treading water,

He was under it.

After Dad, I don't know who was taking it all worse: myself or Scott.

Mack and Meg had each other, had their own home to retreat to.

Tate still had school, had clubs and year end events he could hide in when that house was beginning to suffocate him.

Though I had you, I was already beginning to pull away by that point, already feeling like I didn't deserve the love you wanted to give me, already using Lucas and Scott and Tate as an excuse to stay home in that dark penitent hole.

But clearly I was the only one who wanted to remain there.

Scott's sleepwalking came back. I'd often feel him get out of bed in the middle of the night or find the bedroom door wide open when I headed back after feeding or, more often than not, consoling Lucas. On a few occasions I found him in the library pulling Mom's books off the shelves, stacking them up on the desk. More often I found him downstairs. Once or twice I found him in that room staring at the bed, mumbling to himself under his breath. Generally, I'd find him at the front door or out on the deck. But wherever I found him I'd take his hand, touch his shoulder and he'd, without waking, somehow know it was me, follow me back upstairs where he'd collapse back into the bed as though nothing had happened.

I never had to ask him about it. I knew what it meant. He needed to move.

Then one morning I found a note on my bedside table.

Sorry was all it said. Below it, the name Dani and a Louisiana phone number, a *just in case* in parentheses.

I don't think you've ever met Dani. Might not have even heard much about her beyond her name. If you even remember the few times she's come up. For some reason Chris doesn't talk about her much, despite them never

having lost touch. Dani had gone to school with us, had been one of the alternative artsy kids who hadn't owned a single piece of clothing without splattered paint on it. She had hung out with Scott more than me.

They never really dated, at least not in public. But I remember finding nudes he had taken of her on his laptop once. I had scrolled through them at first because they were honestly good, even then (though part of it had also been out of that teenage sexual curiosity). But when they had gotten more and more pornographic, I had closed the laptop before I had seen anything involving Scott.

At the bottom of the note was a time: *3 am.*

I decided to give him twelve hours.

But the instant I left my room, Tate popped his head out then came into the hall entirely, Rocky at his feet.

"Where is he?"

"Scott?"

He nodded. Rocky's tail flicked back and forth against the carpet.

"With Dani."

He was picking at the skin around his nails. "She still in New Orleans?"

"Pretty sure. Looks like the same number."

Tate nodded, but continued to stand in front of me in the hall picking at the skin around his nails and watching Rocky sit resolutely by his side.

"It's a nine hour drive without stopping," I finally told him. "I figure if he hasn't called by three…"

Again, Tate nodded then glanced at the stairs. "You gonna tell Dad?"

"I don't know. Maybe not until we hear from him?"

It probably wasn't the most responsible decision, but, like I said, Dad wasn't exactly paying attention to any of us at that point. I'm still not sure if he knew Scott was gone or if he just figured Scott was off somewhere with someone grieving like the rest of us, never realizing the somewhere was another state entirely.

I remember it was closer to two than three when you stopped my pacing.

"Just call," you said when I looked at you on the living room floor with Lucas.

It was all the convincing I needed.

"He just got here," Dani told me when she picked up.

"How is he?"

She lowered her voice. "Quiet. Still hasn't told me anything. What happened anyways, Al?"

But it took me a solid moment to answer, the words continuing to catch in my throat while watching you split your attention between me and Lucas rolling closer to you and taking your fingers to stick in his mouth, Rocky stretched out next to you and pawing softly at Lucas' feet. I remember being caught off guard by the confusion between that flutter low in my stomach from seeing you with him and the stab in the chest from seeing him without Her.

"Mom…Mom's…"

"Fuck." Dani sighed. "Fuck. Alex. I'm so fucking sorry."

I nodded, unable to do much more.

"I'll keep an eye on him. I'm sure he'll go home when he's ready. Most likely just needed to move a bit. He'd've gone farther if it was anything else."

"Yeah. I figured. Um. He's, uh, he's sleepwalking again."

"Oh. Thanks. Um, I think I remember how to deal with that."

"Just don't wake him unless you have to."

"Right."

I didn't know what else to say. Was about to end the conversation after that long awkward silence when Dani finally spoke again.

"I *will* make sure he goes home. When he's ready, of course, but…I-I know you need him."

I just nodded, tears threatening to drown any sort of response. "Thanks," was all I managed to get out.

I remember, after hanging up, just standing there for a while staring at you with my arms crossed, watching you, Lucas, and Rocky on the living room floor.

I remember a flash of wanting you so badly, of wanting you to be entertaining our child, of wanting to be in a different life entirely, maybe one where She was still alive, maybe one set years later after we had gotten back in the lifeboat.

I want to remember that I left the phone on the counter and went to the living room floor, sat next to you and guided your arm around me, that we sat there on the floor together, you holding me together, me holding you up, that we were moving forward the way we should have been, that everything wasn't

exactly fine, but it was healthy.

I don't actually remember what happened in that moment.

So, I'm going to believe that that was what happened instead.

I remember the first big fight we had after Her was over finals.

I had already made the decision not to go, but you wanted me to anyways, to at the very least finish out the semester even if I didn't pass, then at least I would have tried. I didn't understand why you were pushing me so hard, why you thought it was so important. At that point I didn't think anything was important anymore.

But I went anyways.

You made sure I did.

Sitting in Jonathan's class staring at that stupid final, it all fell around me how insanely trivial it all was. I started to wonder what I was even doing there, why I was even trying. My mother was dead and here I was trying to finish the semester as though nothing had changed and all I had to do to move on was to pretend like I was fucking normal.

I know you've apologized for that and I don't blame you. The amount of time I blamed you over any of this was a blink compared to it all.

But this was the next step in my falling out of the lifeboat.

It all happened before I could stop it.

At first I had just put my head down, pressed my forehead against the tabletop, wrapped my arms around the back of my head. My plan was to just breathe through it—a few breaths in, a few breaths out, move forward, keep moving forward. But every breath just hammered the thought deeper into me, just shoved it down my throat until I was suffocating around it.

Then the sobbing started.

I remember being half aware of the guy next to me, could only just feel him staring at me. But I was too deep at that point. Even social embarrassment couldn't keep the dam from crumbling.

I remember Jonathan's hands on my shoulders and seeing him blurred from above the waves when I looked up at him.

I remember him taking my hand and guiding me up, but I still stumbled over the legs of my own chair.

I remember the guy next to me scrambling out of his seat, yanking his chair entirely out of my way while I tried to stay up right despite my limbs feeling fallible as rubber, heavy as steel.

I remember out in the hall, Jonathan stuck me to the wall, but I only lasted as long as his hands were on me, sliding to the floor the instant he let me go to rush for the next classroom with a light on.

I remember keening there on the floor both aware of and blind to the sets of eyes hovering over me while their footsteps moved past me on the opposite side of the hall.

I don't remember how long I was there for before Jonathan came back, pulled me to my feet and took me to his office.

I don't remember how long I sat in his office unable to speak, to explain myself, to do anything but sob until there you were on your knees in front of me, your arms pulling me against your chest.

I want to say I remember clinging to you because being in your hull made me feel safe the way it did before, the way it does now, but we hadn't rebuilt yet, water was still spilling through the damage Her absence had done, I clung to you because I was so scared of drowning and the lifeboat had already been swallowed by the current.

I never did tell you what had happened. I tried. I think. But the words kept sticking like tar to the back of my throat and the panic kept coming back up, sea foam spilling out of my mouth instead. Still, you found out.

When you told me Jonathan had found you on campus the next day and told you how I had splintered in his classroom, I was nearly toppled over by the confused emotions that it struck me with. I wanted to hate him for it. Who was he to tell you what had happened? It was my problem, my tar, my sea foam. It was for me to tell or not. But at the same time, I was glad he did it. I wasn't going to. And you deserved to know. You also deserved to hear it

from me. But I guess that wasn't going to happen. My lungs had been too full of water by that point.

"When did you start talking to him?"

It was one of my numb days which were becoming more and more frequent and were a welcome escape from the panic filled days which felt like an endless march with the hours marked by my mother's waterlogged voice. We were on the balcony in front of your apartment next to the stairs, legs hanging off the side while we watched the already brittle and yellowing palms at the far edge of the pool drifting in the wind. Your apartment was beginning to feel claustrophobic. Anywhere that wasn't the dark cave of my penitence felt claustrophobic.

"Midterms? I think?"

In my peripheral, I remember just being able to see you nod and stop watching me, looking down to the shifting false blue beneath our feet instead.

"Did you, I guess, go to him?"

"He didn't say?"

You just shook your head.

"No. My grades were slipping."

You nodded again.

"So, you just…"

"I didn't tell him that time. I told him I was fine."

"And…the, I guess, the next time?"

I looked at you, the wind lifting up and shifting those dark curls, the deepening olive the summer sun was making your skin. You sensed my eyes and lowered your head to your arms to meet them.

"It was only two times. The first and then…"

But then my mother hit me, your hands that used to be home leaving my body, your voice yelling at me to stay in the car, your arms shaking around me.

I hate that my own guilt took you from me so easily.

It should have been harder than that.

I should have clung to you harder than that.

I looked away from you again. "He was worried I wasn't gonna pass."

"And you told him then?"

When I looked at you, you knew my question by my eyes alone.

Jonathan never could do that. Not with your accuracy.

"He asked how…" but the words were just as much of a struggle as they were for me and after fighting your tongue not wanting to say the words, you shrugged instead. "He knew."

I blinked at you, both loathing and loving that you were drowning as easily as I was.

I wanted you to carry me.

I wanted you to fix everything.

Underneath it all,

I wanted to drown beside you.

If I had to stay here on the ocean floor then I wanted it to at least be with you.

And that scared me more than it should have. I should have seen that for what it really was: how much I loved you, how much you loved me, how much you were a part of me, how much we were a part of each other, how much you needed me in those days the way that I so desperately needed you. And that was the part I was unfortunately the most blind to—that while I was trying to figure out where the safety I had once found in you had gone, you were trying to hold on to what little safety I had left for you.

And then you told Mack.

He invited me to his and Meg's where I found him in the driveway in front of the ground level apartment the previous owner had added where there had originally been stilts. He was sanding down the legs of a vintage looking side table when I walked up with Lucas on my hip.

"Hey," he said when he finally spotted me in his peripheral and straightened from his work.

I remember he didn't bother to smile. None of us did in those days.

"Hey," I returned and adjusted Lucas who had thankfully fallen asleep on the walk over.

He had been just shy of four months when She had passed, but he had still felt Her absence. I'm still convinced of it. He slept less, ate less, cried more, clung more. It was the reason I brought him to Mack's that day: he went into a panic anytime we left him with anyone who wasn't family. Even just leaving him in a room alone while he was awake brought on bouts of his own keening that nearly broke me alongside the way Dad, if he was even home, would never do anything about it, never could bring himself to.

"How is he," Mack asked, nodding to Lucas before placing his sander on the cardboard the top of the side table sat against.

I shrugged the shoulder Lucas wasn't asleep against. "Same as the rest of us."

Mack nodded. "Meg can take him while we talk. If you want," he added with a shrug.

I just nodded and we ascended the stairs to the main floor of the house where Meg took Lucas and went back inside where it was dark and the AC was on full blast. She didn't bother to smile either, just nodded to me when she opened the door with her arms crossed tight over her stomach, a greeting I returned and stance I assumed after she took Lucas from me and went back inside, shushing him when he started to whimper and assuring him I'd be back for him.

For a long minute, Mack and I stood in silence on the deck not looking at each other: my arms crossed tight, his hands deep in his back pockets; the wind catching my hair and his thin t-shirt spotted with wood stain and house paint.

"Scott home yet?"

I shook my head.

"You talk to him at all?"

I shrugged. "Twice."

He nodded and looked out over the dunes and the bay they had a clear view of.

"Marc's worried about you."

I didn't answer, just stared beyond the thick line of palms along the side of the house and deck behind him.

"He thinks your pulling away from him."

"What else he tell you?"

"Alex—"

"What else did he tell you?"

He took in a deep breath while crossing his arms and looking across the landscape then let it out before looking me over. "He said you broke down in class? That your professor had to take you out?"

I just shook my head and tightened my arms. "I shouldn't've even been there."

"Maybe not. But you were and what happened happened." He stared at

me for longer than I would have liked before continuing. "Do you think maybe you need to—"

But I didn't want to hear it. "I'm not Mom, Mack." I brushed past him to sit on their wicker couch, tucking my knees up close to my chest, my arms crossed over the back of the couch, my eyes staring hard out at the dunes doing my best to block him out.

"I didn't say you were."

I could feel him staring at me before he sat next to me with a sigh that was as heavy as his shoulders. I don't remember how much time passed before he spoke again.

"Don't do this on your own, Al. Please."

I didn't answer, already too deep in my penance.

"You and Marc both—that couldn't've—" But the words stuck in his throat the way they always did mine, the way they always have for all of us. He rubbed his mouth and chin hard with the entire length of his hand before resting his chin against his fist. "It's okay to need to talk to someone."

"I don't need to talk to anyone."

"Alex—"

"I don't."

He looked at me.

I looked back.

And for a long while we both just stared at each other.

"She wouldn't want you to do this alone," he finally told me.

"You don't know what she would've wanted." I stood and started for the door.

He was right and I was done talking.

"You really think *this* is what she wanted for you?"

When I opened the door, Meg was already standing in the living room staring at me with Lucas close to tears in her arms.

"Maybe you should leave him with us for a bit, Al," she suggested. "Go get some air."

"I've had air."

Her voice shifted from sweet to stern in that seamless way she's so good at. "Go for a walk."

I stared at her a moment before turning and starting down their front steps.

"Alex—" Mack called after me.

"I don't fucking care what she would've wanted!"

I don't deserve what she wanted.

That's what I wanted to say.

That's what I was too afraid to admit.

Because to say it out loud would be admitting the mistake that, in those days, I believed I alone was meant to carry.

I didn't go back. Instead, I sat in that empty house destroying myself. When he came home from school, I sent Tate to go get Lucas. The three of you kept calling me, but I kept ignoring y'all. Back home and Lucas in his crib, Tate found me with Rocky in the library. He just stood there in the doorway, his shoulder against the doorframe in the hall, his eyes never leaving the Oriental rug we used to drive cars along while Mom worked.

"Thanks," I muttered to him, my thumb moving along the deckled edges of one of Mom's collections that was balanced on the arm rest, Rocky having shoved his way into my lap where he was looking up at Tate between slow blinks and loud purrs.

Tate just nodded then stood there silent for a long time, clearly trying to fish the words out from his stomach.

"Al?"

"Yeah?"

"Don't…" His lips pursed and squirmed together. "I…I can't lose you, too."

I didn't answer right away, too many words covered in tar clogging up my throat. Instead, I stared at the same spot of rug he was.

"I'm sorry," I told him. "I'm not…I can't go to someone like…"

Tate shrugged and sniffled. "I just…I don't want you getting stranded on me. I can't…I don't wanna, I guess, be here alone."

After watching him a moment longer, I nodded and stood from Mom's chair, Rocky jumping down and beating me to Tate where he rubbed his head against Tate's Vans and circled his legs. I touched his shoulder. Tate met my eyes then wrapped his arms around my neck while mine went around his torso. We stood there in the hall for a while under our individual flares, just steadying the other.

"Wanna watch a movie or something," I asked against his shoulder.

He nodded then gave me a final squeeze before letting me go before picking up Rocky and following me down the hall to the stairs.

That was the thing that was so easy to forget in those days:

None of us were in this alone.

But in the dark, nothing but black water around you, it's hard enough to see the back of your hand, let alone the person treading water next to you. Even when one of you throws up those flares, it's so easy to just close your eyes and duck your head under water.

Pretend no one's up there.

Pretend you're alone.

Even when you're not.

Even when everyone else is shouting your name from the lifeboat.

The next day, without words, Tate convinced me to go find you on campus. I knew you'd be there, hoped you'd let me sit with you in the quiet the way you did before She left me.

On the way to the English department, I passed the hall leading to Jonathan's office. I remember standing at the crossroads for longer than I should have before my feet started moving again.

I found his office door open.

Before I could knock, he looked up and met my eyes.

"Alex. Hi." He didn't bother to smile either and I knew then you had told him everything.

"Can I ask you something?"

"Yeah. Of course."

I stepped into his office and pressed my back against the wall just inside the door, my arms crossed tight the way they seemed to always be in those days. For a while, I didn't say anything, though, just stared at the economic grey carpet in front of my feet.

"Is it...Is it okay to, I guess...not talk?"

"At all?"

I shook my head. "About..." But I couldn't say what about, my throat filling up with tar and sea foam again. So, I shrugged instead.

He took me in before answering. "If that's what you need?"

I nodded.

"Then, yeah. It's okay to not talk. For now."

I blinked a few times at the carpet before nodding again and leaving his office to continue to yours.

I guess the move was the next thing to happen.

I'm not entirely sure when Dad started thinking about it, when he started looking for houses, when he started talking to a realtor, but I had been having dreams of for sale signs and padlocked doors, paperwork and stranger's hands, for at least a week before that day when I came home from the store, one in our own front lawn. Panic hit me hard in the chest and I abandoned the groceries to rush up the stairs. Flashes of cardboard boxes hit me as I fumbled for my keys. Then there they were in the kitchen, crisp and unfolded, leaning against the counter, Tate just standing there staring at them, his backpack on the floor, the strap hanging loose from his limp hand.

"We're moving," I asked him.

He shrugged without moving his eyes from the cardboard. "Dad's not home."

"Of course he isn't," I muttered and stood next to him, my arms crossed tight over my stomach. "He leave a note or anything?"

Tate pointed to the counter. There I found a post-it with four keys on top. There was nothing to the note, just the new address and a brief excuse of a sentence explaining there was a key for Tate, Mack & Meg, Scott, and myself.

"Seriously?" I looked to Tate, but he just shrugged again, still staring at the boxes looking lost.

I called Dad's cell multiple times just to get his voicemail over and over again. I did the same with his office phone. That thing—intuition you and Sara and Roxie would call it—told me he was avoiding me, was avoiding us. I called the department instead. He finally answered only because someone was

telling him to.

"You get the note?"

That was it.

No *hello*.

No *hi*.

No *I'm so sorry*.

No *forgive me, Alex, but I'm drowning. It's unbearable. I can't take it. Please forgive me.*

Just, *You get the note?*

"Yes, but I don't understand. We're moving? Just like that?"

"Yeah."

"And you did this without talking to us?"

"What was there to talk about?"

"Maybe the fact that we're moving?!"

"It's done, Alex. Just pack up your stuff and go to the new house."

I looked around at our still fully furnished home. "And what about everything else?"

He took in a deep breath that could have been frustration, could have been exhaustion, could have been anything really. "Just pack up what you want. There's some shop on the mainland that's gonna take everything else."

I just blinked at first, too many words racing to get past my tongue first. "And-and the kitchen stuff? The furniture?"

"Covered."

"That's it? Just—"

"Yes, Alexandria. There's no discussion here. It's done. Just—"

"I don't think you're understanding what you're saying."

"I don't think *you're* understanding what I'm saying."

"Explain it to me then, Dad."

He was quiet for longer than I would have expected. "I can't live there anymore. I don't want it. We're moving."

"And…" I looked to the end of the hall where the door was closed, had been closed since that day. "And Mom's stuff?"

While Tate and I were treading water, reaching out for him, he hesitated, faltered, stayed silent for longer than I wanted him to, for longer than either of us needed him to. "Take what you want. I can't…I can't deal with the rest."

After hanging up, I just stared at the counter for a long time.

"Just like that?" Tate said.

"Yeah."

"And we're supposed to pack all this up alone?"

"Yeah. That's what he wants." But I was already dialing your number, Mack's after that.

"What about Scott," Tate asked me between calls from his crossed arms on the countertop.

"He might not be ready."

Tate started to nod, but then shrugged. "He should at least know."

He was right.

Dani must've seen my number because Scott was the one to answer.

"Dad's selling the house."

"What?"

Tate shoved himself off the counter and started looking around the house, his hands deep in his pockets.

"He said he can't live here anymore. Told me and Tate to pack up what we wanted and go to the new house."

"As in he's already bought a new one?"

"Yeah."

He was quiet for a moment. Tate went upstairs calling for Rocky.

"If I leave now I won't get there 'til morning."

"You ready to come home?"

"Seems like it doesn't matter."

"Sorry."

"Don't apologize for things that aren't your fault, Al."

"No one else is."

He chuckled. "I'll be home in the morning. Y'all got help in the meantime?"

As if on cue, a pair of car doors slammed out front, a third not far behind it. Tate came downstairs and went to the front door.

"Yeah. I've already rallied the troops."

Scott was quiet and I watched Meg rush into the house and instantly grab Tate to hug him close.

"I can't find Rocky," he said against her shoulder.

"She'd be proud of you, Al," Scott said. "Carrying everyone like this. You know that, right?"

I blinked through the tears and watched you come in followed by Mack with Lucas, then Meg and Tate going outside already calling for Rocky.

"If you say so," I muttered to Scott.

I remember you, Tate, and I sat in the living room in a shell shocked sort of silence with Lucas while Meg and Mack went to get Rocky back from the shelter and settled him in at their house. Meg said he went straight under their bed, didn't seem to come out until the packing was all over and they brought home one of Mom's sweaters that they folded up and left next to the bed on the floor. Even then, she said, he just laid there, his nose buried in the fabric, until they got into bed that night and turned out the lights. At some point he snuck between them and curled up tight against Mack's chest.

I don't remember how much packing we actually did once they got back. I remember us sitting around the kitchen table then the living room when Lucas started to fuss. I remember all of us avoiding that stack of boxes. I remember discussing, while trying not to yell at Dad who, of course, wasn't there, what exactly we needed to pack. I remember you, Mack, and Meg asking Tate and me how big the kitchen was, will it fit the table; what about the living room, will both the couches and the armchair fit; where was Dad sleeping that night, where had he been sleeping on the nights he didn't come home. We of course had no answers. We were just as in the dark as y'all were.

I don't remember when any of us fell asleep.

I don't remember *how* any of us fell asleep.

I do remember the two of us.

Upstairs in my room.

Trying our bests to distract each other from it all.

I wish I didn't remember the way I wondered why we couldn't hold on to that steadfast safety when you weren't inside me, around me, skin to skin.

I wish it wouldn't have taken me as long as it did to understand that the fact that we still had safety even in that small capacity meant it wasn't entirely gone, that we could get it back, that I just had to believe in you the way you did me, believe that you were still out there, your hand outstretched from the lifeboat, believe that, through the fog, there were still stars in the sky.

That next morning when I woke and left you to feed Lucas, I found

Mack and Meg downstairs in the kitchen making breakfast as quietly as they could manage, Scott in the living room deep asleep on the couch. Over the next hour, as you, Tate, and finally Scott woke, we steadily gathered around the kitchen table where we went back to our collective stalling.

I want to say Meg was the first to start actively sorting. I remember it began with her standing in front of one of the cabinets with the bowls Mack had just washed staring up at it.

"Aren't some of these from your grandparents up north," she asked without looking away from the stack of dishes.

"The brown ones," Mack said without looking away from the sink.

"No, it's the green ones," I corrected.

Mack stopped and looked at me with half-confusion. "You sure? The brown ones look older."

I nodded. "Connie bought 'em for Mom when we did that girls' trip to Fredericksburg."

He continued to stare at me while Tate, you, and Scott looked between us. "Really?"

"Oh, yeah!" Scott hit my arm with the back of his hand. "When we were, like, 13, right?"

I nodded. Scott had been pissed over that trip. Had sulked for days all the way up to Mom and me driving off without him. It had been an email filled with shops and hikes that Connie had turned down along with a follow up phone call which I had spent begging him to start planning a trip to visit them with me that had kept him from continuing to sulk until we came back.

"And on the way home," I said, "Mom was debating what to do because we already had all Grandma Ida's dishes," I pointed to the green plate Meg had taken down to look over, "and she thought Dad wouldn't want that many."

"Then why do we still have both," Tate asked.

I avoided everyone's eyes and shrugged one shoulder. "I may have kept insisting that I wanted them when I got my own place."

Scott laughed. "And the princess always gets what she wants."

"Does the princess still want 'em," Meg asked and I glanced up to see her smirk.

Considering where my head was at the time, I'm not entirely sure why I did it. If I even did do it or if this is just one more of those moments where my heart wants to correct my mistakes so badly that it's created memories

based off what I would have done before, what I would do now. But there's a chance that maybe I did do it and that maybe it was out of habit; maybe it was because I wasn't actually as far removed from you as I remember being; maybe it was just one of those days, one of those moments when your light finally circled back around, slicing through the fog, reminding me that you were still there, that you weren't as far away as I kept convincing myself you were.

Either way, instead of answering, I turned to you.

And you heard my question without me saying a word.

You half-shrugged and raised your brows, a faint smile at the edges of your lips. "I've always been partial to them."

I turned back to Meg and nodded.

She nodded back, took in a deep breath, and started to sort the brown dishes from the green ones (Mom always kept them in alternating order, remember?). "Okay. One thing figured out."

"Out of how many," Scott grumbled.

"Maybe we should make a list," Tate suggested.

"Good idea," you agreed.

When Tate stood to get a notepad and Scott moved to help Meg sort dishes while Mack continued the washing, I turned to look at you. You were already watching me. I remember both of us just sat there, taking the other in for a moment. I don't remember what I was thinking through that moment, but I do remember the light that I felt coming off you, the way that your eyes were begging me to let you carry me through this.

I'm glad I did—leaning into you to press my forehead against your shoulder—even if it was only through those days of cardboard and packing tape, shouted discussions through the house and doing our best to assign worth to shadows and ghosts none of us were ready to let go of.

I don't remember how long it took us to do any of it, what we did at what point. With the exception of two moments, it's pretty much all a blur.

The first was when I was tired and frustrated over sitting on my bedroom floor sorting books and clothes and childhood things I knew I should just let go of, but that I had been hoping to do in another five, maybe ten years after we had been living together, all that stuff left in my childhood bedroom then shoved into some boxes one day that my parents would call me

home to sort through and I'd be able to say *I haven't thought of this stuff in years* before eventually taking those boxes with you to goodwill.

But sitting there with all those half-filled boxes and half-thought of things around me, feeling so entirely fragile as though the entire world would drop out from under me if I didn't hold on tight enough, every item I touched felt like an anchor to a life that would be lost to me forever the instant I let them go.

Frustrated and wobbly and near tears, I went looking for you.

That was when I found you in the library staring at the shelves.

You looked over your shoulder at me with that sad sort of smile we were only just capable of in those years then looked back at the rows of books with a sigh. "What about all this?"

I crossed my arms and leaned against your chest, your arm hooking around my shoulders. "Dad said he's already taken what he wants."

"So, he wants nothing of hers?"

I shrugged.

"I'd keep everything you touched."

I let out what I could of giggle. "That's a little ridiculous."

"Okay, then," you smiled down at me, "just anything that still smells like you."

You kissed me then my forehead where you left your lips while I took you in.

Apparently, it was a good day.

At least I remember it as being one.

"What about her books," you asked. "All her notebooks?"

"I can't get rid of them."

"I wouldn't let you."

"Dad won't want 'em in the new house."

"We'll take 'em to my place then."

"Yeah?"

"Maybe the department'll want some of her old drafts."

"You think?"

"It's worth asking."

This I absolutely remember. This I haven't romanticized or made up to blanket the guilt and maybe find some sort of forgiveness for myself: I looked

up at you and was hit with how grateful I was for you, how grateful I was that you loved Her as much as I did, missed her as much as I did.

I don't know why that didn't last, why I let that slip away so easily.

How hard would it really have been for me to fight for you?

That's easy for you to say now, Sara told me when I asked her that.

And I guess she's right. It's remarkable, terrifying almost, how easily that darkness can trick you into believing there are no more stars left in the sky, that each one has been swallowed whole by those wolves on their way to the moon.

The second moment I remember clearly was at some point late in the process. I want to say it was one of the last things we did in the house that wasn't carrying boxes and staring at empty rooms, things we'd never see again.

Everyone was running in circles at that point with that nearly done determination. I remember watching y'all while holding Lucas who seemed to be in the way no matter where we put him, especially after his room had been packed up and loaded into Meg's SUV lined with towels and blankets to separate all the furniture and boxes from the constant layer of sand that had been in every vehicle Meg owned while living on the coast.

He whimpered from my shoulder and reached behind me for their door. I wanted to tell him no, that we were going to stay in the hall where no one was already stepping over filled boxes and stray drinks and Meg on the floor wrapping Grandma Ida's glassware she and Mack were going to try and sell, both of them already talking about setting up an account for Tate, Lucas, and me in case anything else happened.

I remember doubting we'd need it.

I guess I was wrong.

But Lucas kept whimpering, kept muttering in that not quite toddler sort of way that's nearly words, but not. I finally turned to the door no one had dared to touch since the police had finished with it. I felt that same pull towards it. We assumed Dad had already taken what he could from there, that what was left was the big stuff those strangers were supposed to come collect. But then I had this flash of the room instead exactly the way the police had left it, only a handful of Dad's clothes being taken.

It didn't want to believe it.

But I also couldn't shake the image.

The only way to know was to go in.

Lucas tight against me, I went to the door and opened it.

I still hate that I was right.

"Are you shitting me?"

I glanced up at Scott standing just behind me then adjusted Lucas, now in that nearly crying state while he clung to me and buried his face against my shoulder. "Yeah."

You came in after him, stood close to me, the front of your body just touching the back of mine. "Everything?"

"What's going on," Meg asked, coming in next, then stopped next to Scott. "Wow." After a few seconds, she leaned back out into the hall. "Mack!"

"What?" he shouted back from the kitchen.

A second or two of silence followed by her sigh. "Just get in here."

"Tate, too," I told her.

"Tate. You, too."

Once we were gathered in the bedroom, staring at all we had left of her abandoned by the person who, we were all just then realizing, was drowning faster than the rest of us, no one could think of anything to say.

I remember back before all this, before those years of dark waters and starless skies, you and Mom had bonded over Joan Didion. *The Year of Magical Thinking* had just come out, the two of you had poured over it, sharing notes, reading passages to each other, long discussions in the night out on the porch, the gulls calling in time, the wind in your curls, her waves. I had read it for you, for her, to be able to join the two of you in your academic just for the fun of it discussions.

But that's not the important part, I realize.

The important part was the clothes, the shoes. Joan couldn't make that step to give away all of her husband's clothes, his shoes. Her block wasn't because she needed a reminder of him, a memento, a way to hold on to him through the coming cycles of sighing, falling grief, but because he would need them. Because something in her was still convinced that he would come back—not that he hadn't died, simply that he would come back and when he did, he would need his organs, his clothes, his shoes.

Standing in the room that day, staring at all of Mom's things, that thought echoed along my muscles:

How could she come back if she had no shoes?

I don't know if that's where Dad was in those days. Maybe he wasn't

since he had already called someone, already knew that the house would be emptied out by strangers. Then again, maybe he was, maybe he'd already realized it, maybe that's why he'd called the strangers—because he couldn't do it; because he hadn't expected us to be able to.

Either way, in that room without him, Meg finally half-asked, "He really wants nothing?"

"I guess so," Mack answered.

It was then that I saw Her notebook on the floor next to the bed. I slipped out of your arms and passed Lucas to you. He cried out, but buried his face against your shoulder. Picking up Her notebook, I held it to my chest against my heart that has never stopped aching for Her. I had intended to come back to you, but instead just stood there staring at the bed, at where we had found her, cold, staring, gone.

"Anymore of her books over there," you asked.

I looked up at you, blinked, then turned to the side table. Finding a small stack of them on the floor, I bent to collect those, as well. Under the side table was her red felt tip pen. The books and her pen in my arms, I stood again and stared across the room.

"Here," you offered your free hand. "I'll—I can add 'em to the ones upstairs?"

I just nodded and let you take them from me, taking Lucas back from you. The pen, though, I slipped into my pocket before pressing my nose and lips against the top of Lucas' head while he burrowed against my chest.

"You'll want more than just a pen, Al," Scott said and moved to her dresser.

"I don't need anything else," I told him. Everything of hers that I wanted was upstairs already being packed into boxes.

"You will," Meg said and started for the closet.

It took us three hours to go through that room. We kept stopping to reminisce, to pass items back and forth, to debate what Dad would want once he had come to his senses.

Meg and I split up Mom's clothes and small collection of jewelry. She and Mack took the dressers. Scott took all the pictures promising to get copies made for us. Tate took that blanket Mom always wrapped herself up in during the winter months when the house was never warm enough for her. It still smelled like her. I don't blame him. I've stolen it more than a few times even after that smell of jasmine and sea salt faded.

I don't think I realized just how much Dad wanted to move until we started for that new house. It would be another few years before I understood how much he needed it. It was in Corpus as far from the bridge as he seemed to have been able to find; away from everything we had grown up with; away from Mack and Meg who had bought their house specifically because it was within walking distance from home; away from you, always a minute or two down the road, always there for me to run to, not that I had been running to you often in those days.

I remember fuming at you the minute I realized just how far it was, just how long it would take to get to you, to them, to everything.

I remember you doing your best to calm me.

I remember you failing, just as confused and upset as I was.

And then we drove up to that house, tiny and square in the middle of a dry yellow yard that was mostly dirt. It's entirely possible I'm misremembering that, but one thing I know I'm not misremembering is the interior: the cramped floor plan, the small rooms, the smaller windows, the darkness despite the lack of anything blocking those windows.

It was the kind of home you buy when you have nothing else.

It was the kind of home you buy when you have no one else.

At the time I hadn't thought of Dad as being that far gone.

I guess, I'm starting to understand he was.

Of course, he wasn't there, the cracked driveway with dying palms to one side empty.

It was probably best that he wasn't.

I wasn't the only one who moved through that house with shock and anger. Tate pointed out we shouldn't finish packing the kitchen, there wouldn't be enough room for the pots and pans Mom and Dad had brought down from Vermont from Grandma Ida's kitchen. Mack brought up the new cheap dishes and the fact that there was also no room for Grandma Ida's green set. Thankfully, Meg insisted on taking them back with them along with the vast majority of Mom and Dad's original kitchen stuff. Scott pointed out the mismatched furniture already in the living room and we wondered what to do with all the pieces Mom had meticulously picked from antique stores and flea markets over the years, what to do with the library.

It was Mack who counted the rooms.

It was Meg who started to raise her voice first: "And where's Luke supposed to sleep?"

"Where's Scott supposed to sleep," I added, more numb than angry.

"I can go back to bunking with you," he said with a nonchalant shrug, "but Dad really didn't plan a room for Lucas?"

"Maybe he expected Al to move in with me?" you offered.

"Dad hasn't so much as looked at Luke since Mom," I reminded you.

"Maybe he was planning on changing that?"

"I doubt it," Meg was the one brave enough to say.

"Luke does like Alex best," Tate pointed out.

He wasn't wrong. Lucas had been asleep on my shoulder as we went through the house; had cried when he realized I wasn't getting in Meg's Explorer with him; he always fussed when I left the room, when I left him with Mack and Meg.

I don't know if it really hit me until now that my leaving might have affected him just as hard as it did the rest of you. When I came back he remembered me, but only in an abstract sort of sense. He seemed perfectly happy with Mack and Meg. I never thought to consider there might have been a period of adjustment, that there might have been a point when they had to convince him it was going to be okay, if they even tried.

Maybe I owe them a letter, as well.

I remember standing in that empty room with you and Lucas, looking around at the empty, dark walls that would hardly fit my bed and shelves, let alone a crib, a changing table, the rocking chair.

I remember you reaching out to touch my arm when I let out a sigh, you moving close to me and kissing the top of my head, you assuring me it was going to work out.

"Is it?"

"Y'all can come with me."

I straightened away from you and shook my head.

"You live in a studio."

"We'll make it work."

But I kept shaking my head.

"We can find somewhere else, then. M n' M's? They have that apartment down—"

"I can't leave Tate alone here. Or Scott."

You didn't say anything. I didn't look to read your face, just stared at what little light the window let in stretching across the wall.

Maybe I should have moved in with you then.

Maybe we should have tried to make it work.

Maybe we should have looked for a place where we could live with you and me and Scott and Tate and Lucas.

Maybe we should have just moved into Mack and Meg's downstairs apartment. Tate and Lucas could have easily moved into the rooms upstairs, Scott the one next to the apartment. It's where we all ended up eventually.

At least then we'd have all been together.

But then Dad would have been alone, the fire might have happened sooner, might have been worse, might have locked him away even longer.

And, in truth, would it really have changed anything with us? Would it really have made anything better? Would it really have kept me from him? Or would it have just driven me away entirely?

I don't know.

I can't know.

I almost don't want to know.

Towards the end of everything, the rest of you debating how to move the bigger stuff, Mack snuck down the hall to the room I was still refusing to call my own where I was standing in the middle feeling imprisoned by cardboard and Sharpie words. He didn't come in at first, just stood half in the hall waiting for something before finally looking at me.

"What?"

He stepped into the room and came up close to me, still glancing over his shoulder to the hall. "I, uh, I know we decided not to keep anything for Dad, but…"

He shrugged and brought a small moving box I had thought was empty in front of him. Reaching in, he pulled out the round glass bottle that I had suggested, but that Scott and Meg had rejected, claiming that if Dad insisted he didn't want anything then he shouldn't get anything.

That bottle changed a lot through our combined childhoods, sometimes long and thin, sometimes see-through, sometimes ornate, sometimes plastic, but it always smelled the same, always smelled like Her.

"He'll change his mind," Mack explained. "I don't know when, but," he shrugged, "he will. Make sure when he does…?"

I nodded and slid the bottle from his hand to cradle it in front of me.

"I hate to put it on you, but…" He took in a long breath and I tore my eyes from the bottle to see him gripping the back of his neck. "Keep an eye on him?"

"If he ever comes home."

He half rolled his eyes, half nodded. "Fair. Well, then…when he is home? Don't, I guess, take it out on him?"

"How am I supposed to act towards him?"

He met my eyes with that parental look he always was so good at. "He lost her, too, Al."

"And we need him right now."

"And apparently this is what he needs right now."

"So, what? We're just supposed to follow along without question?"

"Without *judgement*. Like in your psych classes. Question all you want. Just…try not to judge him for how he chooses to heal. 'Kay?"

I wish I could say I took that to heart.

I wish I could say a lot of things.

Tate and I were at HEB. I was pushing the cart through the aisles and doing my best to entertain Lucas (who never did like those cart seats) while Tate and I puzzled through being in a different store with a different layout and different items. It was bigger than IGA and we were both entirely lost first thinking we had a handle on where things were just to get lost again when we rounded the next aisle.

I sent Tate back to get something we had missed while I kept looking for something on the aisle we were on. But Lucas was just as frustrated as we were, probably felt it radiating off of us as we tried not to bicker with each other, something that was getting harder and harder the longer we were there.

I remember regretting not waiting for Scott to get home from the engagement photos he was shooting.

I think I still regret it now.

Jonathan never did like Scott.

Maybe none of this would have happened if he had been there.

Or maybe it would have.

Maybe it would have only delayed it a little.

When Lucas started to wail, I relented and lifted him out of the cart to settle him on my hip where he immediately snuggled close to my shoulder and shoved his thumb in his mouth. I let out the longest of relieved sighs, my eyes closed and my head low. Then I heard my name behind me. It made me jump and I whipped around to see Jonathan standing there with one of those red plastic hand baskets mostly filled with a mix of bachelor and health food.

"Sorry," he smirked. "Just surprised to see you this far from the island."

"Yeah." I did what I could to hide my frustration. "Um, my dad sold the house. Moved us out here."

"That puts him pretty far from work."

"Yeah."

I must have not hid my feelings all that well because he looked me over then, his brows lightly furrowed and his lips only just puckered. But he didn't say anything, just moved his eyes to Lucas.

"Who's this," he asked with a smile.

"Oh, this is Lucas," I told him, taking that instinctive step forward that we always seem to make when introducing a child in our arms. But Lucas just burrowed deeper against my shoulder, eyeballing Jonathan with his head down and his thumb still firmly planted in his mouth.

"Hey, Lucas," he said with a smile, bending forward to meet his hidden eyes.

But Lucas turned his back to him and reached up to grab hold of my collar.

"You shy," Jonathan asked with a laugh.

"He didn't used to be," I admitted and shrugged the shoulder Lucas wasn't wrapping himself around.

"He feels safe with you, though." Jonathan straightened to look at me, his free thumb hooked in his belt loop. "You must remind him of her."

I looked away from him and shrugged. That wasn't something I wanted to face despite us all knowing it and none of us saying it.

"Or maybe you just have a maternal vibe about you. Maybe he can feel it. Knows he's safe with you."

I don't remember how I visibly reacted in that moment, but I do remember that a part of me was flattered, even if the part of me that was still digging through my DNA for signs of Her shortcomings froze with fear in those few seconds.

I do remember looking up at him then, the way he was watching me with soft eyes, a hint of a smirk in the corner of his mouth, dressed in a casual sort of way I wasn't used to after a semester of him in button ups and cardigans, slacks and loafers.

Looking back, I want to say it was because he reminded me somewhat of you in that moment with his brown waves left to roam, his artificially faded Kansas t-shirt, his steadfastness while he stared down at me. I want to say it reminded me of the way we were before all this, the way we are now. I want

it to be that way because then in some convoluted way I wasn't cheating on you. I was just trying to find you. Even if the truth is more complicated and hurtful for both you and me, because I think the real truth is:

I just wanted to hurt.

And he never asked me not to.

I don't actually remember, though.

I just remember Tate coming around the corner and narrowing his eyes at Jonathan's back then me.

I just remember awkwardly introducing them, the whole while avoiding Tate's stare, before Jonathan took his chance to leave.

I just remember brushing off Tate's examining and questioning, hyperfocusing on Lucas and the groceries in the hope of distracting him.

I just remember suddenly wishing Jonathan had stayed.

And

Fuck.

I'm so sorry.

I'm not sure if I ever really thought of that day over the years.

It was in my peripheral sure, but I never really considered it as being a part of our downfall. It was just another pinprick in those days of my numb drifting between trying to carry all the people around me. At the time, I didn't think about why I had to do it nor why I had to do it alone. I just did it. I used it as an excuse not to see your hand desperately reaching for me from the lifeboat, if you weren't in that dark water with me, the waves always pulling you away from me as you called out my name.

Despite dragging us to that new prison, Dad was still never around. Sure he came back to the house to sleep, but otherwise he was on campus or who knows where. Between Corpus Christi and the islands, you'd think we would have been able to at the very least narrow down where he was, but we never could. I'm not even sure we ever tried.

Instead, we drifted alone while together.

Scott kept a steady rotation of shoots going. Sometimes I'd tag along. Sometimes I'd bring Lucas. Sometimes Scott would wrap Lucas up in some spare piece of cloth and hand him to the model. Sometimes the model would flake entirely and, neither of us wanting to go back to that house, he would use me instead. We'd stand on some isolated section of that long beach stretching nearly the entire length of the island and he'd tell me how to position my limbs, how to let the wind catch my hair or the fabric of the dress. He never directed my face, though. I think the pain that seemed to constantly pulse under the surface no matter how hard I tried to ignore it was what he had been searching for in all the women he photographed through those days. A lot of those shoots have these undertones of wandering and loss and

longing, sometimes with implicit overtones of mothers, sometimes sacred, sometimes just as lost. I never had to ask why. I'm sure no one did.

Tate retreated into movies. You know he'd had a vague interest before, but this became nearly an obsession. When Dad let the Netflix subscription lapse, Tate got a summer job at the aquarium. There was a near daily cycle of those red envelopes going to and from that house. When the rest of his money began to burn holes in his pockets, he started that circle between work, the theatre, and the house.

When he wasn't at the theatre with that girl whose name I've long forgotten or that one boy who dressed head to toe in purple, he was in the dark in his room with his little TV on his dresser filling the room with shifting lights and sounds. Sometimes he had friends or that girl in there with him. Sometimes he was able to convince Scott or me or both to watch something with him, usually while Scott worked on his macbook. Sometimes I slipped into Tate's room and fell on the bed next to him, never asking him to catch me up on what was happening on the TV, just not wanting to see him sitting in there alone for the third day straight.

I had a feeling this shift in interest was because books reminded him of Mom, making movies easier to get lost in, never having to be reminded of how she held her books, how she hooked her leg over the armrest of her big, deep library chair you thankfully held onto, how she would sometimes mouth the words as she read, how her eyes would sometimes grow glassy, a line of shimmers along her lower lids.

I only guess that because it was how I felt at the time. It was the reason I went back to running, the reason I went so hard back into music the way I had in high school, the reason Scott and I went out of our way to find live shows in dark, claustrophobic bars you only liked until the music started and the crowd began to pulse and you hesitantly pulled back, but you tried your best to stay. You tried your best for me.

I'm sorry I couldn't see it that way in those days.

I did before and I do now, but something happens when you spend too much time in those dark waters. Your eyes become adjusted to the black and suddenly everything exists under this moonless filter.

Nothing shines.
Nothing makes sense.
Everything is a lie.
Everyone wants you dead.

I've been talking to Roxie and Sara about this next part.

I'm getting closer and closer to things that are already filling my stomach with stones. If I'm being honest, those stones have been dropping into my stomach since the day I left, have been dropping at different rates over the years. For a long time, I told myself that if I didn't acknowledge those stones, they'd stop dropping, but that's not how it works is it? They'd just wedged themselves in my esophagus, waiting for the instant something caught me off guard, a handful pummeling my intestines before I could bolt the door again.

The closer I get to those words I'm not sure how to say because I don't want to say them, the more and more distant I find myself from this letter. I want to not think about it anymore. I want to put it in a box and bury it deep under the deck.

But even Roxie says I need to finish what I've started.

And when Roxie of all people tells you that, you know it's the truth.

Had you asked me back then, I wouldn't have been able to tell you how Jonathan had grown to encompass my days, how he had become a buoy in the dark.

Because that's what he was, Marc.

He was never a light.

He was never a lifeboat.

He was never even a hand in the dark.

He was a buoy I bumped into, clung to, insisting I'd go back in once my arms stopped shaking, once my head stopped spinning. But that never happened. I kept finding reasons to stay there staring up at the starless sky, fearing the dark water, the porpoise fins I was convinced were sharks.

I'm sorry I was too stubborn to see all that.

I'm sorry I was too dependent on the dark.

Sara was the one to finally ask why Jonathan was someone I felt I could go to that night, how I even knew where he lived.

It was something I hadn't allowed myself to think about. Hadn't realized it was something I should. The only way I could explain it to her was to work my way backwards, to start with that night that I can say out loud in her living room, Sara, Roxie, and the dogs the only ones who can hear my guilt, but I can't even seem to make myself write here alone in this empty house. Maybe it's because I know you'll come home the instant I begin to write it, maybe it's because I know Tegan or Lucas will, maybe it's because I don't want those words, that moment, to taint our home even in writing.

But working my way backwards, I began to see something of a pattern, something that was somewhat tangible. It still isn't the entirety of what happened. I'm sure there was more. I'm sure there were things I'll never remember because they were so subconscious there is no memory to access.

Either way, the pattern that I discovered was twofold:

Jonathan kept showing up.

Jonathan never tried to pull me out of the waters I was so keen on staying in.

The earliest moment I can come to after that first run-in at HEB was with Tate again.

And like that first run-in part of me now wishes Scott had been there.

Scott was always a barrier between me and Jonathan.

But Scott was at another shoot.

He had left that morning once he was done unburdening himself of the way Dad had woken, dressed, then immediately left without ever saying a word to Scott who had been in the living room double checking and packing equipment, scribbling thumbnails and ideas the way he always does in those hours before a shoot. He left half an hour later than he planned.

"Tam'll understand," he told me when I pointed out the time. "She probably won't even be ready when I get to her place."

Tam had gone to school with us, went every year of middle and high school never once making it to a class on time to the point where teachers stopped trying to reprimand her for it. By the time we reached 10th grade, if you asked what time the bell rang, the answer was always followed with some

variation on "and Tam's bell is five minutes after that."

But that's not important.

But I'm stalling, aren't I?

Lucas was with Meg for his six month check-up that Dad kept putting off and that Meg and Mack decided I wasn't stable enough to go to. They were right. I knew that even then. Which is why I didn't argue even if I wanted to.

Tate was restless. So was I. Even when that house was mostly empty, it still felt like the walls were built a quarter of a centimeter too close. It was like the house in that Shirley Jackson book—there was this inherent uneasiness that seemed to exist within the architecture itself. It was as though the dimensions were all off just enough to make me feel as though the air itself was pressing down on me.

Or maybe that's just what grief feels like.

Or maybe that's just what being homesick for a home you know you'll never get back feels like.

After circling the house, Tate found me standing in the kitchen, staring at nothing. He leaned against the counter across from me and shoved his hands in his pockets, his shoulders at his ears. "Movie?"

I didn't ask which one. I didn't ask what time. I just nodded and went to find my shoes and keys.

When we got to the theater, I had first left my sweater in the car then changed my mind and went back for it while Tate got in line. I was headed back through the parking lot when someone called my name. I turned and saw Jonathan walking towards me, his thumbs hooked in his pockets, that casual smirk that seemed to extend through his whole body. I gave him my best attempt at a smile and waited for him to catch up.

"I guess I'm gonna have to get used to running into you now," he said with a laugh.

I gave him an awkward chuckle and nodded, looked at our feet.

"Here by yourself?"

I shook my head and started walking. "My brother's in line already."

"Scott or Mack?"

I remember wondering how he knew their names. I remember the thought didn't last, deciding you had told him, deciding someone on campus had. It's not like our family was unknown among the liberal arts department.

"Uh, Tate."

"Ah, the younger one?"

I nodded.

"Not the younger, younger one though."

I glanced up to see his smirk and shook my head with my own.

"Because that's…Lucas?"

"Yeah."

He nodded and when I didn't continued the conversation, did so himself. "What movie you guys seeing?"

"Not sure yet. We just kind of came."

He laughed and nodded. "What reckless rebels you two are."

It was stupid. It made me laugh anyways (not giggle like you made me do back in those early days when my cheeks would go warm and I would avoid meeting your eyes, afraid you'd see all the things you ignited in me. I was never afraid of Jonathan seeing me. I never cared what he found.)

When we reached the line, Tate was at the end. He half turned to look over his shoulder and I can still feel the way his eyes darted from me to Jonathan, his brows tensing, his jaw clenched. Jonathan gave him a warm nod and "hello," but I remember Tate just looking him up and down, his face still tight before silently nodding back then turning all his attention to me as though it would make Jonathan disappear.

"*Cashback* is soonest." It was as though I had walked up alone.

"Cool."

"Hey," Jonathan laughed. "That's so weird. That's what I was coming to see."

Ignoring the way Tate glared at him from the corner of his eye, I crossed my arms and looked up at Jonathan. "Yeah?"

"Yeah. Looked interesting."

"Um," I glanced at Tate who was back to pretending Jonathan wasn't there. "Well, the other day, Tate was telling me about the short it's based on."

"Interesting. I didn't realize there was a short."

We both looked to Tate who didn't respond.

"Yeah," I answered for him. "Um, in the UK, I think? Is that right?"

Tate glanced at me, realized I was looking at him and nodded.

Then it was our turn at the register. Tate all but jumped at the chance to move forward, but Jonathan spoke before the kid behind the counter could ask what movie we wanted.

"Let me pay," he said more to me than Tate. "I'm sure a student budget doesn't have much wiggle room," he added with a smirk.

"I can pay," Tate said before I could answer.

"I'm sure you can," Jonathan told him, already pulling out his wallet. "But you should save your money for date night."

Tate stared at him then looked at me.

Looking back, I realize exactly what he was trying to say to me: *tell him to go away*. But, and admitting this just releases more rocks into my stomach, it was a relief to be around someone who wasn't drowning. So, instead of being the sister Tate needed, I looked away from him to Jonathan and nodded.

"Thanks."

I think I owe Tate a letter.

Then I learned where Jonathan lived.

I had been out running. As usual in those days, I wasn't really running to anywhere, wasn't really running for a reason except to not be in that house. I didn't care that it was one of those normal swelteringly hot summer days because sweat and heat was better than tar and walls pressing down on you, reminding you of what could be, of what you can't have. I was at that point of near weightlessness, my muscles moving through the actions without resistance or pain, everything just was and I was separated from everything back there.

Then I faltered.

I don't really remember what I tripped on or how I had missed it, just that one second I was floating, the next gravity had me tied to the sidewalk while I reoriented myself, trying to remember where I was and how I'd gotten there and why my bones were back to being filled with lead.

"Alex?!"

I remember blinking, pushing myself up from the concrete, turning my head to locate him. And there he was, stooping over to grab my headphones before taking that long step to my side where he knelt next to me.

"You okay?"

I just nodded, confused as to why he was there, still only half-oriented to being once again restricted by physics. I reached for my headphones and moved to stand, but he stopped me.

"You sure you're not hurt? That was quite a tumble."

"Yeah. Yeah, I'm fine."

But when I stood, he grabbed my shin just below my knee to hold me still and examine the blood, the scattered scrapes along both. I winced and he looked up at me.

"Sorry. It does hurt though?"

I shrugged. "I guess. When you touch it."

He nodded, gathered his mail I hadn't remembered seeing him drop, stood, hooked his thumbs in his pockets, looked me over. "My house is the next street over. Let me help you clean that out then I can drive you home?" He must have caught the way I grit my jaw and crossed my arms, because he added. "Or somewhere else?"

I didn't answer right away. Didn't know where else to go. I remember deciding that wasn't for me to figure out right then, so I shrugged and nodded then followed him down the street.

Nothing happened that day.
I'm not going to lie to you and say he didn't touch me,
Because he did.
But it wasn't like that.
It was directing and cleaning and drying and bandaging.
My clothes stayed on
And so did his.
I never touched him,
Barely looked him in the eyes.
Though I remember feeling his all over me.

I don't want to go over what happened in his house that day.
Partly because I don't want to have to say it;
Partly because I don't want to have to say it to you;
Partly because I'm ashamed that it even happened;
Partly because I'm ashamed that part of me enjoyed it.

I liked feeling him touch me.
I liked feeling him fuss over me.
And it wasn't because you weren't trying in those days.

It wasn't because you weren't doing enough.

It was because he touched me and fussed over me not as the daughter of Anna Mathews the daughter of Clara Warren the daughter of Prudence Grey the daughter of mother after mother, woman after woman whose shortcomings were buried in my DNA lying in wait to snap its jaws around my ankles when I wasn't paying attention—but as just Alex, the student he kept running into, the person he wanted to keep caring about.

And I know now that you never saw me like that either, that you always just wanted to love me and help me and carry me, but I was so scared in those days that I told myself you did. I told myself you were trying to fix me because you saw me in my mother, her mother, her mother, and so on and so forth down that straight line of fractured upbringings. I refused to let myself believe that you were trying to fix me simply because you wanted me back, simply because you needed me to love you and help you and carry you.

Because then I'd have to ask myself if I even could do those things.

And then I'd have to admit that I was afraid of the answer.

There was one more moment that pushed me to Jonathan, but first came the big storm.

Looking back, that was the penultimate moment that drove us apart.

And though it didn't immediately send me straight to him,

It did break us.

I remember it wasn't the worst storm we'd ever had, but it was bad enough that you insisted I stay and not risk the ferry, if it hadn't already been shut down. You didn't have to tell me the bridge would be even worse. I still argued with you about it anyways.

Before my mother's death, before the move, before Jonathan, before everything, being stuck at your apartment through a storm would have been something I would have embraced with excitement: spending who knows how long in that studio with emergency candles flickering on bookshelves and the coffee table and the TV stand lighting the path from the front door to the kitchen to the couch to the bed and so much howling and whipping and battering that no one else in that tiny excuse of a complex could hear us no matter how loud we got.

But this was after all that—after that first summer without my mother;

after those first two months in that soulless house; after feeling like the only one who could carry Lucas the way he needed to be, the only one keeping Scott from running off once our backs were turned again, the only one keeping Tate from drowning along with the rest of us. And it had only been three months, but I remember already feeling my limbs giving out, already forgetting how to tread water. And as much as I wanted to be there with you, for you to at least try and work the life back into my tired arms and legs, I also felt I needed to be with my family. I knew Lucas would be scared, Tate would be frazzled, Scott, already riddled with cabin fever, wouldn't know what to do, wouldn't be able to take the crying, would leave without a word and drive to somewhere the storm wasn't, somewhere we weren't, somewhere that wasn't home, not that that house was home either way.

I wanted you, but they needed me and three months of trying and failing to rectify that guilt was wearing down my bones and eroding my insides and...

I don't know.

I don't know if I was aware of this at the time, if I had the capacity in my drowning to evaluate those sharks circling my feet.

But, underneath everything else,

Ultimately,

I didn't deserve for you to keep me safe.

I didn't deserve for you to make everything better while you made love to me through the storm.

I deserved to hurt.

I deserved to be alone, to be miserable.

Because if I couldn't make Her happy, if I couldn't save Her then who was I to ask for it myself?

I don't remember anymore what we were arguing about. Most likely something stupid. Everything we argued about in those days was so stupid. I just remember sitting on the couch with my head against my knees and you in the kitchen, both of us recuperating through the lull in the yelling. I remember the phone rang and you answered it, started pacing.

I couldn't take it.

I couldn't take anything.

I remember looking at the front door one of us had for some reason left open, the wind and rain hammering against the glass of the screen.

I don't remember why anymore, don't even really remember those steps, but then I was on your balcony, standing next to the railing, staring down at the pool directly below.

I remember in that moment feeling so empty yet overflowing all at once.

It was unbearable.

I wanted to be rid of that weight.

I was tired of it.

I was so tired.

My own emptiness had amplified and I was no longer strong enough to carry it. Any more and I would be crushed by it. I could already feel it grinding against my bones.

I remember climbing onto the railing, not knowing, not caring where you were or if you knew where I was. It didn't matter. Nothing mattered. I just wanted to be rid of it, all of it. I...

I just wanted Her back.

I remember the wind tugging at my clothes, the rain slamming against me from every direction, the thunder tearing through me, the lightening battling with the waves out in the gulf. I wanted to be a part of it, wanted it to suck me up and take me somewhere else, somewhere with color, somewhere people didn't leave, somewhere people didn't disappear.

I remember, somewhere under the storm, you screamed for me.

But I was too gone.

I still remember that feeling of the wind carrying me down, the feeling of all that empty weight being left on the balcony, the feeling of the water (part chlorinated, part ocean, part rain) around me, of being cradled in a way I hadn't allowed myself to be since Her. My back to the pool floor, I could see the lightning above the dimpled surface, the fractured palms being yanked through the wind.

But I was no longer a part of it.

I was removed from everything.

I was nowhere.

I was without time.

I was somewhere between safe and not.

I sometimes wonder if that's what purgatory's like, if that's what it's like to watch while the world goes on without you. If only there had been an undertow in that pool. If only it could have held me there until I regained my strength, until I remembered why I should keep trying to move forward.

But all that was gone when the air hit my lungs, when the rain beat against me from every direction, when the wind's keening struck my pulsing ears. I tried to fight the net around me, wanting to swallow heavy stones and dive back down to the bottom, back to that serene, removed, womb. It took me longer than it should have to realize it was your arm around me pulling me to the shallow end and towards the steps.

I was too determined to go back.

It was only when you forced me to look at you that it hit me what I had done and that heavy emptiness shot like static back along my bones. Then that part of me that had been digging through my DNA sounded the alarms— *here they are, we've found Her, there She is!*

I still don't know how you got me out of that pool on your own.

I just know I was too busy being riddled with the steel balls that were etched with Her shortcomings to be of any help, that every step away from the water allowed the gravity to latch onto me like a jar of leaches.

I just know that I wanted everything and nothing from you.

I wanted you to hold me.

I wanted you to throw me back.

I wanted you to give me something more than hope.

I wanted you to slit me groin to throat and dump out my wasted insides.

I wanted you to tell me that I deserved everything.

I wanted you to believe, like I did, that I deserved nothing.

I realize now that that was too much to ask of one person.

I realize now that it wasn't fair.

I realize now that nothing in those days was.

I want to say that we moved forward from all that, even if just a little. And part of me thought we had until this morning when I asked you what you thought about that night and our momentum.

"I didn't," you said. "I think I was stuck there for a long time."

First: the fact that you held my eyes the entire time you answered me, the entire time I asked it, the entire time we went through those memories

together; the fact that you still kissed me after it was all out; the fact that you still made me giggle and press into you despite all of this...

I love you, Marc.

I just wanted you to know that.

Second: Hearing you say that made me realize that I don't think I had either. I think my reaction to everything that happened after that night, my reaction to you, the thought of you...

I think, like you said, we were stuck in that pool for a long time.
For longer than we should have been.

But that's easy for me to say now.

And here's where things get difficult.

I guess I should start with the third moment that led me to Jonathan after that dinner.

I was at HEB again. This time it was just me and Lucas. From the moment we walked in the trouble began. It was busy. Not packed, but people everywhere I stepped. Lucas wasn't happy with this. By eight months, he'd started to notice people, notice noises, notice, I think, how it affected me. He kept reaching up for me, grabbing onto my hand when it was close to him. I gave him his rabbit, but it wasn't enough and he clung to it with one arm while continuing to grab at me with the other. It only took a few aisles before I finally pulled him out of the cart's seat and he immediately fell into my shoulder before I even had him adjusted on my hip. I had left the carrier at home, hadn't even expected to be doing this alone, but there we were and I was too tired, too numb to be upset about it.

But I remember I actually did feel better with him against me, with him chewing on his rabbit's ear at my shoulder, pointing to things while making that squeal he did, actually giving shy little smiles when the middle aged women stopped to wave at him, giggling as I recited for him all the songs and rhymes I could remember from when Tate was born. It was one of the few times, the few ways that remembering Mom didn't hurt.

At some point, I was in an aisle trying to balance Lucas while reaching for a shelf that was just beyond my fingers. I would have put him down, would have stepped up on the bottom shelf like I usually did, but I knew he'd cry the instant I moved to put him back in the cart, knew I didn't want to let go of him anyways.

"You alone?"

I turned to see Jonathan standing just behind me, his thumb hooked in his pocket, a basket in his hand, that smirk in his eyes.

"Yeah, actually."

"What're you reaching for?" He stepped around me, close to me.

"Oatmeal." I pointed up to the box. "The green one."

He grabbed it easily and handed it to me with a smile.

"Thanks."

"You could put him down, you know," he told me with a chuckle as I turned away from him to put the oatmeal in the cart.

"Well, he, um, he's being kind of clingy, I guess."

I started to push the cart with one hand the way I had been when Jonathan jumped forward and took it from me, tucked his basket at the bottom. He smiled and nodded, walked beside me while I fidgeted with Lucas' rabbit while Lucas burrowed deep against me.

"Can't say I really blame him," Jonathan said.

I looked up at him.

"It's not exactly fun in here today," he said with a smirk and glanced around at the crowded aisle.

It had been why I hadn't questioned him being so close, it seemed like everywhere I stood in that store on that day someone was directly behind me.

Then his eyes went wide and he straightened a little. "You don't actually mind if I..." He pointed at the cart.

"No. No, it's fine. Thank you, by the way. I wasn't supposed to come alone."

"Tate busy?"

I nodded. "Registration."

"Ah. That happening already?"

"Yeah."

"Scott?"

"Went with him. Tate kept coming up with reasons not to go. Oh, could you, um..." I pointed to the cereal. "Do you mind?"

He grinned. "Of course not. Which one?"

"Cheerios."

He grabbed the box and placed it in the cart while we continued to the next aisle.

"Marc?"

I looked up at him with my brows raised.

"He didn't wanna come with you?"

I looked away from him and shrugged. You had called me that day. More than a couple times. Texted, as well. I had ignored most of them, given short answers to the others. Since the storm the arguing had gotten worse. It felt like every time I saw you, you were talking about that night and asking questions and bringing up therapists. I wasn't ready for that. I wasn't strong enough yet.

"Megan?"

"She and Mack went up to Victoria to pick up a painting."

"Dad?"

I just shrugged.

"You really were left alone."

I shook my head and focused on Lucas who was starting to leave my shoulder and steal glances at Jonathan.

In my peripheral, he nodded and looked up and down the end of the perpendicular aisle.

"Well." He smiled down at me. "What's next?"

Looking back, I didn't question or even dwell on most of what was said that day. Now, some of it seems odd, but I guess that doesn't really matter anymore, does it?

Can't change the past, Al.

You're here now. He's not.

But, I guess, on that day, he was.

He was only there because I wouldn't let it be you.

Then I found the flat.

I remember just standing there holding Lucas feeling like Odysseus.

What else could go wrong?

"How do you think that happened," Jonathan asked from where he was crouched next to my back tire.

"Who knows." I wanted to say worse, but Lucas was already starting to whimper against my shoulder.

"Ah," Jonathan said and I took a step closer to see what he was pointing at.

A nail.

A fucking nail whose metal head flashed against the black rubber as though mocking me.

To keep from saying worse, I closed my eyes and took in the deepest breath I could manage while Lucas tugged at whatever part of me he could get his fingers around.

"You got a spare?"

"That was the spare."

When Jonathan offered to drive me home, I took it mainly because I was done with being out in public. So, we loaded my groceries and the car seat into Jonathan's Subaru. I didn't know much about cars (don't know much about cars), but I remember it looked new, looked expensive. I almost felt bad when he put that third child car seat in the back while I stood next to him holding Lucas. I also remember being impressed how easily he got it in. I tried to tell him how everything worked, but he got it pretty quickly without my help. When he was done, he smiled, stepped out of the way, and watched as I strapped Lucas in.

Lucas started to fuss immediately, reached out for me, called me Mama.

"Uh-oh," Jonathan said with a chuckle.

I remember shrugging. "He's too young to correct. Won't get it."

It was only partially the truth. The majority of it was that correcting him would mean facing the reason why he was assigning that word to the wrong person, facing why his siblings had to fall into the role of caregiver.

It was then I realized I didn't have his rabbit. I remember looking around, despite knowing it wouldn't be in the car, then feeling Jonathan's hand brush my hip. I looked up at him and he made the rabbit's head wiggle at me.

"It was sticking out of your purse," he said with a shrug.

"Thanks," I chuckled and took it from him before giving it to Lucas who still looked upset, but wasn't fussing anymore. Instead, he hugged his rabbit tight and promptly stuck its ear in his mouth.

I looked up at Jonathan who smiled down at me then started for the driver's side while I closed the door.

After I called the house to tell someone about my car still in the parking lot with the flat, we continued the drive back to the house the way we had in the store: easy conversation that had nothing to do with me, with my shortcomings, with the black ocean and starless sky that everyone else seemed so keen to remind me of. I remember feeling at least a little bit lighter, feeling as though maybe I wasn't the broken person I kept telling myself I was.

Then we drove up to the house.

"Whose truck is that?"

"My dad's." I stared hard at the pickup—sand stuck to the undercarriage, lodged between the grooves of the tires, bed full of tackle boxes and hard plastic crates—and wondered why it was there.

Then the front door opened and Scott and Tate came out.

"Dad's home?" I said to Scott while he stood at the back door of the Subaru, holding the handle, waiting for Jonathan to unlock it, staring at the window, at Lucas, avoiding me.

"Yeah."

"Why? When'd he—"

"You can ask him yourself when we get inside."

He opened the door and unbuckled Lucas, pulled him out then handed him straight to me before he started to unload the car seat. Tate was already hovering behind him.

"Hey, Tate," Jonathan said from the back of the Subaru.

Tate hardly even half looked at him and nodded. Looking between them, I left my brothers and went to Jonathan who was opening the hatchback.

"Got your rabbit?" he said to Lucas who was still sucking on its ear then reached out to touch his elbow, rubbed his thumb along it.

Lucas looked up at him. He didn't smile, didn't giggle, but he didn't shy away either.

"I think he's warming up to me."

"Why'd he be doing that," Scott asked.

We both turned to see him standing close behind me, arms crossed.

"Scott," Jonathan said, holding his hand out to him, while I stepped out of the way and onto the curb. "Hey."

I remember Scott eyeballing him and I wondered if Tate had told him anything about Jonathan, wondered if you had. One of you must have, may have even talked to the friends he still had in the Fine Arts Department at the college. Maybe he hadn't been told anything. Maybe he could just sense the way Jonathan was around me, the way I wasn't around you in those days. Maybe that twin thing goes deeper than current happenstance. Maybe he could already hear my leaving the way he does the wind. Either way, he ignored Jonathan's hand.

"Do I know you?" he said instead.

"No, I guess not," Jonathan said with an easy laugh and hooked his thumb back in his pocket. "Maybe it's the whole twin thing, but you two look—"

"Doesn't fucking work like that," Scott said over him and started for the bags. "These ours?"

"Yeah. Those ones right of the toolbox are all—"

"Cool." But there was not a single trace of warmth in his voice. He grabbed as many as he could then turned to Tate. "Car seat in the house?"

"Yeah."

"Awesome. Get the rest?"

Tate leapt into Scott's place and gathered the rest of the bags before rushing to follow him towards the house.

"Thanks again," I said to Jonathan with an apologetic smile. "Sorry about them."

He smirked, shrugged, then reached up to close the hatchback. "No worries. Hey, if history keeps repeating itself, I guess I'll see you around at some point."

I chuckled and nodded. "Yeah."

Smiling, he winked and waved to Lucas who continued to watch him as he curled back against my shoulder while I turned to follow Scott and Tate. Dad was standing at the open door leaning against the frame and watching Jonathan. He looked tired and sea worn which his pursed lips and squinted eyes didn't help.

"Who's that?"

"Jonathan," Tate grumbled on his way in.

"Some asshat," Scott said following him in.

I ignored them both. "He was one of my professors."

"Looks like an asshat," Dad said before following us in once Jonathan's car had driven off.

"Dad."

He ignored me. "What's wrong with the car?"

"Got a flat. A nail got stuck in the spare."

He nodded and followed Scott and Tate into the kitchen. "We can call someone before we go."

"Go where?"

He all but fell back into one of the second hand wooden chairs that hadn't come from home, that Dad had bought without us. "Dinner's at five."

"Dinner?" I looked to Scott and Tate.

"M n' M planned something," Scott said without looking at me.

"Oh. This last minute?"

Scott nodded.

Tate ignored me.

Dad shrugged.

There was some discussion about how to get there. Without my car, the only one that could fit the four of us plus the car seat was Mom's old Explorer that Tate had been driving. This was news to Dad, but he didn't want to talk about it, didn't want to take it either way. The majority of Scott's car was still filled with boxes of equipment, clothing, and props from his last shoot. Dad's truck only had the front bench seat. This finagling of passengers just to get to Mack and Meg's was something none of us were used to. It was something Scott, Tate, and I were trying not to vocalize.

Finally, it was decided we'd separate. While Scott and Tate were out loading the car seat into Scott's car, Dad came into the living room where I was entertaining Lucas between making sure we had everything for him.

"Al."

I looked up at him to see he was glancing at the door before looking down the floor near me. "Ride with me?"

"What about Lucas?"

"The boys got him."

"You sure?"

He shrugged and glanced at the door again. "Humor your old man?"

He smirked at me then, a shadow of his old self slipping through for the briefest of seconds. I couldn't say no.

In the truck, following behind Scott, Tate in the back seat keeping Lucas from realizing I wasn't in the car with them, Dad and I rode in silence until we were on the ferry.

He stared straight ahead at the car in front of us covered in stickers of a stick family and little league teams and ballet companies. The three kids piled out of the car and ran for the side of the ferry.

"Who's that Jonathan guy again?"

"A professor." We were towards the middle, the metal structure next to my window, but there was a small opening near the floor that I could just watch the water through as the ferry pulled away from the pier.

"Not, like, a current one. Right?"

"Passed his class, so, he shouldn't be."

"What's he teach?"

"Philosophy."

He nodded. "And he just happened to be in the parking lot when you found the flat?"

I shifted against the seat, crossed my legs, leaned back to try and catch a glimpse of Scott's car next to us. "No. Luke wasn't happy in the cart. Jonathan was passing by. Offered to help me."

"Why wasn't Scott with you?"

"Registration?"

His brows tightened at the windshield.

"For Tate?"

"Right. That already?"

I knew what he really meant:

It's been three months already?

It's only been three months?

"Yeah."

Dad twisted his hands along the steering wheel.

"And did he have *all* his students call him by his first name?"

I looked away from him and back out the window, back at the little hole, tourists' legs moving across. "No. He was…he was helping me with…with…"

But I couldn't say it. Not to him. Not yet. Not with the way he had been in those days.

"And you got that close in that time?"

"I don't know. I don't think so." I looked to the blue and black of the falsa blanket covering the leather bench between us. "Why does it matter? He was just helping me."

He shrugged. "Doesn't really, I guess. If that's all it is." He glanced at me. "Is that all it is?"

I looked away from him again. "I think so."

He let out a long breath and we sat in silence while the ferry swayed into port, the cars each rolling softly against their brakes.

"Al," he said as the first cars began to move. "Promise me something?"

I waited for him to continue, but when I turned my head to watch Scott pull off the ferry before us, I saw that Dad was twisting his hands along the wheel again, bouncing his left knee under the dashboard. "What?"

"Whatever happens through all this?"

All what? I wanted to ask him, but decided against it.

"Don't let it pull you away from Marc? Don't let it pull you away from us?"

Like you get to ask me that, I wanted to say.

There is no 'us', I wanted to tell him.

There hasn't been an 'us' since you checked out.

But I knew it wouldn't make a difference, knew it would just cause problems, remembered what Mack had asked me the first day in that house, remembered the bottled jasmine still in my room waiting for him.

"Don't get stranded, Al?"

He looked at me and I met his eyes.

I remember in that brief moment catching that they were pink.

Glassy.

Moonless.

I nodded and he gave me a weak smile before he pulled forward off the boat.

I guess, I'm telling you this part so that you know.

So that you know that I was the only one who couldn't see everything you were trying to do to hold onto me.

So that you know that I was blind to you because, despite my nod, I was already stranded. I had been stranded a long time before this. It might've happened with the pool. It might have happened before. I don't really remember. I don't know if I was ever really conscious enough in those days to recognize when it happened. But it did.

So that you know, when I go into what I have to next, it wasn't your fault, you didn't do the wrong thing, you didn't push too hard, too quick, too…whatever.

You did everything the way you were supposed to.

And it would have worked.

Had I not already been stranded.

It would have worked.

I remember that dinner moving rather normally, albeit the starless night above us all. At the time I thought it was because it had been the first time we'd all been in the same room together since the funeral. Looking back, I understand that I was the only one whose sky was burdened by only Mom's absence that night.

After dinner, when Meg took Lucas from me under the guise of giving me a break; when everyone sat around the table quiet and not looking at me; when I realized that everyone was tense with crossed arms, fidgeting feet or hands, glances between y'all with a whole world of things y'all were saying to each other, but not to me, I started to wonder what was going on.

"Al," Mack said and my head spun. "We wanna talk to you."

My shoulders went numb.

My body from my hips down went cold.

My jaw went tight.

Then you took my hand. You called me Babe. You brought up the storm, the pool, the fact that everyone in that room now knew. You said words to me that I had once said to my mother, words we had all once said to my mother, words I wasn't ready to hear directed at me. I don't remember most of that conversation that night. My ears were pulsing too hard for them to penetrate past the alarms, the panic, the walls closing in on me, the constant cries that I wanted to let out:

I'm not Her!

I'm not my mother!

I'm not!

I'm not!

The only thing I remember is me standing, me ripping from the table, me grabbing Scott's keys from the counter;

You coming after me, you repeating my name, you grabbing hold of me;

Every one leaving the table, everyone coming towards me, everyone but Dad;

You holding me close, you taking the keys, you begging me to stay;

Me fighting you anyways, me wanting to stay for you, me giving into the panic and alarms that were so much louder.

I'm not Her, they repeated as I shoved away from you.

I'm not Her, they repeated as I rushed for the door.

I'm not Her, they repeated as I bolted down the outside stairs, down the driveway, down the sidewalk, away from the house, away from you, away from Her because I wasn't Her, I didn't deserve to be Her, I didn't deserve to have people around me who loved me, who cared about me, who fought for me.

I deserved what I gave Her.

I deserved people who let me float.

I deserved people who let me be broken.

I deserved people who would let me die.

I don't remember going home. I don't remember telling my feet which turns to make. I just remember standing on the first step of the stairs where it finally hit me where I was, that I couldn't go up, that this wasn't home anymore. I collapsed on the stairs and buried my face against my knees. I remember screaming into them while gripping the back of my head.

"Alex?"

I looked up to see Mrs. Hernandez standing in the drive watching me.

"Mija, you alright?"

I just shook my head, tears still clogging my throat.

She knelt in front of me and brushed my hair behind my ear. "Why don't we get you home?"

"I am home," I muttered.

"No, you're not, mija. Not anymore."

I clenched my eyes shut and started to shake. Her arms looped around my shoulders and she pulled me down to hers.

"What I mean is: this is just a house. It always was. Home is where your family is. Let me take you to your family."

I didn't want to be with them, with you. But I knew home was the first place y'all'd look. So, I lifted away from Mrs. Hernandez's shoulder and nodded. She walked with me next door to her house and I followed her into her car, rode in silence while Delilah curated my headspace over the radio. Mrs. Hernandez let me be silent. She didn't ask me what was wrong, mostly because I'm sure she knew, not the specifics, but the general what and why. She probably also knew that nothing she could say would have made any of it better, wouldn't have made even a dent. She probably knew silence was

what I needed in that moment.

I tried to take to heart what little she had said, but it all kept coming back to the fact that I didn't want to be home, not if it meant being without Her.

When we got into Corpus, I remember starting to tell her the way to the new house, but the words never came out. Instead, I pointed her to Jonathan's. Why, I'm still not entirely sure. Maybe it was because I didn't want to be home. Maybe it was because I didn't want to be in that house. Maybe it was because I didn't want to face any of you. Maybe it was because I knew Scott would bring you back to the house, that you'd keep trying, that I wasn't ready to keep trying, that I was too exhausted to keep trying.

Whatever the reasons, she stopped her car outside of the house I directed her towards. Before getting out, it hit me that y'all'd be looking for me at some point.

"Mrs. H?"

"Yes, mija?"

"I, um…They're all at M n' M's? I don't really wanna talk to them right now. Can you tell 'em you brought me to the house?"

She smiled and squeezed my shoulder. "Of course."

I don't want to do this.

I'm so sorry.

At Jonathan's door, I just stood there for a long time. I had pretended to pull keys out of my pocket, reached out to pretend to unlock the door while I waved to Mrs. Hernandez from over my shoulder, waited until she drove off, and then just stood there. I didn't want to knock. I'm not even sure I actually wanted to be there. I just didn't want to be at that house, to be anywhere I could be found.

I wanted to disappear.

He answered the door anyways.

He stared down at me and me up at him.

Without words, he let me in.

This is where it gets hard, Marc.

This is where I want to filter things.

This is where I want to lie and say something else happened.

But, I can't.

Because, the truth is,
I fucked up.
I fucked us up.
This is entirely on me.
I see that.
I saw it then.
But it was what I deserved.
I deserved for everything to be fucked up.

I think it was the fact that he never did say anything to me. He never asked what had happened, why I looked the way I did, why I sat on his couch the way I did. He just sat next to me. Then his hand was on my knee and I want to say it was reassuring, though my hindsight is wanting to say otherwise, but in that moment, that's all it was to me.

It was a wordless reminder: I'm here if you need me.
I didn't need him.
I needed you.

But that knowing pummeled stones against my pelvis until my head was firmly underwater and while I dropped to the ocean floor, I just wanted to not feel so weighed down. I just wanted to drown it all out.

That's why I kissed him.
That's why I straddled him.
That's why I let him take my clothes off.

Because I wanted you.
Because I wanted you to love me.
But I didn't deserve to be loved.

So, I drowned out all my longings for you,
By letting myself be taken by him.

I'm sorry I'm sorry

I'm sorry I'm

sorry I'm sorry

I hate that this isn't the end.
I hate that I'm not finished.

I guess this all works in steps, doesn't it? Because while it wasn't the best we had been, it would turn out to not be the worst either. We plateaued about here while you kept trying to pull me back and I kept drifting, kept trying to not do anything. I remember I wanted you, I wanted to be with you, but I was with you when I let Her go and that must mean something, right?

At least, that's what the alcohol told me through those days.

I don't know how aware of it you were, how aware anyone was of it, because I don't really remember how far I did or didn't go to hide it, but I was convinced in those days that drinking would get me through it all.

It's horrifically cliché, I know, but it's the truth and when your father's already doing the same, his alcohol everywhere around the house, and you drop out of school because you just don't see the point in it anymore, can't take the point in it anymore, and you pass your days following your twin around while he hops from one artsy/musician/bohemian hangout to the next and each of those have their own varied supply of drinks and drinkers to politely insist you drink those drinks, not that you needed insisting because you just needed to numb those gigantic, hopeless feelings for a little bit longer, you fall down a path you wouldn't have otherwise, a path that, if in a better place, you would have foreseen.

Not that it's that hard to fall down a path you weren't the first to fall down.

Not that it's that hard to fall down a path when there's someone on it

right beside you.

I remember when I was with you, I let you try. I let you try to love me, try to make it all right. But I also remember being too far gone by that point. I don't know if you ever felt it and if that's why you kept trying, kept fighting to pull me back, or if you were somewhere between willful ignorance and desperate aching for everything to go back to normal the way those same parts of me were, urging me to keep going back to you even while those broken parts of me kept urging me not to, kept reminding me that you wanted me not to be broken.

I wish I could say I didn't keep going back to Jonathan.
But I did.
I wish I could say I didn't keep fucking him.
But I did.

I remember I mainly went to him when I was drunk, mainly slept with him once I got there because of that dizzy hum between what was real and what I wanted to be real, between who I was when I was sober and what I was when I wasn't. I always told myself on the way there (drunk enough to lie to myself, but not so much so that the people I passed on the way there knew what I was thinking was lies) that I wasn't going to sleep with him, we were just going to talk, we were just going to sit there while he let me float. But every time I woke in his bed, my clothes folded on his dresser along with my phone and house keys. Sometimes it would be dark outside and he'd be asleep next to me. Sometimes it would be the next day and he'd be gone.

On those occasions, I would always hesitate in leaving. Not because I enjoyed being there, not because I wanted to play house with him and start dinner so it'd be ready by the time he got home. It was because that was one of the few places I knew no one could find me. And that was something I craved so much in those days. I didn't care about carrying anyone anymore. I just wanted to be hidden as deep in the ground as I could get.

One time, when I got to his house, he had this movie on. Some black and white Italian film. At least, I think it was Italian. At one point the blonde female lead was following someone out to these caves on the outskirts of the city. Only they weren't caves like here, with tour guides and gift shops, long cement pathways to fortified entrances, made large enough for families and school groups to trek through without fear of collapse or getting stuck.

These were just

Holes

In the ground.

The earth just stopped without warning and there was

Nothing.

I remember staring at the TV, Jonathan's hands and lips on me, under my clothes, and all I could think was how much I wanted to find a cave like that, how much I wanted to just disappear, no longer exist. I don't think I wanted to die. I don't think I ever did through all this. I just

Wanted to not be anymore.

Wanted to not be anywhere.

And, as much as I hate to say it, that's what Jonathan did for me in a way. At least, he did when we were in Port A, for a while once we got to Austin. He was a place where, according to everyone else outside of that house, I didn't exist. I was nowhere. I wasn't being looked at or evaluated. No one was dissecting my movements or trying to find where I was broken, how I could be fixed. No one fell silent when I entered the room or picked back up in careful, hushed voices once I was back in the hall.

I just was.

I just floated.

Looking back, I shouldn't have allowed myself to float as much as I did, to be pulled along whatever current had a hold of me at that moment.

At some point Jonathan began convincing me to meet him on campus, to go with him while he prepped for the new semester.

It never hit me until just now why he had been doing that.

At the time I hadn't thought about it, and if I had I always told myself it was because I was already at his house or simply that I'd gone to campus with you or Mom a million times when I didn't need to be there, every time just to sit and keep you company while you worked, so why not him.

Now I wonder if he had wanted me there because he was hoping you'd see us.

You never did though.

And now I wonder if that's why he pushed things the way he did.

The day it happened, I remember he had me on his desk, kept kissing me despite his office door still being open, guided my hands to undo his jeans despite my continuously glancing at the door, convinced someone would walk in.

And then someone did.

He shot into his chair.
I shot off his desk.
But I knew it didn't matter.

I still remember Glory standing there looking between us with those already big eyes wide. I was convinced she had seen enough of him before he was under the desk. I knew it was all over.

I want you to know that I left his office that day as soon as Glory was gone.

I want you to know that I left his office alone.

The reason I went to your apartment that day was because I knew Glory would tell you the instant she could, because I knew that if I waited for you to call or text then I'd come up with reasons not to go, reasons not to see you, reasons not to face any of it.

Because I could still see you through the building storm

You found me on your stairs waiting for you and I knew the instant you looked at me that you knew.

"I'm sorry," I tried to say.

You stormed past me.

You deserved that.

In your apartment I stood in the doorway with my arms tight around my stomach watching you avoid me with an aggression I wasn't used to.

Looking back, maybe that's why it was easy for me to stand there on that day. Because I knew you were mad at me. I could see on our body where we stood. I could see on your face what was to come and that I deserved what was to come.

Finally, you stood still and leaned back against the dresser, your hands gripping the edge, your eyes avoiding me. "Get in here."

I did.

I closed the door.

I stood in front of the couch with my arms still crossed.

"Why?"

"I don't know."

"That's bullshit."

But at the time, I honestly didn't.

At the time, that was the truth.

I don't remember everything we said after that point.

I do remember most of it was yelling, most of it was you, most of it was me letting you scream because I knew that I deserved it, knew I had no right to yell back.

I remember you kept storming around the apartment, kept leaning against one piece of furniture then the next.

Then you stopped in front of me.

You stopped yelling.

You stared at me.

I wanted you more than anything at any point in my entire life in that moment.

I wanted you because you were staring at me with that same longing, fire burning beneath it.

I don't remember who grabbed who first.

I just remember suddenly being in your arms while you kissed me harder than you'd ever kissed me before, ripped my clothes off faster than you'd ever ripped my clothes off before, held me tighter than you'd ever held onto me before.

It started out rough while you insisted it must be what I was doing with him because he didn't know me, not like you, couldn't love me the way you did and you kept asking if that's how I liked it now because that's the only reason I would keep going back to him.

And I didn't correct you, because, for the first time after Her, you on top of me didn't thrust me right back into that guilt, didn't remind me of every way in which I had failed.

I should have corrected you.

We should have stopped there.

We should have talked.

But the longer we went the more you just held me, made love to me the way you knew how, the way I had loved, the way I do love, the way I couldn't let myself love then. And the whole time you kept repeating to me: *I'm yours, Alex, I always will be I love you I love you I love you;* pleading with me: *please don't leave me please don't leave please don't please.* And all that guilt came back plus more and now not only did I not deserve your care, your love,

I didn't deserve you.

I know that if I keep saying I'm sorry the words will inevitably lose their

meaning completely until they become just letters in empty space with no gravity.

But I am.

I'm entirely sorry.

After, you tried to keep me in your arms, but I slipped away from you anyways. And while I gathered and pulled on my clothes, the last of you still slipping from me, you just watched me.

"Alex," you said, my hand already reaching for the door. "Do you love him?"

No.

I never did.

I never came close.

But, I couldn't have told you that.

I hadn't deserved to tell you that.

I only allowed myself to look at you from the corner of my eye from over my shoulder. "Why are you asking me?"

You shrugged and shook your head, a ghost ship smirk in the corner of your mouth. "I'm stalling."

I had been too numb.

I am too numb.

I don't remember the face I made. I only remember you and your body and your eyes and all the love you were trying not to give me and all the love I desperately wanted, but that I couldn't ask from you.

"Please, don't make me ask it," you begged me, your voice, your eyes, your body shoving me off the pier with a concrete block chained to my feet.

Yes.

Had you asked me...

Well, I'm not sure if I would have told you the truth.

Not then, at least, not with my heart at the bottom of the ocean.

But, yes, Marc.

I still loved you.
I never stopped.

That wasn't what had changed.

I no longer deserved to love you.
That's what had changed.

And as I left you there in Port A, driving through Mustang Island in the dark, over the bridge to Corpus, I wanted to cry, I knew I should cry, but I was too numb and I had lost too much. In my car that night, I blasted Metric too loud over my stereo in the hopes of drowning out how much I missed you, how much I missed the way I had felt with you, how much I missed the way I had been for you. I was empty then and in a way you couldn't fill no matter how much I wanted you to. Very nearly was no longer enough. I wanted you to make everything entirely right; to lift me into the life boat despite your drowning right beside me; to replace every plank the canon ball that had been my mother's death had left in me.

But that wasn't fair, was it?

Nothing I asked of you in those days was fair.

Throughout all this, after that night at Mack and Meg's, Dad tried to be around more. Well, he was there, though he was almost always at the kitchen table drinking while pretending to work, his laptop with his data in front of him, the screen never changing, his glass always refilling until he either fell asleep on the keyboard or stumbled off to the bedroom.

Sometimes he tried to talk to us, mostly me.

Sometimes he tried to make us dinner, asked a million times if I'd be home.

I resented his hovering at the time; resented the way he felt he had the right to tell me I couldn't be broken, the way he kept bringing you up, the way he kept pretending he wasn't drowning right next to us.

I remember mostly trying to avoid him.

I remember mostly trying to avoid everyone.

I think that's why I started drinking as much as I did, because:

First: it was around and Dad was always too blacked out by the time I found him to remember if he'd drunk half a bottle or a whole one or if he'd even picked up a half-empty bottle to begin with.

And second: if alcohol helped him to turn off and pretend we weren't there then who's to say it couldn't work for me.

It didn't, of course, not entirely and I always had Tate or Scott around to give me that hard stare while they calculated how far under I was before finally making some remark that only made me feel worse, made me want to be that much more numb. Then they'd take Lucas away from me, not that I blame them now, not that I wouldn't have done the same, but at the time, in that space, when what I needed was something that I could actually take care

of, someone whose carrying didn't pull me under alongside them, it was more concrete strapped to my ankles.

That's when I would storm out of the house, make my way to Jonathan's, let him do what he wanted as long as he let me float in that numb place of not existing.

Then one night I stumbled home where I found Dad's truck gone, the front door wide open, Scott inside on the phone running in frantic circles around the house while Lucas howled in Tate's arms. I didn't ask what was going on. Just stood there watching them from the distance that was alcohol and guilt and feeling used the way I deserved to be.

Then Scott spotted me.

He stared at me for a good few minutes while I convinced myself it wasn't obvious. "Al, you okay?"

I blinked at him. "Where'd Dad go?"

Before he could answer, my stomach and the room turned, my mouth lubricated, preparing itself for the bile that was already crawling up my throat. I ran for the kitchen and threw up in the sink.

"Fuck, Al," Scott said behind me, making me jump. "Don't tell me you're drunk, too."

"Too?" I muttered over my shoulder and watched him lean against the counter next to me.

When I continued to blink up at him, he stared hard at me, that twin thing betraying me.

"We're coming that way," he said into the phone. "Call Al's cell if he gets there."

"Get's where? Who? Dad? What happened?"

But Scott just hung up the phone, grabbed my arm, and dragged me to the front door. It wouldn't have been dragging, except my feet refused to keep up.

"Mama!" Lucas continued to howl and reach across the room for me.

"Stay here with Luke," Scott told Tate.

"He doesn't want me," he shot back over Lucas' screaming. "He wants Al!"

"Al's not staying with him," Scott yelled over him.

"I want to say with him!" I shouted over them both.

"You," he rounded on me, "are two drinks from plastered. You're coming with me."

"But—"

Scott half-yanked me through the door and to his car.

"Where are we going?"

He didn't answer me.

I planted my feet as best I could and ripped out of his hand.

"Al!"

"NO! What the fuck is happening?!"

"Dad left!"

"So?!"

"He's drunker than you and stranded as fuck! Now get in the fucking car!"

I glared at him hard. I didn't want to be part of it. I didn't want to be part of any of it. I was done carrying people who didn't want to be carried. I was done carrying people period. I decided in that moment that I wasn't made to carry people. Everyone I tried to carry just drowned.

I wanted to go back inside the house. I wanted to take Lucas from Tate. I wanted to hold him against me, feel him calm against my shoulder, know that all he needed was for me to be close because in that moment, during those days, it was all I was capable of—just being close. But no one wanted that. No one needed that. They all wanted and needed more from me, more than I was capable of and didn't want to give them.

I yanked the door open and shoved myself into the seat before slamming the door closed as hard as I could to make sure he knew where I stood.

Scott did the same and started the car. "You get it out?"

"Fuck you."

The ferry would take too long. We both knew it. A discussion wasn't needed for Scott to speed straight for Mustang Island. We were on the bridge when Meg called my phone. I moved to answer it, but Scott took it from me while I fought and cursed at him.

"Meg?"

"How far are you?" Over the speaker, her voice was frantic, two steps from shouting.

"Almost over the bridge."

"Mr. Goodman called. Said Dad just bought a bunch of gas."

"Fuck," Scott breathed.

It was then I could smell gasoline, could hear the flick of a lighter, could feel the heat of flames.

"The house," I said, suddenly more sober than I'd been in weeks, frightened tingling crawling across every inch of my skin.

"How long ago?"

"Just now."

Behind her was the sounds of scrambling.

"Think you'll beat him?"

"Hopefully."

They won't, something in the back of my heart told me.

The line went dead and Scott gave me back my phone that I wanted to hurl out the window.

Scott sped the rest of the way there. Luckily, it was still the off season, the road was practically empty, Scott crossed lanes to swerve around the few cars we came across, ran the light in front of Stripes.

But it was too late. The fire was visible from blocks away. We pulled up before the fire department, after Mack and Meg, at the same time that you were running down the sidewalk.

Dad and Mack were yelling at each other in the driveway that thankfully only held Dad's truck, Mack's car.

"Al, talk to him," Scott said, all but shoving me towards them.

"What the fuck am I supposed to say?"

You caught up to us and stood next to Scott, staring at me with all the desperate confidence in me that he was.

"Just fucking talk to him," Scott nearly shouted.

Standing next to them, both too lost in their shouting to realize I was there, I just stared up at them, wondering what I was supposed to say that Mack hadn't already. Then I looked up at the fire consuming the house, our house, home.

I was numb.

I was nearly intangible staring up at what was every memory of my childhood, every memory of Her. It was then that I was hit with a flood of longing, of aching, of waves and currents holding him underwater. I stared at him yelling at Mack, my ears pulsing with the crackling of Her going up in

smoke. I couldn't hear what they were saying, but I could somehow hear everything beneath his shouting.

"You really think you're the only one to fucking miss her?!"

They both fell silent and stared at me.

"We all fucking miss her!" I stepped closer to him, Mack taking a step back. "We're all fucking drowning here! You'd've fucking known that if you'd've fucking stuck around for more than a few fucking seconds!"

He just stared at me, his eyes bloodshot and reflective, his jaw slack, his shoulders collapsing.

"We all fucking needed her and you keep taking her away! You keep thinking that if you get rid of her it won't hurt, but guess what! She'll still be there! She'll always fucking be there! And maybe we all needed to be home to get through this! Did you fucking think of that?! That maybe we all needed to have her around to fucking get through this?! And you took that the fuck away! You took her away from me!"

"Al," he breathed and sirens wailed through the dark that was being gnawed at by that destructive glow of the fire.

He reached for me and, though I tried to pull away, he took hold of me anyways, held me against his chest, in his musk of salt and wind choked with gas and smoke. I just remember collapsing in his arms, sobbing against his chest over everything.

Over everything that was burning around me.

I didn't want to forgive him.

I didn't want to lean on him.

I wanted to hate him.

I wanted to be rid of him.

But I couldn't.

After Dad was arrested, we thought we'd be able to post bail and bring him home. Mack and Meg had already told us they'd take him in for a few days, keep an eye on him while Scott kept an eye on me. I'm still not sure how much he had told them. I'm still not sure I want to know.

Then Tony gathered us in his office at the police station.

"He's not in a good place."

"Would've never guessed that," Scott muttered between Meg and me and we both hit him with the back of our hands.

Tony stared at him, at all of us, from behind his desk. "We're not gonna let him go."

"Why not?" Tate was the only one to say.

"He could be a danger to himself, son," Tony told him. "I'd feel better keepin' an eye on him."

Lucas babbled and shook his rabbit at me.

"How long," Mack asked.

Tony took in a long breath before answering. "That's ultimately up to the judge, but I'd prefer if it was until the trial."

Meg, Scott, and Tate each spoke at once.

Meg: "What?"   Scott: "Excuse me?"   Tate: "Why?"

"He needs this," Tony said over them without flinching. "I'd prefer it if we could send him to Bayview, but there's red tape shit we gotta get through first."

We were all quiet except for Lucas who was still babbling quietly to his rabbit, his head tucked into the crook of my neck.

Finally Mack asked it. "Do we need to——?"

"Your Mom's has been comin' and goin'. She said she's waitin' to talk to y'all 'til she finds a good criminal lawyer for y'all. One who actually knows what they're doin'."

I'm realizing none of this is really that important, is it?

At least not here.

Because you know all this.

You may not know the details, but you know it.

I guess what you don't know is why I went on avoiding you in those days, went on avoiding Jonathan even.

It was easy in the beginning what with the lawyers and interviews; the CPS evaluations to determine where to send Tate and Lucas; the arguments with Tate who just wanted to stay in the house, stay with me and Scott; the claustrophobia that was pressing in around Scott who stopped looking at me the same way, who went through the house dumping every drop of alcohol he could find, who, despite this, still hovered every time I had Lucas, who questioned me every time I left the house. I remember through those months feeling useless, feeling not just rudderless, but boatless. Not that it was any different than before, but now I didn't even have a buoy to rest on. Now all I had was my own buoyancy to cling to.

Free of alcohol and the hangover that lasted about a week, a knowing fell down on me like an anchor—a baby girl. It was the same as with Lucas, with Tate before. My entire body hummed with it. A baby was coming into the family, a girl this time. I was convinced it would be Meg. In the past, saying it out loud was the only way to relieve the hum of it. But with everything going on, with the prospect of suddenly having not just a baby, but also a teen to look after, I didn't want to say anything. So, I just kept waiting for her to announce it, kept eyeing her stomach waiting for it to swell, waiting for the humming to dissipate.

But it never did.

It just pulsed stronger and stronger within my own womb.

It wasn't until late October that I finally realized the truth, mid-November when I was finally able to hear it from a professional's mouth.

"Second trimester, Mama."

It was all I heard, all Dr. Young had to say before the current drowned

out everything else around me. I'm not even sure I looked at the screen. It wasn't until Dr. Young handed me that strip of fuzzy black and white abstracts that I finally yanked myself above the surface.

"Alex," Dr. Young repeated and I looked up at her, the water rushing from my ears. "Do you remember the date of you last period?"

I looked back at the ultrasound images and shook my head. It took her a while to continue. I think she knew without asking why I had been quiet the entire appointment.

"Well, judging from her size—"

"Her?"

"You weren't listening during the ultrasound, were you?"

I just shrugged.

My chart slid against the counter, the stool rolled forward, she reached out to take my hands, still holding that strip of images, in both of hers with a long sigh.

"You're not your mother, Alex. Don't let what happened change how you love this baby."

It was never a consideration in my mind that I would.

It was the plausibility of hurting you that terrified me.

I shook my head.

"From her size," Dr. Young continued, still holding on to me, "my best guess it that you're in your second trimester. About fourteen weeks."

"What's that in months?"

"A little more than three."

I counted back, my heart beginning to sink.

"August?"

"There abouts."

I begged the tears to not come up. Not yet. Not here.

Dr. Young released my hands and went back to my chart, scribbled on it while she continued talking. "I'm going to put your due date at early/mid May, mid/late April at the earliest, but I doubt you're that far along."

My ears began to ring.

"Any more questions for me, hon?"

I was quiet at first, my knee bouncing as I continued to stare at those first pictures of her.

"It's okay," Dr. Young told me. "Nothing you say leaves this office."

"Do...Can you...?" I took in a shuddering breath. "I guess, is it even possible yet to...?"

She let out that long sigh again. "You don't know who the father is. Do you, Alex?"

I shook my head. I didn't dare look up at her.

"Only if you're brave enough to bring both in—Marc *and* the other man—to put forth DNA samples."

I stared at what had already become my entire world for a long few seconds wondering if I should tell you, if I should tell Jonathan, if I even wanted to know, if I even wanted either of you to know, if any of that mattered anymore.

I finally shook my head.

I wanted to tell you. I nearly picked up the phone to call you, text you, send you a picture of those sonograms that I kept hidden in my purse alongside Her red felt tip pen for another month. But every time, my stomach turned around her, my heart would plummet all over again, I'd feel this panicky urge to keep her from it all: from my guilt; from your drive to fix me; from the legacy I didn't want to bring her into.

So, I kept her a secret as long as I could manage.

I know now that I shouldn't have.

I want to make sure you understand that.

Were I to do all this over again

Well

There are lots of things I'd do differently

But every time I start espousing about what could have been different, Roxie and Sara remind me that that's not the point.

That I can't do things differently.

What's done is done, Al.

Make it right here, *Al.*

And I'm trying.

But you need to know that I'm not proud of hiding her from you.

I don't condone what my terrified, boatless self did in those days.

I know none of it was right.

And then they remind me.

What's done is done.

It wasn't like with the twins.

Nothing about that first pregnancy was like with the twins and not just because there was two of them. It was mainly because, with the twins, I had you beside me through it; because I went through it without guilt, with only your love and support and excitement.

With the twins, I didn't go those next two months constantly surveying my body, wondering if the changes I was feeling were noticeable to anyone else. I didn't go well into my second trimester without showing, without you there to remind me to eat, to take care of them as well as myself. I didn't stock up on oversized sweaters despite not showing, steal the ones Scott never wore, hoped that when I did start to show, no one would be the wiser. I didn't spend my days wearing as many layers as I could manage even when Scott would turn up the heater thinking I was cold despite those fluctuating Texas winter temperatures. I didn't use every excuse I could to get away from Scott and his twin thing constantly pinging as he watched me, as he tried not to directly ask me what was different. I didn't spend most of my time at Mack and Meg's watching Lucas while they worked, watching him play and grow, start stringing sounds together and teasing something close to words from his tongue, wondering what *she'd* sound like, move like, look like.

Even then I hoped she was yours. I hoped she would have those dark Caro curls, those eyes that are sometimes grey, sometimes green. I hoped she would have that casual wit, that smirk that always makes everything so much easier. I hoped she would have your heart, your forgiveness, your ease. I hoped she would make me want to be everything I couldn't be in those days.

Why that still wasn't enough to push me back to you, I'll never entirely understand.

Then Tate found out.

I was at Mack and Meg's with Lucas while they were at work, Tate had been finished with school and was hanging around the house. I remember he seemed lighter during those brief weeks, it was almost as though things were shifting back to some semblance of normal, it was almost suffocating me.

It was a warmer day than usual. Lucas was clingier than usual. I was

sweating under the sweater I had come over in. At some point I had given in and snuck into Meg's closet, borrowed a tank top that I realized was tighter than when I had last borrowed one of Meg's shirts, especially in the chest. I stared in the mirror for a long time while Lucas reached up to me from the floor, tugging on the fabric and hoping the bump that was noticeable when I was naked wasn't while I was clothed.

I decided that it wasn't.

I guess I was wrong.

I was at the kitchen table feeding Lucas when Tate came up from the downstairs apartment. He looked me over as he sat across from me and I told myself I was just imagining the way his eyes lingered over my belly.

"You changed?"

"Yeah. It's too hot in here."

"We can turn on the air," he said, starting to get up.

"Are you hot?"

He stopped and shrugged. "Not really."

"Then it's fine. I just—Guess it was cooler than I thought when I let the house this morning."

Tate nodded and settled back into his seat.

Lucas, excited that Tate was upstairs with us, squealed and waved his arms around, knocking the spoon out of my hand, making it tumble down the front of Meg's shirt.

"Oops," Tate said to him with a laugh and Lucas giggled.

"Don't encourage him. Mind distracting him?"

While Tate continued feeding Lucas, I did what I could to save Meg's shirt before tossing it into the washer and sneaking into their bedroom to borrow another one. Somehow in the middle of it all I had forgotten, somehow some part of me waited until I was walking out of the bedroom still pulling the shirt over my belly to remind me.

I froze, hoping it wasn't too late.

It was.

I met Tate's eyes that shifted up from my now covered belly to mine. "Al…"

"Don't…Don't tell anyone. Please." It was all I could think to say.

"So, you are…?"

I nodded and slid onto the bench side of the table, pulled my knees up

in front of me, crossed my arms, avoided his eyes.

"Marc know?"

I shook my head.

"You even still talking to him?"

I shrugged.

He nodded and went back to feeding Lucas who had started trying to use his fingers instead of waiting for Tate.

"You are gonna tell him, though?" he said without looking at me. "Right?"

"I guess I'll have to eventually."

He nodded again and the conversation was over.

At the time, I had genuinely believed I would tell you. I didn't know when, but I believed that I would.

Then came the trial. Then came the realization that, for the next five years, we'd be floating in an entirely different, yet strangely similar ocean. We all knew Dad would be found guilty. He had already told us he wasn't going to fight it. I don't think that's what had surprised us. It had been the five year sentence, that he'd been deemed a felon, that he'd be taken north to Beeville.

I don't know why that hit me the way it did, why it hit any of us the way it did.

I just remember us all sitting there in a row not moving.

I just remember you taking my hand and squeezing it.

I just remember all that guilt washing back over me, that pulsing in my ears that was beginning to become a Greek choir singing all my transgressions:

Mea Culpa Mea Culpa Mea Culpa Mea Culpa Mea Culpa Mea Culpa Mea Culpa Mea Culpa Mea Culpa Mea Culpa Mea Culpa Mea Culpa Mea Culpa Mea Culpa Mea Culpa Mea Culpa Mea Culpa Mea Culpa Mea Culpa Mea Culpa

I just remember ripping my hand from yours, standing, handing Lucas to Tate, climbing over everyone, leaving the courtroom as fast as I could.

No one followed me.

I preferred it that way.

Out in the lobby, I was headed for the front door when I heard my name. I didn't stop. I didn't want to talk to anyone. I didn't want to be convinced not to drown.

Then his hand was on my arm and I turned to look up at him and he was looking down at me with what felt like all the apology and care in the world.

"I'm sorry, Alex."

I nodded, tried to hold back tears, failed, turned and rushed the rest of the way outside. He followed me all the way around the corner of the building where I finally stopped and when I gave in, he wrapped his arms around me and I cried against him while he ran his fingers through my hair.

I should have asked him why he was there.

But I was too lost in guilt and hormones and that starless, boatless dark.

It wasn't until I had begun to calm that I realized his arms were stiff around me. My fingers slid along my belly, his abdomen, and I pushed away from him. He stared at me while I avoided looking at him, my arms wrapping around her.

"Alex?"

I nodded.

In my peripheral, his hand ran along his mouth and I thought I heard him laugh. I looked up at him and saw him smiling, his eyes shining.

"Holy shit! Are you serious?"

I squinted at him.

"Alex." He wrapped one arm back around me, his hand on her. "This is amazing."

I'm not proud of this, Marc.

I'm not even sure ashamed covers it because shame implies some sort of conscious decision.

And there were no decisions that I made in those days that were entirely conscious, that weren't even partially clouded by dark waves crashing into me any time sense began to kick in.

Not that that excuses what I did.

But

Devastated is closer to how I feel about what happened next.

Disappointed.

Hurt.

Urgent aching to go back and pull myself out of those waters I was too stubborn to let anyone else try and pull me from.

I'm sorry.

"Damn it," he said without letting go of me.

"What?"

"It's just…" He shook his head and took in a deep breath. "I wish I'd known sooner."

"Why?"

"I'm headed for Austin tomorrow."

I just blinked up at him.

"I'm transferring to UT. Kind of miss trees, you know." He smirked and shrugged then looked down at me with those eyes that kept shining.

I finally caught on.

I should have corrected him then, should have shaken my head and backed up, gone back inside, told you right then and there.

But I believed there was nothing left for me in Port A or Corpus.

"How fast can you pack?"

And I believed that the only way I could keep going—keeping going for her and her alone—was to leave. Being around you would just remind me of everything I didn't deserve. Maybe being somewhere else with someone who never asked anything of me, someone who would allow me to exist as the motherless child I deserved to be, would keep me from drowning.

I wasn't looking for light then.
I was just looking for a buoy to rest on.

I nodded.
He kissed me.
I sent a detail-less text to Scott.
He drove me to the house.

We still had boxes left over from the move. I think before the fire Scott, Tate, and I had been holding out hope that Dad would change his mind, that he'd take the house back off the market or buy it back from the new owners. After the fire, we used what we needed to move Tate and Lucas to Mack and Meg's. The rest Scott and I just never had the will to get rid of, knowing it wouldn't be long before one of us finally spoke up about not being able to take it anymore and then we'd leave, either together or apart, but still whole.

That wasn't how I'd imagined using those boxes—in secret without Scott, without Mack or Meg or Tate or you; in secret with Jonathan, packing

as fast as I could manage before Scott got back, most likely with you in tow to rip my heart back to the bottom of the ocean, not that it wasn't already there encased in cement.

I remember Jonathan insisting I didn't need to pack all my clothes, that I'd need maternity clothes soon anyways and that Austin wasn't really the place for sand and sea salt worn shorts and cover ups and flip-flops. He absolutely didn't like my recently acquired sweaters (except for the ones he said were ironic).

"These all hide your belly," he told me with that shining eyed smile that was already dropping pebbles of queasiness against my gut.

When I blinked up at him, he just insisted he could get me new clothes. That I didn't have to worry. I'm not sure why, but I took his word for it, leaving behind more than half my closet. He did that with most of my things, insisting I didn't need them, that he could get me nicer versions. Then he got to my record player.

"My dad bought me that."

"Well," he shrugged and looked it over, "mine can transfer albums to mp3s. It's a nicer model all around, actually."

"I was ten. He got me that and my first Fleetwood Mac album."

He smirked at me, humor behind his eyes. "Okay. If it means that much to you. I guess we can find some place for it. Hey! Here's an idea. We can get a place with a spare room. Set up an office for you. Then you can take classes online or look up recipes or just generally run the house from there."

I blinked up at him again, not sure what to say, not sure what he even meant.

"It'll be great. We can put this in there and your weird old books." He kissed the top of my head. "It'll be your own little space."

I nodded and watched him wrap up my record player before going back to stacking my thrift store and estate sale books that I loved despite how Jonathan described them into a box.

"What's this?"

I looked up to see him holding Her jasmine.

I ripped from the floor and took it from him, cradling it close while staring at the amber liquid, the texture of the glass.

"Sorry," he chuckled. "Didn't realize it was gold. Why don't you ever wear it?"

"It was Hers."

"Oh. I didn't know."

I shook my head. "I was supposed to give it to Dad."

"Why didn't you?"

"He was never ready for it."

He didn't say anything. Just squeezed my shoulder and kissed the top of my head again before returning to packing.

After we filled his Subaru with the bigger items, he left me to sort through the little stuff, told me to meet him at his house once I was done.

I was standing in the middle of that room with my purse and overnight bag on my shoulder, Her red pen gripped against my chest, looking over everything I was leaving behind, wondering if it would end up in a box that Scott would hold on to until one day when I decided to come back or if he'd be so mad at me that he'd just call some strangers to pack it all up and take it away, to strip me from their lives the way Dad had tried to do to Her.

"Al?"

I looked up to see him standing in the doorway looking over what was left, his face scrunched up with confusion.

I just stared at him.

He just stared back at me.

Our eyes both wide with hurt and questions we didn't know how to ask.

Words failing us both, I lowered my head, shoved Her pen back in my purse, back with those pictures of the only thing left that mattered, and rushed to brush past him.

"Hey." He tried to grab for me, but I jerked away from him.

"Al." He followed me down the hall. "At least tell me where you're going."

"Austin."

"You can't afford Austin."

"Jonathan can."

I felt he wasn't directly behind me anymore. "What?"

I hesitated in the living room, still not looking up at him. "I'm…He-he's transferring to UT. I'm going with him."

"Why?"

"Because."

I turned for the door before he could stop me.

"Al, he's an asshat."

"No, he's not!" I whipped around on the porch to face him. "You and Tate keep saying that, but neither of you know him."

So, what? He's a great guy then? This guy who's taking you away from your family right when they need you most, when *you* need *them* most?

I kept trying to argue over him, but the words refused to follow. "He-he's not…"

"Not Marc?"

I glared at him. "He's not the worst person in the world."

"And how is that better than Marc?"

I shook my head, willing myself not to cry. "Fuck you."

I turned and continued to my car. At first, Scott didn't follow me. But then the screen door slammed and called after me. I shoved my bags into the back seat of my car and slammed the door.

"Al, come on."

I didn't get in the front, but didn't look at him either, just wrapped my arms around her, insisting this was for her, this was all for her.

"You're really just leaving? Just like that?"

I shrugged. "You think *you* get to tell me not to?"

It was a low blow, but I believed I was throwing stones for his greater good, her greater good.

He took in a long breath. I watched his feet shifting in the grass while he paced in half-circles. "Fine. Fine, but…Go somewhere with me first?"

"You're not changing my mind."

"I'm not trying to," he said over me. "Just…" He shrugged. "I can get a ride from there. You can leave straight away. Don't even have to come back."

My lips pursed, I stared back at him, then finally nodded.

He took me to a cellphone store. Some big name place with families and flat screens and peppy indie music that was supposed to make the company and employees seem cool but still relatable. I followed him around confused and with my arms crossed tight over my guilt, seeing your face on every father who passed by me following their kids around, having inane exchanges with their wives, sneaking touches on their arms, their waists, their lower backs.

"Al," Scott yanked my attention away from a family gathered around a rack of phone covers.

I blinked up at him leaning against the counter. His eyes shifted from mine to the family. I don't know if he had started to figure me out then or

before or after, but either way, he had ignored it and held his hand out to me.

"Give me your cell."

"Why?"

He smirked at me. "Just hand it over."

Pressing my lips together even harder, I unfolded my arms—my body feeling exposed without them, my arms already wanting to keep them around her, to keep her safe from all the darkness I was convinced had consumed Port A—and dug through my purse before pulling my phone out and shoving it into his hand. He flipped it open and returned to the employee on the other side of the counter.

"Okay. Uh, give it to me again?"

I looked back at the family at the rack, the kids no longer looking at all, spinning the rack in fast circles while laughing, their parents paying too much attention to the employee talking to them to notice.

I remember one of them had dark curls like yours.

I remember missing you already.

I remember telling myself it was for the best.

"Ready?"

I looked to Scott, a little plastic bag in one hand, the other shoved in his coat pocket.

I just nodded.

Outside, he handed me my phone back.

"You've, uh," he blinked and shook his head with a smirk, "got my number now. That's a weird thing to say."

Despite myself, I let out a soft laugh through my nose.

"Call me. For," he shrugged, looking at my phone still in my hand, "whatever reason, really, but..." his face started to fall a bit, "mainly if you start to," he shrugged, "change your mind, I guess? Even a little?"

He met my eyes and I nodded, mostly for him. I was still convinced I wouldn't.

For a long while we both just stood there staring at each other, a multitude of things we should have been saying, things we wanted to say, things we were too afraid to say, things we were too damaged to say, refused to pass between us.

"You don't have to do this alone," he finally told me.

You don't have to do this with him, was what he wanted to tell me. I could

see it in his eyes, in his posture. *Mom wouldn't want you to do this with* him.

"Yes, I do," I told him without taking my eyes from his.

There are days when I wish he'd tried harder.

Just like Jonathan said, we left for Austin the next day. I wasn't that surprised to learn he'd already had an apartment rented and ready to move into. I also wasn't surprised to see it was in some fancy building with a valet, polished floors in the lobby, a reception desk where visitors had to check in and be buzzed up.

Still, when I think back on that first night, that out of place feeling rushes back to me. Stepping foot into that lobby, I was suddenly grateful for Jonathan's insistence to buy me a new wardrobe, my reflection surrounding me in clean glass, polished marble, strategically placed mirrors, making me achingly aware of my worn-to-tatters hoodie, my stretched out t-shirt hanging from my shoulders and swollen breasts, my shorts with the hems wearing thin and stray strings dangling along my thighs, my salt and sun faded Birkenstocks hiding the tan lines along my feet. While Jonathan talked to someone about changing apartments, I just stood there looking around the lobby and thinking that places like this only existed in movies about classy people or in upscale places like Manhattan or certain neighborhoods in LA where hair metal bands did drugs and collected groupies. My arms vibrated with how empty they felt and just clung onto the strap of my purse, Jonathan refusing to let me carry anything. I was hit with how much I missed Lucas, how much I wanted to hold him in that moment, how much I wanted him to weigh me down, keep me from floating away, keep me here in the present and not back home in Port A where I was trying not to think about y'all wondering, discussing, keeping calm for Lucas, for Tate.

"What's that," he asked me at one point, nodding to my hand.

I stopped running Her red felt tip pen along my bottom lip, eyes wide,

not even remembering pulling it out. "Nothing," I muttered and shook my head, shoving it back next to those pictures of Tegan in my purse that was still mine, that still had nothing to do with him.

I was surprised to learn Jonathan hadn't taken most of his furniture from Port A, nearly all of what was in that new apartment being equally new and already set up when we got there. I was also surprised to hear that most likely nothing from this apartment would be moving with us into the new one that would be ready for us by mid-January.

"Why not," I remember asking him while trying not to hover over the building staff carrying my boxes of what he had decided was essential, everything else going into storage for the time being.

He just shrugged from his laptop where he was researching maternity shops in Austin. "Some of it might. It'll be up to the designer in the end."

"Designer?"

He finally looked up at me from the tops of his eyes and that smirk that I had once thought endearing, but was already beginning to understand as condescending, snaked along his lips. "Well, yeah. We want the new place to look nice, don't we?"

I blinked at him for a few seconds before saying, "We can't do it ourselves?"

Moments like that had come up before, but this was the first time it really hit me—how different our upbringings had been. And not in the way that yours and mine were. Sure, you were raised rich with slick parents who only accepted the best, but you rejected all that, roll your eyes when anyone mentions Dallas. The way you spoke of it, speak of it still, it was a hindrance, something you overcame, the reason you love my family with our do-it-ourselves, raising four kids on a researcher and poet salary kind of world view.

For you, we are a relief.

For him, I was something to be fixed, corrected, molded.

He laughed. "Why when there are so many skilled designers here in the city? Besides, there's one who works for the building who's great. She designed this for us." He flicked his hand at the apartment that he'd barely taken two seconds to appreciate and went straight back to clicking around his laptop.

I nodded then (thought it was odd, even then, how easily he kept referring to "us" and "ours"), but in early January when he was busy on campus and I was left alone in that apartment with my new maternity

wardrobe that didn't just show my growing bump, but accentuated it, I was restless and concerned what this designer was doing with my things that Jonathan had given her free reign of.

Down at the reception desk, the girl who looked not much younger than myself at the time (and wearing an uncomfortable, but classy looking uniform) called a teenage boy out from the back (wearing a similar uniform) who she asked to show me to the apartment. I don't really remember talking to him. He reminded me too much of Tate with his lank and his blue eyes, his casual references to Tarantino when I'd initially tried to start a conversation in the elevator.

The entire way up to the apartment, I was bracing myself for a stark angular woman who would glare down at me with a permanent scowl, her judging eyes eliminating every one of my secondhand possessions that I refused to part with. But following the boy down the hall, I was hit with something entirely different—sunshine and yellow, a comfort I hadn't felt for nearly a year, a safety net I wasn't prepared for. And then there she was, smiling up at me from the floor of the half-empty apartment, a notepad on one knee, a catalogue on the other, a ballpoint pen with the name of some gym stuck behind her ear (I learned later she had never been to that gym, but her sister worked there and would steal pens for her simply because she liked how they wrote and she didn't care when she'd inevitably misplace it).

She unburdened her lap and stood with the ease of someone who frequents yoga studios before moving straight to me with her hand out, that smile still wide across her lips tinted with a rose balm she made herself in her kitchen. That first day when I met Delilah her hair had been done in a loose braid that kept swinging from over her shoulder to down her back, the roots a dark brown that faded into a honey gold around her cheekbones and grew lighter and lighter as the braid went on until it reached a nearly silvery sort of white at the end. The entire time I knew her, she wore mostly billowy blouses tucked into high-waisted jeans and shorts before they came back into fashion, tassels hanging from the collars of her shirts, bangles that would jangle as she walked, rings with large pieces of jet, amethyst, jade, or turquoise set in them, Chelsea boots in nearly every color and pattern. I know that, beyond her hair, most of that hasn't changed, but I guess I thought you'd like to know that Delilah has always been Delilah.

"Yes, like the song," she even said with a sarcastic eye roll and a laugh when she introduced herself and I immediately felt as though the barnacles were being chipped from my shoulders.

"*You* must be the music buff," she said with a lift of her naturally thin brows and immediately turned to lead me towards what would become my own library. "I was hoping to meet you," she added over her shoulder.

I followed behind her, only just catching as the boy slipped back out the front door behind us. "Really?"

"Yeah! Your records are amazing! It's kind of ironic, considering, ya know," she gestured to the single large window in the small, square room, "Austin, but it's rare that I meet people with *good* taste in music." She stopped in front of the large dark wood desk in the middle of the room that was otherwise empty beyond my boxes opened and lined up along the desk and around the room where she flipped through my records. "I mean, they have good stuff, don't get me wrong, but stuff they're supposed to like, ya know? *You* like what you like, don't you?" She gave me a wink when I stood next to her. "This one," she pulled out *Lady of the Stars* with its faded to white edges, "was especially well loved."

I tried to bite down tears and took it from her. "My mom bought it for me when I was fourteen."

I didn't go into the way I had listened to it on repeat for months, how Scott had spent those same months taking almost exclusively photos that mimicked the cover and the songs, that three years later I'd initially be attracted to you because you reminded me of Donovan in those days before age slimmed out your face. I'm sure she didn't need to hear any of it, I'm sure she could read it on the length of my body.

"Smart woman. Lucky daughter. Yours'll be just as lucky."

I nodded and glanced at her smile, returning it despite the dragging anchor attached to my heart, my gut.

"I was thinking," she said and moved to the wall, "if you like it," she added over her shoulder. "The desk could go here," she gestured to the space under the window, "or here," she turned and splayed her hands out in front of her, "so you can see the door? And your books," she added with that smile then rushed to the middle of the room on the opposite side of the desk from me, "I'm thinking they deserve to be shown off, ya know. Hubs said—oh, is he hubs yet? Sorry, I just assumed."

I just shook my head.

She nodded. "Your man, then, he said we don't have to put them all out, but I was looking through them and they're great! So, I was thinking floating shelves all around the wall up to the ceiling—I'll make sure to install a ladder

so you can get up to those high shelves—"

The thought made me laugh. "Like *Beauty and the Beast?*"

"Yeah! I installed one in my home office the instant I found a landlord who would let me. And I was thinking we can put counters with open shelves beneath those to keep your records on and I was thinking here:" She went to one side of the desk and waved her hands in front of her towards the wall. "Your record player." She grinned at me from over her shoulder. "And, if you're up for it," she turned and leaned against the desk, "which I hope you are, because I'm getting seriously seasoned thrifter vibes off you—I was thinking I could take you to some of my haunts and we can try and find some little décor things that'll, ya know, just…pull it all together. What do you think?"

I spent those next few weeks with Delilah in her vintage yellow bug wandering in and out of antique shops and flea markets, estate sales and thrift shops. She was a good distraction in those early days, a reminder to me that life is capable of moving forward no matter how stuck that anchor was, would always be, that there were buoys that weren't rooted in guilt or penance.

Then the apartment was finished and, for a little while, I continued to go out with Delilah, but then Jonathan convinced me to transfer over to UT, as well, convinced me to take online courses now that I had my own space to study, reminded me the baby wasn't due until the semester was over. When I tried to argue, pointing out that the semester had already started, he insisted it was fine, that he could get me in anyways.

I agreed because I thought he couldn't.

I was wrong.

The one good thing about all that is that he was the one to convince me to change to social work.

"You can get more jobs that way," he told me with a shrug. "Not that you'll need to work," he added. "It's really only if you think you'll want something else once Elizabeth doesn't need you as much."

"Elizabeth?"

"Yeah. I thought it would be a good name."

"It's kind of…stuffy, don't you think?"

He laughed, gave me that condescending smirk. "There're a ton of nicknames for Elizabeth."

I didn't laugh, didn't smile, didn't budge.

"What were you thinking," he asked with an air that was closer to annoyance than curiosity.

I looked away from him and shifted my feet against each other, ran my fingers along her. "I always had my heart set on Tegan."

I didn't tell him it was what *we* had had *our* hearts set on, that you had lit up that one time I had suggested it, that you had continued to bring it up despite us both being pretty close to drunk when I had first said it, that on that day in that Austin restaurant I was on the side of the pendulum that was convinced she was yours, that wanted her to be yours.

His face scrunched up. "Like that band you like?"

"Yeah." I shrugged. "It's a nice name. I looked it up once, it means 'darling.' I think. Or something like that."

"And it's not just because they're twins," he asked with a chuckle.

But I didn't laugh, didn't grin, just glanced up at him from my plate. "No. I just like the name is all."

He stared at me for a long moment then finally laughed and reached across the table to take my hand. "Okay." He kissed my knuckles. "If you really have your heart set on it. Tegan it is."

I smiled and looked at our hands, put on my best diminutive housewife expression that I'd been learning he liked. "Thank you."

Through schoolwork, adapting to the third trimester, and Jonathan's mounting hints at wanting me to be his dedicated housewife, I stopped finding the time to see Delilah the way I would have liked, though she usually tried to find me, stopping by the apartment during her lunch or slipping in to ask my opinion on a room she was working on.

Then May snuck up on me.

Then that anchor snagged hard and I found myself nearly immobilized while I recovered from the whiplash. Through those previous months, I was able to deceive myself. Without seeing her, I was able to repeat that lie over and over even when the pendulum swung to you: I'd made the right choice; I could never ask you to raise Jonathan's child; this *is* Jonathan's child.

But then came that day.

But then they placed her in my arms.

But then it crashed into me all at once.

They thought my tears were from finally holding her.

I let them think that.

Partly because it was true.

Partly because I could no longer deny it.

Even then I knew no part of her was Jonathan.

Even then I knew every part of her that wasn't me

Was you.

I was so afraid she would be one more reminder of what I had done, of what I had stolen from you, but she never was, not in that way, at least. Maybe it was because she was never wholly me nor wholly you. Maybe it was because she was one way that I could go on holding onto you. Maybe it was because if I could love her without guilt, then maybe one day I could point that unburdened love back towards you.

Then those laboring hormones passed.

Then I was reminded that it had been a year.

In some ways it felt as though no time had passed at all, as though all those wounds were still raw and exposed the way they were on that day. In others I was shocked that a year was all that it had been, that each of those months hadn't been a year themselves.

Holding my own daughter against me while my mother's memory hovered around me, I became more and more terrified of what was to come. Was I just grieving or was this more? Was I falling into my mother's path? Was I also the one in nine? I wanted to make it through for Tegan, but every time it crossed my mind, the fear that I wouldn't be able to grew larger and larger until it nearly surrounded me entirely.

I should have gone back to you then. But I was also afraid of how you'd react if I came home with an infant who I had carried without you, who I had let another man believe was his, who I had convinced myself for two trimesters wasn't yours. Even then I could see the pain in your eyes, the confusion that would climb onto your shoulders and weigh you down every time you looked at me, and, as though I were already in front of you, that guilt would drive a hook through my stomach and yank it hard to the bottom of the ocean while it scrambled to take my heart with it.

There were admittedly days when I would seriously consider going home. When I would stand in the closet staring at the $800 plain black Samsonite luggage set that Scott would have scoffed at and debate how long it would take me to pack up Tegan's things, a bag for myself, and go home to Mack, to Meg, to Tate, to Lucas, to you.

And that's where I'd falter.

Because next my mind would race to my father, would try to remember how long he had gotten, would fall into the court room where I had last seen

him, would scramble outside to the palms and flowerless oleanders, would struggle through the streets that had been my entire life, the streets that were filled with Her and then I couldn't breathe

And then Tegan would cry out in the other room.

And then my stomach would be back on the ocean floor.

I think I only ever moved during those days because of Tegan.

Without her I would have deteriorated there on Jonathan's expensive leather couch.

I don't remember exactly when I started to feel it, but before the end of Tegan's first five months, the guilt and the loneliness began to close in on me making everything in that city feel claustrophobic.

My guilt had grown so strong that it was almost to the point where I felt everyone secretly knew us, reporting my every move and betrayal back to you. The littlest things reminded me of you in ways I wasn't expecting, in ways that hit me in the sternum and batted me around that isolated ocean like battling trade winds.

Between fighting my guilt over you and my desperate need to prove that, though I had failed as a daughter, I wouldn't fail as a mother, I missed knowing where I was. I missed knowing side streets and secret ways around tourists. I missed knowing nearly every employee in every store and restaurant I walked into. I missed being able to navigate my surroundings based on a map I had built since childhood (turn at the corner where Scott and I found that stray dog when we were seven; go one street over from where my sixth grade best friend lived until her dad was transferred inland; it's next to the gift shop where, while waiting around for Meg's sister to pick a souvenir t-shirt and enough aisles away from Mack, you finally kissed me despite those flamingo shaped sunglasses I had put on and asked if you'd still be seen with me if I wore them in public. "Of course," you had said with that smile and those soft eyes that always nearly evaporates the gravity beneath me. "Prove it," I had tested. You had laughed at first then glanced around for Mack while everything inside of me hummed. And then you kissed me. And then I was yours. And then you were mine.)

There was one particular week when it all kept building and building until looking at my own reflection sent shockwaves through me. It was my hair, I finally decided. It was strangling me. I could count our years in every inch. And then one day while pulling it over my shoulder to feed Tegan, I felt

your fingertips run along my neck instead, dragging a chill down and across every place your hands ever explored. When she latched, I tried to push it away, but she kept looking up at me with those Matthews blue eyes surrounded by skin that was already darkening to that Caro olive. I could almost make myself believe that I was home, that I was in the same rocking chair She had nursed five children in, that it was you would come back from campus, that it was you who would take Tegan into your arms and she'd smile up at you the way she did me, the way she never seemed to do with Jonathan.

Because Jonathan never brought the waves to my shore.

Only you ever truly had that effect on me.

And there I was again, at the bottom of the ocean while the current twisted my hair around my throat.

I rushed out before Jonathan could come home, wandered the streets until I found a salon that took walk-ins. I remember the women being too distracted by Tegan to notice the desperation I was convinced covered my face. Maybe it wasn't as obvious as I believed it was. Maybe they all deciphered it as new mom weariness. Maybe not addressing my SOS, simply detangling me from the seaweed without question was the best they knew to do. Maybe it wasn't a guess. Maybe they knew it was what I needed.

When the stylist finished and pulled the styling cape from my shoulders, dusted the stray hair from the back of my neck, shifted the shorn flips around my ears and temples with her fingers, she met my eyes in the mirror and smiled.

"How's it feel, mama?"

"Better," I told her with a nod and a long exhale.

It did.

And it didn't.

Because when I stood, took Tegan from the stylist in the next station, and followed the receptionist to the front desk to pay, I caught in the corner of my eye our years being swept up and tossed away without a second thought, without words or fire tipped arrows. But at least they were no longer around my neck even if they still clung to my skin, jabbed me under the ribs, whispered sweet nothings that echoed off my bones.

At the end of the day, Jonathan came home with his usual distracted chatterings about campus, the department, grading, students, meetings. It took him longer than I expected to notice my hair, to even properly look at me, but when he finally did, he stopped still, jaw slack, eyes unblinking.

"You...you cut your hair."

"Yeah."

I didn't bother to put on a smile for him. I was too exhausted from my own flagellation and I could already feel his disappointment radiating off of him, disappointment I had already decided I wasn't going to take from him. If he wanted me, he'd have to take me without you, without us.

I wasn't his prize for winning the war.

He was my punishment, my purgatory.

Not that he would ever understand that.

"Why, um, why'd you do that?"

I shrugged, all my focus on Tegan sucking on my necklace and staring up at me. "It was too much. Too hot, I guess."

"It's gonna get cold soon. Don't think your neck'll get cold?"

"That's what scarves are for."

He huffed, shoved his hands in his pockets and started to walk away. "I like it long."

"Hair grows back, Jonathan."

He stopped and stared at me.

I refused to give him any more than my words. "You'll get used to it."

He never did. He always wanted that old me. The me that he'd stolen from you. But he'd never won that her to begin with. Because she'd been chained to the bottom of the ocean the day I'd lost Her.

I know I should tell you about that first year, about all her firsts, about everything you missed, but I'm not sure there's much I haven't already told you, if there's much I can repeat here without drowning in that guilt all over again the way I did every time those memories came up in person.

Because the truth is, that first year was a balancing act of guilt and new mother frenzy.

Jonathan wasn't much help, never would be, not the way you had been with Lucas, not the way you would be with the twins. But he still wanted to make sure everyone knew we were his. He insisted we get pictures taken and I held my tongue through the entire thing. I never said that Scott would have taken better pictures, never brought up those early pictures of Lucas and my mother, never let on the way I judged the photographer and the way she never showed us her own work, always showed us what other photographers were doing even in those days before Pinterest, kept show us shoots with celebrities and the way she kept trying to get me to look like someone else.

I don't hate those pictures.

But I very nearly do.

They remind me of those days without you, those days that should have been ours, those days when we should have been yours, those days I stole from you, those days through which I knew all those things, but still kept them from you because I was stubborn and I was broken and I was neck deep in the storm of my penance because I had already taken so much from you.

How could I give you anything after taking so much from you?

Delilah came and went through those days when I was trying my best for Jonathan (despite my already resenting him, despite my hating myself too

much to allow myself to get away from him), to make friends with other moms, to find Tegan playmates, to find us family friends. But every woman I met with a happy, well-adjusted family just made me hate myself all the more, doubled down on my aching for you.

I didn't love Jonathan.

I knew that then.

I knew that from the beginning.

I knew that I should be with you, that I should go home to you, but I was scared of hurting you, I was so scared of not knowing where I stood with you, what you'd do and what you'd say.

I knew you'd be angry.

I wanted you to be angry.

But I also know you, knew you then. I knew that anger wouldn't last, that you'd forgive me the moment you had her in your arms, tell that at least I was home now, at least we were home now.

And I didn't want you to forgive me.

I didn't deserve for you to forgive me.

I no longer believed that I deserved to float. Not after Tegan.

But I did believe that I deserved to be stranded.

I believed that I deserved to be without you.

Then Tegan hit one.

I had gone through three semesters at UT (well, online at UT). Delilah and I had started hanging out more and more again. Tegan started taking her first steps while in one of those empty apartments with Delilah on the floor passing me fabric and paint swatches, moving little cut out furniture pieces that she kept in a cigar box around a file folder room. Tegan said "mama" when we were at a flea market perusing vintage cameras, called Delilah "Yaya" when we were in some fancy furniture store looking for side tables.

Jonathan and I constantly fought about my time and where I was spending it. He didn't like when I would leave the apartment without him, when he couldn't show us off around town. We'd had a particularly bad argument when Delilah offered me a job working as her assistant, something I was already doing for free. He hadn't known that I was taking Tegan shopping with her, that Tegan liked Delilah more than him, lit up when she saw her, let her carry her without screaming, had a name for her. He didn't want anyone thinking she belonged to Delilah, that we were a "couple of dykes" raising "his" kid. I nearly left him for that one. I probably should have.

He just wanted me to be a mother, to be his housewife, to focus on my

degree he'd then insist I'd never have to use. He wanted another kid he could ignore, another kid I would have to somehow both provide for while also hiding away in his perfectly staged apartment. He'd give me lectures like I was a child when he'd come home to Tegan's toys and clothes and formula out in the open after a day of use as though someone would walk in one night and discover that he lived with a real, living, breathing child who had needs and wants and agency, a mother who wanted only to give her all those things without limits, without restrictions, without confining her to a single room in a luxury, high rise apartment.

But it was by this point that it had finally been cemented for me that Tegan and I were symbols for Jonathan, that we were set pieces in his stage performance of the perfect husband with the perfect housewife and perfect child who looked nothing like him. Everything we did was for him, so he could bring us out at get-togethers, brag about the parts of the apartment I'd helped Delilah design, talk about the "kitschy thing" I brought home the other day that he'd been convinced wouldn't work, but *look what she did with it.* He'd slip it into conversation, always framed as my "hobby", always one more qualifier on why I'd earned my place on his arm: *she's a housewife, a mother, going to school, and helps her friend design rooms in her free time. Isn't she perfect? Aren't I just lucky? And to think she was just some kid from Port A in her frayed shorts and Birkenstocks when I first brought her here. Look at her now.*

It was the way he would talk about my life before Austin that really made my head spin, made my tongue bleed from trying to uphold the image of his silent and doting housewife until everyone was gone.

Maybe I shouldn't have.

It was the way he would always say that I was studying social work because I wanted to help people, despite it being entirely his idea. Time would eventually prove him right, but in those days it was all to make him happy, so his donations and schmoozing wouldn't go to waste. It was the way he would say I was wasting my potential focusing on psychology back in Port A, though "still admirable, considering."

But I hadn't majored in it to help the masses.

I just wanted to know how to save my mother.

And I had failed.

Who was I to help anyone?

It was the way he'd always refer to Dad's time out on the boats but never his PhD, never the research he had been doing, the journals he'd been

published in, always tacking on where he was through those days.

It was the way he always referred to my brothers, always the fact that I was the only girl, but never any details about them, just an explanation for when I didn't live up to his standards of femininity. He never talked about Mack and how many times he'd made Teacher of the Year; never about Meg and the houses she flipped with her dad, the way she was going to business school at night to help him run things by the book, not undersell himself or his workers; never about the work she and Mack had done on their own house, the restoration tricks they'd taught me and I was now teaching Delilah; never about Scott's photography, the magazines his photos were in, the companies he'd worked for, the album covers he'd shot; never the awards Tate had won at school, the astronomy club, the quiz bowls, the AV club he'd started with Mack's help; never a single word about you because, for him, you were only a weapon that he'd throw at me when he wanted to tether me to the ground, remind me that he'd won.

It was the way he'd refer to my mother as nothing more than the local poet. He'd leave out how many books she'd published, the ones that had been reviewed by *The New Yorker*, the ones that had made it to the best sellers lists, the poems she'd had published in *Paris Review, Ploughshares, Tin House,* the first issues of *New England Review.*

It was the way he spoke of her: just a coastal girl who seduced a New England fisherman and wrote poems between raising five kids.

It was the way he spoke of me: just a coastal girl who seduced a New England philosopher and made kitschy things look nice between raising "his" daughter.

Because that's all we were to him: set dressing; accessories; one more object he could point to and say *look what I have.*

Now I know what this was, what he was doing.

Part of me, maybe a majority of me, knew it even then.

But it was what I deserved.

It was my penance.

It was the cost of being voluntarily stranded.

It was put up with him,

Or go home to you.

I should have gone home to you.

But I kept coming up with reasons not to, every single one of which

centered around my guilt and the hurt that, with every milestone Tegan hit, grew heavier and heavier in the version of your eyes I carried in my heart.

I did know that I wasn't going to stay with Jonathan forever. It was around the time that Tegan was 18 months that I decided I was going to leave him once I finished my masters. Why leave someone who's paying your tuition, someone who seemed to be able to finagle you around the rules with money and a face to face reminder of the daughter on your hip? Why leave someone before you can support yourself and one of the few people who was capable of keeping your head above water?

Delilah knew my plan. She saw it in the way I was around him, heard it in the way I spoke of him. She coaxed the rest out of me one day in the living room while Tegan was napping. Not that it took that much to wrestle it from me. All she needed was that long stare after one of my usual remarks and then, when I looked up at her, to ask why I was with him.

It was around that time that she got me that job with *On Rotation*. Her sister-in-law, Terra, was one of the editors, brought her along on one of our thrifting trips, explained to both of us that I needed something that was mine, something Jonathan couldn't touch, couldn't manipulate. Later, when it was just us, she admitted that she was worried, that she wanted me to have some form of income in case I changed my mind.

"If you work for me, you work for the building," she explained when I asked why I couldn't just be her assistant like we'd talked about before. "They do things by the book, ya know. You'd end up with tax returns. He'd find them. Start asking questions. You need something he can't stick his nose into. You got your own account? One he can't get to?"

I did. The one I'd had back in Port A. The one I hadn't touched since I'd left. I'd told Jonathan there was next to nothing in it, that there was no real point in him having access to it. It hadn't been a lie then.

Terra agreed to pay me under the table per article and she sent me albums to review and tickets to shows through Delilah. The CDs were just bands Delilah suggested I listen to; the time I spent in my library writing articles with Tegan scribbling at the desk next to me just more schoolwork; the shows were just me getting out, me needing some girl time. Terra and Vera would watch Tegan at their place when I'd go out even when Jonathan would be home, that way he'd never have to lift a finger, his life wouldn't be interrupted. I'd be able to enjoy the show knowing she was with people who paid attention to her, doted on her, played with her, knew not to give her to Jonathan unless I was there, protected her the way I would. Not that I thought

he'd come for her then. Not that that was a concern yet.

I don't remember how it felt doing all this behind his back. Probably because I was already existing firmly in that space he only saw when he chose to look at me. Probably because for another year it would be the thing that would keep me moving on those nights when I felt too used up to care anymore.

I want to say Tegan was nearly two and a half when Scott called me out of the blue, asked if I was still in Austin and where.

We'd talked on occasion before, always when Tegan was asleep, almost always when Jonathan wasn't around, but I hadn't seen him since I'd left, had never figured out how much he knew about why. I told him where we were anyways and once the call ended that's when the panic hit me with a rush. I wanted to tell him about Tegan, wanted him to meet her, see her, love her the way I did. A small, unacknowledged part of me may have even wanted him to tell me to come home, to tell me all the things I told myself at night while staring at the wall hating Jonathan's arm around me. But I knew there was a right way to do it and to just show up at the café we'd talked about meeting at with Tegan in a stroller wasn't the way.

And then that terrified, guilt ridden part of me stepped in and I told myself that Scott shouldn't meet her, that he'd just go home and tell you and then who knew what would happen after that.

Probably what should have happened.

Probably what I needed to happen.

My plan had originally been to meet him on a day when Jonathan was off. I'd come up with reasons for why he couldn't come to the apartment: Jonathan was grading papers; there was work being down on the building; Jonathan had friends over. Most of them involved Jonathan. If Scott knew he was there, maybe he'd be less inclined to push.

But then, on a day when Jonathan was on campus and I was alone with Tegan, I got one of those feelings in my gut, suddenly felt the tingle of familiarity on my skin, suddenly smelled that lingering of salt and sand on

fabric, suddenly saw those Matthews blue eyes, suddenly heard worn out Converse on expensive tile, that chuckle that was home. Then I got a call from the lobby. Scott was downstairs asking to come up. His name wasn't on Jonathan's list of pre-approved visitors and no one in the office knew of any of my family. The voice of the building manager slithered with disapproval as he described him to me. I told him it was okay, smiled when I heard Scott in the background hitting on the girl who ran the front desk.

But then I hung up and the panic crashed against my lungs all over again.

I spent the entire time waiting for him to come up rushing around the apartment hiding Tegan's toys and books and dishes and booster seat and discarded socks and shoes from our lunch visit with Delilah and Vera at the artisan fair they were helping set up. It admittedly wasn't that hard. It all already had hiding spots so Jonathan could have a sophisticated apartment he could pretend housed a child but none of the things required to raise her. It was the first time I didn't silently fume over the hiding ritual I usually did with Tegan every afternoon before Jonathan came home.

Luckily, Tegan was napping, but Scott isn't exactly quiet, as you know, and Tegan was at that stage of testing how far I'd let her dictate her own sleep schedule. I knew it would only be a matter of time before she heard me talking to someone, before she'd come out to see who it was, before Scott would see all the signs of whose child she really was.

But then he knocked.

Then I opened the door.

Then all the panic and worry washed away.

All smiles and excitement, Scott rushed in, grabbed me around the middle and lifted me off the ground as he went straight into how long it had been and why hadn't I been home to see everyone yet and why I'd let *him* be the one to hunt *me* down.

Immediately the entire apartment felt larger.

The clouds began to dissipate.

I could see the stars again, recognize old constellations.

Eventually, he let me go and when I took a step back, he looked me over, that wide smile filled with a nostalgic familiarity never fading and I realized there in that moment it was so nearly the very thing I'd been aching for.

He laughed. "What are you doing in this bougie hell hole?"

My stomach turned then, but I tried not to show it. To hide not wanting to look him in the eyes, I rolled mine and shrugged between crossing my

arms. "Jonathan likes it."

"Course he would. Do you?"

"Fuck no." I felt safe enough to meet his eyes again.

It was then that he squinted at me. "You look different."

I shook my, at this point, fully established jaw length hair at him. I didn't tell him that Jonathan and I had bickered about it the night before while I was blow drying it.

"Oh, shit! Yeah! Damn." He smiled and nodded as he looked me over. "I like it. Reminds me of high school."

I laughed and narrowed my eyes at him. "Is that a good thing?"

He smirked and shrugged. "Those were wild years. Well," he moved down the hall, "Show me around your bougie hell hole."

I showed him around the apartment, avoided the bedrooms, distracted him by telling him about the pieces I'd bought while out with Delilah.

"She's got good taste," he commented in my library as he looked over the framed 70's art prints she'd found for me.

"She's eager to meet you."

"Yeah?" He gave me that Don Juan smirk that I remember not being able to believe I'd actually missed. "Like, eager to *meet me* meet me?"

"It never came up," I told him with a dry tone despite my grin.

He chuckled and looked over my desk. "Sure."

Then he hooked a finger on my pair of expensive Beats headphones and held them up to me with a disapproving smirk.

Mine was apologetic along with my shrug, almost embarrassed. "Jonathan didn't like my old pair."

"Why not? They break or something?"

I shook my head and looked at my feet. "He said they looked…like hand-me-downs? Or something like that."

"He meant poor." Scott rolled his eyes and half-tossed the headphones back on the desk. "He's a—"

"Don't?"

He looked at me. There wasn't really shock on his face, just a bit of confusion, a bit of disappointment, a bit of seeing right through me. "Why are you here, Al?"

"What do you mean?"

He stared at me, knew that I knew what he meant. "With him," he said

anyways.

But I wasn't ready to have that conversation with Scott, wasn't ready to be told to just go home. So, instead I shook my head and stared at the carpet. I can't really hide things from Scott, I never have. Though he may not know the exact why of what I'm thinking or doing, he always seems to understand just by looking at me, the underlining feelings I'm trying not to show him, the parts of me that words and whys can't ever really express anyways.

For so long you were the only other person who could ever do that.
Now there's Sara.
Now there's Roxie.
But that's not really important is it?
It's just...
I'm just missing them today, I guess.
As much as I love Scott and Joss, Jackie, the girls, having them across the yard rather than down the highway, I miss having Sara and Roxie closer.
I know you know.
I just
Had to say it, I guess.

Once he was done judging Jonathan's fingers on everything, we sat in the living room talking for a long time. We mostly avoided talking about home. I don't know if it was because he didn't want Jonathan's territory to taint that kind of talk or if he could see on me that I wasn't ready yet. Either way, we mostly talked about Austin, about his work, about how long he was there for.

Then the sounds of Tegan shifting came over the baby monitor I hadn't felt comfortable enough with fully hiding. My eyes went wide and Scott finally spotted it.

The times I've thought back on this moment, I've gone back and forth over what was behind those hooded Matthews blue eyes when they moved from the baby monitor to me. Sometimes I think he already knew. Sometimes I think he genuinely never questioned why I had gone off with Jonathan when you still wanted me, needed me, back home. Sometimes I wonder if maybe it was somewhere in between, if he'd had a suspicion, but no proof to confidently say it out loud.

Whatever was behind those eyes, they shifted over me for longer than I had expected them to. "You babysitting?"

I stared at him for as long as I could stand, trying to think of something,

willing myself to say yes. I closed my eyes instead and dropped my head. "No."

I couldn't deny her.

Despite Jonathan living in that apartment, despite those days when he pretended to belong to us, despite Delilah, Vera, Terra, she and I had only each other. I wasn't going to send her downstream even if only verbally, even if only for a single moment. I refused to put my guilt on her.

Scott didn't say anything.

When I was finally brave enough to look at him, he met my eyes and nodded.

There was no real point in explaining. Not that I could have with what little I was allowing to pass through my own consciousness in those days, too focused on securing something, anything for us for when I finally left Jonathan. Instead, I just stood and went to Tegan's room, Scott quietly following me. I knelt beside her bed and coaxed her awake because of course it was one of the few days she actually slept through her nap. She didn't get up or even open her eyes, just reached her arms out to wrap around my neck.

I think she stopped doing that by the time we came back to you. It was her way of telling me she'd get out of bed, but she was going to stay asleep for as long as she could get away with. Already feeling guilty, I let her get away with it, knew it would make this all move more smoothly. Pushing the blanket off her, I lifted her onto my hip and carried her, pretending to still be asleep against my shoulder, to the door where Scott was standing, watching me with that same look I've never been able to interpret. (I should probably just ask him. Not that it'd change anything.)

"Tegan, love," I whispered to her and she buried her face deeper against my shoulder. "There's someone Mommy wants you to meet."

Reluctantly, she lifted her head from my shoulder to look at me with those bleary blue eyes.

"Hi," I told her with a smile that she only blinked at. "This is Scott." She followed my finger and turned her heavy blinking to him. "He's Mommy's brother."

Slightly more awake now, she stared hard at Scott then me then Scott again. "Like Hansel?"

"Yeah," I laughed and was glad to hear him do the same. "Scott is Mommy's Hansel."

"Hey, now. Uncle Scott wouldn't be dumb enough to eat off some house

in the middle of the woods."

"But he would be dumb enough to let an evil witch coax him into her house."

"Only if she was young and—"

My raised brows stopped him, though Tegan continued giggling making that smirk of his into a grin.

I remember wanting to thank him there. I remember the rush of relief that came over me, the way some part of me said, *of course he'd forgive you, of course he'd love her.* I remember almost wishing it had been you that day.

In the living room, Tegan pulled her toys from their hiding spots without ever questioning why they'd been put away. Scott eyed me more and more with each reveal of secreted toddler things, but never said anything while I avoided looking at him, all my attention squarely on her. The eyeing, the silent questioning was gone the moment he was on the living room floor with her playing her games, answering her questions (once I'd translated them for him), reading her books, listening to her strange toddler stories that rambled all over the place without ever actually going anywhere.

Then I looked at the clock and realized what time it was. Leaving them to play, I went into the kitchen, started my housewife act, tried to think up something that would distract Jonathan from Scott's presence. Eventually, Scott came into the kitchen and stood quietly next to me while I cooked, both of us watching Tegan.

Then I had to say it.

It was eroding my insides.

"Please, don't tell Marc."

He stared at me for a long while before answering. "What would I be telling Marc?"

But all I could do was shake my head and continue to avoid those words. "Just...don't? Please? He can't know."

It was another long moment before he nodded and shifted his eyes from mine to Tegan stacking those little pastel blocks into spires that made my heart cry out for more reasons than I wanted to admit.

"You can't keep her secret forever, Al."

I knew he was right.

But for whatever reasons, I was determined to try anyways.

Jonathan came home at his usual time to find us at the dining room table, dinner ready in the kitchen, but Tegan's things still out and around the apartment.

"Hi," I said and leapt from my chair before he could say anything.

I lifted Tegan onto my hip and went to him with that housewife smile, my eyes large, making sure to look up at him while I held onto my daughter.

"Uncle Scott surprised us," I told him, emphasizing the "uncle" hoping it would remind him that Scott was as much Tegan's family as he was mine.

"Apartment's a mess," he commented, switching between glaring and smiling depending where Scott's eyes were second to second.

"We were so busy playing we lost track of time," I said to Tegan more than him. "Didn't we?"

Tegan nodded and squealed from my shoulder where she was watching Scott between glancing at me.

"You remembered to—"

"Yes. Dinner's ready."

"And he's—"

"Yeah." I clung tighter to Tegan. "I already invited him to eat with us."

Angry flickered through his muscles, but then he breathed, nodded, then glanced at Scott one last time before turning for the bedroom.

"He's just ecstatic to see me," Scott said with a smirk while I situated Tegan in her booster seat.

"There's a reason I wanted us to meet somewhere without him first."

I straightened and looked at him to see he was watching me from an

angle, his lips pursed while he fidgeted with the crayons Tegan was reaching for.

"Don't look at me like that?"

"Like what?" He smiled at Tegan and held up the crayons to her.

"He's not that bad. He's just…" I shrugged and started to pick up Tegan's things. "Particular."

He glanced up at me then back to Tegan. "Sure."

When Jonathan came back out, he put on a smile for Scott that back home I would have thought was genuine, probably fell for it more often than I realize, but that I now knew to be for people he knew he had to play nice with. He even kissed me on the cheek, tousled Tegan's hair as he passed her for his seat at the table. She looked up at him with wide eyes, before Scott's fidgeting with the crayons distracted her again. And Scott also did his best to pretend for my sake, for Tegan's, but I knew him better than I did Jonathan. I knew those tense smiles and forced laughs. I knew that, when the attention wasn't on him, he was taking in everything Jonathan did and said to me, to Tegan. I knew he was evaluating it all, trying to pinpoint hints to something I wasn't telling him, wounds I wasn't showing him, be they physical or not.

Despite all this, dinner moved more smoothly than I'd expected with Jonathan putting on his best host act and Scott not ignoring him entirely. Everyone finished, I stood at the sink washing dishes while Tegan stood in front of the fridge playing with the chic wooden alphabet magnets Jonathan let stay up even when he was home. At the table, the two were mostly quiet between my shouted attempts to continue some kind of conversation.

"What're you doing tomorrow," I asked Scott when I was on the last dish.

"Um, nothing really. I was kind of hoping to hang out more?"

"Yeah?" I smiled at him while drying the big serving bowl and leaned my hip against the counter. "You can meet Delilah then."

"The designer chick?"

"Yeah." The bowl in the bottom cabinet, I lifted up Tegan who was already bouncing in front of me then carried her to the table where I slid into my chair and held her against me. "And tomorrow's her flea market day."

Before I could continue, Tegan's eyes went wide and sparkly as she started to bounce in my lap. "Unka Got come wif us?"

I smiled down at her, I couldn't help it. "If he wants to."

"Wants to what," Scott asked with a chuckle and a smirk.

"Come with us," I told him while Tegan turned to smile at him from behind her splayed hands clapping together.

"Oh! Well, if *you* want me to," he said to Tegan.

The curls I'd piled on top of her head bounced with her vigorous nod.

"Okay then," he laughed. "Guess we're going to the flea market tomorrow."

Tegan squealed again and swung her shoulders back and forth while grinning up at me. It made my heart swell the way nearly everything she did in those days did and I wrapped my arms around her to kiss the top of her head. When I did, I caught Jonathan watching me with his arms crossed and jaw clenched. I chose to ignore him, pour all my focus onto Tegan and Scott.

He ruined it by clearing his throat. "How long are you in Austin for?"

"A few weeks," Scott said with a shrug, his eyes on the spot in the grain of the tabletop that his thumbnail was tracing. "I always seem to get a flood of shoots when I come through here."

He gave me and Tegan a smirk that made her giggle.

"Where are you staying," I asked him.

He squinted at me before answering. "You remember Dana?"

I squinted back at him. "From TAMU-CC? The sculptor?"

"Yeah. She's out by Lake Travis now—"

"Lake Travis?!"

He laughed at me. "Yeah. She offered her couch."

"What? Her—No! Stay with us. We have an actual bed you can sleep in."

"The guest room?" Jonathan said and I looked at him, suddenly remembering the other half of my "us" and "we" wasn't you.

"Yeah," I told him. It was somewhere between a doting housewife question and a fuck you, this is my brother, my twin statement. "And," I turned back to Scott, "you said earlier most of your shoots are in the city. It's hell getting in and out. You don't wanna do that the whole time you're here."

He gave me a grin and nodded, ignoring, the way I was, Jonathan staring at me. "You know what? Sure. Pretty sure Dana won't mind. And it'll guarantee us time to hang out."

Even then I had a feeling that if he hadn't felt the way he had about Jonathan, he'd have considered it longer, would have insisted on calling Dana first, would have waited to hear what Jonathan thought. I want to say if it had been you he would have done all those things, but you would have been the

one to offer our guest room, would have offered it back when he first called.

Jonathan on the other hand, kept looking between us, didn't talk for the rest of the night, just grew more and more tense while he watched Scott and me talk and entertain Tegan who was already reaching for Scott, sitting in his lap, bringing him toys or books to read to her. But that night, after Tegan was asleep, Scott was settled in the guestroom, and Jonathan and I were in our room, he finally turned on me the way I know he wanted to hours before.

"Why'd you do that, Alexandria," he asked while I was at the sink.

Every last one of my nerve endings screamed and I tried not to look at him in the mirror, leaning against the doorframe, his arms crossed tight. "He's my brother."

"He had a place to stay. A girl to fuck even."

"Don't." I tossed the used cotton ball into the waste basket. "Don't talk about him like that."

"It's the truth. Surprised he isn't—"

I gripped the edge of the counter. "Stop. He's here. He's staying. It's done."

"Why is it so important to you that he stays here?"

"He's my family."

"He's your past, Alexandria. He's everything I saved you from. Besides, you've always argued when I tried to invite my family to stay and with much more advance notice, by the way."

"They don't want to come here," I said as I turned and slipped past him for the bedroom.

"They do. They want to see you, see Tegan."

"They have pictures," I muttered to the decorative pillows I was throwing on the floor.

"But that's besides the point," he said, either ignoring me or having not heard, "I don't want him around her."

I stopped and stared at him. "Around who?"

I knew the answer, but I was giving him a chance to save himself, a chance he didn't take.

"My daughter."

She's not yours, I wanted to growl at him.

Instead, I clenched my jaw, breathed in deep through my nose, planted my feet to the ground. "And why's that?"

"He's not exactly…the best role model."

"Does he need to be? He's her uncle not—"

"He doesn't have a job—"

"Yes, he does—"

"He doesn't have a house. He just sleeps on people's couches, probably in exchange for sex."

"What are you talking about?"

"He doesn't even have a degree. Not even an associates."

"He doesn't need—"

"He's a leach and a man-whore."

I was too shocked to argue.

"Do you really want our daughter around someone like that?"

I stared at him, every inch of me on fire, every heartbeat echoing your name. I grabbed my pillow and the throw blanket off the foot of the bed then walked out.

"Alex," he grumbled after me.

But the door closed behind me seconds after. I went to the guest room and stood in the doorway staring at the carpet, breathing deep.

"You okay," Scott asked.

I just shook my head.

He was quiet for a moment. "I, uh, wasn't really all that tired…"

"Me neither."

He met me at the door. "Come on. Let's find something to watch."

I dropped the pillow and blanket and hugged him tight around the middle. He didn't say a word, just held me tight against him while I tread water until the shaking in my bones stopped.

"There's a place down the street—" I said against his shirt.

"I was hoping you'd be up for getting some real food."

Whether it was for my sake or for Tegan's, for the next few days Scott acted as though that first night hadn't happened. Instead, we spent most of our days with Tegan playing her games, watching the educational cartoons Jonathan let me buy for her, wandering the city between his shoots. We'd spend our evenings with Jonathan, him and Scott playing nice, biting their tongues, only letting their masks slide when the other's back was turned. But I could sense that under the mask, there were things he wanted to tell me, a discussion we weren't having that he was eager to get through.

Then one morning, after Jonathan had left, Scott had called me into the guestroom where he was still sorting equipment that was already strewn with his haphazard care across the dresser, the bed, the side table, the edges of the floor.

"Would Delilah be up for watching Teegs around noon," he asked.

I squinted at him, "Why?"

He shrugged. "Lunch? Just us? Like the old days?"

I laughed. "In which old days did we go out to lunch alone?"

That smirk. That eye roll. That homesick pang in my gut that I was determined to ignore. "Will you just come to lunch with me? Just the two of us?"

"Okay. Okay. I'll see where Del's at then."

He gave me the address of the place he'd be working, hugged Tegan (distracted with her block stacking) then me, and left. Around noon, I took Tegan down to Delilah who had Vera with her that day, both of them taking a shining eyed and giggly Tegan with equal excitement. At that point I may not have been in Austin for long, but before even getting in the cab I

recognized the neighborhood the address was in. It was an expensive one. Jonathan liked to drive around there and window shop for very nearly mansions when he could get away with it, liked to dream up fancy dinner and holiday parties at me, liked when I played along.

I wasn't however, prepared for the taxi to keep driving past the very nearly mansions, past the McMansions to slow at every gated entrance along the street lined with a thick row of trees while we both craned our necks to search for the house number. Finally, we found the right one and he pulled up to the little intercom before shouting into it the information I passed him through the Plexiglas between us. The driveway was more of a road, was also lined with that same thick array of trees. Even the taxi driver let out an impressed whistle as he pulled up to the expansive house that was as much craftsman as it was modern.

"Don't usually get to see the houses," he admitted to me. "Most people get out at the gate."

My eyes went wide at that. "Was I supposed to?"

He laughed and shrugged. "Your guess is as good as mine." Then he smirked at me from over his shoulder. "You got a ride back? Need me to hang around until you leave?"

I just laughed and turned him down with some good humored apology before paying him and going to the front door, which was bigger than any front door should be, while he delayed in leaving, watching me search for the bell. Before I could find it, Scott opened door, camera in hand, Matthews straw hair out of sorts and not in his standard styled behead way.

"Hey! Come in! Sorry, we're still going. You don't mind hanging out 'til we're done, do you?"

"'Course not," I half answered, distracted by the foyer that could hold the entirety of your apartment back in Port A, the rooms branching off of it which could hold the entirety of the apartment I had just left, the chandelier above my head that sparkled with a vast assortment of dangling crystals that I could just see shattering across the polished tiles at our feet in some bad horror movie.

Catching my swiveling head and open mouth, he smiled and looked around the foyer, as well. "Crazy, right?"

"And *my* place is bougie?"

He laughed. "I'm just taking the pictures. Client picked this place."

"Who's the client?"

"Uh," he took in a breath and raised his brows the way he does when he's stalling. "The name on the check is Shawn—Shawna, but she, um, isn't, well, known? By that name?"

"Oh?"

"Yeah, um. Listen, that's what I, um—well, I should tell you before we head up that, well, um, uh, it's, uh, porn? That I'm shooting? It's—this is a porn? Shoot?"

I didn't know what to say, just stared at him with my brows raised, though I wasn't all that surprised. For one, it was Scott. For another, in the taxi, at the front door, between my shock I had felt a level of...sleaze isn't the right word exactly, but there had been that sense of naked bodies, of voyeurism and pleasure usually hidden behind closed doors.

"I thought we'd've been done by the time you got here. All the clothes back on and stuff. Um..." He lifted his eyes back to mine and shrugged. "You weren't supposed to find out like this."

"How was I supposed to find out?"

"I don't know, actually," he admitted with a chuckle. "I was kind of hoping you never would."

"You mean you were going to keep a secret from me?"

He laughed. "You *really* don't get to pull that."

I took in a deep breath and nodded. "Fair."

We stood there for a few awkward seconds longer.

"You okay with all this," he finally asked and nodded over his shoulder.

I don't actually remember how I did feel in that moment. There's a chance my memory is too mixed up with how I feel about it now. Either way, I want to say that I shrugged. "What kind of porn?"

He shrugged back. "Vanilla lesbian stuff."

My brows rose as I started to follow him. "Interesting."

"You can't hook up with anyone I've photographed naked."

"Well, fuck, I'm sure that eliminates half the female population."

"Ha Ha."

I remember being surprised by how comfortable it all was. You hear about porn being this awful oppressive misogynistic operation, and I'm sure parts of it are, but that day Scott was the only man in the room. Besides the two models he was photographing with a professionalism that admittedly surprised me even if it was his normal sort of casual, there was the makeup

artist who doubled as a hair stylist, the client's female agent, a pair of women who were friends of the women being photographed, the client's girlfriend, and the woman who owned the mansion. Turned out she'd done porn before, but when she'd had her third kid, she'd decided to settle down with her boyfriend. No one actually lived in the mansion, she told me. She just rented it out for things like this—luxurious photo shoots, music videos, film projects.

"But mostly it's porn," she'd told me with a laugh.

While Scott worked, the women kept me entertained with a steady stream of questions. Most of them had worked with him at least once before, the two friends had modeled for him more times than they seemed able to remember, and they'd all heard about me, about y'all back in Port A, even if just in passing. One of them, I think it was the makeup artist, when she caught me alone in the kitchen, said she knew about Mom, said she was sorry, said she'd never seen Scott so torn up before, said she'd been almost worried he wouldn't come through it.

It was all strange and somehow comforting. All those years before, Scott leaving placed him in this black box. I couldn't picture what he was doing or who he was spending time with. Even when I would recognize the name he'd leave me, the only faces I would ever have to match was Dani's and Valor's, for all the others I had a voice at most. For all I knew, he was alone driving around the country in his little mustang, spending nights in models' beds before heading out alone again. Now I had some version of what he did, saw that he was surrounded by people who were open and creative and so strangely transient, so oddly on the fringes that family was family no matter how many times you'd met them.

It made the idea of him always leaving somewhat easier, even if it still left me without a limb.

The staged orgasms fully captured, the real ones began to build with giggles and quiet murmurs while Scott packed his equipment and avoided my eyes before shoving the excess equipment into my arms and rushing us down the stairs. I remember it was odd, remember thinking the real ones would have been something he'd usually want to capture. It was only after the goodbyes were exchanged in the foyer, sending some by proxy to those still upstairs, and we were in the car with the equipment that he started to relax.

"That was an experience," I attempted to aid the process.

"Yeah, sorry about that," he insisted. "It wasn't supposed to go that long. Forgot how much of a perfectionist Shawn is."

I shrugged. "I didn't mind. Seriously," I added when he gave me that

restrained laugh. "I didn't! The makeup artist?"

"Gabby?"

"Yeah. She was fun enough on her own."

He nodded. "Yeah. Gabs is great. Always try to book her when I'm in the area. Not that I would have had a choice with this one. Shawn and her are close. Work together a lot."

"So, you've worked with Shawna a lot, too?"

He shrugged. "Enough."

"How long you been doing this?"

That nervous chuckle as he used pulling out of the gate and onto the road as an excuse to delay answering my question, and even then his answer was just, "Depends."

I squinted at him. "On what?"

"What you're asking about? Porn or," he shrugged again, "just sex."

"Is there a difference?"

"Yeah!" He laughed. "Porn is all fake, Al. It's a lot more interesting to just stand back and capture someone fucking, just...doing their thing, ya know? Do your job right and they forget you're even there."

I nodded, that was nothing new—it's always been his philosophy on photography. "As poetic as that is, you do know you didn't answer my question right?"

He laughed again. "Uh, porn since..." He scrunched up one side of his face. "I don't know? Some point at TAMU-CC?"

"What?"

He rubbed the back of his neck while avoiding me, entirely focused on the road ahead of him. "Yeah."

"And you didn't tell me?"

"It wasn't exactly something I was proud of, Al. It's still not. Wasn't exactly something I wanted...Well, I didn't want Mom to find out."

For a moment, I just chewed the skin around my thumbnail while distracting my eyes with the rows of houses slipping by, hoping it would keep the tears from building.

Finally, I swallowed and looked back at the gear shit between us. "Are they good?"

I knew the answer, but he still shrugged. "I guess."

I groaned. "Scott."

He laughed. "I guess there's a reason Shawn keeps hiring me."

I nodded. "Then you deserve to be proud! Even a little."

He shrugged again, still avoiding looking at me. "I guess."

"The erotic stuff?"

"What about it?"

"When'd you start that?"

He was somehow even more nervous about this confession, his entire body shifting away from me along with his shrug. "Uh. High school, I guess."

I nodded, remembering those photos I'd found on his laptop that one time. "With Dani." I don't **remember if it was a question or a statement**.

He finally met my eyes, his brows deeply furrowed, and I shrugged.

"I may have saw something...erotic...on your laptop back then."

That smirk. "You were snooping on my laptop?"

"No! I needed the internet and I saw the folder collapsed in the taskbar—"

He laughed. "So, you opened it?"

"It said 'Dani' and I always liked the ones you did with her and I was curious and wanted to see." I grinned while he continued to laugh.

"You always were so nosey."

"Maybe don't take good pictures."

Still smiling, he shook his head.

"You proud of those? The erotic ones?"

He nodded. "Yeah. Yeah, actually."

"Then I wanna see 'em!"

"No, you don't."

"Yeah, I do!"

He glanced at me with that smirk. "Seriously?"

"Yeah. You're good, Scott! Even the ones you hate are good. If *you're* proud of them...well, then they must be better than good."

They are. He is. But you know that.

Sitting in his car in the parking garage once we were back in the city, he showed me what he had on his laptop, even showed me shots from the shoot we'd just come from after some convincing. Sure, it's awkward looking at pictures of people fucking and knowing that your brother was in the same room as those people while they were entwined, but those pictures are good,

better than good, and it took very little for the awkwardness to fade, for them to become the works of art they are. They're not two people fucking in a room with a creeper standing in the corner because he does his job right— even as a voyeur looking at a frozen moment of people enjoying each other, you forget he's there.

Is this important?

Why am I telling you this?

I'm not really sure. I don't think there's really a reason.

Maybe I just like bragging about my brother, like saying, look at his amazing person I shared a womb with.

Maybe it's to show you that those years in Austin weren't all bad, that I had someone to carry me through at least part of those limbless days.

Maybe this is to show you where my path actually began to fork, part of the reason I went west instead of south.

Maybe I'm just missing him today. Not that I blame them. Kerrville is a hell of a lot prettier than San Antonio. Not that I should be complaining. At least now he's still. At least now I always know who to call when he doesn't answer.

But there was a reason I went into all this to begin with.

It was because of the conversation we had after that when we finally put away his laptop and left the parking garage, walked along Congress until we settled on a restaurant, sat in the booth with our plastic baskets of burgers and fries while he told me everything going on at home without me, while I grew more and more quiet and my appetite steadily slipped away from me.

"When I left, they were getting him into therapy," he said about Tate, finally at the end of that destructive year he had to go through without me, maybe because of me.

I nodded, every other part of me numb. "That's good."

"Yeah. It'll, uh…it'll do him good."

It's what you should have done, I could feel him trying not to say. *None of this would have happened if you'd let us do that.*

"Scott and Meg?"

"Better than Tate," he half grumbled. "They've had each other through all this, ya know?"

"They've had us to take care of through all this," I said, not entirely sure why.

"Well, *us*," he said.

I shifted in my seat, crossed my arms, avoided his eyes. I deserved that. "And…"

And Marc, was what I wanted to say, what I couldn't manage to force from my throat.

Scott sighed. "Depends on the day." He shrugged. "Well, when I was there last, at least."

"When you left…?" But it took me a few seconds to continue, my lips hovering over the words. "How…I guess, how was he when…?"

I could feel his eyes on me. "He, uh—When I left, he was gearing up to present his thesis. Talking about doctoral programs."

"Yeah?"

My heart soared for you. My womb cried out for you. A hurricane formed in my gut unsettling my masts and sails to tangle against my ribs. I continued to avoid his eyes.

"He…Al, you know, he just—"

"Please." My eyes clenched shut. "Please, I don't—"

"You don't need to hide from him like this, Al. He doesn't want you to."

She wouldn't want you to, was between those words.

I shook my head and pressed my elbows against the tabletop, the heels of my palms against my brows, my arms aching for Tegan, my body aching for you.

"I can't," I wish I hadn't said.

"What do you mean?"

"I…I just…Do we really have to talk about this now? Here?"

"I guess not." He stared at me while I fought the breakdown pressing against my throat, flinging my heart and lungs around my chest. "But, Al, you know—"

"Please, Scott. Seriously."

"Okay."

I listened to him slide out of his side of the booth and into mine where he pulled me against his side, one arm around my shoulders, the other along the tabletop in front of me.

"Okay. Sorry."

I leaned against him and rubbed at my nose with the back of my hand, poorly fighting the whimpers that came with those sobs that were bucking against my diaphragm wanting to break me there in the middle of everything.

"Hey, Al, I'm sorry, really. Don't get stranded on my now."

But I already was.

I had been for a long time by then.

I don't think Scott really knew until that moment.

I don't think he really understood until a few weeks later.

I never really knew when he was originally supposed to leave. Looking back, I'm not entirely sure he did. Whenever Jonathan would ask with a passive aggressive sort of tone, he'd give only answers that grew in vagueness with each time he had to give one. Whenever I would ask, he'd just shrug and steer the topic in a different direction.

Through that time, I could feel Jonathan getting more and more frustrated with him, with me. Could hear it in the way he spoke to Scott, the way every little thing he did or said resulted in a deep, partially controlled breath, an eye roll, crossed arms, tense shoulders. I tried my best to dilute it, to play his diminutive wife, to pretend that I needed him to play nice, that I needed him to accept Scott.

For me, I'd ask him with my eyes tilted up the way he liked when we were in front of people, in front of Tegan.

Why can't you just let me have this? Let me have one thing you're not in control of, I'd ask him when he'd continue to rant at me in private.

He never did hit me, but he'd give me a look then, a look he gave me often, a look that made me wonder if today was the day, if this time was the final straw, if I'd pushed my luck too far. Then he'd let out the breath he'd been holding, he'd blink, he'd turn around and walk away.

Delilah was a different story. Delilah embraced Scott before he even got there. Insisted on a hug when they first met (the same way she did you), asked his opinion on designs and details, bought a bunch of photos he'd taken of us shopping and working to use for marketing stuff (though he kept insisting she didn't need to pay him anything), told Terra about him before I ever considered to, gotten him a freelance contract with one phone call.

He wasn't originally going to take the job, but then I pointed out he'd be coming with us anyways, his camera never not around his neck, talked up his concert photography, and he changed his mind. But, as usual, he took those jobs and ran with them. I wasn't surprised when he knew how to talk his way backstage with Delilah and me in tow, managed to get pictures of the bands in the green rooms or in the back alleys or whatever vehicles they were calling tour buses where he'd do what he did best and casual conversations would turn into impromptu interviews and we'd go back to Delilah's or the apartment where I'd sit up the entire night writing something more than reviews, writing things I never thought I'd sit up late into the night writing.

On one of these nights Scott chuckled from my library doorway and I stopped my typing to look up at his smirk, his eyes filled with that sort of nostalgia that doesn't know whether to shine or flood over.

"What," I asked him.

He shrugged. "You look like Her when you concentrate. Never realized it 'til just now."

His confused nostalgia spread through the room and wrapped itself around my own chest while I flexed my fingers over the keys and stared up at him.

He shrugged again and ripped his eyes from mine. "Sorry."

"Don't be."

He lifted his eyes to meet mine again.

"Thanks," I said, that confused nostalgia clogging up my throat.

He nodded and went back to whatever movie he'd been watching in the living room while I dragged my head out of those dark waters I knew he was trying to keep his own head out of.

It was these late nights that bothered Jonathan the most seeing as he didn't share our familial nocturnal instincts and this meant Scott was yet again disrupting his life, his script.

Fuck.

I hate going into this.
I was kind of hoping I wouldn't have to.

But, my staying up late was the capstone of Jonathan's frustration over Scott staying with us.

It began with things Scott would say, things he'd do, the way he dressed, the way he'd let things go in his c'est la vie sort of way, our inside jokes, the fact that he knew me better than Jonathan did, the fact that we'd had an entire life together before Jonathan, but it was my reluctance to leave Scott when Jonathan decided the day was over that the southern winds crashed against the northern.

And it was all because Jonathan would have to go to bed without me,

Without sex.

I know you don't want to hear this because I don't want to say it.

But since this is becoming just as much a purging of him from me as everything else

Maybe I need to.

Because we've absolutely never talked about it.

I've never wanted to.

You've never asked me to.

I don't think I ever could say it out loud to you.

I don't blame you if you skip this part.

But

I think I need to say it either way.

Much like back in Port A, he rarely had sex *with* me. Jonathan always performed sex on me, acting out some scene that I wasn't always privy to. He preferred it that way. There were times, mainly before Austin, before Tegan, when I'd try and take part, add my own flourishes, but he'd always be quick to correct me, shut me down.

It was never like with you and our dance of limbs and caresses and confirmations and ecstatic yeses and familiar fires between experimental giddiness that end in dizzying oneness whether we're in sync or not because in the end it's always you loving me the way I'm loving you and you wanting me the way I'm wanting you.

No. With him it was a one man show with his prop housewife or mistress or stranger or whoever he was pretending I was that night doing as he instructed, nearly always nonverbally, nearly always with shoves and yanks and tight grips. He wasn't always aggressive. When I was pregnant, later after dinner parties, when he'd had a good day and I'd made a meal he liked, he'd be soft, caressing and whispering, romantic even if he never said my name or looked me in the eye. But when he was in a sour mood, his masculinity had

been questioned, his position as head of the household had been threatened, his wife was no longer a prop, but a human with agency and a brother she wanted to spend more time with than him, then suddenly I was nothing more than a streetwalker with bare feet on 6th street, a body to force his cock into while being shoved up against the wall, held down on the floor or the bed, hand pressed hard over my mouth when I tried to protest.

So why did I stay with him?
Why wasn't that what made me leave?

Because I still deserved to be used.
Because I still didn't deserve to be loved.

Sex with Jonathan became more and more aggressive during those days when Scott was there, though he was always careful as his kind always are never to leave bruises where others would see. Not that he ever did leave bruises, just let me know that he could if he wanted to.

Every night I'd pretend to fall asleep afterwards, wait with my back to him until he was asleep or until I just couldn't take being near him anymore, then I'd slip out of bed, put my clothes back on, and sneak back into the living room where I'd find Scott still on the couch with the TV on, the volume as high as he could get it without waking up Tegan.

Most nights we avoided talking about it, about him, one of us starting out talking about nothing until something stuck. But one night neither of us was up for it and we just sat in silence staring at some old western movie he'd found.

"Why are you here, Al," he asked, his voice so weary that it hit my sternum like a cannon ball.

"I don't wanna talk about it," I told him and stood to go into the kitchen.

"Well, I do." He followed me.

"Why?" I opened the fridge, realized I didn't actually want anything, just wanted to put as much space between myself and Jonathan as I could without leaving the apartment, then closed it again.

He stood close to me, pressed one hand against the countertop, leaned far enough over so he wasn't directly in my eye line, but not entirely in my peripheral either, lowered his voice to a tone that couldn't be heard from down the hall, but that was still far enough from a whisper to vibrate my bones. "Because you don't fucking love him. I don't believe that you do or

ever did or ever fucking could."

I just turned around, leaned back against the counter, stared hard at the tile.

It was all the answer he needed.

He took in a sharp, dragged out breath and ran his fingers through his hair while moving to pace along the small space of the kitchen.

"Fucking why, Al?"

"I don't want to talk about this."

"Too fucking bad."

"Stop it."

"You deserve so much more than that asshat."

"Scott."

"You deserve so much more than all of this."

"Scott."

"You deserve to be fucking happy, Al."

"Scott!"

He stopped pacing and stared at me with part frustration, part confusion, part that heartbroken pain that comes with watching someone you want so badly to save make the choice to let go of your hand and shove themselves under the water.

"You deserve to be with someone—"

"Don't."

"Don't what?"

"Tell me what I do and don't deserve."

I met his eyes and at first he just stared at me.

"If I don't then who will," he asked. "You sure as fuck aren't doing it."

"I know exactly what I deserve."

He held my eyes for a long while then finally blinked. "No, you don't."

The conversation was over. We both felt it in our bones, in the tingling finality along our spines. He tore his eyes from mine and went to the front door that he opened and closed with more restraint than I would have expected.

I wasn't in the mood to watch a movie alone. I didn't want to crawl into bed next to Jonathan, not after everything that happened that night, not with you still drifting along my bones among all the words I refused to let Scott say. Instead, I snuck into Tegan's room and wrapped my arms around her while

she turned to curl against my chest.

That should have sent me home.

But it didn't.

The next morning, I refused to leave Tegan's room until I heard Jonathan's keys, until I heard the front door open and close, the lock turning. She was already awake and stretched out along my torso while running her fingers along the buttons of my shirt and half-babbling to me, half-forming sounds just to form them. When I kissed the top of her head and sat up, she laughed and squealed as she slid down from the bed and ran for the door where she waited for me to open it between bouncing on the balls of her little feet, that black fountain of curls swinging with her excitement.

We were in the middle of her morning routine when Scott came out looking more awake than usual and I didn't have to ask to know he'd been waiting for Jonathan to leave, too. It wasn't until Tegan was settled on the couch with *Little Einsteins* playing that Scott followed me into the kitchen where she couldn't see us.

I stopped and finally met his eyes.

In them I saw all the words he didn't need to say.

I nodded and slid into his arms while he held me close and pressed his temple against the top of my head.

"How long do you think he'll put up with me?"

"How long do you think you can go without murdering him?"

He laughed and let me go while I pulled away from him and gave him a weary smile.

He shrugged. "We'll play it by ear? Promise I'll leave the second I start looking over your knives."

I shouldn't have, but I laughed, as well.

Just like those "I'm sorry"s, I'm realizing that me saying at every turn these moments should have driven me back to you are beginning to lose their meaning. But it's the truth.

And I am sorry.

Scott stayed in Austin with us for about five months.

At the beginning of those five months, I believed what I had told him. I believed that I knew what I deserved and what I deserved was to have all my happiness clouded by someone like Jonathan. I deserved to feel those aches and those longings and to do nothing about them because it was all entirely my fault. I deserved to be a prop in a dollhouse because I'd failed at being a real significant other, sister, daughter. I deserved to be without you, because I had hurt you by leaving and I'd only hurt you again by going back.

But Scott shifted all that.

Scott knew my flaws, *mea culpa*s, what was hidden in my DNA, and he still loved me with that smirk and that laugh and those tight hugs that showed me that he was right, that maybe I did deserve happiness, that maybe I deserved it without the metaphorical flagellation that was staying with Jonathan.

What Scott couldn't show me because I was too stubborn to see his flares spelling it out beneath the thinning storm clouds, was that I deserved that happiness with you.

It would take a lot more for me to finally see that.

I wish I could say it would take Scott leaving me alone with Jonathan again, but it would take so much more than that.

Looking back, I'm still surprised Scott was able to last as long as he did under Jonathan's roof. That it took Jonathan flinging the word "freeloader" at him; that it took them locking horns while I put Tegan to bed; that it took me fighting with Jonathan behind a closed door. That night he came close to

actually hurting me. It wouldn't be the closest, but it was the first. He had me against the wall, his fist was raised, I cried out, he stopped, he let me go. It was only once his back was to me that I left the room. When I passed Scott's room, his things were gone. Then I heard the front door open and close and I rushed to the foyer. There he was with his keys in his hand. And there was the second first of the night: Scott staring at me with that apologetically broken look behind his eyes, that look that said:

I tried,

I can't,

I'm sorry.

He didn't say a word.

He didn't have to.

I nodded, pulled on my coat and shoes, and we left together.

At his car, we stood in silence for a long time, neither looking at each other, both just staring at the other's shoes, both dripping with frustration and hurt and regret and homesickness and preemptive distant aches and things we should have said and things we could have never said and every single She taught us better than all this.

He finally took in a long breath, his hands deep in his jacket pockets.

"When you go back? He's not gonna…?"

I tightened my crossed arms that were shaking from, I did my best to convince myself, just the wet and the cold that is Texas winters, nothing more. I shook my head. "He's not that kind."

He eyed me, but just nodded.

Then the silence was back.

"I'm sorry, Al."

I shrugged, but didn't take my eyes off his battered Converse.

"You can come with me. You and Teegs. We can pack y'all's stuff and—"

"Not yet."

He was quiet. I could feel his eyes on me.

"After this semester I only have one more and—"

His arms around me stopped my excuses. I wrapped mine around his neck and buried my face against his shoulder.

"Promise you'll leave the first chance you get?"

I nodded and swallowed down the tears that wanted me to take it back,

to turn around that night and gather up Tegan and her things, to follow Scott wherever the wind took him next—even home, especially home.

"Promise," I told him instead.

He went to stay with Dana out at Lake Travis that night, a few days after that. Then he called and said he was going out to Oregon, down to California, maybe LA, after that. He said that he was going to see a friend who had a brother who was going to University of Oregon, that maybe he could help me transfer up there, left the space between his words to beg me not to stay.

But I couldn't afford that. I may have had money from On Rotation, but it was only enough to get Tegan and me started somewhere until I could get a job. Jonathan had been paying my tuition, had his money in pockets that I didn't know. Even if I could have afforded tuition, a part of me somehow knew that he'd know if I requested any transcripts, that he'd stop it, that he'd come find us.

I couldn't take that risk.

At least, at the time, I didn't think I could.

But lingering trauma that you've yet to have the time to face or even the opportunity to discover the scar tissue it left behind can change your mind quicker than you'd think.

It was late summer when I started to have those dreams again, of house listings and keys, this time mixed with long distance phone calls and the world pulsing and expanding, making my bones feel heavy yet unreal, Tegan drifting farther away from me as the room grew larger than I could stomach.

Then one day I kept getting whiffs of cardboard, hearing the jingling of keys. I tried to shove it away as I dropped Tegan off at Terra and Vera's, spent the night in a too small bar half-listening to some new band full of wanna-be Kurt Cobains while trying to stop myself from taking account of all my things, all of Tegan's essentials, wondering how few bags I could fit our lives into. But I couldn't do it and I went home early in a fog, left Tegan with Vera because for some reason it felt safer than how I was feeling, eels snaking along my veins.

When I got home, there in the kitchen was a stack of crisp, unfolded moving boxes leaning against a wall in the kitchen. I remember my arms went numb. I remember my head spinning. I remember the sound of my purse hitting the kitchen floor. I remember steel balls bursting through my torso. I remember my heart scrambling for any kind of safety as the water flooded in. I don't remember Jonathan coming down the hall.

"Hey. Have fu—?"

I jumped. I woke up. I turned on him. "What the fuck is this?"

He stopped still and stared at my wide eyes, my shaking hands. "What?"

I pointed at the boxes.

He looked at me, at the boxes, blinked. "Oh. Yeah." He continued for the kitchen. "I meant to talk to you about that, but you and Delilah were in such a rush."

He reached out for me, tried to kiss the top of my head, but I lurched away from him. His eyes flashed black. Then he blinked and they were brown again. He let out a long breath and crossed his arms, instead.

"I want us to move back home."

For a brief moment, the water subsided, my heart stopped scrambling. "Home?"

"Yeah. I'm getting kind of sick of the weather here. Aren't you?"

The water rushed back in, my heart didn't even try to fight, just sank straight to the bottom as though it had filled its pockets with rocks. "Weather?"

"The heat. It's…" he lifted one arm and twisted his hand in a circle. "Stifling. I've been missing actual seasons. Snow. You'll love the snow."

"I've seen fucking snow."

The muscles in his face strained. "Tegan hasn't."

Part of me was fully at the bottom of the ocean.

Part of me was fully in a state of panic.

All I could do was blink at him.

"Speaking of, where is she?"

"Vera."

"The dykes?"

I flinched the way I always did when he spat that word, but I didn't give him much else, just stared at him, my jaw clenched tight.

He sighed. "Anyways, I think it's time Tegan meets my family."

"What?"

"She's never met my parents, my sister, Charles. I want her to be close to them."

He was right. She'd never met any of his family. Every time he'd brought up the idea of them coming down, I'd found a way to stop it there at the suggestion: we just moved in, we should settle first; I won't be able to be a

proper hostess right after giving birth; she's so much work *without* guests in the apartment; she's going through her terrible twos, you don't want that to be their first impression of her.

"What-what about my family?"

He gave me that fucking smirk. "Alex. You haven't been back to Corpus Christi since we came up here. Not that she can meet you father—"

"They let kids in the visitation center." I'd looked it up even though I knew Jonathan would never let me take her, knew I'd never be brave enough to go anyways.

His face went hard. "My daughter isn't stepping foot into a prison."

Fuck you, I wanted to say. *She's not yours*, I wanted to spit at him.

But then I remembered that fist. Then I remembered that he was between me and the rest of the apartment.

"So, what?" I said instead. "You just wanna pack us up and take us to Connecticut?"

"Yeah," he said simply. "My parents have a guest house on the property that we'll be comfortable in until we find our own place. I've looked, but there's not much worth living in on the market right now. But, the guest house is fully furnished, so we'll just need to pack up the important stuff before we leave Wednesday—"

"Wednesday?"

He shrugged. "I figured we'd need a few days to pack and get Tegan ready for the drive. We'd also need to sell your car. I'm sure—"

"My car?"

He laughed. "Is there an echo in here?" When I didn't change my expression of numb shock, he went on. "Yes. We can get you a new one once we're there. I'm sure my dad can give up one of his. But I was looking over yours and it's not really suitable for New England winters. It's a beach car, Alex. The heater isn't even reliable."

I just stared at him, trying to hide my breathing that was growing more and more rapid along with my heart rate the longer he talked. I wanted to argue with him, but I knew there was no point. I wasn't there to argue, to have my own mind. I was there to do what he told me to, to be his prop when he needed me to, and if he wanted to move home, he needed his prop wife and his prop daughter that he'd already bragged to his family about, already sent prop photos to. My head was spinning, my heart was near to collapsing.

But then I felt that tug from behind my navel. Then, for the first time, I

heard voices on the wind.

So, I let the blood stream from my mouth, let him kiss the top of my head, let him lead me to the bedroom where I let him think he'd won. Then, the instant he was asleep, his back rising and falling heavily against my ear, I slipped out of bed, called Delilah, took his expensive luggage down from the top of the closet, shoved my clothes inside, collected what I had brought of Her from home, shoved Tegan's clothes alongside mine, filled a second bag to bursting with everything I knew she'd need, and met Delilah at the back door of the building, Tegan asleep against her shoulder.

It wasn't until Tegan was buckled into her car seat, quickly falling back asleep, that Delilah finally asked for details.

"What about your records, Al? Your books?" I'd had a feeling she'd be worried about my things that she'd taken so much time to help me organize and arrange, give me some semblance of a home inside a ghost ship.

"He's not gonna pack it all up himself."

"Want me to grab it for you," she asked when I didn't say it.

"I don't know." I thought of my record player, *Lady of the Stars*. "Kind of? Just the special stuff?" I knew she'd know what was and what wasn't. "And only if you can without making more trouble," I added before she could start getting any ideas.

We were quiet as we stood there staring at each other.

"Where are you going from here?"

"I don't know yet." It wasn't entirely a lie. My heart and my gut were still arguing.

"Port A?"

I was quiet at first, rocks splashing acid against my heart. "I don't know."

She nodded. "Call me once you do? If you can?"

I nodded then stood on my toes to give her a hug that she returned without hesitation.

"Tell her I said bye?"

"Of course. Tell V and Terra thank you?"

"Of course, babe." Her voice was shaking. "I'll miss you so fucking much."

"Me, too."

She gripped me tighter. "Be safe, Al."

"You, too."

I missed her through those years.
I missed a lot of people through those years.
I missed you most of all.

I guess I should explain some things.

We never did talk about everything that happened between Austin and LA mostly because I assumed you had heard most of it from either the police or Mack. I didn't entirely expect Jonathan to go looking for us. I kind of just hoped he'd accept it and move on to Connecticut alone.

But there was a nagging at the pit of my stomach that came with the sunrise and when I came across a Wells Fargo I pulled into the parking lot where I waited with Tegan until the tellers filtered in and the security guard unlocked the front door. That's why I emptied out my old bank account filled with a year and a half's worth of checks from *On Rotation*, the total a bit more than I remembered making me wonder if Delilah had told Terra before she'd left with Tegan. That's why I did it before we left Texas. It wasn't a drawn out decision, none of what happened that night was, just a feeling that I should, that I'd pay for it if I didn't.

Leaving Texas also wasn't a drawn out decision. I don't know where I thought we were going, but when it came to either going south or west, my heart scrambled to get away from the acid the stones sent upward.

I knew Scott was in LA by that point. I told myself every road I got on would eventually take me back to you if, or maybe hopefully when, I changed my mind.

The entire way, Tegan asked surprisingly few questions about why we were leaving Austin, about Jonathan and why he wasn't with us. All I did was tell her I wasn't sure when she asked in her own way how long we were going to be in LA, say no when she asked if Jonathan was going to meet us there, say yes when she asked if Unka Got would. It was all she seemed to need, her

questions then shifting to Delilah and what toys I had brought with us and Scott and if he had any toys and if there were giants sleeping in the valleys between the hills and who drew the map I was trying to read and why the earth peeking through the yellowed dry grass was that rust sort of red and who lived in every house sitting in the middle of the nothing we continued to drive by.

In one nondescript town somewhere up in the panhandle, I sat in a red booth in some nondescript burger joint watching Tegan slap at the controls of some arcade game with a pair of kids who had also wandered away from their families' tables. I was trying not to think about what I was doing, where I was going, Jonathan back in Austin, you back home. But on the wall at the back of the arcade "room" was a not half bad mural of the standard image of Mario and Yoshi. Yoshi's crotch was blurred as though the paint was wearing thin and my sleep deprived mind couldn't stop wondering why it was only thinning between his legs.

Jonathan would have simply rolled his eyes, if he would have ever gone in a place like that at all.

Scott would have come up with some wild tale to explain it.

Roxie's explanation would have had something to do with sex which she would have said at such a volume that I would have had to hide my laughter while shushing her.

Sara would have gasped and then giggled behind her hands, her cheeks going that adorable pink the way they always do before smiling at me.

You would have laughed, would have leaned in close to whisper your joke, your breath on my neck, would have puzzled out the truth with me while we finished Tegan's abandoned food, would have paused when she called out to you, would have answered in just the right way then smiled at me and pulled me close to you.

I'm sorry we didn't get that.

I'm sorry I kept that from you.

We stayed in Roswell that first night mostly to entertain Tegan who nearly died of excitement when she saw the McDonald's flying saucer jungle gym, mostly to distract myself while I watched her giddy smiles over every alien we came across. It was the same reason we stayed in a kitschy motel near the Grand Canyon the next day.

Then we hit California.

Then there was a landslide in my gut and I had to pull off the road while

the acid settled and Tegan, after asking her questions and not getting answers, crawled into my lap and curled against my chest.

Then she told me she was hungry and I pulled myself together for her while a deeper guilt shoved rocks and boulders aside in an attempt to find the light, to try and force me to recognize it, to try for a turn at breaking me next.

When I started to see signs for LA, I realized that I didn't actually know where Scott lived.

"You don't have the asshat with you, do you?"

"No." I glanced at Tegan to see she had her entire face pressed against the glass of the freezer filled with different colored sodas in the back of the gas station I was circling while talking to Scott. "No. He's, um…" I tapped her shoulder and nodded her away from the glass. "He's not with us."

"Okay, but you do have Teegs. Okay. Uh." He dragged out the sound, I'm guessing, while he inspected the house. "Yeah. It'll be cool. I'll text you the address, but, um, basically, head for Brand Park then call me and I'll talk you through the rest of the way?"

I had no idea where Brand Park was, had no idea where anything was. I asked the middle-aged guy with the big beard behind the register and he was nice enough to buy me one of the paper maps on the stand that Tegan was spinning in circles, to draw out the directions with a red sharpie that hit my gut hard enough to make me lift Tegan onto my hip where she happily ran her fingers along the key chains hanging next to the gum while the man talked me through the directions.

I got lost a few times, circling neighborhoods until I found the road I'd missed my turn at, but I finally made it to Brand Park where I called Scott before waiting with Tegan for him to show up in his little mustang that was somehow still holding on and leaking *Wish You Were Here* as he led us through the twisting streets of the neighborhood until we drove up to a small bungalow with no garage, a flat yard, and a small driveway.

Scott was at my door before I could even open it. I remember the instant I climbed out, he had me around the middle and swinging around the yard. By the time he put me down, Tegan was bouncing at our feet and he lifted her up, as well, spun her in even bigger circles while she squealed and giggled. With Tegan on his hip, all smiles and giggles, Scott invited us inside, insisted I not worry about the bags yet, relax for a minute, tell him everything.

And I did, most of it while sitting on the barren slab of his back porch while Tegan was distracted with stacking and lining up rocks from the empty

garden bed at the edge.

"So, you just left?"

I nodded.

"Good on you."

I looked at him from the corner of my eyes to see that genuine closed smile of his.

"He really was a—"

"Scott."

"What?"

I nodded to Tegan.

He glanced at her then smirked and bobbed his head to one side. "Fine. Fair. But he was."

"I know."

"Aaaand…"

I watched his raised brows and his circling hand then rolled my eyes. "You were right. Tate was right."

You were all right.

"So, I'm guessing you didn't really make a plan before coming here."

I shook my head and he nodded.

"I have a spare room, but not a spare bed—"

"The couch is fine. We'll be fine. Really."

He nodded then pushed himself up from the ground and dusted off his jeans, Tegan turning to stare up at him with that sparkling smile of hers. He held his hands out to her without hesitation and she ran into them for him to lift her up on his hip before reaching out a hand to help me up.

We talked more after that between unloading my car and situating Tegan on the living room floor where we set to finding beds on Craigslist for the spare room that had admittedly just been housing Scott's unorganized overflow of equipment, props, costumes, and lengths of fabrics that doubled as costumes, but we avoided any talk of you. He never asked if I was planning on going back to you, where my heart was on the topic that day. I think he knew that, in that moment, on that day, I just needed a place to be, to recover. I think he was too focused on the relief of my finally taking his hand and climbing into a lifeboat, even if it wasn't yours.

Over that next week he moved around his schedule for us, showed us around the city, went with me to pick up beds and order mattresses, Tegan

always on either my hip or his. He went with me to set up a PO box, the address of which he texted Delilah from his phone, went with me every week to collect the packages she sent me one at a time, starting with my record player, *Lady of the Stars*, all of my albums lovingly wrapped in bubble wrap, little artsy notes for Tegan and me from her, Vera, and Terra. He teased me while I reorganized the house, dragged him to Ikea to get storage for his equipment, props, costumes, clothes, cords, utensils, then sat on the living room floor sorting it all room by room, arranging and rearranging the growing number of things, his and mine, while he and Tegan watched cartoon movies that he'd bought by the armful while out getting groceries. It was mostly stuff we watched as kids, mostly stuff Jonathan wouldn't let her watch.

I didn't realize what I was doing at the time, didn't see it as nesting, as settling in. I didn't want to put words to it. I didn't want to acknowledge it. I just wanted to be. I just wanted to not be his. I just wanted to be mine and I just wanted to be hers. I think I had to do that before I could be yours. I had to cleanse myself of him before I could hand myself fully back to you. I just regret all it took for me to properly do that, for me to see that I'd done it long before I thought I finally had.

In truth, Scott had been planning on moving on within the month. That was before I showed up. And he kept that plan for a while even after I did. He was supposed to head up the coast back to Oregon to stay with Kat and Roxie and everybody in that big house they used to live in. Part of me now wishes he had, part of me now wishes I had gone with him, could have met Roxie sooner, but maybe I wasn't supposed to know her yet, maybe she wasn't ready for me, maybe I wasn't ready for her. Either way, Scott continued to pay the bills while he was there, kept insisting on it while also never saying I could pick them up when he left. I think he kept hoping I'd decide to go home. But I still felt bad, still knew I should at least pay for what Tegan and I were using. With enough pestering, he finally told me about a smaller music magazine that had moved entirely online the year before. He shot for them on occasion when their staff photographer wasn't available.

A week later, I started as a staff writer. That's a title I never would have thought I would wear. It still feels strange to say. I was assigned to do interviews pretty quickly.

And that was when I met Joss.

It's one of those moments when I, in retrospect, can almost see the strings, can almost see that some things, some people, some moments cross our paths for reasons we're not meant to understand—not until we're finally

in that moment we preordained in that cosmic space.

I was sitting at my desk brainstorming talking points for the interview I'd been assigned, trying not to let on how much I was freaking out over the whole thing (the ones I'd done in Austin had never been planned, had come out of conversations and casual settings), when I heard those ever familiar clicks of a camera's mirror. I looked up to see this long woman wearing a worn thin, oversized grey t-shirt with blacker than black skinny jeans and scuffed up motorcycle boots. Tattoos of lilies twisted down her arms to just below both elbows, the loose sleeves of her t-shirt covering most of the designs. Her dark hair was tied into a knot on the top of her head and that rectangular face over that long neck was tilted down as she looked over the pictures on the screen on the back of her heavy looking Canon.

"You photograph well," was the first thing she said to me without looking away from her camera. "Anyone tell you that?"

"Yeah, actually."

She lifted those long, blue eyes that are closer to grey than the deeper Matthews blue with its traces of teal, to look at me with raised brows and a small smirk in one corner.

"My brother's a photographer," I explained with a shrug and pointing for no real reason at her camera. "I've, um, stood in for a few flaky models."

She laughed and fell into the empty chair of my clump mate, her long legs stretched out and her ankles hooked. "My sister would be glad to hear that's not limited to her. I'm Joss, by the way, if you didn't, I guess, figure that out on your own." She lifted her camera an inch from her stomach as she said that.

I nodded. "Alex." Then shrugged. "Though, I guess you had to know that to find me."

She laughed and nodded then looked back at her camera. "Um, I'm not sure how much Cindy told you, but I, uh, I kind of prefer to go with you guys when you do the interviews? I, um…" she shoved at her hair that was already out of her face. "I think they," she lifted her camera again, "look better when the person's…distracted, I guess?"

"When they forget you're there," I said with a smile that was more for myself, for Scott, than for her.

She shifted her eyes to look at me, a smile forming as she realized I understood entirely. "Yeah."

I told her about Scott, about how we had worked in Austin, and her eyes

lit up, she talked to her camera less and less. That Friday we met the band (a pair of sisters with this dreamy sort of '80s Barbie synth sound) at the venue they were playing at the next night. Joss had photographed them before and everything fell into place the way it had back in Austin. By the time we left I felt as though I had worked with Joss a million times over.

I want to say it was after a month of getting to know her that I invited her to the house for dinner. She was still living with Jackie at the time who was still dating that guy who didn't like Joss much, always made a point to try and get her to move out, to tell her it wasn't her sister's job to carry her. Not that Jackie ever carried Joss, not that Joss ever asked Jackie to, not that Jackie ever made it seem (to me at least) as though she even was carrying her, not that he would have been right even if she was. But abusive people will create a thread to unravel your support system if they have to.

Anyways, it was after that first month of us knowing each other that Joss was at the end of her rope and was looking for reasons to not go home most nights.

"I mean, I should," she said to me that day in the parking lot where we were leaning against our cars while she tried to come up with a place to go. "I should go home. Shouldn't I? I shouldn't leave her with him."

I stared at the asphalt with crossed arms, rolled a rock under my Converse. "You think he'll...do something without you there?"

Joss shifted her weight and I could hear her fidgeting with her camera. "He's not that kind."

My gut started to spiral, but then I heard that click and I couldn't help but chuckle as I looked up to see her eyes glued to the screen on the back, one corner of her bottom lip between her teeth.

The thing I learned about Joss in that time, in the years since, is that she doesn't just take a constant stream of pictures because that photographer part of her is always on, is always whispering at the back of her ear, the way that poet always hovered around Mom—it's because Joss doesn't always feel safe in her own head, alone with her own emotions. It's when she's nervous or uncomfortable or just doesn't know how to feel that those clicks start going. It's almost like the camera helps her remove herself from the situation, like she's not actually there in that moment, but at the same time she is. Those seconds that it takes her to see a picture, adjust her camera with that intuitive deftness, and click the shutter is all the time she needs to pull far enough away, to see the moment as an unbiased observer, to catch those spiral inducing things on flypaper film.

"When I was a kid," I said, "my folks had this…I guess you can call it a code word."

I could feel that she'd lifted her eyes to look at me, but mine were fixed on her hands.

"Well, my mom…she, um, she had a lot of anxiety, depression, all that. She-she had…" At the time I didn't know why I couldn't say those words. "I guess, she'd have these…dark moments. She'd isolate herself from us." I shifted my weight. "My folks always called it 'getting stranded.' When we didn't understand why she was upset, Dad would say, 'Mom's stranded.'"

I fell quiet for longer than I should have and Joss waited while I cycled through the parts I couldn't say out loud: that he always followed it with, "And we gotta help her get home, okay?"; that we always somehow did; that we *almost* always did; that I learned the hard way what I was gearing up to tell her, that I was still learning it.

"You can't help someone who's stranded when you let yourself get stranded in the process." I met her eyes and shrugged. "The lighthouse needs refueling from time to time."

She smirked at me. "You always talk in metaphors?"

I smiled back and shrugged. "I don't know. Scott would say yes."

Her smirk became a shy smile and she looked away from me again. "I'm curious to meet Scott," she finally admitted, though I'd seen it rustle through her every time I had mentioned him over the previous month. "And Tegan," she added quickly.

I nodded, my own little lighthouse beacon breaking through the fog I'd put myself in. "Wanna come over for dinner? I'm sure Scott won't mind sharing the kitchen table with one more laptop tonight."

She lit up. "Yeah! That sounds like fun, actually."

I led Joss in her car to the house where she parked on the street in front. I was started down the drive towards her car when that excited, high pitched "Mommy!" from the now open front door stopped the world and I turned to see that ball of everything running through the yard towards me. I lifted her into the air and planted her on my hip where she hugged me around the neck all giggles and squeals. I could hear those clicks behind us.

"Teegs, this is Mommy's friend, Joss."

Tegan lifted from my shoulder and looked to Joss who looked away from her camera to give her a big smile and a small wave.

"Hi, Tegan. You photograph as well as your mama does."

Tegan gave her that shy smile and looked at me.

"Say, 'thank you,' mama."

She looked back to her, one hand over her mouth still smiling, though she was eyeing Joss carefully. "Thank you."

I rubbed her back and gave Joss a smile which she returned before following me into the house.

"Where's Uncle Scott," I asked Tegan once we were inside and I saw the living room was vacant, the TV playing *Ponyo* the way it had all week, Scott's laptop at the kitchen table, his headphones lying on top of his notebook.

"Being boring."

"Ah. Which means he's been working," I translated for Joss who nodded and laughed. "But where is he now?"

Tegan shrugged. "Getting something," she said over enunciating those double t's the way she did then. "I get him!" She began to wiggle her way out of my arms.

"Okay. You do that."

She ran off to the hall and disappeared into the dark. "UNKA GOT!"

"She's precious," Joss said with a smile.

"Yeah. I think I'll go ahead and keep her."

Joss laughed while looking around the small open floorplan. "This is nice. You did good."

From down the hall, Tegan shouted something about pizza. Joss glanced down the hall then turned her back to it and smiled at me.

"Is it that obvious," I asked regarding the house.

She shrugged. "I just figure most bachelor men don't care enough to do more than set up a couch in front of the TV."

"In his defense, I didn't need to move the table. And he did have dishes when I got here, but all the utensils were just tossed in the same drawer."

Joss feigned a gasp. "Utter mayhem."

Behind her, Scott came into the room carrying Tegan, but he stopped only a few steps into the living room. I squinted at his wide eyes and slack jaw, then looked to Joss who had turned and was staring back at him, her jaw also slack, her eyes pink and glassy.

"Holy shit," Scott muttered and Tegan giggled at the word he was normally scolded for using, but I was too confused over why Joss earned such a reaction to fuss at him.

I crossed the room to take Tegan before his arms went limp, too. "Y'all know each other or something?"

"Um, yeah. Kind of," he said.

"Years ago," Joss added. "Um, 2005?"

"Six," he corrected.

"Oh. Yeah."

Tegan and I continued to look between them. "How did you…?"

Scott cleared his throat and tore his eyes away from Joss, rubbed the back of his neck, and blinked a few times. "A, uh, a photography retreat? Out in the desert."

"Joshua Tree."

He looked at her, a small smile appearing. "Yeah. Joshua Tree."

I looked between the two back to staring at each other and, realizing a lie was the best I was going to get and that there were things they were wanting to say without me there, I looked to Tegan. "Uncle Scott water the plants today?"

Not even attempting to look away from the awkward pull between them, she just shook her head.

"Well, let's go do that while Joss and Uncle Scott catch up."

They've never told me the truth about how they met or what could have happened at Joshua Tree that would bring them to meet like aching magnets the instant the back door was closed or would make Joss cry against his chest. I probably should have asked them, but the way Joss slipped away from him and tried to hide her tears when we came back inside after Tegan stopped trying to hide her curiosity and just pressed her whole face against the glass of the door as though it would help her hear them better kept me from ever bringing it up.

It's weird knowing your twin's hiding things from you, but Scott had already caught me hiding Tegan. It was only fair I let him have this one. Though that didn't mean I still wasn't curious. I still am. I tried to sneak it out of them from time to time, always when I had one of them alone. If I tried it when they were together, I'd just get cryptic answers while they glanced at each other between not looking at me. When they were alone, they'd still avoid looking at me, but the answers would be slightly less cryptic.

Joshua Tree never changed. Though, even then I didn't remember Scott ever talking about Joshua Tree before and I still don't think I'd ever seen pictures from there. I remember him traveling around that area at some point

when he first left Port A on his own, but I hadn't thought he'd gone as far as California on that trip. I just remember Kofa and that week we spent in Arizona looking for him, waiting for him to show back up.

Not that it's all that important, I guess.

Like I said, it's only fair I let him have this one.

Even if I know you'll come to me with your own speculations that we've no doubt already gone through after you read this bit.

The important thing is, Joss became kind of a permanent fixture in our lives after that day. I want to say it took less than a month for Tegan to decide she'd earned the title of Aunt. She was so excited the first time Tegan said it, asked me to clarify just to make sure she'd heard her right.

Then she gave me this huge, sparkly eyed smile, her hands clasped over her heart. "I'm so honored!"

She's always loved Tegan.

Sometimes I feel like she's always been family.

You'd think I would have gotten sick of her at some point with her always being at the house and always being at work, but having her around made everything feel somehow easier. Joss grew up in LA, has her own internal map that was dotted with two and a half decades of personal landmarks. I rarely felt that frustrated sort of lost the way I had in Austin. And when Joss or Scott weren't there to keep me from getting lost, Ara was.

It helped that she seemed to be one of those people who never slept. It didn't matter what time I texted Ara, what time we'd gone home the night before, she was always awake and had been for hours. Though, we mostly saw each other at night and mostly after she'd finished a gig when she was all high energy and wandering hands and lips.

Granted, Ara was always wandering hands.

At least, she'd always been with me.

When I first met her, Joss warned me about her beforehand.

"You can be straight with her," she told me on the drive to the bungalow with the pool Ara had told us to meet her at.

The house belonged to a mutual friend of hers and Joss. They'd done a few shoots there already, though usually only by the pool or on the back porch. The owners had recently redesigned the kitchen, had suggested Joss and Ara try it out.

In the car, I smirked at Joss with scrunched up brows. "About what?"

"She's kind of..." She shrugged while turning through a sharp curve.

"Forward, I guess." She glanced at me once the road had straightened again. "She's—flirty doesn't seem to cover it. But she gets it when girls're straight. Doesn't make a big deal? You know? So, if she gets...flirty, I guess, tell her if you're not into it. She'll back off. She's good about that."

I nodded. "Kay. She flirt with you?"

She shrugged. "In the beginning. I thought it would make her uncomfortable if I said anything, you know? Thought she'd..." Her lips puckered into one side of her mouth.

"Tense up?"

"Yeah. Kind of? Clam up, maybe? Anyways, I thought it'd make it even weirder if I said anything."

Her full attention on putting in the code for the gate at the end of the drive, she paused for a minute.

"And," I asked when she pulled her arm back through the window.

She shrugged again. "Not saying anything was what made it weirder. She could tell I was pulling away from her and she thought it was because I didn't like her. When she found out it was because I'm not into girls, she kind of lectured me about not saying anything." The car parked, she sighed and leaned back in her seat. "Said something like the world turns better when everyone knows where they stand."

My brows scrunched up even deeper just as she turned to look at me making her laugh.

"Just—do as I say, not as I do."

I smirked and nodded. "Copy."

I know you know though that none of that conversation mattered, but I also know you've never heard it just like you've never heard how I met Ara. We talked about her, just like we talked about the people you were with while I was gone, but I never told you how we met, how it started.

She was already in the kitchen and leaning back against the counter when Joss led me into the house, that thick, black hair clipped back from her face while a guy holding a makeup pallet detailed the subtle shadow on her lids.

"Joss!" She said, grinning as best she could without moving while the guy with the brush near her eye made noises at her to stay still.

"Hey, Ar," Joss said while she pointed me to the dining room to unload the lights she'd brought just in case the sun wasn't enough.

Between helping Joss with the lights and the guy finishing Ara's makeup, it wasn't until she came into the dining room with an excited smile, her hair

now unclipped and draped along one side of her face with those features that are somehow both strong and delicate like an iceberg. She pulled Joss in for a tight hug then eyed me from her shoulder.

"You brought me a cute one this time," she said to Joss with a grin while still taking me in.

"This is Alex," Joss told her with a half what-did-I-say sort of look.

"Oh!" She looked to Joss. "Your boy toy's twin?"

Joss chuckled and rolled her eyes. "Yeah."

Ara turned those eyes light as green sea glass ringed with a deep blue back at me, those full lips in a siren's grin. "Good thing you're fraternal, huh?" She wrapped one arm around my shoulders and leaned in close. "Joss tell you I have a weakness for short girls?"

I stared up into those eyes and could do nothing but giggle.

I couldn't help it.

To say that Ara was beautiful would be an understatement. With that height and that skin, that weightiness that radiated from inside of her and pulled you to her with this intimidating sort of gravity, she might as well have been made from marble. She felt untouchable. And yet you wanted to defy that fact and reach up to run your fingers along that nearly colorless skin and through those black as a moonless night loose curls while she took you in as though you were the only person in the room.

I don't remember anymore what I said back.

Probably something awkward.

You know how I am when it comes to flirting back with women.

It was never really love, what I had with Ara. It was never really that murky in between either. I'm pretty sure it was entirely about physicality: about how I could be overtaken by her, about how she wanted to overtake me, wanted to watch as I gave myself over to her, melted under her touch.

We didn't date, is what I think I'm trying to say. We were just…together. In bed and out, she never asked me to be…well, *anything* for her. She just let me be without restrictions, without demands. It was what I needed then.

Not that I saw it in that way—not that I was ready to—but, after Jonathan, I needed to just exist for a while. I wasn't drifting. I wasn't stranded. I was remembering what it meant to be in my own skin, what it meant to move with my own bones, what it meant to breathe in open air with my own lungs.

I was distracting myself, I guess.

Is that what I was doing?
Now that I think back on those years,
I didn't mourn Her the way I had before,
I didn't fear you the way I had in Austin,
I didn't flagellate myself the way I had for years.
I think you could say I was happy.
I wasn't whole—I never could be without you—but I was happy.
For the first time in years,
I stood on solid ground.

And maybe that's why I continued to stay away:
I was no longer running
I was settling
I was stagnating
I was waiting for something
But I was never given enough details to know what.

The rest of the year, the beginning of the next, moved pretty much like that. I searched for my own voice in my work, my new self in Joss, my own self in Ara, my old self in Scott, you in Tegan. I was starting to finally heal, to feel like myself who belonged only to Tegan, deep down to you. More and more I told Joss about you, let Scott talk to me about you, let him hand me the phone at Christmas when Mack called (I don't know where you were, if they were hiding me from you, all I know is yours was the only voice I didn't hear that day).

I remember having days when thinking of going home to you didn't fill me with guilt, days when I was beginning to make plans to take Tegan home even if just to visit.

I was so close to you.

I could feel my waterlogged fingers slip against you.

Then he found us.

I can't even really say I made a mistake.

Tegan turned four.

Once again without you.

Once again without Her.

We celebrated her birthday along with Joss and Jackie, who was in the off again stage with that guy, on the back porch with cupcakes and sparklers and we painted rocks to put in the garden while Scott struggled with the grill the guy a few doors down offered him after his wife got him a new one for Christmas. He called Mack who gave him shit the entire call.

It was then that Jackie brought up the topic I'd never thought to consider. "Is kindergarten four?"

I stopped painting the ladybug Tegan had requested and stared at the concrete then Jackie and her ginger waves so unlike Joss' piled up on top of her head, thin strands framing her face and those blue grey eyes that are exactly like Joss' staring at me with shared unsuredness. "I don't know."

"Pre-k's before kinder," Scott said from the grill, waiting for Meg to come back from digging for her fajita recipe.

Joss twisted away from her attempt at a frog, her hands covered in more paint than her rocks, to look back and up at him. "So, is pre-k four?"

He stared at us all staring up at him then shrugged. "I don't know."

"Something's four," Jackie said as she scratched at a mosquito bite in the middle of one of the large roses on her upper arms that matched Joss' lillies then went back to her impressively intricate sunflower.

"Will you just ask Meg," I told Scott.

"Why would Meg know?"

"Mack's a teacher?" I reminded him with raised brows and a smirk.

"But why would—They wanna know what age a kid goes into pre-k," he said to Meg who was back on the line. "She says four," he relayed to us, "but that's Texas…it might be different here."

Joss, Jackie, and I exchanged looks then looked to Tegan who was happily ignoring us while she smeared pink and purple paint on a rock Jackie had said was too lumpy to paint a picture on.

After that, Tegan sat painting and talking at Joss from between my feet while Jackie and I researched pre-k registrations on my laptop from the wicker couch we'd found on craigslist.

The conversation continued throughout the rest of the day. It was only once Tegan was asleep that Jonathan's name came up.

"What about the proof of custody thing," Scott asked me.

"What about it?"

He held my eyes, waiting for me to figure it out on my own. "You didn't exactly leave the asshat legally."

"Asshat," Jackie asked.

"Jonathan," Joss and I grumbled.

"We weren't exactly married," I added with a shrug.

"Is his name on the birth certificate," Scott asked.

I ripped my eyes from his and stood to go to the kitchen where I pretended to look through the fridge with my back firmly to him.

"Al," he sighed. "Why the fuck would you do that?"

"He was there." I fought the urge to slam the fridge door.

"So were you."

Joss was next to Scott, her legs stretched out across his thighs, Jackie was next to her, one knee under her chin, both their brows were raised while they looked between Scott and me with confusion. I only ever talked about Jonathan in terms of how he treated me, how he treated Tegan, how it related to Jackie's situation when they were in the on phase. I'd never referred to him as Tegan's father, never said out loud that he wasn't; never said out loud that you were.

"I wasn't exactly all there."

It wasn't a lie. Jonathan kept insisting I was in pain which also wasn't a lie considering how quickly Tegan had come and how much of the process they'd had to skip over, but not to the degree that he kept saying it. At the

time I wrote it off as him just being attentive and it hadn't helped that the pain killers had felt good and I had been dealing with tsunamis of pain that Jonathan couldn't see, that had begun long before that hospital stay, that I hadn't been able to entirely drown out until those nurses brought those clear vials and IV drips.

Now I see it for what it was.

But those strings are only visible from a distance.

Joss and Jackie looked at Scott staring at me, looked at me avoiding him.

"So," Joss was the one brave enough to say, "Jonathan's…?"

I just blinked.

I had locked those words in a chest, chained it to a boulder in the Mariana Trench.

It would take dynamite to get them out.

But my silence was all they needed.

Scott let out a heavy breath that was something between relief and not knowing what was next. It made me dare to lift my eyes. Joss looked to him and reached across the table to touch his arm, pulling his focus off me and onto her.

"It probably won't come up," she told him.

She was right.

And she wasn't.

From what Scott overheard at the station, someone had tipped off the police after we had registered Tegan for school. Joss wondered if it had had anything to do with the whole custody thing, but Scott swears he had heard someone say that a woman had seen a picture of Tegan that had been circulating around online. Without hearing more, without knowing if that was the actual cause of what was to happen, I believe that there were pictures of Tegan online.

I believe that Jonathan would have done something like that.

I believe that I was stupid for previously not thinking that he would.

The part I never really figured out was why they did it the way they did. Why they didn't show up while I was at work, why they didn't take me without her there to see. The only thing I've ever come to is once again Jonathan. They had to have known that Scott's name was on the lease for the house despite my referencing the house as my address on all the paperwork at work. I have little doubt they told him this, I have little doubt he told them some

thing about Scott, something that would make them believe Scott wouldn't hand Tegan over without a fight.

Why he thought I would is something I don't entirely understand.

Whatever the why, the fact is: it was a Sunday and Joss and I were off that day. Tegan had requested spaghetti and meatballs for dinner. She had made her way through Scott's back catalog of movies Jonathan would never let her watch and had discovered *Cloudy with a Chance of Meatballs*. Joss had been unnerved by the changing of the plot enough to buy Tegan a copy of the book. She was going through a meatball phase is what I'm trying to say.

We didn't have anything to make meatballs, just a box of spaghetti that something had chewed a hole through and I had volunteered to go to the store while Scott entertained Tegan and Joss sat on the couch half watching them, half editing shots she'd gotten from the previous night's show they'd gone to.

I believed everything that happened between then and my drive home to be normal. Looking back I can see the police car circling the parking lot while I was on my way out, hovering close by while I was loading up the car and returning the basket. At least, I think I did. You know how faulty memory can be, how easily supplemented it is.

This was another one of those times when I needed one of those stupid maybe visions the most and I was instead left with nothing. Maybe that's why I still doubt them—if they're real then why weren't they there when it meant protecting my daughter, saving Her, not leaving you? Was it really that important that these things happen? What did I gain from sitting in a jail cell an entire night while a wanna-be puppet master tried to take her from me? What have I or any of us gained from losing Her? What did we gain from all this? What's the point if I can't change it when I need to the most?

Roxie caught me writing that.

She said the future may not be written in concrete, but it doesn't always fork when you want it to. She reminded me that there are choices our cosmic selves made for reasons we can't know and those choices can't be changed.

I still wish they could.

But it doesn't matter, I guess.

You can't change the past, Al.

It wasn't until I had passed Brand Park and I was no longer surrounded by a steady stream of cars that I finally noticed the police car behind me. They

didn't turn on their lights at first, just followed from what could be considered a reasonable distance. It was only one I had pulled into the driveway that the siren blipped and the lights whirled once or twice.

Obviously, I was confused. Unsure of what to do, I just sat in the car watching in my side mirror as the cops climbed out, consulted one another, started up the drive towards me.

"MOMMY!"

My eyes went wide and my head snapped up to see Tegan racing towards my car with a wide smile, ignoring the man and woman who had both stopped to watch the child they hadn't expected to leave the house with such reckless excitement.

I opened the door and started to climb out.

"Ma'am!" the man yelled at me. "Remain in your vehicle."

Tegan, already in my arms, looked at them then at me, her body tense, her eyes large and glassy, already whimpering as she pressed herself against me.

"It's okay, mama," I told her while rubbing her back. "You're okay."

They stood over me and the woman asked, "Ma'am, is there someone else in the house who can take her?"

"Y-yes. Um, my brother and-and her aunt."

The cops exchanged glances.

"Al?" Scott called from the front door.

"Is this your brother," the woman asked.

I nodded.

"Sir." She waved him over while the man circled my car. "Can you ask your wife to come out, please?"

"Wife?"

"They're not married," I told her.

"My apologies. Your girlfriend. Can you tell her to come out of the house, please?"

Tegan was starting to cry against my shoulder.

Scott leaned back into the house and called for Joss who came out seconds later.

"Ma'am," the woman called to her. "Could you please come retrieve your niece and take her inside?"

"I can take her," Scott was already saying.

"Sir, we'd like you to stay in the yard where we can see you."

"What?"

"Scott just do it," I begged him.

Joss reached for Tegan who refused to let go of me, shaking her head and crying.

"It's okay, sweet girl," I assured her. "Mommy'll be in soon." She started to cry louder and my womb fought my instincts to do as I was told. "Baby, please. Just go with Aunt Joss. It'll be okay."

Sometimes I wonder if she already knew it wasn't.

Joss and I managed to get her to let go of me and the cops waited until they were inside and the door was closed before the woman turned on me, Scott still standing in the yard watching.

"Ma'am, I need to see your license."

I nodded and leaned into the car to reach for my purse. When I opened the glove compartment, the man still on the other side of the car reached for his holster.

"Ma'am, step away from the vehicle," the woman ordered.

"Al?" Scott was already moving towards us.

"Sir, stay where you are."

We both did as we were told and she stood between me and the car while she watched the man look through the glove compartment.

"My insurance is in the glove compartment," I told her.

"I didn't ask for you insurance. Just your license."

My heart had already been racing. Now it was flailing. I began to shake. Every inch of my body went numb. I understood I wasn't going to be in soon, maybe not even that night.

"It-it's—" I took in a shuttering breath hoping it would slow my heart, restart the saliva to my mouth. "It's in my purse."

She turned and lifted it from where I'd left it on the driver's seat. She lifted her eyes to me.

"Front pocket." I wrapped my arms around my womb as though I could still protect her with my body alone.

"The one with the zipper?"

I nodded.

She pulled out my wallet, found my license, looked it over, looked over Scott, nodded to the man who came around the car behind me.

"Ms. Matthews, I'm assuming the girl inside is your daughter, Tegan?"

"Al?"

"She's not his." I'm not sure why I said it. It was the only thing my brain, my heart, my womb, allowed me to say.

"I'm sorry?"

"She's not his. Jonathan's. She's not his. He can't take her from me."

"That's not for me to decide, Ms. Matthews. My job is simply to locate the girl and bring you in."

My eyes snapped up to meet hers. The man stepped forward.

"Al!"

"Sir!" The woman put a hand up to stop both Scott and her colleague, before taking a step closer to me.

But I was already devolving into protective hysterics. "She's not his," I kept repeating, tears already on my cheeks, my heart nearly through my ribs. "He can't! He can't do this! She's not fucking his!"

"Ma'am!" She grabbed my shoulder. "You need to stay calm. For your girl. Do you hear me? This is going to be hard enough for her without you making a scene. Do you understand?"

I somehow managed to nod through the shaking.

She turned me around, read me my rights, pulled out her handcuffs while the man spoke into his walkie.

"You're arresting her?" Scott was already screaming. "You can't do this! She hasn't done anything!"

"Sir!" The man was already moving for him.

"Don't arrest him, too," I begged the woman under their shouting, Scott repeating everything I'd already said. "She needs him. Please, don't take him from her, too."

"That's entirely up to him," she said over me.

"Please. Explain it to him." I somehow managed to get hold of her eyes before she lowered me into the backseat. "She needs my brother. If she doesn't have my brother, he will take her and she's *not* his. Please. He can't take her. Please."

She nodded and guided me in before closing the door.

I watched from the back seat as she talked Scott down, explained it to him and Joss. By then a second squad car had shown up. The woman spoke to the new cop who got out. Joss got into the back seat with Tegan. Scott rushed into the house. As we were pulling away he was running back out with his keys and the sandals he only ever wore to take out the trash or get the mail.

The entire drive I stared out the back window, trying to catch glimpses

of Tegan through the windshield and the grate. At the police station they escorted her and Joss into the building first, directed Scott where to park. Only once they were out of sight did they let me out, guide me in, process me, take me to a thankfully empty cell where I sat in the corner and sobbed, begging Mom to help me, to tell me what to do, to hold me and tell me it was going to be okay, because if there was anything else beyond me, beyond this, it was Her and only Her.

I never did feel her.

Maybe she was with Lucas.

Maybe she was with Dad.

Maybe she was with Tate.

Maybe she was with Tegan.

Maybe she was out there making sure the strings worked the way they were supposed to.

Maybe she was out there getting me Grace.

Scott said by the time he got inside they'd already taken Tegan from Joss.

"But I just kept saying it," he told me later. "Anyone who would listen, I told 'em she wasn't his. That he couldn't take her. That he was doing it to get to you."

I don't know if it actually did make a difference, but from how they treated me, from the way it sounds they treated Tegan, I think it did. The station brought in a social worker who Scott said talked to Tegan, talked Jonathan once he got there, talked to Scott and Joss. Scott said he believes she made the biggest difference. From my conversation with her, I believe she did, too.

Grace was her name.

It was hard to forget.

Names like that in those moments almost always are.

"Your brother told me some things," she said to me.

I was still in the same cell. I had no idea how much time had passed. They'd taken my phone, Her watch that I really only continued to wear in those days because it was Her's. There was no clock within view of the Plexiglass wall that was one side of my cell. At some point they put a drunk guy in the one next to me. He kept singing between yelling. I assumed it was late by then, but I had no real way of knowing.

"She's not his," I told Grace.

By that point it had become a mantra. Maybe it had become more of a spell—if I said it enough times he'd disappear entirely and I could go home

with my daughter, our daughter.

"Why does Mr. Peterson believe she is?"

I looked away from her. I was tired of thinking about that. The guilt had nearly eroded away my esophagus.

"Alex, I believe you when you say he isn't. You wouldn't be the first woman to lie about the father of—"

"I never lied."

"Omission of truth is a kind of lie."

I shifted my weight on the bench that I was already fed up with.

"And after talking with Tegan…" She took in a long breath. "Well, I'm hoping you can tell me Mr. Peterson's role in her life?"

I squinted at her. "How do you mean?"

She stared at me for a moment. "The thing that concerns me the most is her reactions to him. She's not afraid of him, she's more…confused by him."

I just stared at her. Of course she was.

She took in and let out a long breath. "What did Tegan call Mr. Peterson? Before you left?"

I blinked at her.

I hadn't thought of it up until then. I don't think I had even registered it up until then. Before that day in that cell, I think I'd only ever avoided the whack against my heart, my gut, my womb that hearing her call him the name that was only ever yours no matter how far or how frantically I ran from it would have brought me.

"I…I don't know."

"She had to have called him something. What does she call him when she asks about him?"

"She doesn't." It was the truth.

"Never?"

I shook my head. "When we left, she asked if…" What did she call him then? I couldn't remember. I just remember it wasn't daddy. "She asked if he was coming with us, but…I don't know."

And then it hit me.

Jonatin?

Jonatin come wif us?

"Jonathan," I muttered. "That's all we ever called him."

"Is that what she called him, as well?"

I just nodded then raked my fingers from my hairline to the back of my neck that my hair had finally surpassed after a year of growth. I was briefly distracted with the realization that it had been a year since I had hacked off every inch that tried to grow, every inch that he would have claimed as his if I hadn't been careful.

"Alex, your brother told me that Mr. Peterson never treated Tegan like his daughter. Is that true?"

"She was a prop," I told her without looking away from the concrete floor. "We both were."

"What does that mean?"

I straightened to lean back against the wall with a long sigh, not entirely ready to relive all this, not when I was so far from your hull. At least, that's how I understand it now. I don't know if I did then.

"He…ignored her when it was just us. Was annoyed with her at times even. Annoyed that she existed. Until people came over or he took us out. That was the only time he treated her like a daughter. When being a father benefited him."

"And how did she react to this?"

"Just like you said." I met her eyes. "Confused."

"And you never told her to call him daddy," that whack that could have toppled me had it been physical, "or papa, or…?"

"Why would I? She's not his."

She held my stare for a long time before asking it: "Why were you with him, Alex?"

I deserved to be.

I shrugged. "He…" I shrugged again and looked away from her.

I could feel her staring at me. "Your brother said you were going through some stuff before? When you left your ex? Um, what was his name?"

I went numb.

I was floating.

I was boatless.

I was back in the pool outside your apartment, the storm fractured water above me.

"Marc." It almost wasn't my voice. It almost wasn't my body.

I wanted my mother.

"What was that? What was it that you went through?"

I was quiet for a long time. I wasn't ready to do this. I wasn't ready to dig

into all this. I wasn't ready to analyze myself. I wasn't ready for anyone else to.

"You can tell me. It might even help to understand the hold Mr. Peterson had on you."

I shook my head. It wouldn't.

Her hand wrapped around mine and I looked up at her.

"Let me try."

I just blinked at her at first, the words too deep under water, Mariana Trench deep, it would take cranes and trained divers to get them out.

"My…I lost…" It was then that I realized I had never actually said those words after I'd left Port A. I'm not even sure I had told Delilah, had told Joss. I'm sure they'd put the pieces together, but I'd never actually said the words: "I lost my mother."

She slid across the bench to wrap her arm around my shoulders. "How?"

I shook my head. I didn't want to say the words.

She nodded. "I'm so sorry. How long ago?"

"'07. May."

She took in a deep breath. She didn't have to say the words for me to know that she was doing the math, that she could see the lines without my needing to draw them.

"Is there a chance that Tegan's his?"

I shook my head. "He thinks there is. But she's not."

She let go of me and clasped her hands together. "Because you don't want there to be?"

"Because she's not. She doesn't look like him. And she doesn't look like me."

She nodded and was quiet for a moment before continuing. "Any court will want more than that."

"Test her then."

"He has to agree to that. We can't force him to do it."

I fell quiet.

I was beginning to feel trapped again.

"She's not his," I muttered.

Was he gone yet?

Had I said it enough times?

After talking to me a while longer, Grace left.

Within a few hours, a cop came to my cell, escorted me to a small room that looked like the interrogation rooms you see in those *Forensic Files* episodes always through grainy, deteriorating footage that looks older than it should.

I never did learn what Grace told him, but the superior look on his face when the same cop brought him in made me think it must have been something different from what she told me.

"Hey," he tried to give me a smile, tried to set me at ease. "You're growing your hair back out," he added as he sat across from me. "I like it."

My head spun. I could feel that short length snaking around my neck.

Fuck you, I wanted to spit at him.

"What am I doing in here," I asked instead.

"I hate that you're here as much as you do, but—"

I glared at him. "Do you?"

He squinted at me then put on that concern that, back when I was drowning, I misunderstood as caring, genuine. "Yes, Alex. You scared the shit out of me."

Had it just been me, I would have continued to believe it, would have slipped right back under that current, given in, become a mannequin. Because being plastic was easier than hurting, easier than having to face everything I'd done to you.

But I wasn't treading water anymore. I wasn't adrift alone anymore, I had been reminded that I had flesh, muscle and bone beneath it, blood flowing through it. My heart scrambled into whatever boat it could, my womb pulled the sail taught. He wouldn't catch us, he wouldn't get her, I wouldn't let him.

"No one had any idea where you were."

My brows scrunched up. "How?"

"What do you mean how? You left in the middle of the night without telling anyone anything."

I wanted to laugh. By this point all the things I'd left in my office at the apartment were at Scott's. I wondered where he was living, how he hadn't noticed. I knew Delilah was sneaky, that he never saw her as anything more than staff who was beneath him, but this was something else entirely.

"Are you really that shocked that I'm here," he asked, misinterpreting my expression, his eyes shifting. "Did you really think I'd just go to Connecticut without looking for you, without looking for our daughter?"

Looking for

They were filming us.

He couldn't say "coming after."

Our Daughter

He was done trying to make me swoon.

He wanted me to know that he was in control.

I just stared at him. I didn't even blink.

I swear his eyes were shifting colors, moving towards black. He was getting angry. He just wanted this to be over with. He shook his head and rubbed his eyes with his fingertips.

"You could have at least left a note or called. I thought you'd have at least told Mack or Meg—"

"Why would I have told them?"

He dropped his hands, met my eyes. "They're in Port Aransas."

I squinted, shook my head.

He just stared at me.

"You thought I was going to Port A."

He nodded as though I was dumb. "Yes."

"You went to Port A *looking* for me."

"Yes." He said it slowly, so I'd understand the obvious.

I stared at him.

He stared back at me.

"You didn't ask where Scott was."

His eyes flashed black. "Why would I?"

"Why wouldn't you? You really didn't think—Holy hell, why do you hate him so much?"

"I don't hate him."

I let out a shot of a laugh. I think part of me wanted him angry, wanted him to do what he'd always kept himself from doing, wanted them to see it. "Yes, you do, Jonathan! That's why you drove him out of Austin!"

"I did no such thing!"

"You made it very clear he wasn't welcome anymore."

But his eyes were gripped shut, his teeth were clenched, he was finally catching on. "Please don't tell me you've actually been living with him, that *our* daughter has been living with that low life pornographer."

"Yes," I said over him. "We have. And it doesn't matter because she's not your daughter."

"My name is on the birth certificate. You can't just take that back."

"Yes, I can and if you try and take her from me I will."

His eyes shot open. His irises had taken over. Every muscle in his body was coiled back, ready to pounce. "I won't let you."

Do it, I wanted to tell him. "Too fucking bad," I shouted at him instead. "I don't need your permission."

He shot out of his chair, his finger jutted out at me. "Yes! You do! I'm her—"

"No, you're fucking not!"

"You can't just decide now—"

"I didn't! She's not yours! Do you need me to get fucking clinical with you?" I stood from my own chair, reminded him I wasn't his anymore. "You didn't conceive her!"

"I don't fucking believe you!"

I thrust my arm out at the door as though she were on the other side. "LOOK AT HER!"

"THAT MEANS FUCKING NOTHING!"

"Then get a fucking paternity test, because I'm not handing her over to someone who isn't even her FUCKING FATHER!"

"WHO THE FUCK ELSE WOULD IT FUCKING BE?"

"FUCKING MARC!"

That was the first time I had said it out loud.

Ever.

She's yours.
She always has been.
She always will be.

It had been a mistake to think I could let him have her even in theory, even in his prop life.

It was more than a mistake.
It was stupid.
It was cruel.

I understand that now.

He lunged at me then.

He grabbed a fistful of my hair and slammed me against the wall.

He got a swing in before the cops burst through the door and pulled him off me.

Grace was at my side, but I didn't hear anything she said. I just crumpled to the floor, the gravity and the pain in front of my womb increased while my ears rang, leaving me in a deafening sort of silence which only allowed my last words to reverberate off the walls so they came back to me tenfold, your name penetrating me with more guilt, more pain, than his fists or those black eyes ever could.

On some hard drive in LA, there's grainy, deteriorating footage of me on my knees in that room, sobbing over what I had done to you.

I'm so sorry.

I love you.

He agreed to a paternity test after that.
I think it was just to spite me, to prove me wrong.

She's not his.

They released me shortly after what they kept calling "the confrontation."

They asked me if I wanted to press charges.

I should have.

But I was tired.

I just wanted Tegan back in my arms.

When they took me to her, she burst into tears and fell into me, refused to let me go the way I refused to let her go. I carried her to the car, held her against me the entire drive back to the house, laid next to her in her bed until she fell asleep.

Through it all I didn't know how to feel.

My scales had shifted.

I had cut every tie that remained to Jonathan.

But that final tie was replaced with the now heavy weight of you.

I had nothing left to distract me from you.

But I still couldn't be yours.

I still had cleansing to do.

Cleansing by fire, as it seems.

When I left the bedroom that night, Scott and Joss were on the back porch, Joss on the wicker couch, Scott pacing in front of her. They stopped talking when I stepped outside, both staring at me while I closed the door behind me and stared back at them.

I didn't know what to say and it was apparent they didn't either.

What was there to say?

But Scott needed to hear me say the words.

"What was I not supposed to tell Marc, Al?"

I held his eyes, silently begging him not to make me say it.

But, like I said, he needed me to more than I needed not to.

"That she's his."

He blinked at me. "His?"

"Marc's."

He nodded and took in a deep breath before jumping head first into words I could sense he'd been fighting saying to me for a long time, maybe since Austin: "Go home, Al."

I couldn't look at him anymore. "No."

"Why not?"

I just shook my head.

"I don't understand you."

I could feel him watching me move to the couch where I sat with a foot of space between me and Joss.

"Why can't you just go home?"

"He deserves to know," Joss said.

"He might already."

My head shot up to look at Scott and he shrugged.

"It was the asshat. I kept your secret."

"When?"

"When he went after you. Went straight to Port A. Brought the Texas fucking Rangers with him."

"How do *you* know?"

"Mack told me. They didn't wanna call you directly. Were worried it would lead back to you if they did. I should have told you, but I...I don't know. I just got you back."

I had wondered why they'd been so...calm...understanding, maybe, about it all back during Christmas on the phone, why they'd never asked why I was there all those times Scott and them talked.

"And?"

"He asked if you were with me. If it was true you had a kid." He took a few seconds to say the next part. "If she was really his."

I didn't have to ask which *his* he referred to. I just gripped my hands together between my shins and avoided looking at either of them. The thought of you knowing without me, the thought of anyone else telling you let alone the Texas fucking Rangers, the thought of you believing even for a

moment that she wasn't yours—it all made my stomach turn, made those rocks double, triple in weight.

I could have drowned right there on the porch.

I think I nearly did.

Scott sighed. "I'll go with you if that's what it'll take."

"No."

"Why not?"

I was quiet at first.

I didn't entirely know the answer.

I do now.

But back then...

"I can't," was all I could manage to say.

"But why, Al? You know the longer you avoid it the worse it'll be."

I didn't speak.

"I mean, when are you gonna take her home?"

I don't know.

"When she's five?"

I don't know.

"When she's ten?"

I don't know.

"When she's fucking eighteen and goes looking for him herself?"

"I don't know."

He just stared at me.

"I don't..." It was only then that I realized I was shaking. "Can we talk about this later? Tomorrow, maybe? I just—"

Joss' arm was around my shoulders by that point.

Scott's mouth opened.

"She needs to sleep this off," Joss said before he could argue. "It's been a long day. For all of us."

I nodded.

So did Scott.

"Take a nice long shower. Sleep in tomorrow. We'll take care of Teegs. And we'll revisit it again later." She added that last part more for Scott than me who I could feel watching me, more words in his esophagus.

I nodded and stood before anyone could take Joss' offer back.

I mostly hid in the shower that night.

Hid from Scott.

Hid from Tegan.

Hid from you.

When the water went cold, I left the bathroom, but I couldn't sleep.

Her drowning was echoing through me and I remembered why I deserved to be abandoned in a starless sea without you.

I hate to admit that I can't tell you much about those next several months because I don't really remember a lot of it. I remember the parts with Tegan, the parts spent nursing hangovers at work, the parts spent pretending that everything was fine, the parts spent avoiding Scott's heavy handed hints to go home. But those are just more the same. Everything else was a blur of pummeling music and flashing lights, dark, cramped rooms you would've hated filled with too many people equally hiding from the world.

Ara was my guide through all that.

I'd meet her at some parking garage or club or bar, always at least an hour after Tegan's bedtime, after Scott or Joss or both had settled in on the couch with their laptops and a movie that wasn't animated.

It wasn't every night.

I want to make sure that's clear.

It was a lot of nights, more than I feel right admitting, but there were enough nights when I stayed home. Though they were always the nights when Scott stayed the night with Joss at Jackie's, the nights when Scott was out doing shoots or not in town, the nights when he and Joss took their own turn staying out late into the night enjoying each other without worrying about Tegan overhearing.

The nights I stayed out, the nights through which I let myself hide beneath liquor and loud music and Ara's hands, were the nights when Scott stayed home, the nights when his hinting pushed me to the edge of panic attacks, the nights I didn't feel like hiding from him in the few spaces that house allowed.

I avoided him because you had become more of a weapon and less of a

beacon.

I avoided him because he wanted me to go home to you.

And I couldn't.

Not yet.

Because though I had been close to going home to you before everything that happened with Jonathan, I had also somehow forgotten why I had run from you in the first place. So focused on just being free of Jonathan, so focused on just getting anywhere that wasn't under him, under anyone, I had ignored the guilt over Her, I had allowed it to dictate my life less and less.

It wasn't gone, it wasn't healed, just hidden down there in the Mariana Trench wrapped in chains and heavy locks and Jonathan finding me, forcing me to say it, forcing me to relive it, forcing me to remember had broken those locks and undone those chains and launched that chest back onto the deck of the boat I had built myself and suddenly there She was standing over your shoulder again. The thought of going home no longer meant just to you, but rather to you *and* to Her, to what I had done, what I had allowed to happen.

And, falling back in line, I felt the tide rise around me every time Scott brought it up, felt the fog creep along my skin, watched as the moon and the stars slipped behind the building, darkening clouds, watched as the signal from your lighthouse grew fainter

Fainter

Fainter

Until

I was once again surrounded by the black, empty ocean that was steadily rising above my head.

With Scott against me, Joss on his side, Tegan reminding me more and more of you and Port A and everything I had and was destroying there, Ara was the only light I had left.

Ara and old habits that, as they say, die hard.

They must crash and burn in order to be broken.

And, more often than not, you must crash and burn along with them.

I know we've talked about this next part, but from what I can remember, it's always been in vague, abstract, avoidant ways. And that's for a few reasons, I guess:

First simply being that I've never entirely wanted to tell you about it. It's always been so tempting to filter for you, to keep all that tar inside so it won't infect you, as well. Until recently, until Sara and Roxie, I've believed that one of us had to be clean of it for Tegan, for Lucas, for Hope and Kurt.

The second reason is that I believed you didn't want to know as much as I didn't want you to know. I don't know if I'm right or wrong about that. Judging from the way your eyes went glassy when I brought it up last night, the way you continued to hold my eyes anyways, your lips rubbing against each other in that way they do when you're avoiding saying something, I'm not entirely sure if you know the answer yourself.

Thirdly and the most matter of fact of these reasons—there are large chunks that I don't remember and some of the chunks that I do remember I'm not entirely sure how valid or even reliable they are.

But the farther I get into this, the more I avoid even talking about it with Sara and Roxie, the more I'm realizing that this part might be the most important. That—as much as I don't want to face it or bring you into it—it is in fact what finally led me home.

I'm just sorry I had to crash and burn in order to do it.

It started with Scott and me fighting.

He didn't want me to go out, had caught on to what I was doing. He first tried to get me to stay by offering movies or games or food or anything that

would delay my leaving. When I continued to turn him down, became more and more snippy with him, he turned that snip back around at me until the snipping became cannonballs shooting back and forth over Joss on the couch.

"Hey!" She finally shouted over us.

We both stopped and stared at her as she glared first at Scott then me.

"Just go," she flung her arm at the door. "Tegan doesn't need to hear this."

I didn't need to be told twice.

I knew Ara was performing at a bar across town that night, knew I'd stay the night with her and that she'd drive me home in the morning, so I left my car and took the bus. Turns out that might have been the best decision I made all night. Ara's set had already started when I got there, so I stood with some of her friends unable to vent over the music, instead stewing in one drink after another until I was cut off, then drinks the people around me didn't finish, then more of my own drinks when the bartenders changed shifts.

This is where my memory begins to go fuzzy.

From what I would hear later, after the show ended, I found Ara backstage. Apparently, I wouldn't stop talking about the ocean, about wanting to sit on the beach, about wanting to feel the wind and hear the waves between telling her about Dad and everything about marine biology that had stuck to me like barnacles throughout my childhood.

By the time we were standing on the pier, I was that crying stage of drunk and Ara told Scott she couldn't really make out a lot of what I was saying, but he knows me well enough that even through secondary ramblings, he was able to somehow decipher the references to Lucas and Tate, Mack and Meg, Dad, Mom, you. She told him I kept talking about the beach, kept wanting to walk in the sand, kept wanting to swim, but she knew better than that, kept insisting I stay on the pier.

But you know I can be a stubborn mule when I want to be.

And that my head becomes twice as hard when I'm drunk.

I like to think you would have stopped me.

I like to think I wouldn't have even tried it had you been the one on that pier with me.

It was the wood beneath my bare feet that began to tug my consciousness back to the surface. It was the yelling that brought it nearly there. It was the wind in my ears, that familiar feeling of empty weight being left on a railing that ripped me the rest of the way to the surface.

It wasn't like the pool.

I was tossed back and forth by something so much larger than myself.

And I let it take me.

It's strange being in that place: your mind so aware and your body so entirely separated from it.

My head, my gut, my heart was screaming at me.

What had I done?

What was I doing?

Where was I going?

But through it all, my body refused to fight.

I'm done fighting. Entirely done.

I'm going wherever She is.

I'm going home.

The part that was like the pool was the serenity. The surface wasn't dappled. I never even got the chance to register the surface and what it looked like. But my body moved along with the water wherever it dictated, I felt removed from it all.

I was back in purgatory.

But this time you weren't there to dive in after me, to drag me to the shallow end, to show me what I'd done, to remind me of what I had above the water.

Without you

Without Tegan

Without Her

I let go.

What happened next is difficult to explain.

Everything changed in some ways, but, in others, it didn't.

I was still floating, but I could no longer feel the water moving around me, could no longer hear it rushing past my ears. A soft, gentle warmth surrounded me. It was then that I finally noticed the light behind my lids. I opened my eyes to see the sunlit sky around me, clouds passing through my fingers. Looking down, I saw the ocean, but it wasn't California.

My heart, my feet knew that shore line, that jetty, the college campus nestled among the dunes next to the road that shifted from sand to asphalt before leading to those rows of coastal houses on those strong, weathered stilts.

I was staring down at Port A.

I was staring down at home.

Before I could wonder what was happening, if I was dreaming or dying, a voice spoke just behind my ear, layers of whispered echoes behind it:

Is this what you want, sweet girl?

Do you want this to be over?

Are you ready for nothing?

No.

I wasn't ready.

They need you.

So many hearts need you.

So many lives ache for you.

I know.

I'm sorry.

You were made for so much more than this pain.

We made you so much stronger.

All you have to do is remember.

I nodded.

I promised.

A multitude of matrilineal hands touched my back.

They are your strength, they told me as one. *Hold them close. Remember.*

Then I felt an ethereal chin on my shoulder, a singular voice whispered in my ear: *Go home, sweet girl.*

I started to turn in hopes of seeing who the voice belonged to, if it was who I hoped it to be, but before I could those hands all at once shoved me back towards the earth. I still remember that feeling of falling, that feeling of the rushing wind, that feeling of panic as the shore grew closer and closer. I clenched my eyes shut, wrapped my arms around my head, pulled my knees to my chest.

My back hit solid ground.

I yanked the air back into my lungs.

"Alex!" Ara's voice cried out from nearby under professional sounding orders, over a crowd's worth of spectacle chatter.

I blinked up at the stars, the so close to full moon.

I was still in LA.

I wasn't home.

The world spun.

Everything went black.

My memory of those first few days is fragmented and spliced together with long stretches of blackness occasionally broken up by visions of ocean waves, storm whipped palm trees, lightning strikes in the gulf while "Lady of the Stars" played on repeat.

Scott says it was three days before I opened my eyes, two more before I was awake for long enough stretches to make it worth trying to talk to me. I want to say that I remember some of this, that I remember Tegan asleep against my side.

But I also remember you being there, brushing my hair from my forehead.

Then I remember Her at the bedside holding my hand, a chorus of matrilineal voices whispering to me:

Mea Culpa

        Nostra Culpa

Mea Culpa

        Nostra Culpa

Mea Culpa

        Nostra Culpa

At the end of the week, they were all relieved to see me conscious, but Tegan was the only one who I didn't also feel a hovering hesitancy from. It was painful how obvious it was that they were avoiding looking straight in my eyes for very long, how they eyed me while Tegan sat on the bed close to me and explained to me every story that went with the pictures she'd scribbled in red, black, and blue ballpoint pens through the spiral notebook one of the nurses had given her on the third day.

Then there was a day when I remember being half asleep and hearing Ara talking to someone before Tegan was lifted from my bed between Scott whispering to her followed by footsteps and soft voices leaving the room. I shifted and pretended to wake. I rubbed my eyes and opened them to see Ara sitting in the chair Scott had been occupying over that last week and a half. She glanced up at me with her body bent forward with her elbows planted against her knees and her face set in a solemn nervousness that kept me from smiling at her.

"What?" I pushed myself up to really look at her.

She lifted her eyes to me while her hands continued to grip together. "We need to talk."

I nodded and looked to the stack of thin blankets on my knees.

"What were you doing, Al?"

I let out a long breath and looked at the wall. "You know what I was doing."

"Do I?"

I refused to give it to her.

So, she took something else instead.

"You never told me about her."

I blinked, scrunched up my brows, half turned my head to her. "I didn't?"

In my peripheral, she shook hers.

"Hmm," I breathed.

She was quiet for a long few seconds, but I could feel her staring hard at me. "That's it? 'Hmm?'"

I finally met her eyes. "What do you want me to say?"

"Why you were hiding your daughter from me? Why you were hiding the fact of her from me?"

I squinted at her. "I wasn't hiding her from you."

"What were you doing then?"

"She never came up."

She scoffed. "She never came up?"

"Yeah. When exactly do you think I was supposed to say it? Before the vodka or after the fucking?"

She glared at me. I could tell it wasn't the answer she wanted, that she'd expected so much more, but it was the truth, at least the truth that I wanted

to believe in that moment, and I glared back letting her know it was all she was going to get.

"So then what were you doing?"

"What do you mean?"

"No mother should be—"

"No. *You* don't get to give me that lecture."

"Who's going to then? You don't have any friends who are parents. Was that on purpose?"

"Fuck you."

"I'm not gonna be your suicide, Al."

Canons went off. I shot shrapnel at her. "That's not—"

"You're delusional if you think that's not what you were doing."

She stared at me while I struggled to find any possible way to argue with her. When I couldn't, I pursed my lips and glared at the blankets instead.

"Get it the fuck together." She stood and crossed her arms. "You don't get to throw it all away. Not while she needs you."

She left me there with her words pinging along my bones, off my heart and against my gut.

I needed *Her.*
She knew that.
At least, I want to believe she did.
And She threw it all away anyways.
Maybe that's what we all did wrong.
Maybe we should have been sure.
Maybe we should have said it more bluntly.
Maybe we shouldn't have tried to dress it up.
Maybe we should have just told her the truth we all assumed she already knew:

We needed Her.
We still need Her.
We will always need Her.

I was sent home not long after that. Ara didn't come back. I'm still kind of hurt by that. I probably should have texted her. I still feel bad about that.

Jackie came home with us. That guy yelled at her when she tried to leave his place to go to the hospital that night, then he'd finally hit her. She left before he could finish apologizing, trying to convince her it wouldn't happen again, but just stay, please stay.

"I couldn't stop thinking about you," she'd tell me later. "You walked out. You've always been so good to me and you told me to leave, to not go back and I didn't listen and suddenly it was him or you. I realized that I wanted you, Al. I wanted my sister. I wanted Scott. I wanted *this* family. Not his. I wanted something more. I wanted so much more. I don't know why that was what it took, but I just…" There would be a catch in her throat, her voice all watery. "I finally got it."

But that night, Scott, Joss, and Jackie were quiet, though they tried to hide it around Tegan. They hadn't been able to hide the half hour in the hospital before we left when Scott and Joss disappeared. I tried not to show that I noticed, instead directing Tegan around the room while we did what we could to clean up the room despite the nurse insisting we didn't need to. It was a coping mechanism, I tried to explain to her without using those words.

I still kind of resent him for that.

When we got home, Scott and Joss avoided me by fussing over dinner while they kept insisting I sit with Tegan and Jackie on the couch and watch *My Little Pony*. They did their best to act like everything was fine while we ate, though the vast majority of our attentions were on Tegan and not on each other.

Tegan's bedtime hit and they let me take over while I enjoyed just having her to myself, just being hers and everything she needed from me. I took my time tucking her in and reading to her, even stayed with her when the book was over until she had drifted off to sleep with her arms around me. Once she had been breathing deep for a while, I slipped from her bed feeling more rejuvenated than I had when I left the hospital.

But then there was Scott in the kitchen and all that strength flooded back out of me.

He stood from the table and nodded to the back porch, Joss and Jackie avoiding looking straight at us. My arms crossed tight over my stomach, avoiding their eyes, as well, I followed him.

He leaned against the wall and I sat on the wicker couch staring at the concrete.

For a long time we were both quiet.

Then he broke the silence. "I'm taking you home."

That habit that was a pile of embers in my stomach spoke before I could stop it. "No."

"I'm not asking this time."

The sternness of his voice made me look at him, meeting his eyes that were already staring at me.

I could have sworn I could see the faintest outlines of hundreds of veiled women surrounding him.

When he spoke, however, all the strength was gone from him. "I'm done begging, Al. I'm done raising your daughter without you. And—" He looked away from me, his voice drowning, the string lights catching the tears at the brims of his eyes. "And I don't know if I'd be able to do—to do it if—if you…"

I was slammed against the surf again, the waves pulling away from me while I gasped for air.

"Losing Mom was…" He took in a shaky breath and shook his head. "Losing you like that it…" His mouth tried to form the words, but only struggling silence came out. "It'd break me, Al. The kind you-you don't exactly come back from." He shifted his weight and shrugged. "You know?"

"I'm not gonna—"

"I don't believe you, Al." He met my eyes again. "Not anymore."

For longer than I should have I just stared at him. I saw those women, recounted those voices, those hands, but regret, guilt, fear are so much

stronger than spirits. "Don't make me go back."

"I don't think this'll ever be over until you do."

My mouth hanging open, I just shook my head, fighting my own panicked tears. "I can't," was all I could get to come out.

"Why not?"

But I couldn't answer him. I had only just begun to understand it myself. Instead, I looked away from him and stared at the concrete.

"You know he'll forgive you."

I did.

"Even if you don't want him to."

I didn't.

He took in and let out a long breath then sat next to me on the couch where he stared at the same spot on the concrete, those matrilineal spirits surrounding us.

"Stop doing this to yourself," he said after a while. "You deserve to be happy, too."

"No, I don't," I finally said out loud.

He turned his head and stared at me for a long few seconds. "Because of Mom?"

My silence was all the answer he needed.

"Alex—"

I was drowning now. Shut my eyes and shook my head. "I left her alone."

"*I* did."

I looked up at him then, brows furrowed, mouth open for an argument that was too in shock to leave my throat, the only movement on my face being the tears that refused to stop.

He swallowed and shrugged. "I shouldn't've left the house."

"You were getting groceries," I told him as though it would explain it all away.

"I should've waited until someone got home. I-I should've called Mack or Meg. I...I should've known better."

"How *could* you have?"

"How could *you* have?"

I just blinked at him through the tears.

"You were stretched so thin, Al. We kept throwing you at her. You..."

He rubbed his lips and shook his head, his eyes as wet as mine. "You didn't need that." He gripped the back of his neck. "I'm sorry. But you always…" He shrugged. "Knew what to say."

"No, I didn't."

"Yeah, you did. Maybe not consciously, but…she always came back after talking to you."

"You always made her laugh."

"Jokes only go so far. You…shifted her perspective. Even just a little."

The guilt set off those canons and I burst before I could stop them, doubled over, sobbing so loud I could hear my own keening echo through the neighborhood. He tried to pull me to his side, but I fought him and ripped from the couch, still hyperventilating.

"I—I—I turned—"

"Breathe," Jackie said from my shoulder.

I hadn't even heard them come out, felt Jackie's arms around my shoulders, but she forced me to look at her. "Breathe, Al."

I gasped and the words dislodged. "I turned my phone off!"

She looked to Joss and Scott who were standing between us and the couch staring at me.

"I turned it off," I wailed at Scott.

"I know," he told me, not understanding. "I remember."

"She—she—" But I doubled over, collapsed to my knees.

Scott followed me to the concrete, his hands on my shoulder and back.

"She—she called," I somehow managed to get out.

His hands went limp, but never left me. The words out, the blockage cleared, the other finally gushed forward. "She tried to call me, Scott. She tried to…"

He yanked me to his chest and gripped me close while I continued to sob and hyperventilate.

"She was stranded. And I let her die. I let her go."

He began to rock. "We all did, Al." His voice was as waterlogged as mine. "This isn't all on you. We all did it."

Those were his exact words.

I know because I can still hear them.

They've echoed off my skull, along my spine, across my ribs for years

now. I've heard them in my sleep more times than I can count, always beneath Her drowning, Her humming as I'm pulled to the surface and out of the dark waters that are those terrors.

I don't want to keep doing this.
I don't want to keep reliving this.
I can't carry her alone.

But I don't.
I shouldn't have to keep reminding myself of that.

Yesterday, when you found me once again crying over all of this, you asked if I could just tell you, why I have to write it out. Because if I don't then I'll falter. I'll stop short, leave things out, filter events and words based on your expressions. I've already done that enough here without you next to me, with only my memorization of you predicting those expressions.

Roxie agrees with you, by the way. I'm sure she already told you that. Says I shouldn't keep this up if it's hurting so much.

But Sara says it's important. That I have to purge it all without consequence before I can move forward, before you and Tegan can have me back entirely.

She says it's the guilt. If it were anything else she'd agree with you and Rox, but this guilt is a parasite, she says. Ignoring it, burying it, cultivating nice things around it, only sustains it.

She says I have to take the power back before I can be rid of it.

She says the only way I can do that is by confessing.

Scott says the last boss is always the hardest.

It was only once we had both stopped, both exhausted and numb, that I realized Joss and Jackie were next to each other on the wicker couch, a glass of water at Jackie's feet while she stared at the concrete between her and us, Joss staring out at the dimly lit fence.

"Come home," Scott begged against the back of my head.

Go home, those spirits said under him.

"Please."

I gripped my eyes shut, guilt and fear and self-flagellation whipping the walls of my torso.

"You can't keep fighting, Alex," Joss said, her voice weak.

I opened my eyes to meet hers.

"Tegan needs you more than this fight does."

I pulled away from Scott and stared at the concrete, embers still sparking in the pit of my stomach. "How will going home change that?"

"Marc," Scott said and my head spun with the whack of your name.

I pulled my knees against my chin. "I don't deserve him either. Not after what I've done to him."

"Maybe not," Jackie said. "Not that I entirely agree," she added to Scott who must have glared at her. "But if the way you guys talk about him is true, then…" She took in and let out a long breath. "Tegan deserves him. If you're gonna insist on doing this to yourself, then she deserves a parent who will love her without also destroying themselves."

I didn't say anything.

Neither did Scott or Joss.

I stood from the porch and went inside.

In our room, I crawled into the bed next to her. Without question, she curled herself against me and I fell asleep with her against my chest missing you, hating myself, loving her.

The next day, we went on in relative awkward silence accept when Tegan was around.

Then, close to noon, the house phone rang.

Scott answered it then immediately handed it to me.

It was Mack and he didn't bother with small talk despite how long it had been since I had talked to him.

"Scott called me last night," he said and I glared at Scott who was already across the room avoiding me. "He said we need to talk."

I shifted away from the TV where Applejack and Rainbow Dash were crouched, ready for a race. "About what?"

He didn't answer right away. "Scott called us last week, too, Al. He told us everything."

Without a word, I stood and went to the back porch, closing the door tight behind me.

"You still there?"

"Yeah," I muttered.

Inside, I could hear Tegan starting to cry, Jackie and Joss calming her, the entirety of my insides screaming at me.

"Come home, Al."

I clenched my eyes shut and doubled over on the wicker couch, my forehead against my knees.

"We're excited to meet her."

I took in several shuddering breaths that I'm sure he could hear. "Does…does he…?"

"Yeah. Um, you can, uh, thank what's his name for that."

"Mack, does he…?"

"Just come home, Al. For Christmas? Dad won't be out yet, but—"

I lifted my head. "Dad's getting out?"

"Yeah," he said with a chuckle. "Kind of hard to keep up on that kind of stuff when you're hiding from us, huh?"

"I'm sorry."

"Come home and all'll be forgiven."

"It's not that easy, Mack."

"It is. It can be. If you'll let it."

I didn't say anything, just gripped my forehead and continued to breathe.

"How old is she?"

"Tegan?"

"Yeah. Tegan."

"Four." In the background, Meg said the same thing at the same time which made me smile despite it all.

"Good. Lucas'll be glad to have someone to play with. Julian can't really keep up with him yet."

I closed my eyes again. "Yeah.

They'd told me about Julian the previous Christmas, the guilt that he was already two and I had yet to see him ate at me.

"Right," I sighed. "I-I'm sorry."

"For what?"

"For missing everything."

"No one blames you, Al. We just all really miss you is all."

I didn't believe him.

I should have.

"Bee," Meg said.

"Oh, right. And, uh, Tate's really been itching for y'all to meet Bianca."

"Don't tell me Tate's had a kid, too."

"No," Mack laughed. "Not yet. Though, Meg and I live in constant fear of it. No, uh, Bee's his girlfriend. She's actually pretty cool. A good kind of cool," he added quickly. "Not trouble maker cool." Meg laughed. "You and Scott'll get a kick out of her."

"Yeah?" I stared at the attempt of a garden, the rocks Tegan had painted with us over that past year and a half, a soft smile behind my fingers as I realized how much I missed them, all of them, especially you.

"Yeah. Uh." In the background, I heard people moving around, Meg saying something, Mack moving, a door closing. "What do you say, Al? Until Dad gets out?"

I smirked and rolled my eyes. "I thought you said 'til Christmas."

"He gets out the week after."

All the floating feelings fled. "New Year's?"

He was quiet for a moment. "Yeah. Weird coincidence, huh?"

My lips puckered from fighting the tears. "Yeah."

We both lingered over the words we weren't saying.

"She'd want y'all here," he finally said. "When he gets home."

My eyes shut, breathing deep, I nodded. "Okay."

"Yeah?"

"Yeah."

Once the conversation had ended, the phone had been hung up, I went back inside where Tegan was lingering by the backdoor waiting for me. Without hesitation, I fell to my knees and pulled her tight against me while she squeezed me back and a chorus of matrilineal ghosts gathered around us.

The rest of this, I know you were around for, but believe me when I say I need to tell this part. Not so much for you or for us, but for me. I've spent so much of this letter in pain and angry with myself for how it all happened. I just…

I need to remember the good, Marc.

I need to remember that this didn't all end in total darkness.

I'm still surprised by how little of a mess I was on the drive back to Texas. I had expected to be a wreck of nerves and tears and second thoughts. Instead, I sat in the back seat with Jackie, Tegan between us "reading" to us from her picture books or asking about things she saw out the windows or sang along to Joss' music. In the between moments, I rehearsed what I'd say to everyone, mostly what I'd say to you.

Though, it wasn't until we hit Corpus that it actually became real.

Even when Scott called Mack from the diner we'd stopped at in El Paso, gravity failed to grab hold of me the way it did when Scott drove Joss' Jeep onto the ferry, when we piled out to stand against the edge, Tegan in my arms while we watched the gulls and searched for porpoises swimming along with the bow of the ship.

The instant we were out of sight of the traffic guards, I unbuckled Tegan from her car seat and pulled her into my lap to hold her close against me while she pressed herself against my shoulder and watched out the window, pointing to the giant wooden sailors and the big shark outside the stupid large gift shop. Her weight was the only thing keeping the panic down, keeping me from floating back out into the middle of the ocean.

Then we got to Mack and Meg's street and the tide might as well have come in. I tried to hide my tears, but they knew me better than that, Scott reaching back to squeeze my knee. I looked up at him and, between watching the road, he gave me a smile and a nod that filled in the holes between the strength that holding Tegan gave me.

When we pulled into the drive, Meg, heavily pregnant at that point, was already on the stairs with a wide smile and carrying Julian, Mack not far behind her, a little blonde head peeking out from behind the railing between them. Scott was the first out of the car and immediately went to Meg for a hug then Mack who clapped him on the back and laughed against his shoulder, Lucas staring up at Scott with half familiarity.

It's funny how we freeze people in our heads, how, despite knowing that five years had passed, despite knowing that he's a year older than Tegan, seeing Lucas walking, talking in full sentences, it threw me for a loop. By this point, I had managed to leave the back seat still holding Tegan against me and I just stood there in the drive watching them, not sure what to do—wanting to run to them, wanting to run from them, afraid they'd hate me, knowing Lucas wouldn't remember me.

But then Meg spotted us and her eyes went all watery. Scott took Julian from her and she rushed over to me, her arms already open. I let Tegan slide to the ground and let Meg take me, gripped her back just as hard, her belly pressed firmly against me.

"I'm sorry," I cried against her shoulder, everything I'd planned to say washing away with the current.

"You're home, Al," she told me without letting me go. "That's what matters."

Mack's hand on my back separated us and I flung my arms around his neck while he took me around the middle.

"It's good to see you," he said.

I just nodded against his shoulder until he let me go to step back and smile down at me while we both laughed and dried our tears. It was strange the way it felt as though no time had passed and, at the same time, as though this was all from a whole other life. Tegan's hands on my hip brought me back and I smiled then knelt next to her.

"This is your Uncle Mack," I told her. "And Aunt Meg."

"Hi, Tegan," Meg said to her with a smile and bent to be at her eye level, her arms cradling her belly. "We've been excited to meet you."

Chewing on her nails, she looked to Meg then Mack then me then Scott who was introducing Lucas to Jackie, Joss hanging back taking pictures. I'd already told her about you, told her we were going to meet you. I think up until she spotted another kid her age, figuring out which of these adults was you was her only focus.

"Hi," Tegan said without looking away from Lucas.

Meg followed her eyes and didn't skip a beat. "That's Lucas. You wanna meet him?"

She didn't bother to explain that he's technically Tegan's uncle, as well, knew, like I did, that that was a conversation for another day, another year even.

Tegan nodded and leaned closer to me, all the while still watching Lucas.

"He's so big," I said to Meg and Mack as I stood.

"Five already," Mack said with a smile and a sigh.

"When did that happen?"

"At the same time that did," he said, hooking his arm around my shoulders and nodding to Tegan who had caught up to Meg.

"Sorry," I told him, but he shook his head.

"Just promise we'll get to see you more than once every five years."

I nodded and leaned against him.

"Luke, this is Tegan," Meg was saying.

"Hi," he said, looking her over with curiosity.

"Hi," she returned with the timidness of an only child whose mother struggled to be around other parents, who was pulled out of pre-k because being without someone she knew, thinking something would happen to them in the in-between sent her into waves of panic that she couldn't be talked down from until we were in her line of sight again.

Lucas looked to Meg than Mack, his eyes falling on me. With a harder look than I would have expected, he examined me, as well.

"Is she Alex," he asked Meg.

My head spun, but that inner logic yanked it still again, reminding it they still had pictures of me, had probably been preparing him for our arrival for a few days.

"Yeah," she told him with a smile. "This is Alex."

"Hey, Lucas," I said.

He continued to stare up at me as though trying to piece something

together.

"Luke," Meg broke his concentration, "you wanna show Tegan your chalks?"

His eyes lit up. "Yeah!"

He turned to zip under the stairs where the cushioned wood couch and armchair I would later learn was yours sat among a dense collection of potted plants. Just as Tegan was starting to follow him with her hands in little balls under her chin, he came back out with a plastic bucket and held it out for her to look inside.

"I got all the colors," he told her with pride.

"Do you have green?"

"Of course!" He dug in the bucket to pull out a chunky piece of pastel green chalk and hand it to her. "Meg lets me draw all over the driveway but not in the street but the sidewalk's fine and *all* over the driveway!"

Tegan's eyes went wide. "Really?"

"Yeah! Look!"

We watched while he led her to a spot between the stairs and a newer version of Meg's old Explorer where there was already a series of scribbled images, obvious adult drawings among the five year old only just distinguishable forms and toddler erratic lines and circles.

"Chak," Julian said from Scott's arms and pointed to Lucas and Tegan already on their knees and focused on their art.

"You wanna draw, too, buddy?"

"Yeh!" Julian giggled and bounced while reaching for the ground.

Scott put him down and he and Mack followed him to the chalk drawing where he crouched over the bucket and carefully chose a piece before joining in. Tegan looked up at Scott with a huge smile and pointed to her picture while he knelt next to her.

"Bee and Tate draw with them," Meg told me. "Marc sometimes, too, but he says it's less fun when you have actual artists next to you."

A hurricane whipped through my chest and my lips struggled between smiling and trembling.

"That's what they tell me when we paint rocks," Jackie told Meg with a smile.

They introduced themselves to the other while I struggled to stay above water.

"Wh-where is he? Marc?" I said when they were in a lull in their conversation.

"Work. We, um, we didn't exactly tell him when you were coming. He'd've wanted to take off if he knew and Mack and I thought, I guess, that all this would be easier without him first." She looked to me. "Ease you in."

I met her eyes and nodded. "Yeah. It's better for her, too. Meeting y'all first then him."

Meg smiled. "He's excited. Nervous. A little scared, I think. But excited. He's missed you."

"And-and Tegan? Does he...?"

"He wants to hear it from you." She shrugged. "I think that's what he's scared about."

I don't know why I hadn't thought about it before: you being scared, that there could be something for you to be scared of. For me there was no question she'd love you because how could she not, but I realize now that was just me projecting, that there was a possibility she wouldn't.

Meg looped her arms around mine and hooked her chin on my shoulder. "It's all gonna work out, Al."

"Promise?"

"Of course."

We fell quiet and just watched Mack and Scott with the kids. Behind us were those ever familiar clicks.

"Who's the documentarian," Meg finally asked and nodded to Joss distracting herself by snapping picture after picture.

"Joss," I said.

"My sister," Jackie added.

"Scott's girlfriend."

Meg's brows went up and her eyes went wide.

"I know," I laughed.

"She's nervous," Jackie added.

She'd never actually told any of us that, but the amount of time she spent behind that camera before Scott dragged her out was all we needed to know the truth.

"Babe," Scott finally said with a laugh and stood to pull Joss over to him, though her eyes were glued to the back of her camera. "Stop hiding."

"How is it that all of you photograph so well?" She remarked more to

Scott and her camera than anyone else.

"So, there's two of 'em now," Mack said with a grin.

Joss' eyes went wide and that nervous smirk came over her while she looked from him to Scott who was just laughing.

"Take it as a compliment," Mack said and waved her over for a one armed hug. "I've always believed only another photographer would ever be able to put up with him."

"Funny," Joss said as Mack released her. "Dad always said the same about me," she added, smiling up at Scott.

"Where's Tate," I asked Meg while Jackie was being introduced to Mack. She let out a sigh. "Inside."

I nodded.

"He's..." She shook her head. "I don't know. Depends on the day."

Before I could ask for elaboration, the front door opened. A short, lean woman with warm terra cotta skin and nearly waist length deep brown curls came out, dragging Tate by the hand behind her. The sight of him nearly toppled me. He wasn't 15 anymore. He was no longer gangly and itching at the limitations of his own skin. The way he stood at the top of the stairs with his shoulders slouched, his hands in the pockets of his black faded and fitted jeans while he kept his eyes squarely on Bee who was looking up at him from one step down, talking quietly to him with her silver ring covered fingers on his stomach—there was so little of the teen I had left behind five years earlier. I think it was his hair that caught me off guard the most. It was the first I had seen it down to his shoulders. Scott had tried to grow it out like that in high school before you. Still firmly in those scarecrow days, his Matthews straight, unwieldly hair only worsened the effect. Mack had warned him of it, but teens will always insist on learning their mistakes first hand, won't they? But Tate has her Warren waves, that natural flip at his left temple. Tate was born for that bohemian look. Him and Bee both.

Bee finally gave up on him and turned to start down the stairs alone. Once at the bottom, she crossed her arms and looked to Mack who had gone to the bottom step to see what Tate decided.

He shrugged to her. "Give him time."

She nodded and met my eyes. Smiling, she stepped forward.

"Hi," she said with that soft nervousness of hers. "I'm Bee."

"Alex," I told her and before I could reach my hand out to her, she gave me a hug instead.

"I feel like I already know you," she admitted.

"Yeah?"

She took a step back and nodded, her hands fidgeting with the stacks of bangles on her wrists. "Tate talks about you a lot. Well, they all do, but Tate and Marc especially."

That hurricane whirled again, threatening to sever my anchor. "Yeah?"

It's odd learning that people talk about you when you're not there. It's odder when you freeze those people in time, believe in your heart they're still the person you left behind. There's this strange mix of realizing that those people continue on with life whether you're there or not and realizing you're still prominent enough in their mind to talk about, to talk about you enough that someone might feel they know you before they've ever met you.

I guess I always assumed I had faded from your lives, that Tate would never have a reason to bring me up in conversation, that you would hate me enough to not want to talk about me, that maybe you'd even moved on and found someone else to fill your thoughts.

I guess I was wrong.

Inside, Meg, Jackie, and I kept the kids occupied (which wasn't hard once Tegan discovered Rocky) while Scott, Mack, Joss, and Bee unloaded the car. At one point, Tate must have snuck out through the apartment downstairs, because without having passed us, he came through the front door behind Bee with his own armload of stuff.

He continued to avoid me, though I noticed he was at least talking with Scott and Joss.

By the time everything was settled, Meg and I had decided they'd take Tegan and Joss to see the beach while I went to campus to meet you. Scott offered to go with me, but I knew I needed to do it alone—we needed to do it alone.

It wasn't that hard to find you, my feet moving along those halls to the English department like muscle memory. Thankfully, the work study girl behind the desk didn't know me, didn't narrow her eyes when I said your name or tack on a jab when she pointed me to your office.

Your office.

I remember thinking those were strange words and yet, as I shifted them along my tongue, I felt bubbles of excitement for you underneath the storm of panic and guilt and anxiety and regret that took up most of my torso,

hurling lightning bolts at my stomach.

I found your office empty the way the girl had told me it would be, had also told me in a low voice that you never locked it while on campus, because of course you wouldn't. But I was too anxious to sit, instead circling your desk, looking over the bookcases with my hands deep in my sweater pockets.

It was then that I found them.

My mother's books lined up on your shelf, titles among them that hadn't already been stitched into the walls of my heart. I pulled one off to find one of Scott's photos on the cover: Mom on the beach, myself next to her, a ring of seaweed on my head, Lucas in my lap. *Sirens*, it said in looping font across the front.

Out in the hall, I heard your voice, but I was too deep in Her current to move.

And then your voice stopped along with the footsteps and I was only just able to pull myself to the surface to look up at your face with your slack jaw, your eyes shimmering and confused. It took all my strength not to immediately fall back into you, and I probably would have if a student hadn't been standing next to you, looking between us in a deeper state of confusion than you were.

All I could do at first was blink, clear my throat. "I'm sorry. I-I can wait if-if you need."

I moved to return the book to the shelf, but you stopped me.

"Take it," you said, the sound of your voice once again in my ears rather than my memory making my body hum.

I met your eyes and it hit me for the first time how much I had not just taken from you, but from myself, too.

"We—um—this won't take long. But, you should…flip through it. Read a few? While you wait?"

But all those impulses to run that I had been indulging through all those years had dissipated and finally my anchor had been lowered, making it a struggle to move away from you. I didn't want to take my eyes off you, didn't want to feel yours leave mine. I just wanted to stand there, continuing to bring the waves to your shore while you brought the rhythm to my measures. I nodded anyways and ducked my head while I squeezed by you both, your hand grazing my hip as I went.

I never bothered to ask if that was intentional.

For once, I like not knowing.

For once, I like simply believing it was.

Standing in the hall, I wasn't able to get very far through Her book, though. Just seeing your name on the title page next to the word editor brought up tears I had to breathe deep to get to go back down and each new piece shoved them back onto my shores all over again. Instead, I just stood there clutching it against my chest with my eyes closed, internally repeating the same words over and over:

Breathe Breathe Breathe

Shit Shit Shit

Sorry Sorry Sorry

Mea Culpa Mea Culpa Mea Culpa

Then the door opened and my eyes fluttered open to look up at you standing in your office door staring at me while your student avoided my eye line and continued down the hall.

"Hi," you said.

"Hi," I returned.

What else were we supposed to say in that moment?

Anything else, I want to tell myself now.

You nodded me into your office and I followed you in, the door closing behind me.

I remember neither of us sitting.

I remember standing there both staring at you and avoiding meeting your eyes the way you were mine.

I remember fighting against the current that kept pushing me to you, kept wanting me to fall into you, kept wanting to press myself against your chest and cry into your sweater and beg forgiveness for everything I had done to you, everything I had taken from us.

"Your hair's different."

I nodded and for the first time over those five years, I regretted letting the seaweed get to me.

"It looks good."

I wanted to fight even that small smile your voice brought to me because that floaty, light as air turn in my stomach felt so right, felt so easy—this wasn't supposed to be easy. "You really think so?"

You let out a rippling chuckle that made me want you right there on that desk, erase that lingering memory of Jonathan and the day that ended us.

"You always look good."

I let you make me smile, but I had to fight a giggle, the urge to brush my hair behind my ear, look up at you from the tops of my eyes.

"It's, uh." You let out another confused chuckle. "It's—it's really good to see you, Al."

"Yeah."

"I missed you," you said before I was ready and I was nearly ripped down into the undertow.

"I'm sorry," I said instead and stole a glance beyond your chest to see you nod.

"Where were you?"

"LA."

"With Scott?"

"Yeah."

"And, um, be-before that?"

I hesitated over that part. "Austin."

"With—?"

"Yeah," I answered before you had to say his name. "I'm sorry."

You nodded again and crossed your arms, still avoiding looking at me. "He, uh, he…" You took in a deep breath while I watched your lips struggle over the words I didn't want you to say. "He find you?"

"Yeah."

"Is he—?"

"No." I said before you could go on entertaining the thought. "No. He, uh, went back to Connecticut…I think. I don't really know. Haven't talked to him since."

You nodded, staring squarely at the carpet between us now. "Did he…He didn't…Did he…?"

"He forfeited all rights to her."

Your eyes met mine and my heart scrambled against my ribs for you. "Why'd he do that?"

"She's not his."

You stared at me and I remember not being able to read your eyes. At least, I remember seeing only hope in them, but wanting for there to be anger, hurt, all the things you wanted to yell at me while I was gone.

That's why it took me so long to finally say it: "She's yours, Marc."

You just stared at me at first while your entire being lit up. I didn't want to see that, I wanted you to reflect what I was projecting, so I ripped my eyes from yours and looked at my feet where I could pretend you hated me. "I'm so sorry—"

But then your arms were around me and all the tears I had held back in the hall burst onto your sweater between sobs I couldn't hold back once I felt that steady, unhesitating hull around me again.

"I'm so sorry," I repeated over and over.

And you just held me close, your lips and chin against the top of my head.

It wasn't what I had imagined, what I had acted out in my head the whole way there, but it was you. It was so entirely you.

I've never understood what I did to deserve you.

I'm still not entirely convinced that I do.

Once the tears had lulled, you kissed the top of my head and my anchor shook again. You were making this too easy. I convinced myself that you were keeping what you really wanted to say to me buried, that you didn't want to say those hateful things because then I wouldn't bring you to her. Once you saw her, then you'd hate me, then you'd realize the depth of everything I took from you.

But, at the same time, I wanted it to be this easy, I wanted you to forgive me, love me, because I loved you—I still do—I didn't want to leave the place I had been aching for since Her death.

But I didn't deserve it.

But for the first time in a long time, I wanted to.

"Where is she now," you asked which finally gave me the strength to move, to slip from your arms, make it look casual, make sure you knew I wasn't running.

Drying my eyes, I went back to avoiding looking at you. "She's, um, with everyone else. Lucas wanted to take her to the beach."

You laughed and every inch of me ached for every inch of you. "Yeah?"

I smiled. I couldn't help it. How could I? "Yeah."

"After California beaches? She's not gonna be impressed."

I stared up at you, at your smile, both glad and worried that you weren't more upset. I wanted to say something, but I couldn't—I was nearly toppled by how much I really did miss you, how much I really did need you.

"I'm sorry," I said instead.

You smirked. I was 17 again. "You said that."

"I am, though."

You nodded. "We'll talk about that another day. We've got time. Right now…" You smiled and took in a nervous breath. "I just wanna meet her."

I nodded back. "She wants to meet you."

But neither of us moved, both just staring at the other.

"I never stopped loving you," you said.

"Me neither," I finally admitted as much to myself as to you.

Driving back to Mack and Meg's with you behind me was a bit of a blur, I was too deep in my own thoughts, my own concerns, my own fears that once you met her, once you saw what I'd kept from you, you'd hate me, if you didn't already, if you weren't putting on an act and telling me that you didn't.

I remember the walk down to the beach was mostly quiet, mostly tense, you breaking that silence only on occasion to ask about Tegan: what she likes, what she doesn't, what her first four years were like without you even if you tiptoed around those questions as though you both did and didn't want to know the answers.

I remember coming to those little covered picnic tables dotted along the edge of the road and seeing everyone taking up two of them.

I remember we were coming from a bad angle—we couldn't see her digging in the sand with Lucas and Julian just behind the crowd of adults.

I remember when you finally saw her, you stopped still and I was surprised that I still knew you enough to understand that it was as much from nerves as it was from seeing for yourself that she is indeed yours, so entirely yours.

I remember lifting her up, her wrapping herself around me, tentatively watching you while I walked.

I remember, after introductions and timid hellos, all three of us being at a loss of what to say, what to do—nothing seemed right, nothing seemed wrong, it all just felt…

Unreal.

Then someone broke the spell (I don't remember who. Probably Meg. She's good at that sort of thing.) and time moved forward again, though Tegan stayed latched to me while she watched you and you kept trying not to stare at us and I was trying not to stare at you. But in those moments when

your eyes met hers, you made faces at her, made her giggle and loosen from me.

And slowly she began to leave my arms, began to gravitate towards you. Then my entire torso was filled with this blinding light that was shining off my heart and reflecting off my womb while she sat close to you, answered your questions, asked her own, giggled at your answers. From time to time you'd lift your eyes to meet mine and every time I thought I might burst into a nebula.

Through all this, however, I could still sense a hesitancy from her as she continued to watch you closely despite her smiles and giggles and hugs. When I realized what it was I couldn't help but grow still, quiet. It was the only thing I could do to keep from letting y'all see everything I wanted to hurl at him for even taking this moment from her, wanted to hurl at myself for allowing him to do it.

But Scott still knew me and he caught my eye, mouthed those words: *You okay?*

I started to nod, knew there was no point in lying to him. So, I shrugged instead. He looked to you and Tegan, the way her nails, already trimmed short, kept sneaking between her teeth. He didn't have to ask, I didn't have to say it, he nodded.

She'll be okay, he mouthed.

I nodded back, wanting it to be true.

When we got back to the house, Tegan and Lucas ran up the stairs while the adults followed at a more sluggish pace, Mack at the front helping Julian try to keep up with the big kids.

Towards the back of the line, I reached out and touched your arm. "Hey."

You turned to look at me, all joy and light which only made the guilt in my gut that much heavier.

"If you're alone with her?"

You smirked and your brows furrowed at me making me doubly aware of how odd what I was about to say was. My resentment flared up along my bones yet again.

"Make sure she knows you're paying attention to her. Make sure she knows you're with her, that..." I took in a shaky breath. "That you're not ignoring her."

You stared at me, that joy gone, that light now a suspicious sort of

protective and I knew you understood at least a small part of what I was asking.

"I can explain later, but for now, just so you know—it'll make all the difference to her."

You nodded, looked down at my hand that was a fist at my side, then guided it to loosen, took it in yours, squeezed. My entire arm hummed. I wanted so much more. It was radiating off of you that you wanted the same. But, for some reason, neither of us acted on it. I think I was waiting for you to make the first move, afraid that I was seeing ghosts in your body language. I get the feeling you might have been doing the same.

That first day was awkward, I know. Neither of us wanting to act as though anything had changed, but also not wanting to pretend as though the last five years hadn't happened. And then there was the hurricane in my chest that both wanted to just be with you the way I had been—the way I was finally ready to be again—and for you to just be mad at me. I wanted you to avoid me the way Tate was while Bee tried to compensate by going out of her way to get to know me. I wanted you to resent me because then the guilt that was gnawing on my heart would have felt justified, I wouldn't have felt as though I was getting away with something that I had no right to be forgiven for.

I took her from you.

I took you from her.

I took all of this from us.

That was the most apparent when I came upstairs from Tate's room that Scott and Joss were sleeping in (Tate staying with Bee at her Moms'), you were in the kitchen with Tegan and Lucas who were chattering to you between giggles while you were on your knees in front of the open fridge.

"What's going on here?"

You grinned up at me from the floor and my heart swooned while my gut twisted.

"There was a witch!" Tegan said, bouncing in front of me, her little curly ponytail swinging.

"There was?"

"Yeah!" Lucas chimed in with a grin so big I thought his face would split in two. "And she put a spell on Marc!"

"What?" I gave you a smirk that you returned.

You raised you brows and shrugged.

"She took Daddy's voice," Tegan said. "Like Ariel!"

"Oh, no," I feigned for her amusement. "That's terrible. But, why's he digging in the fridge? Is that part of the spell, too?"

She looked to Lucas and they both burst into giggles. "He's looking for Meg's chocolate!"

By now your full attention was on us, that soft light pouring from your heart.

I crossed my arms and narrowed my eyes at her. "Why's he looking for Meg's chocolate?"

"It's the only way to break the spell," Lucas said with a vigorous nod that Tegan mimicked.

"Yeah! He needs chocolate to be better!"

I looked at you and you shrugged again.

"And let me guess, the two of you are also going to need chocolate?"

They looked at each other, both giggling, Tegan's splayed fingers in front of her grin.

Those two would have made the worst criminals back then.

"Maybe," she admitted between giggles.

"I see what's going on here." I dropped to my knees and grabbed her, tickling her as she fell against my shoulder all laughter and wiggles. "There is no witch, is there? Just a hungry chocolate monster who's taken possession of my sweet girl."

When I stopped tickling her, she flung her arms around my neck and continued trailing giggles just under my ear. I enveloped her and pulled her tight against me, feeling your eyes on us through it all.

I wanted to tell you I was sorry right there.

I wanted to tell her I was sorry.

Lucas squirmed his way into the hug and I wanted to tell him I was sorry because they could have had each other all these years, he could have had me, he could have had us.

But I knew this wasn't the time or the place, so, instead I just squeezed them both tight then let y'all go back to your game while I hung back and watched as Tegan pretended to be a monster who couldn't be tamed until she got chocolate and Lucas revealed himself to be the witch who had teamed up

with the monster to make you do their chocolate based bidding. I'd done enough damage over the years. I knew that it was for the three of you to put the pieces back together. I trusted that you would. Already, by that point in the day, you had been ten times the father Jonathan ever tried to be for her.

By bedtime, I was sure that, despite us still having work to do, you and Tegan were nearly whole. Though you stayed downstairs with Scott, Joss, Jackie, Tate, and Bee that night at bedtime, she still ran to you before following Lucas upstairs, still threw her arms around you and said good night. It wasn't the "I love you" it would grow to be, but I knew it would only be a few more nights before she'd be sure enough about you to let it come.

Watching y'all from the stairs, my heart was overflowing, but by the time she was in the tub and I was washing the sand and salt from her hair while she chattered on about you, I was back to feeling weighed down by guilt, back to feeling those flagellating whips against my shoulder blades.

In Lucas' room, she sat between my feet, her and Lucas concentrating hard on the same giant box of Legos that had moved from kid to kid since Mack was born, while I detangled her hair and prepped it for the same nighttime restlessness that had plagued Scott through our entire childhood.

Meg was on Lucas' bed, Mack on the floor building Legos with the kids, while I continued to question their choice of sleeping arrangements.

"You're sure you're okay with Julian in your room," I asked yet again. "Teegs and I've been sharing a room for..." my hands paused and my eyes shifted to the floor while I calculated the months. Tegan tilted her head back to look up at me. I smiled down at her then went back to brushing the leave-in-conditioned through her hair, twisting the more stubborn clumps with my fingers. "Well, I'd be fine sleeping in here. And Jackie's been on our couch on and off. We'd be fine—"

"It'll be fine, Al," Meg insisted yet again with a laugh. "Besides, he's such a heavy sleeper, he'll hardly notice he's in a different room."

I bunched Tegan's hair into a loose ponytail as far up on her head as I could manage with her reaching for pieces. "You sure?"

Mack laughed.

"Yes," Meg repeated. "We want y'all to be comfortable."

I nodded, distracted myself by shaking out the fountain of curls with my fingers.

I didn't deserve to be comfortable.

With a deep sigh, I squeezed Tegan's shoulders. "Okay. Now you're a

pineapple."

"Finally," she groaned and scooted forward to be closer to the pile.

"Like Sponge Bob," Lucas asked without looking up.

"Yeah," I laughed. "Like Sponge Bob."

"Which means," Meg said, pushing herself to the edge of Lucas' bed before Mack leapt up and pulled her the rest of the way, "That it's time for lights out."

The two groaned.

"But I'm not a sleepy pineapple," Tegan said without stopping her Lego digging.

"All pineapples are sleepy pineapples," I told her and lifted her off the floor. "Come on."

"We need to clean up!" She announced and went for the big plastic bin while Lucas stared at her with confusion.

"She sure likes things orderly," Meg said to me with a smirk.

"Surely didn't get it from you," Mack teased.

But I avoided both their eyes and shook my head.

It took a bit of convincing to get her to not organize the entire room. She was in a strange environment surrounded by new people and by then that organizing had become a coping mechanism. To talk her out of it just triggered more anxiety. It was the reason we never trained her out of it in LA, though we probably should have. The best we had done was to teach her that we didn't have to hide her away, that it was okay that her bins of toys stayed out in the open in the living room, that it was okay if her My Little Ponies stayed lined up on the window sill above her little toy shelves, that it was okay if her shoes stayed out on the rack with ours—Mommy wouldn't get yelled at if people knew there was a child in the house.

I could tell that night that Lucas, Meg, and Mack not understanding was making her even more anxious and she kept chewing on her nails between asking me where to put things and I had to once again bury that resentment, that guilt while I scrambled to think of ways to distract her from it.

Only once her things were packed back into her My Little Pony suitcase and Rainbow Dash backpack then placed neatly at the end of the spare bed alongside her shoes was I able to get her under the covers. But she was still unusually quiet and fidgeting with her Rainbow Dash doll between watching Mack and Meg who were tucking in Lucas.

I ran my fingers through her curls. "You okay, mama?"

She nodded then looked up at me. "Mommy?" Her voice was small, secretive.

"Hmm?"

"Tomorrow night? Can Daddy tuck me in, too?"

My womb hummed and I gave her a soft smile. "You can ask him, but I do think he'd like that."

She nodded then shifted her eyes to where Mack and Meg were leaving Lucas' bed. Seeing the secret in her face, I grinned at her and kneeled.

Her arms around my neck, I let her guide me to her so she could whisper close to my ear. "Is Daddy coming home with us?"

"I don't know, baby," I whispered back. "Actually, I was thinking that maybe we would stay here? In Texas?"

Her eyes sparkled. "With Luke and Rocky?"

"At first. We'd have our own house eventually, but, yeah, you'd get to see 'em whenever you wanted."

She smiled, but then a thought seemed to pass through her eyes, her face shifting while she looked away from me to my shoulder where she ran her little fingers along the collar of my sweater. "And Daddy?"

"And Daddy."

A little smile came over her despite her best efforts to hide it (which, being four, wasn't much of an effort). "And will Daddy live with us?"

I watched her not watch me, wondering what exactly and how deeply I had taken from her those past four years. I hoped she wouldn't remember it when she was older, hoped there would be nothing she'd need to remember, hoped we could pretend we'd spent her first years together, whole, the way we are now, so she'd grow up believing she'd never had anything different.

"That's up to him," I admitted.

Her face began to drop.

"But," I added before it got too far, "*I'd* like that. Wouldn't you?"

That little smile came back and she nodded.

"Okay, then. Dream for it, sweet girl." I kissed her forehead and she giggled. "For you and me both."

While I stood, we exchanged "I love you"s before I started for the door.

"Alex," Lucas said.

I stopped and smiled down at him. "Yeah?"

He held his arms out to me and I bent to give him a hug.

"You gonna keep my baby safe for me," I asked him.

Squeezing me tight, he nodded against my shoulder. "Me and Mama."

I froze, but then swallowed it and the tears down before squeezing him back.

After more "good night"s and "I love you"s, I joined Mack and Meg at the door. They started into the hall and I reached for the light, glancing over the kids before I switched it off. Before I could though, I hesitated, looking back at the end of Tegan's bed where I'd thought I'd seen a wisp of something white.

But there was nothing that hadn't already been there.

The light switched off, I closed the door.

Downstairs, the house was empty, y'all's voices drifting in from out on the porch.

"I gotta pee," Meg announced making Mack laugh while she left his side for the hall bath.

Then he looked at me with a grin and a sigh. "You've done good, Mama. Considering."

I couldn't help but smile. "Thanks. How long do you think before they go back to playing Legos?"

"If they're anything like you and Scott? The second you closed the door."

I laughed and he continued to smile down at me.

"I don't know if Meg told you, but he remembers you. Kind of. He, uh, he remembers the...idea of you...I guess."

I squinted up at him and he crossed his arms, leaned against the back of the couch.

"He knows about Mom. Meg never felt right just letting him think we were his parents, especially knowing Dad would be out eventually. So, once he was old enough to understand, we tried to explain it to him. Gave him that picture of her and Dad." He shrugged towards the ceiling and the framed photo of them together on the beach the week before he was born that was on the dresser in Lucas' room, on the wall between his and Tegan's beds now. "But, at first, he kept getting confused. Every time he saw a picture of all of us, he'd point to you and ask if that was Mom."

I stared at him, not sure how to react to this.

He held my eyes and shrugged. "It didn't take long for him to get it right, but...you know, there was a long time when you were the closest thing he had

to her."

I nodded and we were both quiet for a few seconds while it sank back in.

"I'm sorry," I said just above a whisper.

He smirked. "Al—"

"No. I am. I already knew I'd messed up for Marc and Teegs, but...I guess I was never really in the right place to understand just how much I broke."

"You didn't break anything."

"Yeah, I did."

He stared at me, saw that I wasn't going to let him let me off the hook that easily. I was back now and I wasn't going anywhere—I wanted y'all to stop acting as though to admit my wrong doings would drive me further away.

"Maybe you did," he finally gave me. "But...you remember what I told you about Dad? The day we moved y'all into that house?"

I did.

And I didn't.

"I'll never judge you for how you needed to heal. None of us will."

"Tate is."

"Tate's not judging. Tate's...questioning. Once he gets answers, he'll snap back. You'll see, but..." He shrugged, looked over his shoulder to the front porch where Bee kept trying to watch us without being noticed—by us or Tate, I'm still not sure. "He's just gotta work up to asking his questions first."

I nodded, though I wasn't sure if I believed him.

Meg came down the hall with a groan and a sigh to lean against Mack's shoulder, his arm unquestioningly wrapping around her.

"What do we got in the way of sweets?"

"Ice cream?"

She squinted up at him. "What kind?"

"I donno." He stood and she followed him to the kitchen.

I started after them, but then Bee caught my attention through the door, smiled and waved me over.

"We're heading out soon," she said once I was outside. "I just wanted to make sure we got a chance to say bye."

"Oh, yeah," I said. "Of course."

"Not yet though," Tate told her and flicked the ashes from his cigarette over the banister.

I remember wondering when he picked that up, deciding it wasn't worth asking, especially with the way he was still avoiding looking anywhere near my direction.

"Still," Bee said with raised brows and still grinning at me.

"Y'all goin' up to Georgetown at all this year," you asked them from where you were leaning against the banister next to Tate, Scott doing the same on the opposite side of the porch.

Bee sighed and moved to lean back against Tate's chest. There was a tug on my jeans and I looked to see Joss nod to the space on the wicker couch next to her and Jackie.

"Bee's dad lives in Georgetown," Joss whispered to me once I was close enough.

"Ah," I responded with a grateful smirk.

"We really should, babe," Tate told Bee. "Reece keeps saying she wants to go."

"It's a five hour drive," Bee said and Tate shrugged around her between taking another drag.

"So, we stay one night." He blew smoke behind him. "We plan it right, he'll get dinner with us and maybe breakfast, then we come home. Reece gets some time with him, he sees you're still alive, everyone's happy."

Bee started to fidget with her bangles, her feet wiggling in her black, lace-up boots. In my peripheral, I caught Scott, Joss, and Jackie exchange glances.

"Can we talk about this once we're at the house," Bee asked with a soft tone, her eyes glued to the wood beneath her toes. "I don't wanna spoil all this with all that."

Tate nodded and kissed the back of her head. "Fair. Sorry."

She shook her head and tilted it back so he could kiss her on the lips.

I fought the urge to look at you, my hands itching. Despite my best efforts, I found myself still staring at the potted aloe vera at your feet from the side of my eyes and I could almost see you struggling with the same.

To my relief, a distraction came in Mack opening the front door and popping his head out. "Meg's begging for ice cream and card games in here if anyone's up for it."

Joss straightened up. "I am."

"Joss is," Scott said at the same time then smirked at her.

"We should be going," Bee said with a sigh and behind her Tate crushed out his cigarette with equal reluctant disappointment.

Mack came out all the way as Bee was crossing the porch to him for a hug. "Y'all coming with us tomorrow?"

"Of course!" she said. "Any chance to see PopPop."

Without thinking, I looked to you with a smirk and scrunched up brows. You were already looking at me from the side of your eyes then grinned and mouthed, *Dad*.

I nodded and tried to ignore the lightning in my stomach, the crackling along my bones.

Goodbyes were passed around (Tate giving me an awkward side hug after Bee gave him a look), Bee followed Tate down the stairs while still waving to us, Joss rushed inside for ice cream the instant it was safe to do so, Mack following her with a smile to Scott and Jackie who were steps behind him.

And then it was just us.

The silence was suffocating, but we still sat there in it, neither knowing what to do, neither wanting to be the first to give up.

Finally you took in a deep breath and leaned back against the bannister, your hands in your pockets, your shoulders tight. "What d'you think of Bee?"

I chuckled and returned to the couch. "Is it possible not to like her?"

You smirked and shrugged. "Tate's ex might say so, but she was…" You shook your head. "What does she know?"

I nodded, wondering if this ex was the same girl from astronomy club he'd been with when I'd left, but not being brave enough to bring attention to just how much I'd missed, I just moved the topic in a different direction. "How long have her folks been divorced? You know?"

"Um, I think Tate said she was young, like doesn't remember kind of young. She, um…" You scratched the back of your head and glanced at the space where Tate's car had been as though debating how much to share. "Her sister went missing? I wanna say ten years ago or something. According to what Tate told me she told him, so," you smirked and shrugged, "take that for what you will, uh, her dad kind of gave up on looking for her sooner than Bee thought he should. She's never really forgiven him, as you might have been able to tell."

I nodded. "And who's Reece?"

"Her half-sister. She, uh, according to the telephone version of Bee's life that you're getting, her moms—lesbians, not bi, sorry."

You met my eyes with a grin and I giggled for no real reason except that I felt 17 all over again, staring up at you while you effortlessly made me feel all floaty and bubbly.

"Well, they wanted Teresa—Reece—to still have a father figure and I guess her birth mom's still on good terms with her dad despite everything with Ava, so..." You shrugged. "Yeah."

I nodded, staring at you despite feeling like I shouldn't be.

And for a quiet moment, you stared back at me.

"Can I ask you something?" You finally said.

"What?"

"Um, it's just, I guess..." You broke first, your eyes shooting to the wood at your feet. "I didn't wanna ask in front of Tegan, but...how-how are you doing, I guess?"

I was quiet for a second as my body was reminded of what gravity felt like. "How do you mean?"

You shrugged, but an answer didn't come despite your mouth being poised to do so. Finally, you cleared your throat and shifted your weight. "Um, Mack? He, uh, he told me about what happened i-in LA? With the pier?"

My ears rang.

Static ran through me.

My shoulders went numb.

I knew Scott had told Mack, I figured Mack would have told Meg, but I had hoped they wouldn't tell you.

"Al, were you...? It's just...it sounded a lot like—"

"I wasn't trying to kill myself. I mean, I don't think I was?" I scrubbed my face with my hands then pressed the heels of my palms against my eyes. "I was..." I shook my head. "I don't remember most of it."

I heard you cross the porch, felt the wicker give beneath your weight. You didn't say anything, didn't touch me, though your want to radiated off of you, I wondered if mine did, as well.

"I'm sorry how I handled it all," you finally said, your voice quiet with the same distant hurt I was grappling with. "That first time?"

Shaking my head, I lowered my hands and clasped them in front of me.

With my eyes open I saw that they matched yours, our elbows both pressed against our knees so close together.

"You did what you were supposed to," I insisted. "I'm sorry I put that on you to begin with. I'm sorry I ran."

"You had every right to. I shouldn't have brought everyone else into it. I should have—"

When I took your hand, you stopped. Initially, I had just wanted a way to let you know that you weren't at fault, wanted a way to tell you without words because I wasn't ready yet to have that conversation out loud. But once your hand was in mine, once my skin was against yours, I just wanted you close.

But I didn't deserve that yet. Not the way I wanted it.

That's why I just wrapped both of mine around yours and guided your arm closer to me.

"There's a lot of things we could have done better," I told you.

In my peripheral, you nodded then leaned towards me. Your lips hovered near my temple. I want to believe that you were debating whether or not to kiss me. Mostly because I was debating whether or not to let you. Instead, you pressed your brow against my head, your nose buried in my hair above my ear.

It wasn't entirely what I wanted.

But it was enough.

It was the most I deserved in that moment.

Things moved pretty much like that through those days before Christmas, before New Year's. I don't remember how the next few events fell in line, just that they came one after the other. I'm sure they weren't all the same day, but for whatever reason I remember them as though they were.

Maybe it's just that it'll be easier to recount as though they were.

Maybe it doesn't matter.

Maybe I just want to remember them.

It began with us driving out to Edinburg to see Dad before his release.

We rode in separate cars up there, myself with Scott and Joss so we wouldn't have to unload Tegan's car seat, you with Tate and Bee, Meg's Explorer too cramped with both Lucas' and Julian's car seats even if it was only Lucas who was coming to the prison with us, Julian staying at the house with Jackie. Through the drive, we told Tegan and Joss about Dad, Scott told us what to expect once we'd gotten there.

Joss and I followed y'all through the standard procedure that y'all seemed to be so adept at, especially Lucas who went through it with an impatient excitement guiding Tegan through it all while she held onto my hand listening to Lucas talk even more about Dad and the visiting center.

Once through and inside, we sat around the table in that visiting center minimally decorated for Christmas with tinsel hung along the ceiling and felt snowflakes somehow stuck to the whitewashed cinder block walls. The rest of you were so casual, so accustomed to this process while Joss and I sat mostly silent, just taking it all in while Tegan moved between us and Lucas who was playing with his Hot Wheels at the other end of the table with Tate

who was still avoiding me despite Bee's attempts to bridge the gap.

I remember you sat on the opposite side of the table from me, catty corner with Mack and Meg in front of me. Joss was next to me, her hands cameraless and fidgeting with first her hair tie then her sweater cuffs then Scott's hand when he'd grabbed hold of hers just as she'd started picking at the skin around her nails.

Then a door opened on the other side of the room and men in blue scrub uniforms filed in.

Then I saw him in the line—his hair more gray than that Matthews blond, more wrinkles around his eyes and his skin not nearly as tan as it had been throughout the entirety of my childhood, but it was still him. He had this nervous giddiness all over him and I realized I hadn't asked anyone if he was expecting us, but I guess he had been, because he glanced over y'all then smiled wide when his eyes fell on Scott and me. He paused for the briefest of moments before looking at me again with a watery eyed smile and I knew without following his eyeline that he'd spotted Tegan at the other end playing with Lucas.

I knew that I probably shouldn't have, but I left the table and rushed to him. His face lit up and he grabbed me around the shoulders to pull me tight against him where he just held me for a long moment. I remember he smelled different, no hint of the sea salt that I would have thought was seared into his skin, and his arms and chest were different, more lean, less that kind of muscular that had come from years of lugging heavy equipment around campus or between his truck and boat or out of the water and over the sides of those boats. But something about hearing his breath in his chest, his heartbeat beneath it—it felt safe again.

All of you did.

"We've missed you, sweet girl," he said with that soft voice that rumbled through his chest.

It was like pressing your ear against a shell and hearing home in the distance.

"I'm sorry," I said, biting back tears. "I've missed you, too."

He nodded and kissed the top of my head. "Is that my grandbaby?"

I pulled away from him enough to look back at Tegan who was watching me while leaning against Joss and twisting her fingers around her t-shirt.

Back at the table I sat on the bench and leaned close to her.

"This is PopPop," I told her as she watched him kneel in front of her.

"Mommy's daddy."

"Hi," she said in that shy little voice, her entire body leaned against me. I wondered if she was sick of meeting new people yet.

"Hey, Tegan," he said. "I am so excited to finally meet you."

I looked to Mack who was watching with Meg pressed against him, her chin on his shoulder.

"Of course, we told him," she said for Mack, reading my glare and smirk as well as he could.

You snickered and I shifted my eyes to you, your grin, your own eyes watching me, watching her.

Dad ignored us. "How old are you now, Tegan?"

"Four," she answered.

"You like *My Little Pony*?" He poked her tummy and her t-shirt earning a giggle.

With a shy smile, she nodded.

"Who's your favorite?"

"Rainbow Dash."

"Which one is she?"

She looked at her t-shirt and pointed to her. "The one with the rainbow."

"Oh!" He feigned. "I should have guessed that."

"Mommy's is Twilight Sparkle." She showed him which one she was.

"And why is she Mommy's favorite?"

"She likes books."

"Ah," he grinned up at me, "Mommy would like the one that likes books."

"Dad, she lives in a library," I told him.

He laughed.

"And has a dragon friend," Scott added around Joss.

"Spike!" Tegan clapped her hands and giggled.

"He's Uncle Scott's favorite," I told Dad. "And Aunt Joss' is Fluttershy."

"And is this Aunt Joss," Dad asked while he stood.

"Hi," Joss said with a shy voice that could rival Tegan's as she followed Scott off the bench.

"You look kind of familiar," Dad told her and looked to Scott who he gave a warm hug.

"She and her sister were at Kofa," Scott told him. "Uh, back in '06?"

"Oh! The girl in the pictures? Those were good shots," he told Joss who lowered her head and turned to Scott, her cheeks bright pink.

"Thanks," she said with a shy smile.

I squinted at them then looked to Mack, Meg, you who each looked equally confused. None of us remembered seeing pictures of a girl from that trip. I've seen them since then, but all I've been able to get out of him is that he'd lost track of Joss and Jackie at some point on that trip, had been too heartbroken to go back to the photos afterwards. I guess Dad had caught him looking at them once, but what he told him about them he's never told me, nor why it was suddenly Kofa and no longer Joshua Tree.

By then Lucas had come around them (I'm guessing Tate and Bee finally let him) and reached up for Dad all smiles.

"Hey, big boy!" He lifted him up and gave him the same bear hugs we'd all gotten growing up.

"Are you coming home soon," Lucas asked him.

"By New Year's," Dad promised. "But I'll make sure Santa sends you and Jude something nice for me. And Tegan, too," he added and turned to smile down at her.

I want to recount that entire visit despite the fact that I know you were there. I want to relive it all—the way we all were as though nothing had happened, as though we weren't even in a prison visiting center. The only thing that kept that fact in my head was Dad bringing up inmates and the prison library and double checking with Mack the plans to pick him up the day of his release.

"Greg," a man shouted from the other side of the room towards the end of our visit.

Dad looked over his shoulder and I turned to see a smaller, bald man with soft eyes wearing the same blue scrub uniform, headed out of the room.

"That your girl," he asked with a smile and nodded to me.

I looked to Dad and saw that shining smile. "Yep. And my granddaughter." He pointed to Tegan in his lap.

Looking back at the man, I saw him smile, nod, give him a thumbs up. "Welcome home, baby girl," he called before following one of the guards out of the room.

I never asked Dad about that man, I guess because it didn't really matter

who he was, just that Dad talked about us, about my leaving y'all for so long, about his wishing I'd come home. I want to say it changed everything, but I don't really think it did—it simply solidified it.

Through the drive home, Tegan slept in the car seat with us on either side of her the way she'd kept begging it be, talking endlessly to you about PopPop and Lucas and Uncle Tate and Aunt Bee until she eventually dozed off. Joss and Scott were talking in the front seat when I caught you watching Tegan sleep with a soft smile.

"She's so precious when she sleeps," I said and you looked at me. "I always feel like I'm...overflowing when I watch her sleep."

"Yeah. I get that." But instead of looking back at her, you just focused that soft smile on me.

I wanted it, but that guilt came back and told me I didn't deserve it.

So, I looked away from you to her. "Who came up with PopPop?"

"He did," you said with a smirk. "He was worried Julian calling him grandpa would confuse Lucas, so..." you shrugged. "I think he felt PopPop would be closer to Papa or something."

"I wonder if the whole Lucas thing will confuse her."

You stared at me for a moment longer than I expect, nothing but a light I didn't deserve behind your eyes and smile. "It doesn't seem to."

"Eventually."

You chuckled and shrugged. "It's a confusing situation. We'll figure it out when it comes up."

I stared back at you for longer than I meant to, the swelling light emanating from my womb at the idea of figuring it all out with you, that you wanted to figure it all out with me, slowly dissolving the guilt that wanted to snatch the smile from my lips.

I wanted that—so desperately wanted that—even if I didn't deserve it.

But you were willing to give it to me despite me believing I hadn't earned you back and I think that's part of why I began to open myself back up to you that afternoon sitting with Mack and Meg in the kitchen while Tegan and Lucas played outside with Scott, Joss, Jackie, Tate, and Bee; why when you sat next to me on the bench side of the kitchen table, I let myself gradually move closer to you; why I let myself touch you the way I used to, let you touch me the way you used to; why I stopped avoiding your eyes when you'd look at me with that soft loving smile. It still wasn't perfect, there were still words left unsaid, bricks left between us, but it was getting close—I could see you, you

could touch me.

At some point, Meg went to put Julian down for a nap, falling asleep with him. You and Mack began talking about dinner, decided y'all needed to go to the IGA. I decided to stay, Tegan still not fully over the past year, still getting nervous when I wasn't close enough for her to run to. I watched y'all leave from the front porch, watched Tegan run over to you and skip alongside you while you told her where you were going, point up at me to show her where I was, lift her up for a hug when she thrust her arms up to you. I was nearly overflowing with my want for you, for everything to be fully back to normal, for the last four years to have never happened, to have at least not happened without you.

Once you were gone, Tegan went back to playing and I watched her and Lucas with the others for a while before going back inside.

I stayed on the living room couch largely because I was tired of trying to figure out Tate, tired of watching him avoid me. Despite the fact that I felt I deserved this treatment, it was still heavy to carry, still made my shoulders ache beneath it. And it didn't help that the more the rest of us fell back into our old comforts, the harder it was to feel Tate pulling away, almost pretending I wasn't there, reminding me of how the rest of you should be treating me.

I sat in the dim living room alone for a long time, just staring at the ceiling, working through it all, when I heard footsteps coming up the inside stairs. I looked up in time to see Tate round the banister at the top. I don't think he saw me at first, too focused on glancing over the room. Then his eyes fell on me and he stopped still. It was only a second or two before he looked away from me again to continue examining the room.

"You, uh, seen a silver lighter up here," he asked, his hand in his back pockets.

I looked over the coffee table, the side table. "It's not over here. Maybe the kitchen?"

He shrugged and went to check the counters before coming back into the living room and starting for the door.

"Tate?" I said before he could leave.

Though he didn't look at me, he did stop, shifted his body a quarter turn towards me.

"Sit with me for a sec?"

He did his best to not look straight at me, his eyes on the carpet at my

feet instead, but shrugged and nodded all the same.

Tate hadn't been excluded from the speeches I'd rehearsed in my head over that drive home in those between moments when Tegan was occupied or asleep. He also wasn't excluded in his speech clogging up my throat the instant I had a chance to say it to him.

"Do you hate me, Tate?" was all I was able to get out.

Though he shook his head before I had even finished asking the question, it took him longer for the words to follow. "Not anymore. I'm, um, not…entirely sure I ever did."

"But you are still mad at me." It wasn't so much a question. It wasn't so much a statement. I don't know what it was. I don't know what I expected it to be other than my own fears tumbling out of me.

He was quiet for longer than I would have liked and I was about to fill the void that was hurling rocks at my ribs when he finally spoke. "I'm trying not to be."

I didn't know what to say to that. If there was anything I could say or even do except allow him the time and space to tell me what he wanted me to say or do. So, we sat in silence for what was most likely less than a minute, but that felt like a million. He could have left then, taken my silence to mean that I had said what I had meant to say. To my relief, he didn't, just sat next to me on the couch awkwardly staring at the same spot on the coffee table that I was.

"Why'd you leave me, Al?"

He may have well screamed it the way those words hit my bones to the marrow.

"I…When M n' M took you in, I thought…I thought you'd finally be safe again. I thought you didn't need me around making things darker."

He took in a deep breath and shifted against the couch. Scott had told me what had happened with Tate while I was gone—the undone homework, the skipped classes, that girl whose name I can never remember because we try not to talk about her showing up at Mack and Meg's door, the drinking she said he had taken up when you adults weren't around, the new group of kids he would ditch her for, the kids who did more than drink, who she was worried would convince him to do the same. It almost brought me home, but then I'd look at Tegan, think of you, think of that hurt I knew would be in your eyes, and I'd stay out there on the buoy instead.

"They weren't stranded like we were," he said. "They kept expecting me

to…I don't know. Not be upset, I guess."

"To not hurt."

"Yeah."

I didn't bother elaborating. I knew he didn't need me to. I knew he understood, understood that I understood.

"What about Scott," I asked.

He shrugged and shook his head. "Scott came and went. Then he stopped coming home."

More rocks.

"I'm sorry."

His knee began to bounce and he fidgeted with his ear either avoiding or working through saying something. "Did you—I guess…Bee always speculated that…She says you probably needed him…more than I did, I guess?"

My shoulders went numb, a feeling that drained down my arms, my torso, contaminated my stomach, made those rocks into sulfur while canaries sang warnings. "I don't know."

"Did you have anyone out there?"

"Where?"

"Either?"

"In LA I had Joss and Scott, but in Austin…" I shrugged. "When Scott wasn't there…Only Tegan. This one women, Delilah, but…Jonathan didn't really let me out much."

He finally looked at me, brows furrowed, eyes squinted. "Let?"

I shrugged. I wasn't ready to talk about that. I was still convinced it was what I had deserved. I guess I still kind of am. I think Tate saw this, understood the way some wounds are only made worse with talking. He nodded and looked back to the coffee table that we both went back to staring at for a silent moment.

"Did having Scott help?"

"Yeah. He did."

Both of us fidgeting, we continued to stare at the coffee table, not saying what we should have.

"I guess I still don't understand," he was brave enough to admit.

"Understand what?"

"Why you couldn't stay with us? Why you…why him?"

My lips hovered over the words. "I don't know. But…When I realized I was pregnant I…" *Breathe.* "I was so scared, Tate. I…I thought if stayed here? Stranded like that? I thought I'd…" *Breathe.* "I knew I couldn't put her through that. I had to break that cycle."

His voice was quiet, hurt, but understanding. "You could've at least told us."

"I know. I should have. I'm sorry. I just…I had to do it and I didn't want to have a discussion about it. I just wanted to do it. I kept waiting for things to get better so I could call y'all, but…"

"Never did?"

I shook my head. "I shouldn't have left you and I'm so sorry I did it the way I did, but…"

"She came first."

"Yeah."

It was then that I felt it—that hum, that knowing in my gut that a baby was coming, that knowing that Tate would understand even more than he already did within the next year. But I didn't say anything, let them have that moment themselves.

Tate nodded in the silence, but then craned his neck to look through what we could see of the house, turned and stretched to see the front porch. He then glanced me over and returned his back to the couch.

"You know, Marc never moved on from you."

I nodded and shifted my eyes to the inseam of my jeans which I slid my thumbnail along. "I know."

Scott was always quick to remind me of that.

Tate took in a deep breath and held it for a few seconds. "He needed you more than I did. More than any of us."

"I know." The sulfur began to burn. The canaries stopped singing.

"Scott tell you he wrote a book about you?"

I stopped fidgeting, my eyes going wide. "Marc?"

"Yes. Well, poems, but they're all about trying to find you in Mom's writings. Trying to find how he could make it all up to you."

My heart slammed against my ribcage and it was my turn to look at Tate with that confused look.

He met my eyes and gave me this smirk that was somewhere between sly and sad, a chuckle beneath it all. "Ask him about it."

"But…Make what up to me?"

The door opened and I wanted to yell at whoever was coming in to go away. But when I whipped around, Tegan ran around Bee and under Scott's arm holding the door open, yelled that magic word with those shimmering eyes and climbed into my lap all giggles and excitement, telling me something with that frantic sort of joy that only children seem to be built to contain. I don't remember what she was telling me, just remember the way she cleared out that sulfur with that smile, the easy way she fell against me, would have melted back into me if she could.

The rest of the evening, I tried to not think about what Tate had told me. I didn't ignore it, in fact, I let it change the way I looked at you, let it consume the guilt that ate at me when you and Mack came home and I felt this overwhelming urge to kiss you, every time Tegan called you Daddy, every time she wanted you near her and you without hesitation obliged, every time you went out of your way to be near me.

I knew I needed to take Tate's advice and ask you about the book, but not now, not with everyone else around, not with her enjoying you the way she was.

At some point that night, I was in the kitchen leaning against the counter watching you, Joss, and Bee on the living room floor playing with the kids while Mack, Meg, Scott, and Jackie watched from the couches. Tegan was in your lap smiling up at you between whatever game y'all were playing, her eyes shimmering the way they did when she looked at me. I remember feeling as though I was about to burst, as though I was a magnet and you were cobalt, as though I was a compass and you were north, as though I was the tide and you were the moon.

Tate leaned against the counter next to me, our shoulders just touching. For a long moment, we just watched the growing parts of our family and I tried hard not to tell him how him and Bee would be next, their daughter playing with her cousins with squeals and giggles and big smiles.

"Al?" His voice low despite y'all being in the other room. "Do you…do you think you broke it? Th-the cycle?"

My chest inflated, deflated. "I hope so."

"Then…I guess it was all worth it then?"

I nodded. "Hopefully."

And ultimately

I think he was right.
I think it was all worth it.
Because, as much as I wish I had done it with you,
I did break that cycle.
At least,
I hope I did.

I'm still not sure why she didn't ask you to tuck her in that night. I'm sure there was still a level of unsuredness going through her, still some level of not knowing how permanent this all was, of not knowing how real it was. Not that I blame her. I still blame him. I know you see it, too—the way she still is around people, the way she watches them at first, holds them at arm's length, studies them until she's sure they're not putting on an act, not tying strings to her wrists. I don't know if she's aware of why she does it, if she's even aware that she does it.

I still hate him for that.
I still hate myself for letting him.
But that's not important.
What is is the conversation we had that night.
I'm not sure how we managed it, but, yet again, it was just us on the front porch after Tate and Bee had left and the others had all gone back inside. I remember we were sitting close together on the wicker couch, your arm behind my head, my knees bent in front of me while I ran my fingers along the seams of my jeans. I remember us both sitting in silence for a long moment while I worked through how I was going to ask you and, I'm pretty sure, you were waiting for me to be the first one to stand.

"Marc," I breathed.
"Hmm?"
"Tate told me something today."
"Yeah?"
"He, um, he said you…wrote a book? About me?"
You shifted, scratched at the side of your neck, but you left your arm behind me. "Ye-yeah. It, um, it was part of my thesis."
I hesitated over the next part the way I could feel you were.
"What did you think you had to make up to me?"
"Do."
I looked up at you and you lifted your eyes from my fingers to meet mine.

Then you looked away from me, pulled your arm out from behind me, leaned forward to press your elbows against your knees. "There's…a lot I need to make up to you."

"No, there isn't."

But you shook your head.

"*I'm* the one who messed up," I insisted.

You turned to look at me. "I drove you away."

"Marc—"

The front door opened and Jackie leaned out. We both looked to her.

"Teegs had a nightmare."

I stood without question and went upstairs to find Scott trying his best to calm her while Lucas hovered by her bed. I swear in that moment I saw a white shimmer next to him, but I was too concerned about Tegan to think about it. I held her close while she cried into me. I didn't need to ask to know her nightmare was about me. She'd had them nightly when I was in the hospital, after I was released.

After I'd gotten her back to sleep, I wanted to go back downstairs, back to you, but I couldn't bring myself to. So, I curled up on the bed Jackie and I were sharing in Julian's room and tried my best to not cry myself to sleep, to not let the guilt consume me entirely.

That night, I was pulled out of a dream by humming that I knew, that I knew I couldn't be hearing. Still drowsy, I blinked heavily at the wall for a few seconds before I registered that I could still hear the humming. It was then that I realized there was something moving in my peripheral. It was then that I recognized the scent of jasmine. I looked to the rocking chair (painted with sea greens and blues, shells and waves by Bee) to see a figure covered in a white translucent veil softly rocking back and forth.

"Mama?" I whispered.

She stood and floated across the room to kneel by the bed where she just took me in with that preserving gaze.

"I love you so much, sweet girl," she said with a voice that was soft, just above a whisper, could have been a breeze through the oleanders.

"I miss you, Mama." I didn't bother fighting the tears. "I need you."

She smiled and shook her head. "No, you don't, baby. You are so much stronger than this. You are so much stronger than us."

"I don't deserve to be, Mama. I left you. I—"

"All you did was love, baby. Don't destroy yourself because you asked for it in return."

She leaned forward and kissed my temple. Despite her veil, I could feel her lips against my skin the way I used to.

Before pulling away she whispered. "You are meant for so much more than this pain, my love. Don't let it destroy you. Promise you won't let it win."

"I'll try," I said with a shuddering breath, tears hitting the pillow.

"Remember, she is your strength. They all are. Hold them close when it gets hard."

I nodded against her chest.

She kissed my temple again. "I love you."

"I love you, Mama."

But the jasmine was gone along with her warmth and I opened my eyes to an empty room.

I was suddenly aware of how cold it was, how weak I felt, how much I wanted you, but didn't deserve you. So, instead, I took my blanket and went into the kids' room where I slipped into the bed with Tegan, where she, without question, curled against my chest while my arms and blanket enveloped her and Rainbow Dash.

The next morning, I woke feeling like I'd been through battle, but stronger for it. I also found not just Tegan curled against my one side, but Lucas against the other. I gently woke them both and started Tegan through her morning routine which Lucas followed along without question or hesitation.

And through it all,

I realized

She was right.

I never saw it before that night, but they are my strength. Holding them, guiding them through their routines, their lives, watching them learn and grow—it all brings me strength, reminds me why I'm here, keeps my muscles limber, my feet moving. I'd have given up a long time before this if it weren't for Tegan, if it weren't for Lucas before her, if it weren't for the twins after them. Even the nieces and nephews—I feel stronger after seeing them, resilient in ways.

For that reason, I'm partially glad we didn't come back together until we did. Without the kids and their Christmas excitement, I'm not sure I would have been able to do it as easily. Not that it was easy through those days of

our ebbing and flowing to and from each other with not so secret hesitancy, but watching you with her, with them as we went through Christmas traditions and dinners and presents, it gave me the space to remember why I loved you to begin with, why I had been so focused on earning you, on deserving you again.

That's why it took me another week to fully let you in.

I remember it started the night before Dad was released when Mack came downstairs. We heard him ask Scott and Joss in Tate's room if they'd seen me before he came into your apartment where we had been talking. When he came in, but stopped in the doorway to listen down the hall, we both stopped talking to watch him before he came the rest of the way in.

"What," I asked with a confused smirk from your bed.

But instead of answering, he stopped and glanced between us with his own distracted smirk.

"What," I repeated while you avoided looking at him, your cheeks going pink.

He raised his brows, took in a breath, looked at the plastic convenience store bag wrapped thing he was holding. "It's just, tomorrow? When Dad comes home? I wanna give him this." He handed the bag to me. "I want you to give it to him with me."

I unwrapped it to find Her perfume, the bottle I was supposed to hold onto, the bottle I had left on his porch the day I left along with a note that just said I was sorry.

"You held onto it," I half-asked while cradling it.

"Yeah. Meg doesn't know. She really felt like he didn't deserve it after the fire, but…"

"You think he does now?" I didn't look at him, didn't look at you.

"He's coming home."

I looked up to meet his eyes fully on mine.

"That's what matters. He deserves what we're willing to give him."

After searching his face, hoping underneath it all he was answering what I had really been asking beneath mine, I nodded and handed the bottle back to him. "I'm willing to give him that."

"Good," he said with a small smile. "At dinner?"

I nodded and he went back upstairs to re-hide the bottle.

I don't remember how we continued the conversation after that, if we

even did, but I do remember being in a bit of a fog afterwards. It lasted the rest of the night, the entire next day until Mack came home with Dad wearing the new set of clothes you guys had gone out to get him at some point before that day.

His presence drove away some of that fog, but it came and went throughout the night.

At one point after dinner, after we'd given him the perfume and we'd all fought tears (even Meg), some more successfully than others, we sat on the couches talking and watching the kids play, waiting for midnight to roll around. You got up to help someone in a different room and Dad waited until you were out of earshot before leaning close to me.

"You two still bein' weird?"

"Dad."

"What?" He grinned down at me. "That boy's waited long enough for you."

"Things aren't gonna go back to the they were overnight."

"And why not?"

"I don't know."

"Don't tell me you've changed—"

"No. It's...It's not like that."

I could feel him looking me over then he nodded in my peripheral. "You both deserve to be happy, Al. Happy together."

I started to shake my head, but he wrapped his arm around my shoulders and pulled me tight against his side.

"*You* deserve to be happy, Al. You came home. You brought her home. He wants you back. Why can't that be enough?"

I shrugged and he nodded.

"She wouldn't want to see you like this. She'd want you to fight for him, for her to have a daddy who'll love her the way he does."

"I know."

"Then forgive yourself, sweet girl."

"It's not that easy, Dad."

"I know. I know. But you have it easy, ya know."

I looked up at him.

"He's still here to say it." He nodded towards you. "Even if you don't believe it."

I hate to admit it, but it was only then that it hit me what he must have gone through, the wars he must have waged inside himself and without even the chance of hearing forgiveness from Her, of seeing it in her face, feeling it in her arms. I felt a whole new guilt take hold of me and I pressed myself against his chest while he wrapped his arms around me.

"I'm sorry, Daddy," I begged him, but he shook his head against the top of mine.

"I hear her sometimes," he whispered to me. "In the dead of night. Today on the waves."

"What does she say?"

A chuckle rumbled through his chest. "Nothing. She just hums. Sometimes she sings."

"Like a siren?"

"Yeah. Just like a siren."

Then you came back and Dad and I separated.

I remember really trying after that.

I remember letting myself lean against you, letting you put your arm around me, letting the space between us become smaller and smaller. Then, long after Lucas and Tegan had given into sleep, the clock hit midnight and I let you kiss me, let myself kiss you back, let myself be so nearly yours and you so nearly mine the way we had been before.

It was so close.

But there were still words that needed to be said.

Not that I knew that then, not that I knew that in your apartment where we made out that night like high schoolers trying to force the so nearly out from between us. I wish that I had known it then. It would have made it all so much easier to have had it out then instead of falling asleep fully clothed next to you.

Not that I regret that night nor waking up the next morning with your arm draped over me like so many mornings we'd shared before. The smirks and sidelong glances upstairs were enough to coax up second thoughts, but remembering your warmth, hoping that, with time, we could have more, realizing that I could admit that I wanted it with only a small spark of guilt, it all shoved those second thoughts back down.

Maybe that's what led us to finally say those things.

Maybe it was being at the Chapel on the Dunes again.

Maybe it was thinking about Mom, all of us in a strange somberness.

Maybe it was watching Lucas and Tegan, thinking about what we were going to do next, what kind of life I was going to give her, what kind of life I wanted with you.

I remember we were following Tegan and Lucas while they ran around the beach with Jackie, Tate, and Bee while Joss and Scott took pictures. Dad was up ahead carrying a sleeping Julian while talking with Mack and Meg.

Our own conversation had fallen into a lull. Watching Scott taking pictures of Lucas and Tegan reminded me of the book I'd pulled out in your office.

I looked up at you, the wind making your curls dance.

"What was your book about?" I said.

A shy smile came across you that made me think of Tegan. "Uh…you, actually."

"Tate said it had something to do with Mom's poems?"

"Yeah." You looked to your feet. "Um, I was—well, Mack thought it would be nice to go through her poems, the stuff she'd been working on when…" You took in a breath then chewed your bottom lip before continuing. "Uh, I, uh, while I was going through it all, I, um, I kept finding references to you." You shrugged and looked out at the others. "At least, I think they were. It, um, it kind of became…I don't know, maybe an obsession: looking for you in it all."

I wanted to apologize.

I wanted to beg your forgiveness.

I wanted to hear anger in your voice, hurt, anything that I could chastise myself with.

"And then…" Your lips hovered around the words. "I, um, I started to see you in her. I started to…hear you, everything you were going through before…It…it broke me, Al."

I don't remember when we stopped walking, just that in that moment we were still and you looked at me.

"I finally got it. What I did wrong."

"You did nothing wrong."

"I did."

"No. *I* shouldn't have left. I shouldn't have…" I kept shaking my head, crossed my arms tight around my stomach. "I shouldn't have let him—"

"Al."

I looked up at you.

"You are not to blame for any of that."

"Yes, I—"

"Al, he took advantage of you. He saw a hole and he-he kept shoving himself in until you broke."

"I let him do that."

"You weren't exactly thinking straight."

I stared at you while you stared at me.

I was in the wrong.

I just had to figure out how.

"Be mad at me," I practically begged.

"Why?"

"I kept your daughter from you, Marc."

You nodded and looked to your feet. "Yeah. I *was* upset. When I first found out? But...then I was just worried." You shrugged. "No one knew where you were and," you took in a deep breath, your brows raising, "Mack wouldn't call Scott with all the cops in the house—"

"Why?"

You lifted your eyes to meet mine. "Jonathan. Mack wanted to find you before he did. Knew he'd try and take her, if he didn't take you, too." But then you looked away again. "He knew she's...she's mine...before I wanted to."

"Marc."

When I stepped closer to you, you didn't pull away, but didn't look at me either. "I was scared, Alex. I was scared to know the truth no matter what it was. I just..." you shrugged. "wanted you home. In that moment...I just wanted you to come home. All these years...that's all I've wanted."

You finally met my eyes again and the only thing keeping me from falling back to you was that guilt nipping at my heels.

"You deserve to hate me."

"I know. And..." You shrugged again. "I tried. I did. Even after finally hearing from you that she's mine, I knew that I should be, but...I love you, Alex. If you disappearing for," you let out something between a sigh and a laugh, "five fucking years didn't change that, then...that must mean it'll take a whole lot to actually do it."

"Tegan?"

You smiled at the sound of her name and its undertow nearly yanked me against you.

"She's why I stopped trying," you said with a shrug, still smiling. "I can't not love you, Alex." You looked across the beach to her. "And now I can't not love her."

But I was stubborn. I refused to take that love this easily. "Tell me you forgive me."

But you were just as stubborn. You smiled at me and let out that sighing laugh again. "There's nothing left to forgive, Al."

I closed my eyes and shook my head. "I kept her from you! I ran away without telling you anything and then I kept her from you!"

"Because you weren't ready to let me back in."

I just stared at you, not knowing how to answer, not sure if you were right or wrong, not sure if I was ready to know. But you turned to me, came close, touched my arm, and in your eyes I could see that you knew everything I was unable to say. Even after five years without me, you still somehow knew me by heart.

"I will never blame you for those years."

"I want you to."

"But I won't. I can't. We needed it. Everything that happened."

I shook my head, but the way you looked down at me with nothing but love and understanding made me stop.

"I wanted to fix you. That's what I did wrong."

"I needed to be fixed."

"You needed to heal. You needed to work through it in your own way and so did I. I wanted to fix you because I…" You looked away from me, your mouth working through words I could feel you had rehearsed a million times, but had never allowed yourself to say out loud—not without me there to hear them. "It made me realize how…powerless I was. That there might be things, other things in our lives that I wouldn't be prepared to carry you through. And that scared me. So, I stopped trying to carry you and…I tried to fix you instead." You met my eyes again and ran your thumb along my arm through my sweater in that way that I hadn't realized until feeling it again how much I'd missed. "That's what he did. Isn't it?"

I couldn't look you in the eyes and stared at your t-shirt instead. I also couldn't say the words and swallowed while I nodded. "Kind of. At first. He didn't really…carry me. He just…let me be."

I remember feeling your arms around me then.

I remember your warmth enveloping me.

I remember the sound of your heart in your chest.

I remember your lips against the top of my head.

I remember the smell of your t-shirt, the smell of you, the smell that made my head spin with relief even if I still felt in some way that I didn't deserve it, I didn't deserve any of this, I didn't deserve you.

"I'm sorry we couldn't figure it out together." Your voice rumbled in your chest like summer thunder against my ear while She hummed along with the waves and I nearly cried right then and there.

I'm not sure why I asked it, why I needed to hear it. I don't think I had even planned on asking it. Not then at least, not in your arms. Maybe after the fight I had imagined us having. Maybe after you had let out all the anger and spite I had convinced myself you had been collecting over those years just to erode me with it the moment I came back.

But there it was before I could even register it was leaving my lips.

"Do you still love me?"

You let out a soft laugh that I couldn't decipher. "Didn't I already tell you?"

"Remind me."

"I never stopped. I'll always be yours, Alex. Yours and hers."

I love you, Marc.
I always did.
I always will.

— Alex

ABOUT

Rae Sengele is queer, neurodivergent, and quiets the wailing ghoul in the attic of her brain the only way she knows how—by writing moody, character driven speculative fiction. She lives in South Central Texas with a pair of black cats.

Connect with Me

⊙ @raesengeleauthor

Milton Keynes UK
Ingram Content Group UK Ltd.
UKHW011124050624
443649UK00006B/524

9 798990 787803